AMBUSH!

Several workstations erupted in a buzz of excitement. "Legate. Aerospace fighters report taking fire from the Drop-Ship. *Astral Prize* has opened up with weapons."

"Legate Ruskoff! Liao Defense Wing requesting permission to go weapons-free."

"Legate. Legate!" Lieutenant Nguyen, now taking over the workstation that kept LianChang in touch with local Drop-Port Authority. "DropShip *Astral Prize* reports that it has opened fire on Confederation fighter craft. They are pleading for help . . . on civilian channels."

"We just . . . *Zāo gāo*! We just lost two fighters. Two down, that's *two* down."

So fast? Even if the merchant-converted DropShip had remounted many of its old weapons, Michaelson would have expected a longer fight.

"DropShip twelve minutes—one, two—from Chang-an."

Legate Ruskoff glanced at Tsung and then Kincaid. So did Michaelson. He read a similar conviction on both faces. The Legate nodded. "Weapons free," he ordered calmly. "Force down that DropShip."

BY TEMPTATIONS
AND BY WAR

A BATTLETECH® NOVEL

Loren L. Coleman

A ROC BOOK

ROC
Published by New American Library, a division of
Penguin Group (USA) Inc., 375 Hudson Street,
New York, New York 10014, U.S.A.
Penguin Books Ltd, 80 Strand,
London WC2R 0RL, England
Penguin Books Australia Ltd, 250 Camberwell Road,
Camberwell, Victoria 3124, Australia
Penguin Books Canada Ltd, 10 Alcorn Avenue,
Toronto, Ontario, Canada M4V 3B2
Penguin Books (N.Z.) Ltd, Cnr Rosedale and Airborne Roads,
Albany, Auckland 1310, New Zealand

Penguin Books Ltd, Registered Offices:
80 Strand, London WC2R 0RL, England

First published by Roc, an imprint of New American Library,
a division of Penguin Group (USA) Inc.

First Printing, December 2003
10 9 8 7 6 5 4 3 2 1

For Peter and Cathryn Orullian.
Rén bú huì tài duō hǎo you.
(One can never have too many good friends.)

ACKNOWLEDGMENTS

One year of *MechWarrior Dark Age* books behind us, I look at the storyline and the way it is developing and see so many new possibilities I'm really not certain where we will end up. I feel I can safely say, however, that BattleTech lives on through the MechWarrior line, and that these novels have a long future ahead of them. Here's to another decade of good fiction, and to the people who help make that all possible for me:

The WizKids themselves: Jordan and Dawne Weisman, Mort Weisman, Maya Smith, Mike and Sharon Mulvihill, Scott Hungerford, and everyone at the company who continues to work very hard on such dynamic and growing universes. And certainly Janna Silverstein, who continues to push me into being a better writer. Thank you.

My agent, Don Maass, and his office staff, for their hard work on my behalf. Also Laura Anne Gillman and Jennifer Heddle at Roc. Anyone who thinks too many editors spoil the book have never worked with these very excellent people.

Allen and Amy Mattila, for their longtime friendship. Randall and Tara Bills, Bryn and Rhianna, who have also made themselves such a large part of our lives. Kelle Vozka, Erik and Alex, who are always welcome at our home. Phil "Skippy" Deluca, who really should come over more often.

The gang of usual suspects: Mike Stackpole, Herb Beas, Chris Hartford, Chris Trossen, and the mapmaker Oystein Tvedten. Special thanks to Team BattleTech members Pete Smith, Chas Borner, and Warner Doles who gave so freely of their time this last year. Special acknowledgements for "JT" Yeo Jia Tian and also for Howard Liu for their help with Chinese translations.

For my loving wife, Heather Joy, who makes everything worthwhile. To my children, Talon, Conner, and Alexia, who get more interesting (and more frightening) with each year. Okay, and the cats. Chaos, Rumor and Ranger. What would I do without them? (Probably much better. I hope they didn't hear that.) And Loki, who, like all dogs, is happy just to be here.

Or hath God assayed to go and take him a nation from the midst of another nation, by temptations, by signs, and by wonders, and by war. . . .

—Deuteronomy 4:34

Border Territory
Republic of the Sphere
Capellan Confederation

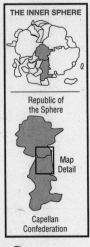

THE INNER SPHERE

Republic of
the Sphere

Map
Detail

Capellan
Confederation

National capital

District capital

Contested worlds

COREWARD

ANTI-SPINWARD

SPINWARD

RIMWARD

MAXIMUM JUMP:
APPROXIMATELY
30 LIGHT-YEARS

Map compiled by COMSTAR.

©3133 COMSTAR
CARTOGRAPHIC CORPS

Zurich
Tall Trees
Saiph Aldebaran
Genoa Kansu
Algol
Almach
Demeter
Liao
New
Canton
Ningpo
Buchlau
Pleione
Halloran V Algot
Jon
Zion
Gan Singh Poznan
New Aragon
Kyrkbacken
Menkar
Shensi
Hunan
Asuncion
Styk
St. Andre
Foochow
Foot Fall
Tsitsang
Suzano
Wei Shipka
Second Try
Palos
Elnath Yunnah
New Macao High
abren
Zurauk
Menkib Mandate
Phact
Corey
Sakhalin
Matsu
Wazan
Ulan Bator
Remshield
ld Kentucky
Quemoy
Kaifeng
Heligoland
Chamdo
Sarna
Tsingtao
Raballa Bora
Truth
Lesalles
Sarmaxa
Minnacora
Randar
Capella
No Return
New Sagan
Ares
Bandora
Necromo
Masterson Geifer
Capricorn III
Cordiagr Aldertaine
Relevow
Nashuar
Kurragin
Gei-Fu Brighton
Ovan
Taga
Overton
Preston Glasgow
Vestallas
Scituate
Kittery
Hexare Harloc Milos
Gurnet
Sian
Denbar Spica

30 LIGHT-YEARS

90 LIGHT-YEARS OR 20.1 PARSECS

PROLOG

A Dark Night on Liao

*This use of the Emergency Communications System
is to inform all citizens and residents of Liao that the
local ComStar network has suffered a loss of systems
coordination. Precentor Rayburne Belzer, citing last
week's three-day interruption, promises to have the
HPG back up as soon as possible. "Disruption will
be kept to a minimum."*

— Station WXU, Alert News Broadcast,
2200 hours, 7 August 3132

Outside Lianyungang
Qinghai Province, Liao
Prefecture V, The Republic
11 August 3132

Twilight had come and gone on Liao, and that wasn't good.

Evan Kurst paced a tight box around his small moving van,
one of four haulers parked in a staggered line atop an isolated
bluff overlooking the Cavalry River. He kept to himself, as
he'd been taught to do. Kicking gravel against the van's oversize tires, Evan divided his time between watching the narrow
access road that had brought the small cadre of *Ijori Dè
Guāng* members here, and looking at the jewel-studded blanket of velvet sky. Not a trace of sunset's color bled over the
western horizon, and the sky remained crystal clear with visi-

bility at twenty kilometers or better. The worst possible conditions for a clandestine operation.

"Drive flare!" someone shouted from behind another of the dark-painted vehicles. Evan winced, wondering—worried—how far the shout would carry in the still night. "DropShip."

The flare was little more than a bright star moving across the heavens, a thin dagger of hard, white light. Too small for the merchant-converted *Union* they were expecting. Too high for any kind of approach to the bluff. And actually, wasn't it close to —

"Twenty-one hundred hours." Evan glanced at his watch. "That is the ballistic shuttle from Nánlù." Liao's southern continent. "Not our DropShip," he said softly, to himself.

It wasn't coming. Something had gone wrong, again. He dried his palms against his jeans. Evan knew only one of the other six recruits. Mai Wa wasn't here, the needler pistol weighed his hip down awkwardly, and they were fifteen kilometers outside of Lianyungang—the city's lights were a muted glow above the forest to the northeast—with no good safe house to run for should the local constabulary swoop down.

"And I have a military history test on Monday."

That bothered him more than it probably should have. A member of the budding *Ijori Dè Guāng*, Liao's newest band of self-proclaimed freedom fighters, should not be worried about his position within The Republic's militia. But he was. Evan had worked too long and hard for this chance to become a MechWarrior. With his recent transfer to the prestigious Liao Conservatory of Military Arts, his personal honor demanded that he make his mark above the line set by any citizen student.

It almost made him laugh. "What I could tell them now about the end of the Capellan invasion in 3112 would qualify as Master's level work." Doctorate, even. A few history books would have to be rewritten.

But he wouldn't tell. The secret he'd been entrusted with was too big to share with anyone save Mai Uhn Wa, Evan's *sifu* in all things seditious. Mai would know what to do with such a secret.

If Mai ever arrived.

If the DropShip came.

Too many ifs.

A warm breeze smelling of pine trees, wildflowers, and the day's moist heat ruffled Evan's mop of dark hair. The warm, wet climate made Qinghai Province one of the planet's best agricultural centers. Rice, peppers, sweet naranji: everything grew well here. Nánlù and the once-more inhabitable regions of Anderia were Liao's industrial heart, but Beilù, the northern continent, was Liao's breadbasket.

It was also the seat of occupation by The Republic of the Sphere, and the very heart of all resistance to Devlin Stone's "benevolent" despotism.

Devlin Stone. The "devil" Stone. Evan Kurst looked up into the starry heavens, found the suns of Nanking, Tigress, and there, on the horizon, valiant Tikonov. Capellan systems, all, and along with Liao once belonging to the mighty Capellan Confederation, one of the Inner Sphere's five Great Houses.

In the local constellation of Qu Yuan, the poet, Evan located the sun that looked down upon Terra. It was from that cursed star system sixty-five years before that the Word of Blake launched its Jihad against civilization, bringing the Inner Sphere to its knees in ten brutal years of scorched-earth warfare. Devlin Stone led the resistance that finally cast down the Armageddon worshippers. Then liberator turned conqueror as Stone bargained for a new realm centered around Terra, taking as spoils of victory a territory spanning a hundred-and-twenty-light-year radius around mankind's birthworld. Which was how Liao and over fifty other Capellan worlds became part of the new Republic of the Sphere.

Whether they wanted to or not.

"You see somethin' up there, Kurst?"

Whit Greggor stepped up next to Evan. Greggor was the one *Ijori Dè Guāng* member present tonight that Evan knew. The large man had a voice that rumbled up from deep within his chest, broad, Slavic features, and crew-cut reddish-brown hair turning premature gray. Too old to be a student, full of ideals. Too young to remember life under the Confederation, fifty-some years before. Evan pegged him as a thug. Mai Wa probably recruited the tough out of a dark alley somewhere.

Did Evan see something? More than Greggor could imagine.

"Freedom," he finally said. "I'm enjoying sunlight that never looked down on the Word of Blake . . . that never knew Devlin Stone."

"I'd rather catch the drive flare of our 'Ship. We need more weapons." He cracked his scarred, oversize knuckles. "Then we can ram real freedom down the throats of all these paper citizens."

"Spoken like a true patriot." Crude and boorish, the sentiment summed up Greggor quite well. Evan considered it very likely that there was a bridge somewhere missing its troll. Would a man like this even care to understand what he was fighting for?

"You sayin' we don't need more weapons?"

"We need something," Evan agreed. Weapons. Resources. *Leaders*. The people of Liao longed to slip The Republic's harness. Mai Wa prophesied that once the landslide began, it would sweep the world.

Evan believed now more than ever.

"So what's the holdup, you think? The new ComStar blackout?"

"Could be."

The man hawked, spat to one side. "What else, ya think? The *oubluduk* cowlheads've never had their shit in one sock."

Greggor's speech was often laced with Russian curses and colorful stock, but his analysis did not differ much from Evan's. ComStar's local service had gone down again, disconnecting Liao from the rest of the Inner Sphere for the second time this month. Without faster-than-light communications provided by the organization's network of hyperpulse generator stations, disruptions occurred in everything from shipping schedules to interplanetary market trades. Once had been a costly anomaly, virtually unknown since the agency's inception.

Twice? Evan wondered.

"The JumpShip could have had technical problems," Evan finally said. "Customs maybe stopped the DropShip in orbit." Besides the HPG network, so much relied on the tenuous fabric of interstellar travel: jump-capable vessels that moved thirty light-years at a leap and DropShips ferrying goods and people between worlds.

Greggor wasn't satisfied with that. "I still say it's ComStar. Got us all frigged up again. Filthy *vrebrachneys*."

Evan shrugged. Greggor's black moods could be contagious. A shout from another cadre member saved him from any reply.

"Lights! Lights on the road!"

"Truck," someone else called out. "Hovercraft."

This time Evan didn't worry about the noise. He worried about who was arriving so late to their party. A chill took him as he drew his needler pistol, felt its uncomfortable weight in his hand. His efforts in the *Ijori Dè Guāng* so far had been limited to "liberating" supplies from remote military compounds and sabotaging public transportation services. Military academies taught MechWarrior cadets basic small arms handling—laser pistols, for example—and those he wasn't allowed to carry outside the firing range. The needler was a more vicious weapon than any he'd trained with.

Perspiration warmed under Evan's arms as he took cover behind his rented haulers, extending the weapon in a two-hand grasp over the vehicle's hood and waiting for confirmation of sight, fight, or flight.

The open-bed hovercraft flashed its lights twice, once, twice.

"Mai! It is Mai Wa." The resistance leader. Liao's best hope.

Relief flooded Evan with a cold touch, like an aftertaste of the regret that came after any compromise. Part of him had looked forward to pulling the trigger, he realized, placing himself apart from those who *talked*, and among the company of those who *did*. Even the Cult of Liao, Evan had discovered recently, honored action over rhetoric. In that, the underground political movement had more in common with the forming *Ijori Dè Guāng* than most people thought.

The hovertruck cut its lights and lift fans just short of the gathered haulers, settling to the ground as its air cushion spilled out from beneath rigid skirting. The dying whine of its lifters reminded Evan of this morning's visit to the Cult of Liao shrine, and the humming of its generator, which echoed off stark, barren, bunker walls.

Mai Uhn Wa slid out from the cab, pouring himself to the ground with a fluidity which Evan had come to envy. His shaved head was tanned to a leathery brown, his mustache oily black and obviously dyed on the fifty-odd-year-old man. Small and compact, rarely given to exaggerated gestures, Mai Wa might have been any Capellan-descended citizen you passed on the street if you never noticed his eyes. Black and hard, and never blinking enough, they were eyes that had seen—and still saw—too much.

Yet Evan would show his mentor something the other man had never dreamt to look upon.

The thought warmed him, buoyed his hopes, until Mai Wa looked over his assembled cadre and shook his head slowly. Once.

"The DropShip will not arrive," the elder man informed them straightaway. "Our off-world network is compromised."

"Compromised?" Greggor sounded as if he was struggling with the meaning of the word. "How? Who?"

Evan had never asked about Mai's off-world contacts. In a resistance cell organization, the less you knew the better. Evan already knew more than he should about Liao-based operations, including the names of other cell leaders, which he put down to being a prominent MechWarrior candidate. Among more common members Evan carried influence, which Mai Wa had used in this last year.

Now he regretted not asking. His ability to advise would be limited.

"Customs Security on Genoa halted all outbound traffic three days ago," Mai Wa told them. "In the process of routine management, some . . . discrepancies were uncovered. The DropShip was destroyed trying to flee authorities."

Like dominoes poised to topple, no doubt a great deal of Mai Wa's network stood exposed. How bad was this setback? And why halt *all* outbound traffic? The disruption such a decision caused . . . would pale next to any larger disruption already occurring.

"The blackout," Evan said, spitting out the word like a mouthful of rancid naranji pulp. The timing could not be coincidence. "Genoa noticed that we were off the HPG net again."

"Yes," Mai said. "And no. And not exactly." The small man seemed to be carrying an extraordinarily large burden, and now simply heaved it aside in the most direct manner possible. "Four days ago, Genoa witnessed something we were spared. In a way. They saw nearly *every* world go dark. In a six-hour period, they lost HPG contact with all star systems but one, New Aragon, which reported much the same thing."

The implications rolled over Evan Kurst like an assault tank. HPGs reached out fifty light-years. Two worlds reported a complete loss of signal from almost every other station within that distance?

"Arboris?" someone asked. "Ningpo and Gan Singh?"

Neighboring worlds. "New Canton?" The capital of Prefecture VI.

Mai had little left to offer. "Only a single JumpShip has come in bearing any news so far. Shipboard rumor claims that sporadic contact has been made with New Canton, yes. And with Achernar in Prefecture IV. But we may be looking at over ninety percent loss of the ComStar network. If that extends into any of the Great Houses at our borders . . ."

Hundreds. Thousands of worlds. Dark. Evan grasped at the full implications. Missed. "Our work here," he asked, "what of it?" The awaited supplies were everything they needed to flesh out a true resistance force. To make the *Ijori Dè Guāng* something other than one more small-time movement. Evan felt their work slipping away into nothingness.

"It is finished," Mai admitted, "for now. Chaos reigns outside of this system, and likely will be here in very short order. If we were prepared, it would be a golden opportunity." For a moment, a flash of fire lit up the other man's dark eyes. Then, "But we are not."

Angry now, Evan stepped forward. His hand itched to grab something, and his needler came to mind. "We are out here, all of us, because of you," he accused Mai Wa. "You made promises."

"And it is no longer possible to keep them." As if speaking to someone in the distance, the *Ijori Dè Guāng* leader added, "It will not be the first time I have had to break such promises."

What was one more person to fail the Capellan people, and Evan? Raised as a ward of the state, Evan had hardened himself against most disappointments. But for the first time in years, he felt betrayed. Felt it deep down near where the fires of hope had burned hot not many hours before. If the secret he carried might change things, Evan would have spilled it in front of all. But it would not. He heard the sound of defeat lurking behind Mai Uhn Wa's words. The movement's *sifu* was crestfallen—emptied, and hiding it.

Evan turned away, ignoring questions that Mai would deftly deflect. He walked to the bluff's edge, staring out over the dark valley as, behind him, cadre members abandoned plans and each other in their empty haulers.

Then all was silent. For a time.

"You are angry."

Evan knew that Mai Wa had not left. The rebel leader's

eyes had never left the back of his neck. They burned there, drilling holes.

"Anger has its uses, Evan Kurst, but if you let it guide your next actions, you will be lost."

"I no longer need to listen to you, Mai Uhn Wa. What I do next is my own business." To stand alongside people who *do*, and not people who make excuses.

"If you think I enjoy seeing years of my work destroyed in a single night, you are greatly mistaken, and not the man I thought you would become." Evan noticed that Mai held back from saying "the man I thought you were." Mai stared through Evan. "I have more important people than you to whom I will answer for this failure. This time I gambled and I lost. Liao is on its own."

Evan couldn't trust anything the other man said. Mai Wa claimed ties to the highest authorities. To have been involved in several uprisings on Liao over the years. He did put together the *Ijori Dè Guāng*, and now he abandoned it—that was what Evan *knew*. That Mai thought it necessary made no difference to Evan.

More importantly, it made no difference to the Capellan people.

Evan waited until footsteps gave way to the whine of powerful turbines, and then until the last echoes of the hovercraft were lost back down the long access road. He watched the heavens rotate on the axis star, a parade of celestial beings. Thinking. Planning.

"We have always been alone," he finally whispered into the dark summer's night.

But that was not necessarily the case.

Not anymore.

PART ONE

The Politics of Destruction

1

Path Toward Redemption

"Prefect Tao's relocation to New Aragon should not be considered any kind of estrangement between himself and the Prefecture's governing body, which will remain on Liao. We all accept the need for shifting resources to match our new strategic demands."
—Lord Governor Marion Hidic, Recorded address
from Liao, 12 January 3134

Celestial Palace
Zi-jin Chéng (Forbidden City), Sian
Sian Commonality, Capellan Confederation
8 March 3134

Footsteps echoed in the outer corridor. Mai Uhn Wa nodded to himself. He sat cross-legged on his thin mattress, feeling the cold stone floor through a half inch of meager padding and his threadbare prison dungarees. Gooseflesh puckered his bared forearms.

He faced the gray cinderblock wall at the rear of his isolation cell, hunching forward in concentration. A few strands of graying hair fell across Mai's face as he dabbed more of his homemade stain onto the wall's porous surface. His ink was rancid pork fat rendered down by slow cooking under the light they never turned off, mixed with soy and the red juice he pulped out of beets. A strip of cloth torn from his prison dungarees acted as his brush. Wrap it over the end of two fingers, dip into the dark stain, and then dab carefully. One day's work completed two or three ideograms.

He'd worked halfway through his second when his cell door slammed back and a pair of Maskirovka agents entered. Mai Wa did not flinch at their arrival, or even turn to look. Whatever was to happen would happen with or without his participation.

"More of your grandiose delusions?" Michael Yung-Te asked, disbelief coloring each word. A shrugged pause. "On your feet, Mai Wa."

Snugging the cloth strip tighter against his discolored fingertips, Mai Wa continued to stain a dark line across the wall's light gray facing.

Yung-Te stepped farther into the room. He scuffed his boot against the side of the thin mat. "I said get up." His tone was darker this time. Angry.

A second request? How novel. Almost enough to convince him to obey. Instead, Mai Wa put finishing touches on the ideogram for "loyalty," then straightened to survey his work.

"The highest and most important ideal in any MechWarrior's life is loyalty," he whispered softly.

That was the opening tenet of the sixth dictum of the Lorix Order, a quasireligious philosophy endorsed by the Capellan state. It was also among the strongest principles endorsed by Capellan Warrior Houses, the elite military enclaves of the Confederation: Imarra . . . Kamata . . . Dai Da Chi . . . Hiritsu . . .

Ijori?

As always, thoughts of the fallen Warrior House led Mai Uhn Wa back to his recent attempts to resurrect it on Liao, and to the disastrous timing of the ComStar Blackout. *Ijori Dè Guāng.* The *Light of Ijori.* If he'd only had six more months.

"Mai Wa—" Agent Yung-Te warned.

The Mask agents still hadn't forced him away from his work. Sensing that this visit was something beyond their normal interrogation and reeducation attempts, Mai Wa now set his wooden cup of stain to one side and folded his strip of cloth next to it. He rose slowly to his feet, favoring his right side with the taped ribs and electroshock burns. Neat columns of ideograms very nearly covered the entire wall. Starting as high in the upper right corner as Mai Wa could reach, they scrolled from top to bottom and right to left in the ancient tradition. The first five dictums, all complete, and the start of the sixth. With effort, he would find just enough room to finish them.

"Such determination would have been admirable put in service to the State, rather than against it."

Mai Wa turned and half bowed toward his keepers. "I am a traitor," he agreed. "I serve the Confederation."

Michael Yung-Te was in his late thirties, with black hair and a lean, angular face. Ambition burned behind gray-blue eyes. He was fast approaching that timeless quality some men of Asian descent were fortunate to gain. His associate looked older, with the sunken-eyed expression of a man who was part of too many secrets, too much senseless violence. Your basic agent of the Capellan secret police. Both wore Han-styled charcoal gray suits and high-necked, stiff white shirts. Their mandarin collars were closed at the throat with a triangular Confederation crest.

"You'll serve as an example to other would-be traitors," the older agent said, but his voice lacked the usual dogmatic conviction.

Mai Uhn Wa looked at both men with a faint stirring of curiosity. A tense smile crept at the right side of his face. The left no longer worked so well, even with the cheekbone reconstruction. "Will I?" he asked.

Yung-Te reigned back his associate with a raised hand. "No marks," he reminded the other man, who stepped forward and kicked Mai Wa's bowl against the wall, splattering reddish-brown stain along the lowest cinderblocks. Several large spatters smeared across the ideogram for "loyalty."

"An untidy end," Mai said softly.

Oh, yes. This was something different.

Mai Uhn Wa limped into the Chamber of the Celestial Throne with head bowed and ankles shackled together by a short length of polymer chain. His bare feet whispered against teak flooring, the black wood lacquered so heavily that it reflected the entire room like a dark mirror. Heady incense lingered in the air. Sandalwood, he tasted. And jasmine. His prison dungarees rubbed roughly against his skin, but at least they were freshly laundered and pressed with military creases.

One did not appear before the Chancellor of the Capellan

Confederation, Soul of the People and God Incarnate of Sian, in anything less than the best their station allowed.

His Maskirovka escorts paused awkwardly at the threshold, unbidden to enter but uneasy with leaving their charge alone. A half dozen shuffle steps into the chamber, Mai Wa stopped as well. The Mask agents finally bowed and retreated, closing the large, bronze-faced doors behind him.

Still, he waited.

"Approach me, Mai Uhn Wa." The command was subtle, shadowed, but no less forceful for being spoken barely above a whisper.

Mai raised his head and took in the austere beauty of Daoshen Liao's throne room. The walls were paneled with red-grained bamboo, suggesting a ring of flames around the entire chamber. A carved frieze ran down the left-hand wall, depicting ancient warriors on an eternal march. On the right only a few simple charcoal sketches hung as decoration, drawn by the hand of The Ascendant Sun-Tzu Liao, Daoshen's father, if stories were to be believed.

A runner of red carpeting shot through with gold threads led from the bronze-faced doors to the foot of the dais. Gold: the prerogative of the emperor in ancient China. Mai avoided it, keeping to the right-hand side as he approached the Celestial Dais with all due humility.

His life, and purpose, might very well hang by such a thread.

A suit of Chinese armor, from the Nán Bei Cháo dynasties of ancient Terra, stood on display at the corner of the dais, a beautiful piece of physical history, as was the chair at the center of the dais, the Celestial Throne itself. The Chinese zodiac wheel formed its upper backrest, a reminder of the diverse nature of mankind, and each leg ended in a dragon's claw. Carved from one solid piece of mahogany, the red and brown wood grain promised both strength and character.

And on that throne, half hidden in shadow, sat Daoshen Liao.

For the third time in his life Mai Wa looked upon the Chancellor of the Capellan Confederation. Although he had mentally prepared himself for this interview a hundred times over, it still surprised Mai that his eyes found the Chancellor only when it seemed that Daoshen wanted to be noticed.

Sian's living God rested back into his throne with arms draped over each massive rest. *Coiled.* Ready to strike. The Chancellor's head was shaved clean. His mustaches were long and jet black, braided at each end and weighted with a tiny golden bead where they came even with his shoulders. He wore a golden Nehru jacket with a green mantle fastened across his shoulders, and green silk pants decorated with red and gold serpents along the outside seam. Nearly two meters tall, and reaching past gaunt for emaciated, the Capellan leader was anything but frail. He . . . radiated.

Truly invested with Divine Will or simply secure in his own power, that was for Him to know.

Mai Wa went down to his knees, then stretched full length onto the floor of the Celestial Chamber, prostrating himself before the Chancellor. "I serve the Confederation," he said.

"Attend, Mai Uhn Wa. Set your feet beneath you, and stand once more as a man."

Mai's hair, damp but clean, fell into his face as he slowly climbed back to his feet. He pulled it back over his shoulders, untangling ropy strands from the wispy beard prison had given him.

Daoshen Liao hunched forward slightly, peering intently at Mai Wa, green eyes burning with an inner fire. Mai could never know what the Great Soul was searching for, and so stood up under the scrutiny with as much military bearing as he could muster. Daoshen smiled, thin and without humor. "It is Heaven's Way to conquer without striving, to get responses without speaking."

"To induce the people to come without summoning," Mai quoted automatically, then realizing that he had just interrupted the Chancellor. Daoshen might have been making a private joke. And the passage . . . but there was no path left to him but to finish it. "To act according to plans without haste," he finished softly.

"You have studied Lao Tse and his *Tao Teh Ching*. Recently?" Daoshen's voice was nearly devoid of inflection. But his words, at least, conveyed a sense of interest.

Picking his words, and his tone, with great care, Mai nodded and said, "I have been fortunate to enjoy the hospitality of the State for many months, Illustrious One. We are granted the magnificent benefit of two recreations. One is the study of proper Capellan philosophies."

"The other?" asked the Chancellor.

A glance at the suit of ancient armor. "The study of history. I have availed myself of both."

"But have you learned anything?" Daoshen asked, and his question was very obviously rhetorical. "On your return to the Confederation," he continued, "I declared you a traitor to the realm. You offered no defense. The Maskirovka, finally, would like to set your trial date."

Daoshen paused, waiting for a denial. "I am a traitor," Mai said. "I serve the Confederation.",He was guilty the moment the Chancellor declared it. A trial was mere formality.

"How do you serve the Confederation?" the Chancellor asked. "How did you serve me?"

"Majestic Wisdom, I have always sought to further the Capellan nation. When I strayed, when I did not return to the Confederation as ordered, I did so only for the chance of bringing you greater glory."

"When you first served on the world of Liao, you obeyed my father without fault." Daoshen did not sound as if he were cross-examining Mai. He went on carefully and methodically. "You were instrumental in the new rise of pro-Capellan sentiment."

That had been nearly thirty years before, just after the new century. Mai Wa's first mission to the birthworld of House Liao. Chancellor Sun-Tzu had ordered a number of young officers to foment unrest within The Republic. Mai Wa's successes saved a lackluster military career, earning him a promotion. His future suddenly looked bright.

That had all come crashing down, however, the next year.

"I was not there for the Night of Fury," Mai said, ashamed. He'd been pulled back for specialized training. Had he been there when the first assault wave landed on Liao, he believed he could have—*would have*—made the difference. Instead, The Republic rallied, and so began a violent, two-year conflict.

"Later, I was attached to the Fifth Confederation Reserves. We saw action on Wei, Hunan, Styk. I was not called on to accompany your father."

His plans ruined, Sun-Tzu traveled to Liao in an attempt to broker peace, a rare expedition from Sian for the aging Chancellor. His arrival did little to calm the angry sea of resentment harbored by Republic stormtroopers, though. They attacked. And Sun-Tzu fell. Capellan forces rallied long enough to effect a full retreat, but they did not come away with the Chancellor's mortal body for there was none left to claim. By all accounts Sun-Tzu *ascended* that day, becoming a divine being. Charged by His spirit, Confederation forces struck back hard enough to force a new peace with The Republic.

The world of Liao, and so many Capellan worlds, however, remained in Republic hands.

Daoshen nodded, agreeing with all spoken and unspoken. "You accepted discommendation."

"I did. And indefinite leave from the military." The memories were fragmented after so long, but still there. Mai Wa remembered those painful years of hard work and contemplation, struggling alongside farmers on the planet of Jasmine. Exploring the ruins outside of Lhasa, "I found the old Ijori stronghold." One of the Warrior Houses lost to Word of Blake's Jihad. Only four of the original eight now survived. "Spent seven years studying their philosophies, their strategies, their victories and defeats." Finding in them a purpose that filled the void left after Sun-Tzu Liao's ascension, he'd petitioned for a return to active military service.

Which was how Mai Wa first found himself before Daoshen Liao, in 3126, summoned into His Presence and tasked again with delivering the Chancellor's dynasty birthworld.

"You were to help return home our lost people," Daoshen said.

Mai nodded, his eyes casting for the floor again. "Yes, Generous Soul. In return you offered to grant me my single wish: the resurrection of Warrior House Ijori. But my efforts failed. The student uprising I inspired at the Liao Conservatory was defused by the Paladin Ezekiel Crow."

"To act according to plans without haste." Daoshen reminded him of the earlier quote from Lao Tse.

"I was eager," he agreed. "I moved too quickly."

"And you disobeyed my command to return!" Daoshen's voice hardly rose above normal levels of conversation, but the power behind his words slammed into Mai Wa as if driven by sledgehammer blows.

"I did. I hoped to create an uprising that would finally sweep away The Republic. I devoted every effort, calling on resources developed as far back as the first Liao campaign." Mai felt hollowed, empty. At the time, it had felt so right. A divine purpose. "I devoted my life toward that end."

"You were supposed to devote your life," Daoshen said, very coldly, "to me."

Mai nodded. "I am a traitor. I serve the Confederation."

"You *are* a traitor. You may *yet* serve the Confederation."

The reprieve—faint, but there—stirred faith back into Mai Wa's soul. The old warrior looked up to Daoshen Liao, Soul of All Things Capellan, and dared to hope.

"Yes," Daoshen allowed, awarding him one regal nod. "Your past failures—even your treason—may yet be put behind you, Mai Uhn Wa. Today is the eighth day of *sān-yuè*."

March eighth? The twenty-first anniversary of . . . "Your father's Ascension." Daoshen nodded. It was no coincidence. "Liao."

"Liao," the Chancellor agreed. "Birthworld of my father's line. It is time to begin again. Your long ties to Liao, the on-planet assets you still possess, your array of protected aliases— perhaps you can still serve the state."

"Chancellor. That is all I ask."

"All? You were more forthcoming during our first interview." Daoshen Liao obviously read the desire still written across Mai Wa's soul. "The true prize awaits you, Mai Uhn Wa. Do not fail me."

"No, Celestial Wisdom."

Daoshen's wrath, should Mai bring it upon himself again, would fall swiftly and certainly. Which was only right. The taking of Liao could only be one step in a much larger parade, and if plans did not go as foreseen, as they so often did, Mai Wa expected to be one of the first casualties. The Chancellor offered him a chance for redemption, but he did not guarantee anything.

As if reading his mind, though, Daoshen nodded. "What I can do for you, I will. There are old debts, promises, that may help smooth the way."

Mai Wa bowed from the waist. "I serve the Confederation."

"As do we all," Daoshen said, staring off into the distance, smiling at a future only he could see. "As do we all."

2

The Campus Cabals

*The unidentified DropShips burning in toward Terra
continue to refuse all attempts at communication.
The Tenth Principes has mobilized and their aerospace assets will intercept in approximately sixty
minutes. After the recent fighting on Achernar, on
Northwind—we can only imagine what has now
come home to Terra and what will eventually befall
The Republic of the Sphere. Why are we so afraid of
the dark?*
—Mace O'Ronnell, Stellar Associated, 29 March 3134

Yiling (Chang-an)
Qinghai Province, Liao
Prefecture V, The Republic
24 April 3134

Evan Kurst staggered over to a storefront wall and held it up
for a moment. The night air felt cool against his flushed skin.
Wiping his hands on the outside of his jeans, drying them, he
then adjusted the straps on his backpack, trying to make it
look natural. A half dozen books, a load of laundry for the
laundromat, a few days' groceries; those would have been
nothing for a fourth-year student at the Liao Conservatory.
Military-grade power amplifiers weighed a bit more. And you
really did not want to get caught hauling them around the
Liao capital of Chang-an.

Or anywhere, for that matter.

Even in the early hours of morning, barely past midnight, the Yiling suburbs could hardly be considered deserted. Separated from Conservatory grounds by the four-lane avenue and a high wall on Evan's right, the local commercial district tailored itself to student lives which included late-night cramming sessions, celebrations, and general night-owl behavior. Neon signs glowed in fluorescent colors. There was no real traffic to consider, but several couples and half a dozen singles still roamed the streets, heading to or from the university or simply between parties.

One kindred soul staggered along with an open bottle of Timbiqui Dark and saluted Evan with the tall-necked container, offering moral support.

Evan waved back dutifully, shoved himself toward the nearby street corner. One edge of the amplifier's housing dug into his back. He shifted its weight again by pretending to slide along the wall in need of support, shrugging his shoulder straps into a new position.

Across the intersection was the corner entrance to a commercial park, where students could bike or blade or lounge on hard plastic benches if all they wanted was a place to get off-campus. To the right, across the wide avenue, was the Grand Arch entrance to the university: the photo-op entrance, with fortresslike stonework holding up a buttressed arch, LIAO CONSERVATORY carved in relief, framing an impressive stretch of landscaped grounds.

Most students and military cadets chose to use any of several minor gates much closer to dorms or teaching halls or parade grounds. Which made for light foot traffic and just enough time to pull this off.

Evan was late, ten meters short of the cross street when a squeal of tires and a plastic-crunching smash echoed up the street behind him. He fought to keep any extra spring out of his step. One of the easiest ways to blow a stealth operation was to do something that stood out from the crowd. Still, Evan staggered a last few steps to the corner before rubbernecking to look back at the auto accident. One block back a car abandoned the scene, fishtailing up the wide avenue that divided Yiling from the Conservatory wall. The other, an Avanti economy hybrid, caught fire as a sparking flywheel touched off spilled fuel, or that was how the accident report would read.

People ran to the aid of the abandoned hybrid, or stood

around watching, or pointing. One concerned youth sprinted over the four-lane avenue and pounded on the window of the small guardhouse nestled beneath the Grand Arch. A lot of shouting and gesturing ensued, followed by the security guard running off with Evan's ringer, rendering aid to the pre-arranged "accident."

"Move along, please," a commanding voice ordered. A uniformed policeman stepped into the intersection, waving Evan forward with a curt gesture.

Evan nodded, thankful for his arrival. They traded tight smiles as Evan hurried across the intersection, knowing each other for members of the Cult of Liao. The officer would keep prying eyes focused away from *Ijori Dè Guāng* activity.

Dodging into the commercial park, Evan pulled a light cotton mask down over his brow. An overhead streetlamp had been broken out the night before, and not repaired. Beneath that his people waited. Whit Greggor lurked into the shadows with a large piece of iron—a prybar good for jimmying doors. Two other *Ijori Dè Guāng* members were busy connecting their own equipment into a working laser.

One of them had already cracked the lamp's utility box and run a pair of cables out onto the cement walk. "Late," he said, helping to wrestle the laser onto a stabilizing tripod. He was a utility worker with the Yiling suburbs. The man did not know who Evan was at all.

"Get set up," Evan said by way of apology.

It took moments, well-rehearsed the week before and waiting only for the power amplifier Evan delivered. The fourth man, retired infantry, pulled amber goggles over his eyes and took up station behind the laser's handgrips. "Charging . . . ready," he said.

Evan looked over the hedge at the Grand Arch entrance, the well-lit guard booth, and a small cluster of late-nighters who debated crossing the grounds or walking down to the accident site. The acrid scent of burning plastic drifted down on a light breeze. He nodded.

"Fire."

The laser pulsed, stabbing sharp spikes of sapphire energy through the night. There were a few screams, more shouting. The police officer's whistle shrilled sharply, directing people back—away from the park—just move it! No radio call as yet. Confusion of the moment.

Evan stood rigidly still, feeling the warmth radiating off the overheating laser as it scoured and sliced and cut and stabbed.

Then it was over. The *Ijori Dè Guāng* members broke down their equipment faster than it had gone together. Evan took the power amplifier and they split in three directions. Whit Greggor stayed with him until clear of the park, then left Evan alone as the student staggered back through the streets, making his escape.

Behind him, the first sirens of the night finally sounded.

Evan lounged at a bistro table outside YiCha's Gourmet Coffees, sipping a citrus-blend juice. He sat with his back to the shop window—the best choice he had, considering—and his eyes glanced left along the street, right toward the intersection, then straight through traffic toward the busy monorail stop. The sun barely peeked over the roof of a nearby mall, its rays slanting down the narrow street, jumping over the curb and a double-wide sidewalk, and warming the left side of Evan's face. It looked to be a beautiful day, part of Liao's deep autumn wonder that ended with a short winter season during the Terran standard months of June and July.

Left again. Right.

Got him.

Evan paused with the insulated cup half lifted to his mouth as David Parks skulked around a corner, keeping his back toward the wall. Parks moved at the edge of Evan's peripheral vision, but there was no missing his Caesar-cut red hair or the black range rider trench he so adored.

Parks reached into his coat. For a weapon.

With a quick spin and toss Evan could have dashed his entire cup right into the David's face—except that it wouldn't do much for the other man's temper, and the juice was still too fresh and cold to be wasted. Instead, Evan finished his sip as he brought up his left hand, resting casually in his lap until now, and formed a two-fingered gun that he aimed back over his shoulder.

"You're dead, David."

David leaped forward and snaked his thick arm around Evan's neck, locking it in a stranglehold. Evan tensed, but forced himself not to react as his friend throttled him. "Tomorrow, Evan. I'll get you tomorrow."

Jenna Lynn Tang walked up just as David gave an extra

squeeze and then released Evan. Behind her followed Mark Lo. "I think you've said that three days running, Dave." She offered Evan a weary smile. "Me, I've been assassinated every day this week."

"All for the good of the movement," David told her. "Got to be ready." He didn't say for what, though everyone knew he spoke of the *Ijori Dè Guāng*. He talked about joining up all the time. Dropping Evan a too obvious wink, he turned for the coffee shop door and disappeared inside.

Jen slipped into a vacant chair at the small bistro table. Gathering her tight braids into a loose collection, she secured them behind her with a red band. Jen had pale skin and green eyes the color of polished jade. She had also paid for some cosmetic surgery during her sophomore year at the Conservatory, adding just a touch of epicanthic fold at the corner of each eye. Evan found the effect very appealing.

"I'm gonna grab a coffee," Mark said by way of offering.

Jenna thought, then shook her head. "Nothing for me." Evan picked up his cup and sloshed it around. He was still good. Mark ducked inside, and Evan's smile faded a notch as soon as the other cadet was out of sight. He hadn't called Mark, who had obviously spent another night at Jen's. Mark would not find this morning's event amusing.

"Something wrong?"

"Where's Hahn?" Evan asked, covering his lapse by staring back the way his friends had come. Hahn Soom Gui was crossing the nearby intersection—against the light, of course, walking as if the world would move out of the way for him. A hoversedan blasted its horn. Safe behind red-tinted aviators, Hahn was oblivious.

"Got stopped by some admirers," Jen told him, amusement playing richly through her melodic voice. "I think they're planning a rally."

"Again?" The academic year was only into its fourth month, and already Hahn had helped organize five pro-Capellan events.

"Something has people stirred up," Jen said, and she leaned across the table. Her eyes were brightly interested. "Of course, you wouldn't know anything about that?"

He might. Evan fought back any reaction. His friends might be ready to march in campus demonstrations—all but Mark, anyway—but they were also candidates for The Republic military. The less they knew, or had confirmed, the better. Very soon Evan would have to make a hard choice: cadet corps, serving in the local militia most likely, or underground.

"Might have something to do with the new rumors," he said, dodging away from the opening she'd given him. "I hear a new JumpShip passed through." Which was the only way to get stale news from of the rest of The Republic these days.

"We heard that, too." She nodded in greeting as Hahn walked up. "Fighting on Terra. Who would have thought?"

Devlin Stone might have, Evan did not say, or The Republic's current Exarch, Damien Redburn. Terra was no more a true Republic world than . . . than . . . well, Liao.

"Fighting on Terra. Northwind. Achernar." Hahn Soom Gui stopped behind Evan because he knew how much it irked the MechWarrior candidate. Evan shifted his chair as Hahn struck a pose. "In the dark times no one can tell friend from foe, only brother . . . from other."

Hahn's delivery was polished and perfect; he could have been reciting lines from any well-crafted political speech. And he'd likely made the expression up in just the last few moments. Evan was the eldest among their little campus cabal, and a training MechWarrior, but there was a real reason why Hahn, an armored corps cadet, was the group's leader.

Not just the fact that Evan preferred to remain out of the spotlight.

"Not bad," Jenna said, playing it down. But Evan saw the light blossom across her oval face. Hahn inspired. Hahn led.

Evan tried to imagine Hahn holding a gun, standing over the body of a Republic MP. The picture didn't fit him at all. Evan winced, banishing the memory, and nodded his approval at the rhetoric.

Hahn accepted the tribute from both friends, then turned to the shop window. He waved at someone in line—David probably—and made a complicated set of hand gestures that Evan actually understood: Mocha, double-shot, iced. Hahn did not get his own coffee either.

Mark and David returned together, Mark on his wireless phone and David cradling two cups and a sweet bun in his large hands. Both men were enrolled in the Conservatory's battlesuit infantry program, though David looked more the part at one hundred ninety centimeters, extra-wide shoulders and chiseled features. One could almost believe David's claim to have Clan Elemental blood in his past. But then, David claimed a lot of things.

Mark looked like a stockbroker, big but bookish. He clipped his wireless back to his belt.

"Now that we're all together," Hahn said as he accepted his cup and passed David a couple of stones—The Republic currency that Evan refused to carry. "Maybe Evan will explain what's going on."

"Yeah." David bit into his bun. Around a mouthful of pastry he added, "Why the call?"

Evan sipped his drink. Naranji had a wonderful sweet taste like strawberries and orange together, but in the morning he mixed some grapefruit into the popular juice. "Can't just want to say hey before classes?" he asked, and smiled at his friends' disbelief. "Okay." He pushed his chair back and rose. "Come on."

On the way, pushing through the monorail crowd to the next street over, Evan explained. "I saw it this morning while on my run. I like to finish out here for some Ji-Go." He rattled the ice left in his cup. Jen and David made faces. They couldn't stand the sweet taste of naranji. He ditched the cup in a nearby can. "Instead, I went back for my phone and called you up to meet here. I thought you would like to see." Most of them, anyway.

They took another corner, rounding a bento restaurant with an enviable location one short block from the Conservatory's main gate, and then along the commercial park. The small cadet cadre shuffled to a stop near the corner. They still had to cross the street for the Conservatory grounds, but the view was better here as there was still quite a crowd milling about underneath the Grand Arch entrance, trampling police tape.

Word had spread.

New guerrilla art. Or, what true Republic loyalists would consider more destructive graffiti.

"Yes!" David jumped up and pumped his fist in the air, celebrating the coup. He spilled steaming coffee over his other hand, but didn't care. "That is so excellent." Hahn merely smiled, his washed-out gray eyes hiding safe and secure behind the tinted aviator glasses.

Evan didn't look toward Jenna or Mark at all, protecting his game face. Instead, he stared out across the slow-moving traffic and gathered students, up at the stone arch which had once proclaimed its entry to the Conservatory. The raised letters had been laser-sanded away, and a new proclamation etched over them.

Yóng yuǎn Liào Sūn Zǐ!

Forever lives Sun-Tzu Liao.
"If you will all excuse me," Hahn said, pulling his own wireless off his belt, "I have some calls to make."

3

The Guardian

*Lord Governor Hidic, we've had a dozen phone-in
requests the last few minutes concerning this morning's guerrilla art at the Conservatory. Would you
care to comment on the sentiment? Do you believe
that Sun-Tzu Liao lives forever on this world? Lord
Governor? Hello?*

—Meet & Greet, Station XLDZ,
Interview with Marion Hidic, 24 April 3134

Yiling (Chang-an)
Qinghai Province, Liao
24 April 3134

Evan Kurst counted more cheers and smiles around the Grand
Arch than complaints, though not by many. And there was
plenty of shoving to go around. With Hahn peeling away to do
some campus politicking, the rest forced their way through the
tight knot of students with Mark and David blazing a trail.

"It's vandalism." Mark Lo kicked angrily at the ground as
the cabal passed beneath the ruined stonework. He refused to
look up. "Not free expression."

Evan felt a touch of pity for his friend. It couldn't be easy
at times, hanging around with a group of pro-Capellan cadets.
Even though they were all enrolled in various programs
which would—eventually—lead toward military service, some
students were more Republic minded than others. Mark, fortunately, was a liberal. He believed that every person, citizen

or resident, had the right to voice their opinion. Sometimes that belief ran hard up against his own political views, though.

And against Jenna's.

"Do you really think the PTB would let us post so much as a sign that mentioned Sun-Tzu Liao anywhere near the campus grounds?"

PTB. Powers That Be. Evan did not care for that assignation. It implied irrevocable status. But that was Jenna's way. Rock the system, but never believe you can effect real change. It was one reason, among others, why Evan had never approached her about the *Ijori Dè Guāng*.

"No way," David said, blowing on his scalded fingers. "The government'd rather pretend the resistance didn't exist."

Mark shot a dark glance at David. "So *un*true. The government would rather work *with* people, but they aren't in denial."

"Remember the Heritage Days military parade? They called it a 'switchbox failure,' but I happen to know that some freedom fighters took over the public works building and sabotaged all the lights that morning. Gridlock forced the parade to pass outside of Yiling. I heard there was a killing, too."

Evan noticed the other three staring at him. "What?" Everyone glanced away at the same time. It was almost comical.

Almost.

His friends had long suspected Evan of being an *Ijori Dè Guāng* cell member. Or one of their resources, a snitch, maybe. Or a spy. Evan had a tendency to know more than he should, or be nearby when things turned . . . interesting.

David came back faster than the others. "Well," he said, "I did hear that something similar happened down in Duan." Duan was the local capital of Liao's southern continent of Nánlù.

"Isn't Bulics Academy in that province?" Mark asked.

Evan had attended Bulics before finally getting his transfer to the Conservatory. Damn David. Why couldn't he keep his mouth shut? David was too gung ho, and liked to spout off on the fact, otherwise the burly infantry cadet might have made an excellent recruit.

Evan nodded. "It might be," he said to Mark. "And you know, I think I remember taking classes with several hundred other cadets."

Mark dropped the subject. Not that it would stay dropped for long.

The simple fact remained that Evan Kurst *was* part of the *Ijori Dè Guāng*. A large part, in fact, taking up the reins of the Qinghai Province cell after Mai Wa's abandonment, and eventually parlaying it into a strong voice in all Beilù operations. That, and other reasons, was why Evan had to be so careful with whom he trusted. Mark Lo was the weakest flaw in his personal armor. But Mark came with Jenna, and they all circled around Hahn, so Mark stayed and Evan watched him most carefully of all.

The four students passed onto the Conservatory's walled grounds, where brushed-ferrocrete walkways webbed out over immaculate lawns. Students clustered within some of the nearby courtyards, holding club meetings or just talking about the morning's big event. A *Men Shen* BattleMech presided over one of these areas: The Guardian. The decommissioned 'Mech, with its hooked nose and long-barreled arms, stood a permanent post on the main grounds, a tribute to the Conservatory's past as the alma mater of notable MechWarriors through the years, as well as a nod toward Liao's Capellan roots. From a hundred meters it looked very imposing.

They turned toward it, striking out over the grassy campus toward the cluster of buildings that rose behind the Guardian.

"I still say that there are better ways to effect change," Mark said, catching up Jenna's hand in his own. "Look at Governor Pohl. Evan, you actually worked on her People First campaign, didn't you?"

Evan nodded. "Two years." After his initial application to the military had been denied. "I was a fund-raiser. Not a bad one, either, and it got me noticed for a liaison position later, between one of the Governor's aides and the HungLi Military Base." That earned him a second look at his aptitude tests, and entry into Bulics. Evan had qualified for the Conservatory, but was bumped by lower-qualifying students who had already picked up Republic citizenship. Residents went to the bottom of the list. "Never met the Governor, though."

"My point is, we got a world governor very sympathetic to the pro-Capellan movement. Anna Lu Pohl was not my first choice, but I respect her view that Liao can acknowledge its past while still looking toward the future."

"And that future will always include The Republic," Jenna said, nearly resigned to it. "Especially since Lord Governor Hidic has to personally approve any candidate for world office."

Mark had no easy answer for that, and an awkward silence descended over the group as they passed by the *Men Shen*.

Lord of all it surveyed, at eight meters high and fifty-five tons the Guardian appeared more avatar than machine. Evan felt an initial thrill for the power it had once represented. Of course, that thrill always darkened to an empty hollow in the pit of his stomach. The Guardian was not a functional 'Mech. The Republic did not waste such resources on decoration, though Evan had read that during the military buildups of the Succession Wars it was considered a status symbol to embellish important locations with actual, working BattleMechs. The Lyran Commonwealth throne, so legend said, had been guarded by *two* 'Mechs. Two!

They were probably more effective symbols than the Guardian. The *Men Shen* drooped a bit at its turret-style waist, where age and neglect had caused the joint to fail. Strong welds sealed all access ports, including the cockpit hatch. Its weapons were nothing more than open ports and sealed barrels, and the fusion engine which was the heart of any 'Mech had long since been ripped out. He could only imagine now what it had looked like, stalking forward in a swaggering gait, its feet stomping out a warning against the ground. *Boom. Boom.*

And just for a second, Evan swore he felt one last footfall shake the ground.

Then another.

"Hey." David stepped to one side and pointed. He sounded disappointed. "Man, that was fast."

The 'Mech-heavy steps not only continued, they grew louder. From behind the *Men Shen's* resting place a ConstructionMech stomped into view. Painted bright, industrial yellow and swinging its clamp and bucket arms alongside in a simian swagger, the IndustrialMech walked around the frozen *Men Shen* and then angled along one of the reinforced walkways as it headed for the Conservatory's Great Arch.

"They're going to take down the Arch," Jenna said, nodding. "Can't have it spoiling the grounds."

Others had come to the same conclusion. Closer to the gate, students began shouting, "*Yóng yuǎn . . . Liào Sūn Zǐ!*"

Even with such shouts being thrown out in protest, Evan couldn't help thinking that the *Men Shen* now looked a touch sadder as the industrial machine left it behind. And wrapped up in his thoughts concerning the gutted 'Mech, he missed Jenna's next comment.

"Huh?" he asked as she prodded him in the side. Her fingers were strong, and left uncomfortable aches where she had dug at his ribs. Or maybe that was something else.

"I asked if you believe it is true. Forever lives Sun-Tzu Liao?"

Evan felt David's stare and, more importantly, Mark's warming the back of his neck. He thought of the many ways that could be answered, including not answering at all. But Jenna sounded as if it was important to her. Maybe she needed to know. To believe.

He shrugged. One of his favorite answers when his friends pried too much. Then, "I don't know, Jen. Sometimes I'm not sure what I believe." Which wasn't exactly a lie. He listened to the fading, distant shouts of the disaffected students, and glanced over once more at the gutted *Men Shen*. "I guess I believe that things are changing, which means anything is possible."

And that wasn't exactly a lie either.

4

CEO

Pro-Capellan terrorists have seized the world Governor's mansion on Menkar! Governor Charles Kincaid and his family are being held hostage. Demands made by the terrorists include putting the Governor on live (interstellar) trial for treason against Menkar's true citizens. Menkar is one of only three worlds in Prefecture V with HPG capabilities. . . .
—Jacquie Blitzer, battlecorps.org/blitzer/, 3 May 3134

Pelago Estates
St. Andre
Prefecture V, The Republic
8 May 3134

Jacob Bannson feared very little.

"Fear is the result of weakness," he was fond of saying. "To show fear is to let your competition know where they may attack you."

For twenty-one years Bannson had put a stranglehold on his fear and built an interstellar corporate empire with few rivals in The Republic. Bannson Universal Unlimited was second to the great GioAvanti conglomerate only because GioAvanti lobbying forced the Senate to slap Bannson's company with operational restraints (and he would find a way around those!). He'd fended off hostile takeovers, the creeping fingers of organized crime and, on numerous occasions, The Republic's Securities Trade Commission with its ferret-like investigators. His enemies accumulated, but he did not fear them.

So why did he immediately fear the tissue-wrapped package resting in the middle of a foyer table?

Dagger Di Jones coiled up against a paneled wall near the hallway entrance. As far from the package as she could get, Bannson noted. She slicked her red hair back with the palm of one hand, wiping snowmelt and loose strands away from her eyes. Ivan Storychny, Bannson's personal aide on St. Andre, stood in between his master and the package. He still carried the CEO's laser rifle and the game bag. His ice blue eyes never left the table. It had taken Ivan only a few seconds longer to realize the importance—and the danger—of the package.

Pelago Estates was Bannson's private retreat on St. Andre, situated on a northern wilderness preserve stocked with caribou and moose, black bear, the nearly extinct royal pheasant, feathered serpents, and even—his favorite—the tenacious Terran wolverine. He'd ostensibly spent the day on a hunting trip, neatly decapitating two pheasant with his laser rifle, spilling barely a drop of blood on the pristine carpet of fresh snow. Bannson had also visited a hidden valley base where some of his raiders were tucked away, and helped plan an operation on the planet Foot Fall. The appeal of this northern mansion was its remote location, accessible only by aircraft. It allowed Bannson to relax his stringent security even as he consorted with raiders and rebels. Jones usually discouraged any sudden movements by those around him, and Ivan had hidden talents as well.

And still someone had secretly invaded his domain, leaving behind a present wrapped in golden tissue and green ribbon. The colors told Bannson who, and that "who" was definitely to be feared.

Ivan leaned the Intek laser rifle against the table. His large hands framed the small box, moving it around so that Bannson could see the small death's-head pin tacked into one strand of the ribbon.

"A Death Commando." Jones shifted a few more centimeters toward the door as her brown eyes flashed dangerously toward the next room. She wasn't afraid, Bannson realized. She was readying herself to attack.

The Death Commandos were Daoshen Liao's private terrorist squad. As good as Jones was, Bannson would not want to bet on her being able to bring down such a fanatic.

"We should leave the mansion, Boss." No pretty titles out of Ivan. No "sire" or even a "chief." To the large man, Jacob Bannson was simply the boss.

Bannson forced himself to step forward. "No need. If Daoshen wanted me killed, I would already be dead." Daoshen wanted him scared. *That* Bannson would not give the eccentric leader. "Ivan, please put away my rifle and bring us all drinks in the gallery." He caught Jones's suspicious glance. "You can look if you like, my dear, but I assure you that our visitor is quite absent."

She apparently trusted his instincts, though the tense set of her shoulders said that she remained ready for nearly anything. "Whatever you say," she replied.

Bannson picked up the small box. It weighed very little, and fit comfortably in two hands. About the size of a small cigar box, and the right weight too.

"After you." He nodded toward Jones.

The foyer opened up into a long hall. The red-haired mercenary stalked down to a double-wide entryway. The downstairs library-study. Bannson followed, thinking about the gift and what it meant, coming now.

That Daoshen even knew of his visit to St. Andre bothered him. Bannson's schedule was never published beforehand. Bannson Universal may have begun on this world, but it now stretched throughout Prefectures IV and V. He had specifically chosen a return to St. Andre because it did serve more as a retreat than a seat of power. The place he'd begun his new life, and where he returned for anonymity.

And it was far, far away from Terra.

Not that he worried overmuch. The assault on Terra had been a doomed venture from the start. Ezekiel Crow should have realized it much sooner. But he hadn't, and Bannson had used the smokescreen of Crow's treason to pay back a few debts of his own.

A Republic Senator who needed early retirement.

A military officer, who had grown resistant to being on Bannson's payroll, lost in the chaos of battle.

Most other men in his position would have simply tipped off The Republic and gathered accolades after. Most other men did not play the long game. Besides, what had The Republic ever done for him except put a ceiling on his rise to power? So he had let the assault go forward, and slipped in to take care of his own business where he could. A good day's work, even if it had cost him one of his most valuable hole cards. Ezekiel Crow. The fallen Paladin.

But Bannson did not casually throw away such a valuable asset, and had laid groundwork to salvage Crow. Such a card, played a second time, might trump almost anything. And the weaker The Republic became, the more chances for Bannson to advance his own agenda.

An agenda that included corporate interests in Prefecture III (next) and political interests here at home.

An agenda that would have to take into consideration Daoshen Liao's interference.

Through the magnificent library, with its rolling ladders and tall cases full of books from every Republic world, Jones and Bannson walked to the gallery where he stored most of his locally gained art treasures. The gallery could be sealed behind a ferrosteel door resistant to most anything but platform-scale weapons. It was cold in the room, a chilly twenty-six Celsius, and dimly lit with spots showing off his most valuable prizes. There was also a small shelf in the room at which three people could comfortably stand. It was here he set the brightly wrapped package and began to carefully unwrap it.

The ribbon was secured with a bow knot that easily slipped loose. Bannson pocketed the death's-head pin. The golden tissue folded back and away from the top. A promise of riches? Of Daoshen's personal interest? The retreating folds uncovered a deep-grained lacquered box that glowed rich and red and reflected back a warped image of both Bannson and Jones.

"What is it?" the raider asked.

Bannson ran a finger along one edge, marveling in the perfection. "What does it look like?"

"Well, is it a cigar box?"

Her lack of imagination annoyed him, until he remembered how he had thought something similar. "I highly doubt it." No, this was something much more. With nervous fingers, he flipped up the tiny golden clasp and lifted the lid.

It was empty.

"Empty?" Jones frowned, her eyes narrowing to dangerous slits as if she had missed the punch line of a joke and wondered if it were at her expense. Ivan came in carrying a silver salver just big enough to carry three brandy snifters. He set it on the edge of the shelf. "It's empty," Jones told him quickly, perhaps trying to get in on the joke.

But what was it empty of? Bannson sipped at his smoky liquor. He stared into the box's velvet interior, reached in and traced the molded recess with one finger. Cylindrical. About twenty centimeters long and three centimeters wide. Soft, soft. The perfect rest for an important, and valuable, scroll.

What kind of scroll would Bannson find valuable? Only two men in the Inner Sphere likely knew that answer.

He had stood in Daoshen's throne room barely two years before, and made it very clear that the cost of Bannson's assistance was nothing less than "my appointment as a peer of your realm."

There it was: Bannson laying his cards out for the first time in decades, and to the Chancellor of the Capellan Confederation. He'd never planned to go so far, even after accepting Daoshen Liao's invitation to Sian. The tour of Zi-jin Chéng impressed him, certainly, especially the level of detail to which Confederation citizens had restored their capital to pre-Jihad quality. And the Celestial Palace itself was breathtaking, a mixture of modern materials and classic architecture outside, classic material with modern design inside.

What had changed Bannson's mind, though, was the tribute paid to him by the Capellan leader. Daoshen had stated baldly that he intended to invade The Republic of the Sphere . . . a dangerous gamble to take with one of The Republic's economic leaders. The Chancellor made no apologies for the situation in which he placed Bannson, or for his insulting assumption that the other man would be interested in committing treason. Nesting back into his magnificent throne, dark eyes nothing more than black pits seen through the haze of incense smoke, Daoshen offered his plans freely, and waited for an answer.

Which Bannson blurted out before he'd really thought it through. Very likely saving his own life.

Daoshen gave the merchant king time to begin fidgeting. Betrayals of nerves were rare, but then Bannson did not make a habit of keeping such exalted company. The Chancellor had even allowed him the dubious honor of sitting in His presence, ordering a simple chair brought into the room. Even years of training did not keep the surprise—or the quick flash of terror—from the faces of palace servants. Sitting in the incense-choked room had softened Bannson, allowing him to relax. And now he tapped nervously on the side of his leg, willing his hands to stillness and finally overcoming the natural need for movement. For flight.

"A noble," Daoshen tasted the idea. "Subject to our laws and holding property at our whim."

Bannson could not tell if Daoshen had made a switch to the royal possessive, or if the Chancellor now included himself among all of the ennobled landholders.

"The only coin I will take." For that, Bannson offered to covertly support a Liao drive into Prefectures V and VI, and eventually through most of IV as well. Tikonov. Tigress. Tybalt. Strong worlds in the chain of Bannson Universal Unlimited, and each one fixed in the eye of Daoshen Liao.

"You are not a citizen of the Confederation," the leader said as if dismissing the claim.

Did a hint of Bannson's anger show? "I know that an appropriate gift to the State can secure citizenship in the Confederation." He never sat a meeting without having done his homework. "The average payment is, I think, quite low. But in The Republic of the Sphere, citizenship costs more and is held cheaply. I would rather see value for my efforts."

No way to tell what the wily Capellan was thinking. Daoshen had perfect control, letting slip only that which he meant to. Bannson would do well to remember that.

Daoshen slithered up to his full height. He stood at the edge of his dais, weaving back and forth just enough to curl the incense smoke around him. With crimson robes swirled tightly around his cadaverously thin body, and the wide mantle resting on his shoulders, he reminded Bannson of a red cobra. And its dance could be so very hypnotic.

"You are an ambitious man," Daoshen finally said. "We have spoken enough this day. Perhaps it would be best for both of us to think on our positions."

Bannson never saw Daoshen again.

He spoke with interviewers, but refused to give up further information without mutual assurances from the Confederation. Military officers invited him to meals and meetings, working out different theories about how the Confederation Armed Forces and his commercial empire might best work together. At one point the Leader of Warrior House Imarra took Bannson to a remote facility hidden deep inside a mountain. There, the corporate magnate was allowed to walk along rank after rank of mothballed BattleMechs. *Atlas. Men Shen. Tsi Tsang.* New designs and classical configurations— enough to instantly outfit a full combat regiment. More than one hundred machines, ready to march. It had been some time since any Inner Sphere state had seen the like.

It was meant to impress, and it did. How many such caches did Daoshen have at his disposal? Bannson was never told.

He was treated cordially, and shown more entertainments. Eventually, the Maskirovka came with his papers for leaving Sian. Bannson was left to guess that he'd asked for more than Chancellor Liao was willing to pay. Or that plans had fallen through some other way.

It wasn't until he was back within Republic space that he remembered Daoshen's last words, and how they might be read in a completely different—and threatening—manner.

Why had Daoshen allowed him to leave Sian? The more he considered it, the more certain he became that Daoshen Liao had planned the CEO's death before ever inviting him to the Confederation capital. Yet something stayed his hand. That glimpse behind Bannson's public face?

Maybe.

"So what's he offering?" Ivan asked. Big, yes. Ferocious, certainly. But the man was not stupid. Bannson did not tolerate ignorance, especially in those closest to him.

"He's offering the world," Bannson said cryptically, and meaning it quite literally. But which? There were perhaps a dozen worlds within one jump of Capellan space. Where would Daoshen strike first? Where would he eventually install Bannson as one of his nobles?

Bannson felt confident in his own long game. Sooner or later, the businessman gathered in what he felt owed. But if Daoshen was extending his hand a second time, could Bannson afford to turn his back on the erratic leader? Liao was coming, make no mistake. Wasn't it good policy to keep his options open?

"I have a better question," Jones finally said. Her rough-edged voice shattered Bannson's train of thought. She tossed off the last of her drink. "Why do we care?"

Bannson wasn't ready to share his reasons with anyone else. "Perhaps it is a case of accepting the inevitable," he offered his agent. Sometimes that led to the most profitable business arrangements. And in the meantime, he still had assets in play, didn't he?

5

Dark Descent

Marion, attached are field reports from Algot, Foot Fall, and Wei. As you will see, Menkar was only the first of several worlds to experience severe pro-Capellan uprisings. While the timing and focus of these events suggests an outside coordinating influence, nothing is proven as of yet.
 —Report by Prefect (V) Shun Tao to Lord Governor Hidic, 14 May 3134 (leaked to press by confidential sources on 20 May 3134)

DropShip *Burning Petals*
Above Liao
Prefecture V, The Republic
20 May 3134

The DropShip corridor was narrow, dusty warm and dimly lit—a seldom used translateral passage squeezed in as an afterthought between officers' country and a power relay station. A short jump down half a flight of steep metal steps, remember to duck under the ventilation ductwork, and through an airlock quality hatch that opened onto the DropShip's lower weather deck. A shortcut, if you knew your way around a converted *Seeker*-class vessel.

Major Ritter Michaelson, late of The Republic's vaunted Tenth Hastati Sentinels, would know.

Michaelson wore dress blacks with enough salad on his left breast to back up his claim as one of The Republic's elite soldiers. He pulled his service cap low so that the bill partially hid his contact-tinted eyes. Michaelson didn't want to speak with anyone—he should have remained in his cabin. But the opportunity, forever his failing, was too great.

The *weather deck*, a holdover term from when naval vessels had sailed Terran oceans, was one of the *Seeker's* three observation platforms. It opened onto ten meters of the curved outside hull where armor had been replaced with thick ferroglass. Ten centimeters separated Michaelson from the oblivion of space. With no atmosphere to fog his vision, the stars stood out in sharp, cruel splendor. He had the deck to himself because the ship was so close to planetfall. That was the way he wanted to come home, back to the word of Liao. Alone and repentant.

He got half of his wish.

The DropShip had started a port-side roll when a crewmember making his rounds slid down a vertical ladder with hands and feet clasped expertly to the outside rail. "Sir," he said, spying Ritter Michaelson. Then, "Major. The Cap'n has sounded our atmospheric alarm. All passengers—".

He turned, letting the spacer see the ruined side of his face. Always a showstopper. "Should be webbed into their beds for landing," Michaelson finished. He read the other man's rank and name off his shipboard dungarees. "Petty Officer Samuels. I know. But I needed to see."

Michaelson turned back to the ferroglass wall. Only four decks above the DropShip's massive engines, he felt their deep, powerful thrum seeping up from the deckplates and warming the bottoms of his feet. He watched, waiting to see what the enlisted man would do, waiting for . . .

Liao.

The world rolled in from the left-hand side of the massive window, blotting out the stars like some great, shadowed curtain. *Burning Petals* fell into the darkside, though a dark green crescent brightened the rim of the planet where tinted sunlight bent just enough to reach around. Reflected light off of Elias' Promise, the planet's moon, allowed him to barely register the outlines of Nánlù and Beilù, the southern and northern continents, though right now they appeared more eastern and western given the DropShip's equatorial approach angle.

"How long away?" the crewman asked, over his initial shock.

How long had it been since he'd set foot on his homeworld? In which life? "Several years."

"They say Liao is one of the worlds—m'be a dozen or so— that if you know their history, you know most of the important events of the entire Inner Sphere."

Viewed from a spacer's eye, each world a small point of light lost among thousands, that was probably true. Liao had spawned one of the five ruling dynasties of its day. When the planet was lost to the Federated Suns in the Fourth Succession War, Chancellor Sun-Tzu sent all eight of his fanatical Warrior Houses to reclaim it twenty-five years later. The "immortal" Sun-Tzu then invested a great deal in the industrial renovation of his dynasty's birthworld, and Liao was eventually named the capital of a reconstituted Commonality.

Which very nearly became its death when the Word of Blake attacked.

Intent on smashing all industrial and political infrastructure, the Jihad swept across Liao like a winter storm. This was one of the truly heroic stands of that entire war as the Capellan military and the people themselves stood up to the invaders at incredible cost. In ten long years, Liao never fell.

No wonder Devlin Stone honored this world by choosing it as a prefecture capital.

"If only its history ended there."

"Excuse me, Major?"

Ritter Michaelson straightened with a start. "Never mind. I was just thinking back—"

"To Terra?" The crewman had apparently waited for this chance. His gaze fell on the red patch Michaelson wore on his shoulder, identifying him as a MechWarrior. "I'm sorry, sir. But . . . well . . . the entire crew's been talking about it. And you. I mean, you were on Terra when the Steel Wolves came, and the Black Paladin turned, weren't you?"

Black Paladin. That was a new one. How many more titles would come to Ezekiel Crow as word of his treachery spread throughout The Republic? No cover-ups, no citing of security concerns, were going to hold back this story. Michaelson rubbed one hand along the right side of his face, over the glassy scars that shortened his ear and crept right up to his goatee and the puckered edge of his eyebrow. At least they were out from under the bandages now.

"I was there," the major admitted.

Hard to deny it, since his travel papers stated very clearly that he was lately put on deactivated leave from the Tenth Hastati. They had held the ground nearest to Paris, fighting alongside the Northwind Highlanders. But Michaelson had not been a part of that battle. His trial had come earlier.

"Did you see Tara Campbell in action?" the crewman asked.

Michaelson dropped his hand back to his side. "I most certainly did. Hero of the hour. Do not pass Knight, go directly to Paladin."

"You didn't hear? The countess turned 'em down. Flat. She took her Highlanders and left. Man, that woman has some brass ones. I mean . . . well, you know what I mean?"

"I know."

No doubt Petty Officer Samuels had other questions too—everyone did. Ritter Michaelson's new life would make certain that he relived the event over and over again. He was spared for the moment, though, when Samuels showed the preternatural senses of those born to space travel and said, "We're turning. Hands on the rail please, Major."

Michaelson didn't notice for several seconds longer, then the planet began to sink in the window as *Burning Petals* rotated its drive flare toward Liao's surface. Not even aerodyne DropShips truly flew out of orbit. Like the spheroid *Seeker*-class, they decelerated and fell. The first tremor of atmospheric turbulence shook the massive vessel, and Michaelson grasped the slender metal rail that ran along the inside of the ferroglass. Gravity shifted under unsteady feet for a moment as the DropShip's orientation lagged slightly behind, but soon they were stable once more as the vessel became a slow-falling star in Liao's night sky.

"We'll be coming in o'er Beilù, heading for the interplanetary spaceport at Lianyungang. Thirty minutes," the crewman guessed, "and we'll be on the ground."

Where he would restart his life? *Ritter* Michaelson: the Deutsch translation for *knight*. How long would he be able to live under that name? He gripped the rail tighter, finding it a bit harder to breathe. The deckplates hummed with power. Then his legs buckled as he slumped to the floor, knees striking the deck hard enough to bruise, and his vision clouded.

For a brief second, he wondered if his history had finally caught up with him, dragging him down into darkness.

"We're boosting back for high orbit," the crewman said, also kneeling on the deck as his body fought to readjust to the increased gravity.

Michaelson struggled back to his feet, using the rail to leverage himself up. Liao did not want him back—was his first thought. Then, facing out through the ferroglass shield, he caught a streak of fire flashing past the vessel only a few thousand meters out. Another one slashed up from beneath his line of sight, and this time matched the DropShip's roll for just a second before it pulled over and cut around the far side again.

Aerospace fighters!

Under attack? He felt no tremor of weapons fire, heard no call to general quarters. An escort. *Burning Petals* was boosting back into a holding orbit, and had been given a safety escort of at least two fighters.

Something was going on below.

"I have to see what this is," Samuels said, walking bow-legged for the nearest hatch. He paused, looked back. "I wanted to ask you, well, a lot of things, I guess."

Michaelson nodded.

"Did you . . . ?" Petty Officer Samuels couldn't seem to find the perfect question. His blue eyes snagged again on the glossy ruin, winced. "Did you see a lot of hard fighting on Terra?" That was obviously the best he could do.

"Some of the hardest of my life," he said, and meant it.

It was enough, and the crewman bolted down the same shortcut passage that Michaelson had used to find the weather deck. Michaelson—Michael's son—almost smiled. It felt good not to lie, even if it was through careful interpretation. It *had* been some of the hardest fighting in his life. Complete with the realization that he had again betrayed everything he held close.

That was why Ezekiel Crow had to die and it was Ritter Michaelson making planetfall over Liao, looking for a new start. For good or ill, the Black Paladin had come home.

6

Joy Ride

Encouraged by Ijori Dè Guāng *terrorists to try their own hand at a public message, a large group of pro-Capellan residents used rope scaffolds to scale the Lord Governor's Executive Office Building in Chang-an and paint* "Wǒ mén huì shì zì yóu dè!" *across the dome. Translation:* We will be free! *Twelve arrests were made.*
— News clipping from the *Dynasty Daily*, 11 May 3134

Lianyungang Spaceport
Qinghai Province, Liao
20 May 3134

A siren wailed out long, mournful notes that echoed across the Lianyungang Spaceport's wide expanse of ferrocrete and steel. Two merchant DropShips squatted on the tarmac, twenty-five stories tall, like improbable skyscrapers raised out of the flat, flat landing fields. From nearby towers, spotlights searched from the sides of the DropShips. From pairs of armored hovercraft that ran the spaceport's perimeter fencing like Dobermans in a dog run.

Evan Kurst stood at the corner of a small hangar, keeping to the shadows as he checked the northern approach. Two hundred meters away a secure customs warehouse blazed with light and security personnel. Beyond that Evan saw the fiery orange glow of the burning repair depot his people had charged with aviation fuel. Caustic fumes hung on the evening air, stinging the back of his throat. As near as he could tell, emergency vehicles and military efforts still centered on the arson.

That wouldn't last much longer.

Jogging back to the side door his people had forced without any alarm, Evan rapped twice, once, once—then slipped inside and froze as the security guard's light slapped him square in the eyes.

"*Zāo gāo*, William." Evan fought against raising his arm too quickly to shield his vision. "It's me."

William Hartsfield clicked off the heavy flash, but did not hook it back to his belt. The weight sat comfortably in his hand and would make a good bludgeon. Evan didn't worry for his safety. The man was simply nervous, and nervous men needed to feel prepared.

"How does it look?" the security man asked.

"It looks like the militia will be contracting more civilian work," Evan said shortly, dismissing the arson with a shrug.

The repair depot was actually a matter of convenience for the Liao garrison, servicing any vehicles stationed at the spaceport. But it made for a nice diversion, and fire always hit the planetary news.

"Going to be a good haul," the guard said.

Evan nodded. Four military hoverbikes commanded the center of the hangar, each parked inside a yellow box painted onto the floor. Beyond the bikes, red-tinted flashes dimly lit the interiors of two VV1 Rangers and circled around the metal cages of battlesuit berths. Feet shuffled over the smooth ferrocrete, and someone kicked a loose bar of metal they had cut from one cage. It clattered noisily over the floor. There had been no way to arrange a hijacking of the larger vehicles, so they'd be sabotaged and left behind.

"Time?" a voice called from inside one Ranger.

Evan checked his watch. "Plus six and time to put up or shut up, Greggor." The large man was no deft hand at sabotage. He was simply holding the light for an *Ijori Dè Guāng* member who was. "If they can't black box those vehicles, burn the ignition now and let's move."

Whit Greggor climbed out of the vehicle. "They're closing up the panels now. Next time someone cranks one of these over, they'll burn out every last circuit as well as the entire starter system." He sounded like a kid at Christmas—a big kid, ready to blackjack the fat man and take the bag for himself.

It would have been easier to simply burn the Rangers now, but this way the sabotage might not be discovered for days. That meant another news cycle this week with mention of the *Ijori Dè Guāng*. People had to know that the resistance continued. They needed constant reminders.

Other cell members exited the two Rangers wearing watch caps and nylon face masks. William already knew Evan and Greggor, and the team Evan had assembled for this night's work, but many of them did not know each other and Evan kept it that way. What a man does not know, he cannot betray.

So close to the end, William fidgeted from one foot to another. "They'll be expecting me to check in soon, Kurst. We've got to wrap this up."

Evan traded warm clasps with the security guard, steering him around as Greggor padded up silently behind. "We cannot talk again, William. You know that." The man would fall under some suspicion no matter how Evan arranged this. William's pro-Capellan politics were well documented.

"Yeah. I think this would be a good time to go visit relatives on Styk. You know, as part of my crisis therapy." He smiled weakly. "Not in the face, okay? And, ah, nothing broken, if you can help it."

Evan braced the man, clapping a gloved hand to each shoulder. "I promised we'd take good care of you," he said, then released him as Greggor brought a small device up toward the back of his neck.

A flash of blue sparks and a singing *zzzap*, and it was all over. William Hartsfield collapsed like a gyro-struck Battle-Mech, his legs and arms twitching with uncontrollable spasms. The scent of ozone and scorched hair burned in the air. Evan forced himself to watch as Greggor knelt down to deliver another charge from the pocket stunner.

"We should kill him," the large man said, standing. "You know this."

Two sides warred in Evan's heart. To maintain perfect security, a loose end like William should be silenced. Mai Wa would not have hesitated, not with the safety of the movement at risk. But in the last year Evan had grown into his own, and he still remembered with perfect clarity the military policeman, laid out on the ground and bleeding from multiple wounds in the chest and neck . . . the stench of shredded plastic . . .

. . . the weight of a needler pistol in his hand.

William Hartsfield was a patriot. Like so many of Evan's resources, he'd come recommended through the Cult of Liao. He had also applied for academy training and failed to place, very likely because of his parents' pro-Capellan leanings. The Republic claimed it did not discriminate, but of course it did. Everybody did, toward one side or the other. Evan could still end up the same way: trained as a MechWarrior and then shuffled aside at the last moment in favor of a die-hard citizen. It could be *him* lying on the ground some day.

"He lives," Evan commanded.

"You're risking my life, too."

"Shall we waste time arguing about it, Greggor?" Evan glanced at the back of his wrist. "Plus eight. A few more minutes, we'll be debating it with some of Legate Ruskoff's officers."

Greggor smiled like an ape baring its fangs and then shuffled off for the row of hoverbikes. Evan's people had cracked the security on two, their instrument panels glowing in blues and subtle reds. They were at work on two more.

Evan rolled William's body out of the way, then jogged over to where a final team had laid out pieces of a suit of Purifier battle armor. Its storage berth stood nearby with the cage-built door half disassembled, but the locking mechanism still in place. These were the true objectives tonight: hoverbikes and a battlesuit. They would be added to a growing stockpile of military arms and equipment. Political statements and hindrance raids only went so far. When revolution came, the *Ijori Dè Guāng* had to be ready to act.

"Ready?" one of the masked operatives asked. Her voice wavered uncertainly. None of Evan's people had experience with powered armor.

He offered some silent thanks to Mark Lo and David Parks for their unwitting help in training him for this mission. A little simulator time goes a long way. "Let's get it on," Evan said, nodding.

Each suit of powered armor was a technical marvel that started with the bodymesh undergarment. Evan Kurst stripped out of his jumpsuit with no thought for the young woman standing nearby, then struggled into the tight-fitting mesh, a combination of cooling vest and padding. Its arms and legs were too long, bunching inside his elbows and knees. No help for that now. He worked his fingers into the gloves. The female operative pulled a thick hood over his head, adjusting the opening around his face.

"Okay?"

He nodded. Nearby, four hoverbikes powered up, turbo fans readied for their mad dash.

Two larger men helped Evan alley-oop into the lower half of the Purifier suit. In theory, a trained infantryman could don the armor solo, laying pieces on the ground and shuffle squirming into the bottom half before pulling down the top carapace. Evan wasn't a trained infantryman, and even the best solo attempt could result in an improper fit or broken seal. That wouldn't do tonight. Evan pointed his toes downward, working his feet through the reinforced ankle joint. He now stood in approximately half a ton of immobile ferrosteel and myomer.

The upper carapace came in three pieces. First, the chest shell, with arms held straight up to slip overhead like a metal-reinforced sweater. His right arm ended in a mechanical claw. A laser stubbed out of the left arm.

Next, the helmet, shoved ruthlessly down over his padded head and locked into the deep neck well. Evan refused the mouth bit a veteran might use to operate many of the Purifier's electronics, and had his technicians switch off the optical sensing array which translated eye movement and blinking into commands as well. When the hangar's main doors rolled back, Evan would be running, not fighting. He didn't need a wrong glance to cut his jump jets and send him crashing into the ground.

His final piece was the power and control pack that detached for ease of suit up, but without which Evan was going nowhere. "Switch on!" one tech called. The suit hummed to life, flexing and settling around Evan in a smothering grip, charging the mimetic armor with its chameleonlike ability to blend into its environment. His helmet lit up with a soft green glow as the battlesuit computer painted a head's-up display across the inside faceplate.

Someone rapped knuckles against the side of his helmet. Dull, gonging sounds. "How's it feel?"

Like wearing a giant bandage wrap, then being shoved into a suit of ancient steel armor. The bodysuit bunched and pinched, and Evan could tell he didn't fit the shell quite right.

His arms felt awkward and heavy moving them around—carefully—to test his range of motion. His palms were sweaty How did he feel?

"Great."

Well, what was he going to say?

His first steps, though, convinced him that he could make it off spaceport grounds. The Purifier's internal computer corrected most of his awkward wobbling. The armor flexed where it was supposed to, and went rigid as necessary to prevent Evan from listing too far to one side. The effect was accomplished through negative feedback—thousands of sensors arranged over the inside of the suit. When he pressed in any direction, a power spike moved the suit's artificial muscles in the same direction to relieve pressure. Evan might pick up strained muscles and more than a few bruises, but he'd also come away with a fresh suit of battle armor for the cause.

He stomped over to the large hangar door—still closed, locked, and rigged with an alarm his people could not bypass.

"Everyone ready?"

Some operatives slipped out the side door, stepping over William's unconscious form. A few others, living in the moment, hopped aboard one of the idling hoverbikes, straddling the forward-mounted machine gun. They'd ride out in style.

Evan raised his right-arm claw and struck it down hard against the locking mechanism. Once. Twice. An alarm would be going off somewhere by now. Again. The housing cracked open, which let him thrust his laser into the housing. He clenched his hand and then stabbed it straight out. The triggering mechanism interpreted his actions and fired a bright, ruby spear of energy deep into the door's lock.

A light flashed from red to green. There would be no power for rolling it open by remote, so Evan clawed into the metal facing and *shoved*, rolling the door back several bowlegged paces. Enough for the hoverbikes to slip through.

Evan stepped outside, out of the way. "Joy ride," he said, his voice picked up by the suit's internal mic and translated into a powerful broadcast.

Four hoverbikes screamed forward on thrusters, quickly breaking into wildly different directions for their separate egress points. Only Evan knew where all four were heading: two for wilderness on the far side of the spaceport, where narrow paths had been cleared to allow them to pass; two more for breaches that would be blown in the fencing in less than thirty seconds.

Evan pointed his HUD compass east-nor'east and set out in a loping stride that ate up the ground meter by meter. The Purifier ran at a top speed just over ten kilometers per hour and could leap in controlled jumps at forty—maybe sixty—meters at a time. Fortunately, he had the shortest distance to go, striking out for a place where the spaceport perimeter was walled off instead of fenced.

This was going to work.

Or not.

Hope that had barely begun to flare inside Evan's breast died stillborn as his HUD painted a target icon moving to intercept. He hadn't figured on anything larger than a light hovercraft, but the identity tag read PK-H9R. A *Pack Hunter* BattleMech!

There was no beating the light 'Mech to the wall, not when it pounded forward at better than one hundred ten klicks per hour. Evan slowed, hoping to gain some stealth effect from the mimetic armor. If the MechWarrior inside wasn't alert . . . wasn't watching very carefully . . .

Evan lost the *Pack Hunter* behind the customs warehouse and put on a burst of speed to try and reach the wall. The MechWarrior was ready for him. On twin jets of bright plasma the BattleMech sailed up and over the warehouse, leaning into a long, flattopped arc that angled in between Evan and safety. It landed in a ready crouch, arms spread wide and the shoulder-mounted PPC aimed right for him. The red-and-gold columns of the Fifth Triarii, Liao's garrison, stood out very clearly, the insignia centered right over the *Pack Hunter's* right breast.

Evan slowed to a walk, then a stop. With numbers on his side—even with the scattered hoverbikes—he might have stood a chance attacking the eight-meter-tall machine. Alone, he'd be vaporized by the PPC's hellish energies or simply crushed underfoot. He readied himself for a suicide dash. Evan would not—could never—be taken prisoner as a member of the *Ijori Dè Guāng*. He knew too much, and they would find a way to drag it out of him.

The *Pack Hunter* straightened to an easy stance, swiveling at the hips so that the MechWarrior could directly survey the nearby grounds through the cockpit's ferroglass shield. No call to surrender. No warning shot fired. Near as Evan could tell, no call for reinforcements. The way the BattleMech had moved—it had come in fully ready to meet resistance. Expecting it. Instead, it had found a lone Purifier, running for the wall. Not much of a threat.

What was going on?

Slowly, so slowly Evan could count every rivet running down the outside of each leg, the *Pack Hunter* stepped back and turned away.

Evan took one cautious pace, watching for any sign that the MechWarrior might change his mind. Then another. The BattleMech stayed facing away, an obvious invitation. Another closet Capellan? Maybe one who had kept his sympathies hidden, or had been placed in the military after his academy years, but never to rise higher than the local Triarii garrison. Evan raced back up to full speed, heading for the wall. Did it really matter, the why of it?

It did, but not right now.

Thirty meters from the gray slab of high wall, Evan leapt up into the air, pointed his feet at the ground. Barely a few centimeters above the tarmac, his jump thrusters cut in, burning reaction mass as they rocketed him into a ballistic hop. They carried him over the ferrocrete wall, and into the woods beyond. Evan tried nothing fancy on landing, letting the suit absorb most of the fall as he snapped down through tree limbs and sprawled full-length upon landing.

Bruised, but far from dazed, he struggled back to his feet. He burst through a thicket and crossed a stretch of train tracks, entering the fringe of Lianyungang's industrial district. An abandoned factory stood dark and decrepit nearby. Evan went through an old door without pausing, shattering it into an explosion of splintered wood. Waiting for him in the cavernous interior was an old moving truck with back door rolled up and ramp extended.

It was the work of a few moments to climb into the back, shed the power armor, and seal the truck up. Two minutes after that Evan was driving into light traffic, the spaceport and the authorities behind him, lost again among the people of Liao.

7

Old Wounds

This morning, local authorities on Menkar attempted to rescue Governor Kincaid and his family following a twelve-day standoff with pro-Capellan terrorists. The mansion caught fire during the attempt. Burned almost beyond recognition were the Governor's family and seven presumed terrorists. Claims that questionable tactics and unnecessary force were intentionally used—and may have led to the fire—are under investigation.
  —Jacquie Blitzer, battlecorps.org/blitzer/, 15 May 3134

Lianyungang
Qinghai Province, Liao
21 May 3134

They cut Ritter Michaelson out of line as he worked his way through customs. One more stamp, just a couple of questions, and he would have been free. Free to claim his luggage. Free to hail a cab and eventually grab an overcrowded train to Xiapu. Michaelson's benefactor on Terra had secured a small ranch house for him not far from the midland city. Two more minutes.

Then the uniformed customs agents crowded in next to him.

The man was Asian, slight of build and wore a gold hoop in his right ear. The silver badge sewn onto the right front pocket gave his name as Tai Nae Luk. Amanda Ringsdotter was slightly taller and very curvaceous. She also wore stronger perfume than her coagent. Customs Security wasn't Sphere Intelligence, and neither of these civilian agency officers were likely to be a Ghost Knight—one of the invisible Knights of the Sphere who acted as the Exarch's eyes, ears and (at times) hands in areas best left out of the interstellar tabloids. Still, there was an obvious purpose about them, and as much authority in their voices as there was riding on their hips in small nylon holsters.

They were polite and insistent, asking, "Could you please step over here, Major Michaelson?" while letting him know it was not really a question.

"Over here" was located down a new hallway and into an office where his identification was examined again. He grumped and joked and picked lint off his uniform cuff, readying three different stories depending on what kind of problem they found.

Nothing, apparently. His papers were handed back without hesitation or comment.

Amanda Ringsdotter furiously typed information into an old keyboard, the sound of striking keys echoing like hail pelting down against a metal roof. She glanced up once, sharply, as if discovering something . . . unsavory? No, that wasn't quite it. A mixture of pity and hesitation. Something she didn't want to tell him. And, in fact, did not. Agent Tai made a phone call, where he did a lot of listening, and then the three of them left the spaceport together.

"I'm sorry, but we have to detain you," Ringsdotter informed him. She didn't quite meet his eyes, avoiding the facial scarring as so many did. "Orders from the local garrison. You understand, sir. We'll have your luggage collected and forwarded on to your destination if you will please fill out these forms here and here."

She handed him a small noteputer, left him filling out releases, while they waited for a black sedan to be brought around.

In the car, sharing the backseat with Amanda while Tai drove, he carefully reviewed his situation. They hadn't discovered any flaw in his new identity, so he continued to think of himself as Ritter Michaelson. Ezekiel Crow . . . Daniel Peterson . . . they were other lives, ones best left forgotten.

Detailed paintings began with a blank canvas and very simple brushstrokes.

He wasn't under arrest, and the agents weren't particularly on their guard. They did have guns—Nasant thirty-eights by the look of the protruding butts—which was unusual for Customs Security Officers, but not unheard of. Special detail? If so, under whose authority? Amanda had mentioned the local garrison, which kept Michaelson from speaking out against the delay to his schedule, merely grunting an affirmative like any good regular army officer. The ride took long enough that they engage in some offhand conversation. He learned that Beilù's autumn has been unseasonably warm—good for the late harvests, hard on city living. The Eridani races were still run every weekend. And the delay in his arrival was not caused by a simple warehouse fire, as had been announced to passengers of the *Burning Petals*, but sabotage of a repair depot by a pro-Capellan terrorist force. Amanda glowered darkly as she mentioned them.

Ritter Michaelson pasted a similar frown over his angular features, then rode along in determined silence as the car turned off the highway and onto one of many access roads for the LianChang Military Reserve. Although located several kilometers outside the sprawling mass of suburbs that was official Chang-an, Michaelson noticed that Lianyungang Garrison now co-opted part of the capital's name for its own, giving it greater weight. That was new.

They slid through one of the gates with a flash of badges and an infantryman's wave. Five minutes later, he nodded good-bye to the CSO's, settling himself into a padded leather seat. He gazed with frank interest at the well-appointed office and the well-decorated man who sat behind the teakwood desk: Legate Viktor Ruskoff, commanding all Republic military forces on Liao.

Ruskoff tapped strong fingers on the dark wood grain. Of average height, he still possessed wide shoulders and a lantern jaw, which no doubt served him well at political photo-ops. His fine, ash blond hair was tightly shorn, showing a few scars twisting across a pink scalp. "There is no easy way to say this," he began, then seemed at a loss for how to proceed.

Steeling himself for most anything, question or accusation, Michaelson nodded encouragement. "Straight out is usually best."

"Very well, Mr. Michaelson. Ritter." The early use of his first name spoke volumes on how awkward Legate Ruskoff must have felt. Still, what came next was something of a shock. "Your parents. I'm afraid they're dead."

Michaelson blinked slowly, felt a dark stab of old guilt and pain deep in his gut. Celia and Michael Peterson were both dead all right. But they had died twenty-three years earlier, during the Massacre of Liao. He remembered the muddy boot prints, leading him up the stairs of their modest town house where Capellan soldiers had already been . . . then the laughter.

"How—" His voice cracked on the first attempt, and Michaelson swallowed hard. "How did they die?"

"A fire, it seems. Just a few months ago. On your family ranch near Xiapu." Ruskoff offered a tentative smile of support. "You raise Eridani stock. Beautiful animals."

Michaelson was far too seasoned not to roll with it. "Yes, they are." His mind worked overtime. He hadn't been briefed on this aspect of his new life. A cruel joke played by his benefactor on Terra, or coincidence?

"Can I offer you anything, Major?" Ruskoff paused one finger over an intercom button. "Brandy? Something to take the edge off?"

"No, thank you. I don't drink." He had considered it, though. Just to calm his nerves? *To the Betrayer of Liao.*

"Soft drink?"

"Please."

The Legate stabbed down at the intercom, ordered his assistant to bring in two sweetened colas. Michaelson looked up with a guilty start. He hadn't thought of sweetened colas in years. A Liao touch, adding a pulped naranji to the soft drink. The memory made his mouth water.

"Passing along such grim news was not why I had you brought here, Major. I'm afraid I must intrude on your time a bit further." Ruskoff smoothed his hands across the edge of his desk as if straightening out a wrinkle in the dark wood grain. "I would never interrupt your grief without need."

Which Michaelson could use to dig for more information. "I appreciate that, sir. If you are pressing customs into military duties, the situation must be grave."

"We're stretched to the limit," Ruskoff admitted. "We've had dozens of pro-Capellan movements pop up since the Blackout, though most of our troubles are centered around the Cult of Liao and the *Ijori Dè Guāng* terrorist cells. The Cult has spread its influence into some of the highest circles on planet. Fortunately, they operate mostly inside the political arena, which is Governor Lu Pohl's headache."

"And the *Light of Ijori* is yours?" Michaelson asked. "I hear they were responsible for my DropShip delay. Lit a fire or two."

"And made off with over fifty thousand stones' worth of military equipment. That hasn't hit the headlines yet, but it will. Our planetary administration leaks like a sieve. I really do wonder if the Cult of Liao and *Ijori Dè Guāng* aren't working more hand in fist than we think."

Against the entire Republic infrastructure on Liao, that still didn't seem like too much trouble. The last time something like this had happened, Ezekiel Crow had talked the situation out with no further loss of life. Michaelson was about to (carefully) say as much when a sharp rap at the door heralded the arrival of refreshments.

A lieutenant showing off crisp military bearing paraded in with a serving tray, paying as much attention to detail in one of his most menial duties as he might spend reviewing soldiers or cleaning his side arm. The tray was set quietly on the Legate's desk, two coasters proffered, and tall, sweating glasses placed on each. Ice tinkled softly against fine glass. The lieutenant removed himself as carefully and precisely as he had arrived.

"Good kid," the Legate said in praise after the door clicked shut. "Be a good officer once we rub off that academy seriousness."

The first taste of the citrus-spiked soft drink sat easily on Michaelson's tongue. "We were like that once," he said, relaxing for all of three seconds.

But that recalled times when he *had* been that same lieutenant, full of strong thoughts and ideals and ready to save the world. Ideals were dangerous things. The taste of naranji turned rancid at the back of his throat, and he braced himself back to alertness. He could never afford to relax. Never.

He took a second sip, more for form's sake than anything. "These situations, Legate. They sound like insect bites."

"But we have to scratch. And it's getting worse the longer we're cut off from Terra and the Exarch."

Michaelson swirled the ice in his drink. "I thought Liao was a focal point for the new courier system." A series of planned JumpShip routes and times that picked up some duties from the lost HPG network. "The Solar Express, they're calling it."

"The system is far from complete. With HPGs on Genoa and New Aragon I have an adequate chain of communication with Prefect Tao. A good thing too. The *hùn dàn* Confederation has the entire border stirred up." He calmed himself with visible effort. "Still, intelligence seeping our way from Terra . . . that is in shorter supply."

Now Michaelson was beginning to see what this was about. One of the red flags he'd tripped with customs had been his forged military documents, which placed him on leave from the Hastati Sentinels. "You want to know what is happening on Terra," he said.

"We *need* to know," Ruskoff stressed. "We have rumors of troops massing on the Confederation's side of the border, and every indication is that Daoshen is coming. If we aren't going to see any support from Terra and Prefecture X because they've buttoned up against the next Steel Wolf assault, that's something we'll need to take into account."

So he had hurt Liao again, without even knowing it this time. Well, Michaelson had come to restart his life and make good on past mistakes. What better place to start than gaining the ear of the Planetary Legate?

"I'll tell you what I can," he promised.

This time, he would do it right.

Chang-an
Qinghai Province, Liao

After his interview with Major Michaelson, Viktor Ruskoff caught a VTOL to the White Towers District of Chang-an where the Governor's Palace anchored Liao's administrative center. It truly was a palace, once a summer escape for Confederation Chancellors and other family members of House Liao. As the rural area developed into a modern city, and then an urban sprawl, great care had been kept to maintain the palace grounds and several public buildings separate from the city. A great wall surrounded the entire district, creating a hidden city within the capital.

The VTOL settled on a wide expanse of park in back of the

lofty structure, rotors still thumping overhead when the Legate jumped out. Ruskoff knew his way through the Governor's Palace, having been a fixture around the capital for longer than Anna Lu Pohl had held the top political office. He found her taking a meeting in one of the many executive suites. Extremely tall, despite her Asian heritage, Governor (Mandrissa) Anna Lu Pohl favored Han-inspired gowns that harkened back to the Capellan culture she shared with so many among Liao's population. She sat down with several aides as they poured hard-earned data into her. Governor Lu Pohl also had an insatiable thirst for detail.

"Trouble?" he asked, seeing the stormy expression that piled up her dark eyebrows. For all her aristocratic background and political training, Anna Lu Pohl wore her emotions on her sleeve.

"Trouble," she affirmed. "Messages from New Aragon." She lifted her chin in a simple, regal manner. "If you would all excuse us."

Everyone left save the Governor's chief of staff, who was immune to all but the most direct command. Gerald Tsung was tall and broad shouldered, and looked like he belonged in a uniform rather than his Mao-tailored suit. He had a sharp mind, and Ruskoff often suspected that he created as much policy in the Liao government as did Governor Lu Pohl.

The Legate sat, nodded a stiff greeting to Tsung, then focused back on the Governor. "Should we teleconference with Lord Governor Hidic?" As the political head of Prefecture V, also making his capital on the world of Liao, Marion Hidic often consulted on local matters. It also helped, in Ruskoff's mind, that Hidic was less tolerant of Capellan intrusions than the Liao Governor.

"Marion is on his way here," she said abruptly, giving Ruskoff an idea as to the seriousness of the latest news. The same data would be making its way through channels to his office. As usual, politicians found ways to shortcut procedure. "What did you learn from this Ritter Michaelson?"

"I'll forward my report as soon as possible. Briefly, though, Exarch Redburn got off lucky. Northwind took the real pounding, and the Highlanders were on hand to soak up more damage for him, too. I think mostly it was the shock that fighting came at all to Terra."

"Which leads us to the big question," Gerald Tsung said. "Can we count on help from Terra and Exarch Redburn?"

The soldier in Viktor Ruskoff wanted to speak up at once in support of the Exarch, the political and military leader of the entire Republic. The rational man inside him deferred. Damien Redburn was not everything Ruskoff looked for in a leader, and the Legate owed The Republic an honest evaluation to the question.

"No. We can't."

"Thank you, Viktor," she nodded. "*Shí-fen gǎn-xiè.*"

Her accent was polished, proudly Capellan. Another reminder that Anna Lu Pohl had gained her governorship on a People First campaign, proving that one could be loyal to the old culture and stand for The Republic at the same time. Viktor Ruskoff still had his doubts about that.

As did Shun Tao, the Prefecture's ranking military officer. Tao's relocation to New Aragon made sense, but he counted on Viktor to play watchdog on Liao as well as keep a lid on the *Ijori Dè Guāng* terrorists. As the previous day's firebombing and thefts proved, the latter was more difficult than the former.

Or so he thought then.

"Has Prefect Tao sent new word regarding the problems on Menkar or on Wei?" These two worlds were the hardest hit with pro-Capellan demonstrations and borderline uprisings.

Governor Lu Pohl nodded. "He has. And a number of other worlds, besides. Lord Governor Hidic did not deign to transfer the holographic message to us, though I expect him to bring it so that we may all watch in his presence. But we have the gist. Gerald?"

Tsung passed over his noteputer. "I expect you will get more detailed intelligence than we normally see. The Governor appreciates being kept completely informed."

"Of course," Ruskoff promised.

Unless Tao ordered him to withhold data from the Governor, he was obligated to report at her desired level of detail. The military generally worried about things other than a turf war being fought between planetary and prefecture leaders . . . especially when it came to real war.

"Is this confirmed?" he asked.

"We see no reason not to assume so," Gerald Tsung said evenly. He stepped smoothly into the conversation as Governor Lu Pohl rose and glided gracefully to a sideboard to pour herself a glass of plum wine. "We expect general dissatisfaction to rise by thirty percent once the news breaks. Increases in vandalism, protests, and labor strikes."

Anna Lu Pohl returned to her chair and the conversation carrying her small aperitif of rich, dark liquid. "*Ijori Dè Guāng* activity will likely double in the short term, trying to capitalize on events."

Damned if they wouldn't, Ruskoff knew. "With your approval, I can increase the military presence around Chang-an and our larger cities. Soldiers on the streets might discourage civil unrest as well."

"They might also engender a great deal more resentment among the pro-Capellan population," Tsung warned.

Governor Lu Pohl considered the arguments. then gave her Planetary Legate a simple nod.

Ruskoff rose, noteputer still in hand. He didn't have time to await Marion Hidic's arrival. Best to start things moving right away. This was going to place a great deal of pressure on his troops, their families, and the entire world of Liao. As if they needed any more. He glanced over the noteputer screen once again, reading down the list of worlds. Wei. Palos. Foot Fall. Shipka. They had done it.

The Capellan Confederation had invaded The Republic.

8

School Daze

*News from the front lines is sketchy at best, but this
much we can say for certain: Wei has fallen! In a
dramatic turn of events, the local population stormed
the capital and staged a public coup d'état. Possibly
recalling the Terror Campaign they faced in 3061,
Wei has thrown open its doors to welcome back the
Capellan Confederation.*
—Damon Darman, New Aragon Free Reporting,
27 May 3134

Yiling (Chang-an)
Qinghai Province, Liao
30 May 3134

Rain stormed down from a dark unruly sky, pounding the
Conservatory campus with the fury of the Confederation
unleashed. Under the covered park, where he and his
friends often took their lunch in bad weather, Evan Kurst
sat on one corner of a cement-formed picnic table, elbows
resting on knees and feet on the bench. He stared out into
the gray curtain, trying to picture what was happening on
worlds light-years away: BattleMechs on the march, cities in
flames.

The Capellan ensign with its fist and sword hoisted once
again above the capital on Wei.

"I'm tellin' you, it's happening." David Parks stuffed half a
burrito into his mouth, talking around the food. "Tracy Fox al-

ready got her letter offering early graduation and an immediate position with the Principes Guard."

That was the latest buzz, of course. Call ups. Advancement. Heightened training schedules. With the fall of Wei and a second assault wave already hitting Foochow and Menkar, everyone was certain that the border fighting would impact the Conservatory with dramatic results.

Evan glanced down at Jenna, who huddled between his feet and Mark Lo. She did not look convinced. "Tracy is top of her class. Early graduation was bound to be offered." She smiled with bitchy sweetness. "Elemental blood will out."

A popular turn of phrase, and not always complimentary. Infantrymen descended from Elementals, genetically bred warriors introduced by the Clans, almost always did better than their naturally evolved cousins.

David winced as the barb struck, since his own claim to Elemental bloodlines had done nothing more than mark him for jibes from his friends. "Yeah, but the Principes? Not the Triarii Protectors? I hear the Guard took heavy losses on Palos, which is why they are looking at direct recruitment." Sitting on the far side of the table, he had to reach across to slap Lo on the shoulder. "Back me up, Mark."

Mark Lo sipped a grape-colored power drink. He had weight training right after their shared lunch and rarely ate anything heavier than a creatine-laced shake. "I think David might be right." Though he couldn't refrain from adding, "This time."

David ignored the addendum. "And the fact that she made it off world at all—you know it's her campaign work for Marion Hidic."

"Now *that's* ridiculous." Mark jumped back in fast. "Political leanings have nothing to do with military postings."

"You keep telling yourself that. But when was the last time any student who signed up for Capellan History and Culture was posted anywhere but to the local militia? Oh, that's right, you don't take that class, do you?"

Neither did David, but only because he hoped for an off-world assignment himself. Evan felt a slight stir in his gut, though, as his and Jenna's next hour put them both in Professor Rogers's auditorium for Capellan History and Culture.

It was popular mythology that any Conservatory cadet who signed up for CH&C was automatically pigeonholed as anti-

Republic and would be blacklisted from any fair military placement. Likewise, being civic-minded enough to support a *legitimate* political campaign showed what a good Republic citizen you were—or would be—and boosted you along your career path. Discrimination, certainly, of the very kind The Republic claimed it stood against. But who was going to hold the military responsible?

"The Conservatory only started offering the course again thanks to the efforts of Ezekiel Crow." Jenna sounded thoughtful. She forked up the last few bites from her bento bowl. "I wonder if the course is tainted more than ever now."

"Not you, too," Mark said. "Whatever happened to Crow on Northwind and on Terra, what he accomplished here was a good thing."

Evan wasn't so sanguine. They were referring to the campus uprising of 3128, when a strong minority in the cadet corps and regular student body took control of the Conservatory in protest of discriminatory campus policies. Most of those protestors believed that Capellan culture should be celebrated, and taught, as it had in the years following the Conservatory's founding. Those privileges had been suspended after the Confederation assault of 3111, the Night of Screams (or the Massacre of Liao, if you accepted Republic propaganda). In its place had come classes on citizenship and moral philosophy.

3128 stirred up a lot of mixed feelings. The Legate fired on student positions, and had been on the verge of launching a full assault when the Paladin Ezekiel Crow arrived. Crow talked the students into ending their violent standoff. His compromise on behalf of the standing authority was to allow true Capellan history, unvarnished and fully credited, to be taught, and that the students be given more liberal rights to assembly. Legate Kang resigned two months later and the people had celebrated the Paladin's idea of justice.

Now Crow had betrayed everything the Knights, Paladins, and The Republic stood for by abandoning The Republic on Northwind, on Terra. His name was no longer celebrated. Invoking it was more often an attempt at black humor. Crow, come to pick on the bones of The Republic.

David certainly wasn't going to defend the fallen Paladin. "Yeah," he said. "Crow accomplished something good here. He made it easier for The Republic to pick out old-school Capellans." Then a sharp gust of wind caught his burrito's wadded wrapper and scooted it off the table. He went after it.

Another gust sent David chasing over to the next table. Jenna pulled her hands up into her parka sleeves and hunched in closer to Evan's legs, trying to hide from the damp touch of approaching winter. Evan sat up, thrust his hands into the pockets of his leather jacket. "He might be right," he said to Mark, quietly, needing to say something just then.

Mark nodded glumly. "Yeah. But I'm never gonna tell him that."

David didn't need anyone's encouragement. Returning with wrapper in hand, he clambered up onto the cement bench and yelled out, "Would all Capellans please raise your hand and wave at your nearest military recruiter?"

A few nearby students laughed. Others started guiltily. Still more frowned—whether at David's lack of tact or his pointed example, Evan couldn't be certain.

David jumped back down, straddling the bench. "I guess I don't have Hahn's knack with people."

Evan didn't feel much like laughing today, but he still chuckled. Even Mark managed a weak smile. "Hahn would be a touch more . . . subtle," Evan finally offered as critique. "Not everything can be assaulted like a fortified base."

"Better than filing endless paperwork just for a right that most other Republic academies enjoy."

Hahn Soom Gui *was* filing paperwork, in fact. Preparing for another pro-Capellan rally. Evan often wondered if his friend actually hoped to commit career suicide with regard to the military, so he could run on Governor Lu Pohl's next People First campaign drive. He knew that Hahn had rebuffed efforts from the Cult of Liao to recruit him into their underground political movement: too small for his tastes, apparently.

"To each his own," Evan said evenly. "Honeyed words, spoken at the right time, can often shake a world."

Jenna elbowed him in the knee. "Confucius say, man get farther with kind word and gun, than he can with kind word alone."

"Master Kung said no such thing," Mark said, laughing, the tension draining out of his face. Jenna stuck her tongue out at him. "Though it does sound close to something you could pick out of the writings of Lao-tse."

Kung fu-tsu? Lao Tse? Evan leaned over Jenna. "You've

been reading," he said, eyes narrowing in mock severity. "I thought that was forbidden to infantry."

"That—right." Mark stone-faced the entire cabal. "Big—men—no—need—books. Got—big—gun."

"I heard it was more like a derringer," David said, leering across the table and waggling his eyebrows at Jenna. "That true?"

Jenna's green eyes sparkled playfully. To Mark's embarrassment and Evan's relief—he really didn't want to get into a discussion of his friends' relationship, not at *that* level—she merely smiled and shrugged. Lo flushed a healthy pink and Evan pretended to cover his ears with his hands.

"Too—much—information," he chanted, mocking Mark's earlier routine.

Everyone laughed, and on a gray day with news of the budding war storming the campus, it was a welcome sound. Their lunch rendezvous broke apart on that note. Mark gave Jenna a quick squeeze and David shot each of them with finger guns, blowing the smoke off the barrels after and then holstering them at his sides. "Sim time," he said, and jogged off to the simulator complex. Mark zipped up his windbreaker and pushed off for the gym. Evan hooked his backpack over one shoulder and ambled out toward the edge of the covered park to stare into the rain.

"Self-absorbed, aren't we?" Jen asked, bumping him with a hip check as she stepped up on his left side. She hugged her CH&C books against her chest. "You thinking about the fighting?"

Evan reached out to grab a sprinkling of water, and scrubbed it over his face. The chill pleasantly shocked his skin and distracted him from Jenna's close proximity. "We'll be late for class," he said, avoiding an answer.

Weaving past tables and knots of students, they chose a covered walkway that led toward the social sciences buildings. The smell of damp cement and fresh mud followed them. They walked close enough that their arms rubbed from time to time, sending an uneasy burst of warmth up to Evan's shoulder.

"Okay, give," she said as they came to the intersection of two paths. From here, all three choices took them out into the rain. Turning left, it was a short fifty meters to social sciences, and part of that was shielded by a couple of large red cedars.

"You've been moody for a couple of days and I'm not the only one who's noticed."

Evan considered the silent treatment, and knew he would never hold up against Jenna's constant badgering. Reaching into his jacket's inside pocket for the tightly folded letter he'd tucked away, he handed it over.

Jenna snapped it open and read. "You've been offered your citizenship." Her eyes glanced between the letter and Evan, glowing like polished jade. "We've always known you were holding out on us, Evan Kurst. All that community service and campaign work. You're really going legit, aren't you?"

Her teasing needled him gently, but Evan still tensed. "You don't think it's a bit suspect?"

"Why? Oh, the war?" To her credit, she didn't dismiss it out of hand. "You think David might be right, that the government is going to step up the pressure to put us in the field faster?"

"The thought crossed my mind."

Republic citizenship was not a right, it was earned. Residents knew mostly the same privileges as anyone else. They simply couldn't hold titles, or large landholds. And they couldn't vote. Part of Governor Lu Pohl's triumph, in fact, was that she had persuaded enough *citizens*—people who thought enough of The Republic to actually work for its betterment—that their old heritage was still something of which to be proud.

Evan's foster parents had believed that, even though their pro-Capellan bias had kept them from earning citizenship despite sixteen years running a foster home for war orphans. In the fantasy all orphans created, Evan liked to believe that his real parents would have thought the same. *That* was the reason Evan had volunteered. Never to specifically earn citizenship for himself.

And to offer it to him now?

" 'Based on your earlier contribution to The Republic,' " Jenna read out loud, tasting the words, " 'and your continued commitment to its defense.' " She handed it back. "You could've gotten this letter at any time, you know. You earned it."

Tucking the letter away, Evan nodded out into the rain. Jenna stepped out first, careless of the rain that soaked into her tightly braided hair. Evan handed her his backpack and hiked his jacket up to form a temporary umbrella for them both. It got them under the trees, where big, fat drops leaked down, but not so hard that either of them cared. Evan settled his jacket back on his shoulders.

"The fact is," he began, almost thought better of it, then continued, "I earned it two years ago. Double service for my political work on the campaign and my academy years . . . why didn't it come then?"

Because he was flagged as a potential Capellan sympathizer? Because The Republic wasn't worried about him then, planning to shuffle him off to the side in a dead-end militia post or cashier him due to lack of billets? Jenna didn't make any other suggestions because deep down both students felt the truth of it. The Republic wanted to buy him off now because he might be called up for off-planet duty. And an enfranchised soldier had more to fight for, didn't he?

"You'll still accept, of course."

When had he said that? "I don't know," he said. "Would you?"

"Well, yeah. I mean, you have to be part of the system to change it, don't you?" She grinned, reached for a laugh. "The *Ijori Dè Guāng* notwithstanding."

As a joke it fell flat, stretching a long silence between them as the two cadets gained the social sciences building and shook off the rain. Jenna whipped her braids around, flinging water in all directions. She glanced at him repeatedly, but held her tongue until they slipped into the main hall, joining the press of students who shuffled around between classes.

"Do you think we should drop Rogers's CH&C course?" she asked. "I mean, if The Republic is really paying attention to this kind of detail right now—"

"I don't like being manipulated," Evan said shortly. He nodded Jenna through the auditorium door first. "Not by anyone."

But then a hand fell on his shoulder, preventing him from following. "No," a soft voice said as the hand turned him around. "Going your own way has never been a problem for you, has it?"

Evan might have overlooked the other man without recognizing him. The long hair, a wispy beard shot through with gray—but the voice, that was familiar. And the eyes. Still dark and hard, like a doll's eyes. In less than a second, they chilled Evan right to his core. He dropped his backpack to the floor, stood their dumbly.

Mai Uhn Wa had returned to Liao.

"Hello, Evan," his old mentor said with false pleasantry. "Don't you have a greeting for—" he paused, as if trying to think how best to describe himself, "—an old friend?"

He did. With all the strength he could summon on an instant's notice, Evan balled up one fist and swung it for the tip of Mai Wa's chin.

9

Sifu

I see nothing courageous or noble in undermining your legitimate government. Devlin Stone brought peace to The Republic and to much of the Inner Sphere. Have we already forgotten him? I tell you now that I have not. If necessary, I will save our Capellan people even from themselves.
— Prefect Shun Tao, Public address, 28 May 3134

Yiling (Chang-an)
Qinghai Province, Liao
30 May 3134

The shock of seeing his old mentor fueled a deep anger within Evan Kurst. Mai Wa's return at this very moment seemed just as opportunistic as the letter Evan carried in his jacket pocket. He swung without thinking, dropping his thin veneer of calm for several irretrievable seconds.

And then he was flying forward, pulled off balance and bodily tossed into the center of the corridor. Mai Wa had been ready for any outburst of anger. A simple matter to block the punch, grab, twist and *extend* . . . Evan tripped over an outstretched leg and levered out full-length before he caught the floor with his hands, chest, and the side of his head.

The small man stood over him. "Good to see you, too."

Evan rocked up onto his knees, shook his head clear. He owned the center of the hall. Other cadet-students stood around in a rough circle, watching. Jenna waited at the door, casting a wary glance at Mai Wa, but also spending some concern in Evan's direction. Ruefully, he dusted his hands against his jacket and climbed slowly back to his feet, bending down to get his backpack before facing his old *sifu*—mentor and master—again.

Mai Wa kept a flat-footed stance and a wary shoulder turned toward him. "First attempt is free, Evan. The next one will cost you."

He considered it. Then Jenna placed a hand on the side of Evan's face where he had polished the vinyl floor, brushed some dirt from it. "Everything all right here?"

Ignoring the ringing in his left ear, Evan nodded. "Just saying hello to an old friend. Jenna Lynn Tang, this is Mai Uhn Wa. My old kung fu instructor." The half-truth rolled easily off his tongue. Chinese martial arts techniques were some of the things Mai had taught him. "I've never been able to catch him off his guard." Also true.

"Well—" she didn't sound sure "—if that's how rough you boys used to play, no wonder David can never get the drop on you."

He nodded. "Can I catch up with you in a second?"

It was an abrupt dismissal, maybe too abrupt. Jenna frowned, then glanced around quickly, nervously. Sometimes having a reputation among his friends served Evan well. This was one of those times. Jenna moved into the small auditorium. Mai and Evan followed, but immediately moved to one side to sit at the upper row of tables. Jenna had found her usual seat next to Hahn, who stared a question back at Evan.

"Your friends?" Mai asked.

"*My* friends." The emphasis was slightly different between the two. Hands off.

"*Róng-yi*, Evan. Easy. You are the only person here I am interested in."

"That makes me feel so much safer." Evan shouldered his backpack onto the table. Professor Rogers stepped up to the podium, readying the day's lecture. As usual, a Conservatory proctor sat in on the class, right down front, taking obvious notes for his report to the dean. "How did you slip back onto Liao?" he asked.

"Customs was a problem. They've tightened down border crossings, certainly, but JumpShip crews are not interrogated as well as they might be. And planetfall?" Mai Wa shrugged.

"I am not without resources, even now. Still, if approached, you may want to stick with your story about kung fu instruction. It will hold up much better."

"What do you want?"

"I understand that you have been busy in my absence. I expected nothing less. Causing gridlock traffic to reroute the Heritage Days military parade—a masterful piece of work."

Evan simmered. "Greggor has a big mouth." Who else had Mai contacted?

"Loyalty, Evan, is never easily abandoned."

"You seemed to find it easy to do so."

"From your point of view, that is probably true. Or you could say that loyalty is what brought me back. I never forgot you, Evan, and we still want the same thing: a free Liao."

"I don't know what it is you want, Mai. You left us. Care to explain that?"

The old man steeled himself against something unpleasant. Evan saw it in his eyes, and slack expression. "I was called back to the capital," he said, careful not to speak direct names. "To the . . . black towers. That is all the answer you should need."

Sian! The Celestial Palace . . . Mai Wa had always intimated that his orders came from the highest levels. Evan wanted to stay angry, not believe him, but he couldn't help asking, "Did the . . . the Celestial Wisdom send you back here?" Meaning to Liao.

Mai answered it differently. "To the Conservatory? Actually, I was invited. By Professor Rogers." With a tight smile the old Capellan stood and walked stoically down the aisle to accept a nervous handshake from the professor.

Professor Rogers was a bookish, slender man, and Evan had no trouble reading his unease in the tight set of his shoulders. He introduced Mai Wa as a visiting lecturer from Bulics Academy, Evan's previous school. Another weighty glance from Hahn Soom Gui followed that announcement. Evan groaned, and put his head down on the table.

Fortunately, Mai Wa did not launch into a tirade against the evils of The Republic. He actually talked, at length, about its formation. About Devlin Stone, fresh from victory over the Word of Blake, convincing the great leaders of his time to help him create a new hegemony with Terra at its center. Stone's swords-to-plowshares program, adopted by—or forced upon—the Great Houses so that war could not be waged at the Jihad's scale again.

The world of Liao was part of those events. An example of the horrors of unbridled war, and the courage of a besieged people.

"But didn't those people lose their basic freedom of choice?" Only Hahn would ask that question with the dean's man sitting two tables in front of him. "Liao did not wish to join The Republic. It was thrust upon the Capellan people, for the common good." The way he phrased it, Hahn could be playing devil's advocate and leading the discussion into the merits of Republic occupation of Liao.

Always the politician.

"One point two billion dead," Mai reminded them all. "That was the price Liao paid for never capitulating to the Word of Blake fanatics. The continent of Anderia was rendered nearly uninhabitable. Two of the Confederation's fabled Warrior Houses died here. And still the people rose up time and again, flooding the streets and the battlefields with live bodies, often wielding nothing more than a pistol, or a club. They formed a living shield and forced the Blakists to march over them. Enemy MechWarriors were never safe outside of their cockpits. Infantry could never hold on to gains made by the 'Mechs and tanks.

"Does this sound like a people who would meekly accept anything?"

It was a refined approach to the same arguments which had given birth to the *Ijori Dè Guāng*. Mai was not given to extravagant gestures or boisterous speech, as Hahn used in rallies. He put the information to you in reasonable tones, and let you decide for yourself. But Mai Wa was a master at leading you to the conclusion he wanted you to find.

It was a skill he demonstrated as another student stood, waited to be acknowledged. "Some books suggest that our suicidal behavior only fueled the Word of Blake's anger." Cynthia Raddle. Evan recognized her haughty tone. "We allowed them no safe refuge, so they razed cities to the ground rather than leave enemy strongholds at their back. In the conduct of civilized warfare—"

Mai Wa let her get no farther. "Warfare is never civilized," he said tersely. "It is the focused use of power to gain a specific objective. *Focused . . . use.*" He repeated those two words slowly.

"The Word of Blake was not interested in warfare, civilized

or otherwise. They were wanton and malicious. They reveled in destruction as only agents of chaos can. Look at their actions on Tikonov, on Northwind, where the public did not as strenuously oppose them. When you make excuses for the Word of Blake, Raddle-*xiǎo-jie*, you weaken The Republic's authority and you cheapen the cost to Liao."

Ouch! Turning Cynthia's pro-Republic leanings back onto her was a method Evan had not considered. It was no off-the-cuff remark. Mai had been prepared with her name. Evan fought through the reasoning, trying to see what Mai gained by promoting Stone's efforts. He did not have far to go, as the other man quickly returned to his point.

"One point two billion dead. That is what we gave up in the struggle. And Liao, in ten years, *did not fall*. This was the strength of your grandfathers and grandmothers. This is why our *Chung Yeung* Festival, the Autumn Remembrance where we feast for the dead, is a larger festivity on Liao than even the New Year's holiday. This is what it means to be Capellan."

Never give up. Never bend your neck—not when you know you are right. These were the lessons Mai Wa attempted to instill in the young minds.

Evan tried to hold himself in his seat, unwilling to leap to Mai Wa's assistance yet unable to pass up the opportunity. Someone had to bring the topic back around, and Hahn was apparently not going to stick his neck out a second time in one class. Evan rose, felt eyes turn on him as his chair scrapped against the floor. Mai's curt nod was no more than he had given the other students.

"The earlier question, Mai *sifu*. If our ancestors were so strong, why did they embrace The Republic when, according to most scholars, they wanted to resist?"

No doubt that added Evan's name to the proctor's report.

Mai Wa allowed the question to hang over the class for several long heartbeats. "Shock," he finally said. "Grief. Liao had suffered through ten long and traumatic years. And on no world was Devlin Stone more celebrated than he was on Liao during the day of liberation. People trusted in the future, and few truly believed then that the Confederation could be pressured into giving up this world. Throughout the entire Jihad, House Liao never once turned away from its birthworld, and that as much as anything empowered the people.

"Remember that word, young sir. Empowered. The people

never threw their lives away without some meaning attached. Not once."

Evan sat back down, a warm flush burning his ears. Mai did not wait for a new question.

"But in a political decision made on a distant planet by powers far removed from the people of this world, Liao was suddenly stripped away from the Confederation with assurances that its Capellan roots would never be forgotten. Would be celebrated, in fact. And it was like that, for a time. The problem that crept up on the population, though, was that it was no longer empowered. Citizenship, once earned under the Confederation flag, had to be earned again in support of The Republic. Add to that Stone's relocation programs, which flooded many non-Capellan communities onto Liao, and you can see why some would say that we were given no choice. But we were."

Was it a good choice, though? The question was there, whether Mai Wa voiced it himself, or not.

"Now, there is a subtler context to your question, which you did not mean, but I will also try to answer. You asked why the people embraced The Republic. I ask you, did they?" Silence. He let his gaze travel the entire breadth of the class. "Have you?" he asked.

"How many of you have truly embraced The Republic and all the good it has brought? How many of you continue to resist, each in your own way, when you can? I put it to you, to answer for yourself, what it means to be Capellan.

"And that," he said with a shrug, very animated coming from him, "is a debate for another day. Thank you for your attention."

Evan stayed seated as most of the class stood to applaud. A few dozen students crowded around the guest lecturer while most filed out, eagerly debating today's lesson and ready to share it with their less enthusiastic friends around campus. Evan noticed that Hahn made a point of introducing himself to Mai Wa, and slipped the elder man a card. Jenna held herself in greater reserve, having already met the Capellan in a more awkward manner.

Eventually, his friends joined the tail end of students leaving the room, and Evan nodded them onward as he remained behind. Mai came up the aisle, as self-effacing as only he could be.

"What do you think?"

Evan held back outright approval, but still felt he owed his teacher some warning. "I think you'll have people looking into your past by tomorrow."

"Let them look. They will end up running around in circles."

"Yes, but for how long?"

"Long enough."

There it was again, that unvoiced promise for the future. Evan remembered it from before. He also remembered how it had turned out, with Mai abandoning them when they needed a strong leader most. "I still do not trust you," he said.

"And you shouldn't. I have not given you reason to." Yet. He left that unvoiced as well, but Evan heard it in his head.

"If you lead the authorities to us . . ." He did not have to finish. The necessary threat was understood. After all, hadn't Mai taught him the rules?

"A truce, Evan. That is all I am asking of you. If you need to contact me . . ." His eyes slid sideways, back down toward Professor Rogers. "I think you know how to go about that." He offered his hand.

Evan took it. Slowly. The handshake was no warm greeting, but it was an understanding. A truce, as Mai Uhn Wa had said. Evan did not want the older man's help, and Mai, whatever he wanted, would ask for nothing more. For now.

10

Eye of the Storm

*Two hostile DropShips violated Liao airspace last
night and made high-G drops over the continents of
Nánlù and Beilù. We believe this is an exploratory
advance by the Second McCarron's Armored Cavalry, the same unit currently leading the assault on
Gan Singh. It appears the Confederation has opened
up a delayed front. I'll take questions . . .*
—Legate Viktor Ruskoff, Press Briefing, 8 June 3134

Xiapu
Huáng-yù Province, Liao
9 June 3134

Ritter Michaelson sat astride an Eridani mare. He hadn't
been born to the saddle, but was growing comfortable with it
after several weeks. He shifted his weight carefully, not wanting to spook the animal. Her ambling walk rocked him easily
back and forth, back and forth, but he knew better than to let
down his guard. The mare had already proven herself to be
proud and headstrong as any of her breed. On his morning
ride out, she had taken the bit between her teeth and ate up
several kilometers with long, powerful strides before he'd regained control.

He had learned one thing from that wild ride: he could
hang on more easily during a gallop than during a canter or
slower trot. A gallop rolled beneath him like the swaying gait
of a light BattleMech. The short, choppy strides of a trot

tended to slam the base of his spine right up between his shoulder blades.

It all took some getting used to.

The small ranch could not have been more different from the city life he had grown up with. Grassy plains stretched for hundreds of kilometers in every direction, cut apart by wind-break forests and a few muddy rivers. Eridani horses and beef cows shared the range. Simple barbed-wire fences kept the herds separate, and someone had to ride those fences every few days. It was a task he found almost enjoyable. It gave him time to be alone with his thoughts. As alone as he could be, for a man who had lived two other lives.

Both of them ruined by bad choices.

Daniel Peterson had been a young man caught up in large events. A fresh-faced lieutenant thinking he could force his homeworld into a confrontation with its Capellan heritage, with the Confederation. One DropShip. That had been the arrangement. Flashes of memory from that night haunted him still.

. . . Chang-an, burning. He ran through the streets, fighting his way back to his parents' home.

. . . Muddy bootprints heading up the stairs, and a wet stain of blood seeping into the hallway carpet from behind the door.

That had ended his first life and begun his second, where he'd tried to accomplish good works in penance. Becoming a Knight of the Sphere, then a Paladin, Ezekiel Crow gave self-lessly to the homeland he'd failed. Twenty-three years, only to have his past catch up with him on Northwind. Blackmailed, he had again betrayed those around him—and himself as well. Was there salvation after that?

Daniel Peterson, the Betrayer of Liao. Ezekiel Crow, the Black Paladin.

"Who will I be this week?" he asked out loud.

The mare snorted and shook its head, long mane whisking along the side of its neck. Michaelson patted the muscular neck with a gloved hand, calming the high-spirited animal. For a second he thought he heard the distant, thumping echo of VTOL rotors, but saw nothing on the horizon. He heard nothing more except the slow clop of hooves and the whistle of dry wind combing through tall grasses.

Who would he be?

Ritter Michaelson was all he had left.

Things were heating up with the arrival of the Second Mc-Carron's Armored Cavalry. A veteran Confederation unit, its arrival put Liao on notice that the world had not been forgotten. The supposed minority of pro-Confederation residents became more vocal, swelled their numbers every day. Republic responses grew more determined in turn. A citywide labor strike in the southern city of Jíla turned ugly when the local magistrate shut off residential power as a way to force people back to work. The industrial sector was still burning, two days after the resulting riots.

Michaelson had seen this kind of schism before, up close, and if someone did not head it off soon, blood would run in the streets again.

Only there didn't seem to be anything he could do about it. He had no BattleMech. No unit. No appointment by Exarch Redburn. All he had was a tenuous relationship started with Legate Ruskoff, and the ranking officer had not returned one of Michaelson's calls in over a week. More important things to do.

Then he heard it again. The thumping beat of rotor blades, soft, but getting louder, bouncing down against the grasslands and seeming to come from all around him. A nearby herd of grazing Eridani horses raised their heads, stamped at the ground.

Lifting his eyes to the horizon Michaelson did a long slow scan of the leaden winter skies. There! A small dark smudge moved against the gray backdrop, dipping down and back up, making long, sweeping runs. Looking for someone. He rubbed a gloved hand over his face—the glove smelling of leather and horse, and always sliding too easily over the glossy healed burns.

Coincidence? He didn't believe in it. Not anymore.

Who would he be? The question mocked him even as the helicopter swooped in close and circled once, twice. Nearby, the Eridani startled, trying to decide which way to run. His own mare tossed its head, pranced sideways. Michaelson bent forward to calm the beast, and she bucked up violently, throwing him overhead and into a bone-jarring heap. The 'copter flattened out and drifted down for a landing. The horses bolted northeast, a fine golden stallion running at their head and his mare trailing only a few lengths behind the herd.

Michaelson untangled himself, rising on shaky legs. An angry shout died on his lips as Jack Farrell jumped down from the VTOL's passenger compartment.

No mistaking the tangle of coarse, dark hair, the eyepatch worn over his ruined socket, or the challenging set to his shoulders which held the proverbial chip up there. The veteran raider walked tall beneath the still-pounding rotors where most men would have ducked just out of forced habit. So far as Michaelson knew, Farrell bent his neck to only one person in all of The Republic.

Jacob Bannson.

"One-Eyed" Jack Farrell looked the part of rogue and pirate raider. His lean features were chiseled and hard. His good eye was pale blue, and seemed to bore right through you. That eye fixed on Michaelson now, who limped forward with fists clenched. The two men did not shake hands or even nod a greeting. There was history, yes, but most of it bad.

"What do you want?" he asked Bannson's man, shouting over the deep rattle of the still-spinning helicopter blades. He pulled off his gloves and tucked them into a back pocket.

"Not to be here, you can bet. I can think of ten things I'd rather be doing than watching you rot out here in the desert."

Most of which involved stomping through cities in his *Jupiter* BattleMech, at the head of a raider company. Michaelson nodded back at the 'copter. "Don't let me keep you."

Farrell hawked, spat to one side, and glared with his good eye. His contempt for Ezekiel Crow, never a secret, had degraded another few notches since the Paladin's fall from grace. That likely translated over to the entire world of Liao.

"Doesn't work that way," he said, obviously not liking the matter any more than Michaelson. "Bannson told me to ride herd over things on Liao." He glanced across the golden sward, at the fleeing colorful shadows of the Eridani. "Didn't know he meant that literally."

"Your boss gave me up on Terra. He told them everything. Tara Campbell. Jonah Levin. Because of him I had to bury Ezekiel Crow and start again."

"You should be getting used to that by now."

Michaelson glowered. He was getting to be an old hand at it, in fact. Speaking of which, "How did Bannson find me this time?"

"What? You thought you had an ace in the hole with our

'friend' on Terra." Farrell was talking about the crime boss who had arranged Crow's escape and new identity. The raider smiled thin and cruel, and glanced back at the helicopter that waited on him. "Bannson Universal has far-reaching business interests."

In other words, the underworld lord sold him out. Probably before he'd left Terra. "I should have guessed." The crime boss had muscle enough to set him up with a new identity, but it would have taken Bannson's influence and long reach to make that cover stick so well on Liao.

"Yeah, maybe you should have."

Farrell reached around for his back pocket, fished out a pewter flask and unscrewed the top. He took a long pull. Michaelson watched him drink, eyes glued to the flask. Farrell had never taken a drink on the job as far as Michaelson could recall. He watched as the pirate finished, wiped his mouth with the back of one hand and then held out the metal container, offering it. It was no casual nip, and not an offer of camaraderie. It was taunting, cruel and dark. Daniel Peterson had sworn off drinking after the Massacre of Liao, that last night he spent in the wine shop trying to staunch the memories of the blood and smoke, the mass graves dug by laboring IndustrialMechs. . . .

Hearing the laughter in the voice of the Confederation agent as he described how they had toasted him.

To the Betrayer of Liao.

That laughter had followed him around for over two decades. In his mind's eye he pictured them with their glasses raised, drinking to the health of Lieutenant Daniel Peterson. And they had paid him a bonus—one stone for every Republic citizen killed in the fighting. Ezekiel Crow had never forgotten, and had never touched a drop of alcohol since. Ritter Michaelson could have used a drink just then, anything to drown out the memory, but would not give Farrell the satisfaction.

"I want nothing more to do with Jacob Bannson," he said, biting off each word.

"That's hardly the point, Crow." Michaelson started to correct him, but Farrell simply waved a hand, unconcerned with whatever name the disgraced soldier used now. "Bannson might have something more to do with you, especially if things continue to heat up on Liao and around the Prefecture.

Opportunities abound for real men who are willing to take chances and seize life."

The Confederation invasion? "What's Bannson got to do with this? Is he backing the Confederation's play now?"

Farrell wasn't about to answer the question. "Ah, so you are still interested in the bigger game. That's good, 'cause I'll be around to make sure you remember who's side you play on." Another swig from the flask. "And don't think about trying to skip out, either. You'll never make it."

"There's nothing more Bannson can do to me."

The raider laughed, long and loud, as if the disgraced man had said something truly funny. "Sure there is. Unless you like the idea of sitting through a very public trial, or have the balls to eat the barrel on that service piece you have back at the ranch house. You still have plenty to lose, and I'll be here to make sure you don't forget it."

With a toothy grin Farrell tossed the unstoppered flask at Michaelson's head. He caught it, some of the amber liquid sloshing out of the spout and wetting his knuckles. Farrell gave him a heavy wink, and turned back for the 'copter, its rotors spinning in preparation for taking off.

Staccato slaps of cold air buffeted Michaelson, stirred the long grasses. The scent of sour mash bourbon warmed his nostrils. He traded the flask into his other hand and sucked on his knuckle, eyes clenching as the alcohol's smooth taste coiled at the back of his throat.

No. Not again. Farrell's presence on his homeworld was poison enough.

Jaw clenched, Michaelson watched the helicopter thunder its way south, back toward the ranch house. He turned over the heavy flask, pouring out every last drop, letting the booze soak into the soil of Liao. He threw the container as far as he could out into the range, then turned in the general direction of the ranch house and began a long walk home.

11

Monsters in the Dark

On Shipka today, elements of the Fifth Hastati Sentinels smashed through to the besieged militia at Sombulton. The Confederation Reserve Cavalry had supposedly choked off all access to the area, but reports claim that resistance cracked almost at once. New analysis indicates that the main body of the Reserve Cavalry may have been pushed as far forward as Menkar.

—Franklin Chou, Reporting on New Aragon,
11 June 3134

Yiling (Chang-an)
Qinghai Province, Liao
14 June 3134

Wrenching on his controls, Evan Kurst manhandled the sixty-five-ton *Thunderbolt* into a sharp pivot that turned him in behind a small office building. Tracer bullets chased after him, white-hot and angry as they flashed through the perpetual gray of urban night. They smashed into the corner of the building. A blurred stream of autocannon fire chewed in with them, pulverizing stone, pitting the steel frame hidden beneath the façade.

"Four . . . three . . . two. . . ." Evan kept count softly, marking the timing in his head. He levered back on his BattleMech's throttle, shifting from a flat-out run to a reverse walk in a matter of seconds. The cockpit pitched forward, throwing Evan against his restraining harness. The entire machine might have sprawled headfirst along the street if not for the bulky neuro-helmet he wore to link his own sense of balance with the *Thunderbolt's* massive gyroscopic stabilizers. Arching his back, chin up, Evan shifted the 'Mech's center of mass to cope with the change in momentum.

"One."

The *Thunderbolt* stepped back into the intersection, right arm levering up and outward, pointing its light Gauss rifle straight back down the street at the Confederation forces. A bulky *Shen Yi* stomped along the avenue, a Schmitt assault tank rolling along at the BattleMech's feet while a pair of Demons and Fa Shih infantry raced up from behind. A *Wasp*, battered from earlier fighting, leapt over a nearby building, cutting off the *Shen Yi* as it landed in a bent-legged crouch.

Evan's targeting crosshairs flashed from red to gold and he pulled his primary trigger.

High-energy capacitors dumped their stored power into a series of coils, creating a magnetic funnel that latched onto the nickel-ferrous mass loaded into the Gauss rifle's acceleration chamber. In a fraction of a second the mass had been driven up to hypersonic speeds, flashing down the short city block and into the left knee of the *Wasp*.

Sheer kinetic force wrenched the leg back. Sparks exploded out of the ruined lower leg actuator. As the Confederation 'Mech stepped forward, the entire leg collapsed like an accordion. The *Wasp* pitched forward, planting itself face first against the unyielding ground. More sparks ground out beneath the fallen BattleMech as it sprawled into a rough, ungainly slide that tumbled it over once and left it pitched up against the office building.

Evan throttled forward, ducking behind the building once again. Out from under the sights of the Confederation forces that followed.

The *Shen Yi* levered its large laser forward to stab megajoules of ruby energy into the night. An orange afterglow of missile exhaust wreathed the upper torso as it let loose with twin flights from its assault-class launchers. The Schmitt pounded out fifty-millimeter slugs. Neither had a chance to hit him, but in this Confederation assault of Liao the enemy soldiers were programmed to vent their anger on civilian targets. Dark windows lit up as the building's interior filled with the laser's red glow. The missiles smashed deep into several floors, blossoming into fireballs of orange flame. Glass exploded out on all four sides, raining broken shards over the streets of Desu.

The historical simulation was incredibly detailed. Biased, but very well-programmed.

Desu was one of the larger cities of Nánlù, Liao's southern continent, among the hardest hit in 3111 after the so-called Massacre of Chang-an. Just outside the city had been the Lord Governor's mansion. It was always demolished before the local militia responded, with the Confederation assault force already moving into the outskirts of the city, burning and destroying.

Simulator pods allowed for such battles to be fought again and again, always looking for how things might have been handled differently. What if the militia had massed forces in the north, preparing a hard-line defense? What if they had flanked and attacked the Confederation DropShip?

How about a lone MechWarrior, running interference for the main militia force?

That was Evan's mission today, to slow things down while other students set up a defense to protect the densely populated north sector. He'd received operational orders while firing up his "BattleMech," plugging his cooling vest into the working life support system and shivering as a slug of coolant circulated through tiny tubes sewn into the protective gear. Vents at his feet dumped scorching air into the pod, simulating the high temperatures known in combat. The pod rocked inside of a cradle to approximate the BattleMech's rolling gait, and a rough vibration shook the simulator whenever he came under fire. Controls were the real thing, but the cockpit's ferroglass shields had been replaced with monitors on which the city assault would play out according to historical fact, augmented by computer probability.

Everything was as real as they could make it. Even the enemy, who acted in callous disregard for human life and frustrated The Republic's every attempt to save the day. Because that was how it really happened, right?

No militia tank crew brought down one of their own *Legionnaires* with friendly fire because they were too scared to double-check their targets.

No armored infantry squad took cover in a civilian neighborhood, firing out of doors and windows to avoid the wide-open streets. Forcing Confederation officers to call in gunship strafing.

And no Republic-trained MechWarrior walked his *Ryoken II* through the brick facing of a downtown apartment complex, parking his war avatar in the center of the building to hide it from approaching Capellan forces, trading ninety-three civilian lives to set an ambush. The *Ryoken's* left-shoulder machine gun would not have been of a height with the third-floor apartments. There was another reason for the twenty-mil wounds that killed Evan's parents and left a two-year-old ward for Chang-an's Civic Child Care Services.

Evan shook himself free of his imagination's hold and tightened his grip on the simulator's control sticks. Dwelling on the past would only earn him failing marks in the present. He owed his parents better than that. He owed himself better.

And the battle for Desu continued.

Failing under the Confederation's onslaught, the office building collapsed into a pile of rubble and fire. Lasers sliced through the dust, searching. Evan turned into the battle but throttled backward, working into a retrograde maneuver that duckwalked the sixty-five-ton *Thunderbolt* back between two parking garages. He shifted his crosshairs over, framing the *Shen Yi's* broad chest.

The programmed MechWarrior fired first, carving into Evan's left side with the ruby scalpel of its large laser. A score of missiles hammered in behind. Evan shook against his restraints, clamping his teeth together in a grimace of determination.

His crosshairs flashed between red and gold. Partial lock would have to do. Pulling into a full strike, Evan gambled on the computer's biased programming. His Gauss rifle missed, screaming its payload past the *Shen Yi's* shoulder and over a low-rise mall. Evan's missiles fared much better. Smoke trails corkscrewed in at the *Shen Yi*, blasting craters across its armored chest. Then his trio of medium-class lasers sliced across the 'Mech's shoulders, one of them splashing over the forward shield.

"Cadet Kurst, southeast quadrant," he said, raising his voice so that the volume-activated microphone opened up a channel. "One *Wasp* disabled. I have a *Shen Yi* with supporting forces on top of my position, lowering real estate values. Request assistance."

Sergeant Cox would ding him later for the black humor, making light of the tragedy. Evan felt just as insulted that the simulation glorified The Republic position when there was plenty of blame to go around.

"Copy cadet." Cox's voice was gravelly and gruff. "We have forward deployments of Fulcrum hovertanks relative two-four-five, and Elemental battle armor at one-six-eight."

Evan's head's-up display painted new icons in friendly blue. Each graphic had a small identification tag to help distinguish it at a glance. Evan could fall back northeast to the armored vehicles—better firepower but a lot more damage to the city—or northwest to rendezvous with the armored infantry—good holding power, and a real threat to an enemy MechWarrior unless he wanted to risk Elementals cutting through his cockpit's access hatch and bodily removing him, in pieces if necessary. Neither gave him a fair chance at winning the scenario because the Confederation forces would call up support as well.

One or the other. Sergeant Cox would not give Evan command of both.

But Evan might force the issue, if he timed it right.

He throttled into a faster, backward walk, drawing the *Shen Yi* after him, down the narrow street. The armored forces took their own path down a parallel avenue, trying to flank him. Flip a coin. "Elemental company, close on my position," he ordered, taking charge of the armored infantry. "Engage and delay enemy forces."

At the next intersection, Evan throttled back, sidestepped out of the *Shen Yi's* line of fire and hunkered his *Thunderbolt* down, facing into the next intersection over where the Schmitt would appear any second. It did, bringing up the rear as the Demon medium tanks ran an advance path.

"*Hùn dàn,*" Evan swore, wrenching his stick over to drop crosshairs on the lead Demon.

Bright gold rewarded his quick reflexes, and he pulled into his primary trigger to punch a Gauss slug straight through armor, cockpit and the simulated Confederation crew. The tank rolled onto its left side, slamming into the parking garage. The second Demon stuttered ruby bolts from its bed-mounted laser, splashing more of Evan's armor into a molten mist.

Ignoring the second vehicle and hot-cycling his weapons, Evan pulled his targeting reticle back in time to cover the advancing Schmitt. Eighty tons, heavily armored and armed, the "mugger"'assault tank was perfect for controlling city streets. Evan hit it with a full spread of weapons, his Gauss slug slamming the tank's turret, missiles shattering armor across the front and right side.

And then it was as if the Schmitt simply picked up Evan's *Thunderbolt* and threw it bodily to the ground. Both Mydron rotary autocannon roared into the night, bright fire tracers tracking in at the *Thunderbolt's* waist. Hundreds of tiny hammers, each one a fifty millimeter slug tipped with depleted uranium for 'Mech-stopping power, beat against him in a thunderstorm of sharp, metallic pounding. Four lasers poured out scarlet fire, slagging more armor composite, and missiles followed after to punch the *Thunderbolt* deep in the gut and in the side of its head.

The head-ringing detonations were bursts of noise through his comm system, meant to disorient, not injure. The simulator bucked and shook, worrying Evan like a rag doll caught in the jaws of a pit bull. He ducked forward, fighting against the rough treatment. His ears filled with the whine of stressed metal as his gyros strained to work with him, but it was too much, too fast. One foot flailing for purchase, Evan stumbled backward.

Gravity did the rest.

"Down," Evan croaked after the simulator quit bouncing him against the simulated street. "Kurst is down." His wireframe schematic showed heavy armor loss across his entire lower torso and damage to the gyroscopic stabilizers. He also counted three warning lights—two for ruptured heatsinks, and another for a ruined jump jet.

Evan worked his controls, half rising, half stumbling into a side street, taking out the overhead traffic signals with a swinging arm. He regained his bearings quickly.

"Backing away north, nor-east." Away from his infantry reinforcements. "Elemental company, move zero-nine-zero for new rendezvous point." The move would tie them together only a half kilometer shy of the staging Fulcrum heavy hovertanks. Evan couldn't call on them for additional support, but he trusted the computer's AI to make some decisions on its own.

Which it did in the next few seconds as the *Shen Yi* put its weight to use, driving through a nearby apartment building rather than take the longer way around. Joined by a squad of Hauberk infantry and more fearsome Fa Shih, the Battle-Mech led the drive forward. The Schmitt and remaining Demon stuck to the street, chasing around the corner the same way Evan had come.

Evan reacted without thought, recognizing the danger in an instant. Close quarters with the *Shen Yi* and the Schmitt, pressed up against a row of high-rise apartments, it was a no-win situation. He stomped down on his steering pedals, lighting off his remaining jump jets and leaping into the air, right out of the *Shen Yi's* line of fire.

Too late for the apartments, though. The programmed Capellan reached out with lasers and missiles again, gouging deep into the building. Evan twisted the *Thunderbolt* about in midair, feathered his jets early and soft-landed it atop the high-rise.

Like an archer looking down from a parapet, he had a commanding view and clear firing lanes. He put a Gauss slug into the *Shen Yi's* shoulder and peppered its head and chest with missiles, staggering the mighty machine. Then, before anyone could track him, he stepped backward off the building. Firing three short bursts from his jets, Evan landed in a ready crouch on the next street over.

"On the run," Evan said for the sergeant's benefit, delaying and distracting as he tried to put his plan into effect.

Throttling into a forward run, Evan pounded down one street, over again, and then raced forward as he brought his *Thunderbolt* in among the armored infantry. They moved as one unit then, the Elementals scurrying around him like soldier ants. Turning back to the west, they paraded into a large intersection, gaining it just as the *Shen Yi* came up another block west with the Demon and Hauberk, and the slower Schmitt one long block south protected by Fa Shih.

And only two blocks short of the militia Fulcrums.

"Come on, come on," he muttered to the computer, levering up light gauss to engage the closer *Shen Yi*.

His gauss missed again, careening off the angular shoulder armor and leaving behind nothing worse than a bright crease in the dark-painted metal. Missiles rained down on the Confederation machine, blinding it in a wreath of fire and thick, gray smoke. Taking their cue from his targeting, the Elemental infantry leapt forward, swarming toward the sixty-five-ton scrapper, letting loose with backpack missiles and the short-range stabbing lasers that replaced their left hands.

And on his HUD Evan saw the Fulcrum hovertanks finally begin to move forward, coming down the street behind him as the limited AI put them on self-preservation, proactive assaults. By his HUD markings, they engaged the *Shen Yi*.

"Yes!"

With his infantry and the Fulcrum hovertanks tying up one force, Evan was left to slow down the Schmitt with its Fa Shih entourage. The assault tank had paused, waiting at the far intersection in a yellow island of streetlamp light. It waited for not much more than a second, though, before it began its slow, unimaginative drive forward, weapons ready.

Missiles punched out from the Schmitt's launcher, hammering into Evan's *Thunderbolt*. A pair of warheads found the ruin of his torso cavity, scoring the reactor's shielding and damaging more internal components. Vents dumped more heat into the simulator pod, raising fresh sweat on his legs and arms, stinging at his eyes.

Evan moved down the narrow street, kicking a streetlight post, which sheared off at its base. Missiles . . . gauss . . . missiles again. He watched his ammunition rates fall into critical levels. He needed another few dozen meters, just enough that his jump jets could put him over and behind the assault tank, but the Schmitt wasn't giving it to him.

Missiles and lasers pasted his BattleMech, shredding more armor from the *Thunderbolt's* right leg, side and arm. The tank slowed its advance, and then began to grind backward with the Fa Shih in tow.

Seventeen attempts at this scenario, dozens of spectator monitoring and hundreds—more!—in case study reviews and this was the first case Evan could think of where *any* member of the Confederation assault force retreated!

"No you don't," he whispered, pushing his throttle forward just a touch more. "Come back here and hold your ground." He goosed his throttle again. "You're the assaulting marauders. Assault!"

"Cadet," a new voice bled over his comm network. Not Sergeant Cox. "*Shen Yi* has been taken. Demon neutralized and Hauberk falling back."

No time to worry about what had happened to Sergeant Cox. "On my position," he ordered. "Forward at the Schmitt." He throttled into a full-out run that the assault vehicle could not hope to match. "Six . . . five . . . four. . . ." Suddenly, he was pounding down the street at better than sixty kilometers per hour, kicking aside parked civilian vehicles and charging down on the tank's position.

Right into the spread of mines laid by the Fa Shih.

The first explosion blossomed underfoot at the count of three, shoving him to the left. The *Thunderbolt's* shoulder dug into the side of a building. A second mine detonated directly under the flat of his spade-footed machine, jerking the sim pod in a rough shake. Evan cursed his eagerness, having overlooked one of the basic functions of Fa Shih battle armor: their ability to pay out portable minefields.

Another explosion, and his wireframe darkened about the left foot. He had to get off the ground now, now, *now*!

Cutting in his jump jets, Evan rocketed up in his *Thunderbolt*, gliding forward on streams of fiery plasma. Up two stories . . . three. He leaned forward to get every last meter, trying to get behind the Schmitt where he'd drill into its back with one of his remaining Gauss loads.

He wasn't going to make it.

The minefield had goaded Evan into his jump too early. The smarter move would have been to break off the attack and regroup with his support team. BattleMechs were fearsome machines, but a supported 'Mech using combined-arms tactics was twice as deadly. Evan knew that. But never before had the simulated Confederation forces used it to their advantage quite so well. Overwhelming firepower and ruthless tactics. That was their game, as programmed by Republic trainers.

An assault vehicle did not retreat, and hold back its most damaging weapons until an overeager Republic warrior jumped into its trap.

Showing an almost casual confidence, the Schmitt powered forward again, tracking Evan with its rotary autocannon. Fire licked out several meters past the end of each barrel as it spat out long, lethal streams of metal. Catching him in the air, the slugs gouged new craters in his right arm, shoulder and down into the already mangled armor that protected his gyro and fusion engine. The pod hitched . . . stuttered . . . listed heavily to one side as Evan fought to control his jump, bring his arm around for one last gauss shot, and crouch into a semicontrolled landing.

Far too much. Evan lost control of the *Thunderbolt*. Lost his orientation with the ground. He was still fighting vertigo when the autocannon cut apart his fusion reactor's shielding and blew him apart like a New Year's skyrocket.

Every screen went blank.

The cockpit pod quit shaking, settling back to its neutral position as the simulator reset itself.

Only the communications system worked.

"Nice try, Cadet." Cox again, but his gravelly voice wasn't as commanding as before. It had a tinny ring to it. Like . . . battlefield comms. "It might have worked, against programs."

Cox had jumped into another simulator pod, and taken control of the Schmitt.

"So the enemy forces are only bloodthirsty Capellans when it suits you?" Evan asked, losing guard of his tongue for a few irretrievable seconds. Damn—

The sergeant let him stew with his slip for a moment. When he came back, though, it was with just as much good-natured mocking as before. "You want to give The Republic some spine in this scenario, then I'm going to give the Confederation a brain. Now get showered, Cadet, cool off and report to briefing. The class can learn things from your example."

"Yes, sir." Evan couldn't pump much false sincerity into his voice.

No doubt the class would be shown once again how the Confederation had been a monster. A dark, Capellan monster, to be fought and eventually defeated. Except that Evan knew monsters only existed to those with cause to fear. For all its accomplishments and white-knight posturing, here The Republic feared the truth. That Liao was Capellan, too. And it would be free.

12

On Deadly Terms

*Republic forces lost ground on Gan Singh when lo-
gistical support collapsed. Prefect Tao cited Bannson
Universal for defaulting on several military contracts.
CEO Jacob Bannson had this to say: "Lord Governor Hidic directed us to support humanitarian efforts on Palos, bringing relief to those fleeing the
occupation. If the Lord Governor and Prefect do not
coordinate their efforts, how is that the fault of Bannson Universal?"*

—Cassandra Clarke, Reporting from
St. Andre, 15 June 3134

Morgestern
Mǎ-tou-xī District, Palos
Prefecture V, Republic of the Sphere
18 June 3134

The Lazarus Lounge, located at the far end of Morgestern's
Interplanetary Spaceport E Concourse, was dimly lit and had
an outdated sound system that played only maudlin techno-
jazz that was fresh before 3100. There was very little glass to
look outside on the more successful travelers and tourists. Pa-
trons of the Lazarus flew coach or the modern equivalent of
steerage.

And, surprisingly, there were no clocks.

Jacob Bannson noted this right away. Not because it was
out of place for a bar—and the Lazarus was a bar, not a real

lounge—but because it wasn't. He'd expected such an intrusion. There were flights incoming and outgoing, people to be met and baggage to claim. Even the people who would be drawn to an establishment like the Lazarus still had to keep an eye on time. It fascinated him, as a curiosity.

Bannson liked a good bar. He liked a bad bar, so long as his money bought him safety. Not that he was a big drinker, he wasn't, but there was something to be said for the feel of such a place. The ambiance. Dark, close and timeless. That was why you never saw clocks in a real bar. No timepieces, no windows to the outside world. When you walked in nothing else existed, and there you stayed (for several drinks, the management hoped) until you finally decided it was time to rejoin the real world. If you ever did. This was the kind of place envisioned by people who talked of clandestine meetings and shady, backroom deals. Smoke drifting up at the ceiling, pushed around by a slow-turning ceiling fan, and the scent of beer and stale popcorn.

And it was costing Bannson Universal five hundred an hour to keep it closed for the day. Paid in ComStar bills. Republic stones, for obvious reasons, had recently gone out of favor on Palos.

Bannson and Di Jones threaded between empty tables and chairs still half scattered into the narrow aisles. His guests already waited, which was how he wanted it. Ten hundred hours meant ten o'clock in the morning *precisely* to a military man. Bannson expected it to be clear from the start that he was not a soldier to be intimidated by rank. He was more than that, and *Sang-shao* Carson Rieves would be wise to know it.

"Interesting place for our meeting," Rieves said.

He was a thick-necked, pug of a man, hands clasped behind his back and always rising up on the balls of his feet. Tense. Commander of the Confederation's Dynasty Guard and ranking officer in the Gan Singh theater of operations, he had direct control over his own regiment and the Third Confederation Reserve Cavalry. He was also "first among equals" with the *sang-shao* of the Second McCarron's Armored Cavalry— a Capellan way of being in charge without really taking charge.

Meaning they weren't required to do exactly as he commanded, but it really was a good idea to do so.

Sang-shao Rieves eschewed his uniform today, dressing in a rumpled business suit that looked less out of place in the Lazarus than Bannson's expensively cut clothes. Glancing at the bodyguard Bannson had deigned to bring along, "The Maskirovka did not appreciate being left out of this."

"You have your demands, I have mine."

Rieves had ordered this meeting under a very thin veneer of politeness, pulling Bannson from St. Andre for a face-to-face. The CEO could have hosted the officer in the lavish comfort of his private DropShip or emptied one of a dozen executive offices at the DropPort for less than the final price of the Lazarus. But he didn't want the Capellan soldier putting on airs surrounded by luxuries bought with Bannson's money. The Lazarus cost him more, but paid less in deference.

"The Confederation has demands," Rieves corrected him. "So far we are advancing along our timetable as planned, but that could change quickly should the local leadership discover new allies."

Jones laughed. Her red hair glowed softly in the bar's muted light. She held up four slender fingers, one at a time, each tipped with black polish. "Wei, Palos, Shipka, Foot Fall," she ticked off the names. "Four worlds taken in as many weeks. What're you complaining about? That has to be some kind of CapCon record."

"And Gan Singh," Rieves said, his pride in the Confederation attempting to trump Jones's snide comment. "It will be ours by tomorrow's end."

"Really?" She smiled, showing white, white teeth. "What about the Sixth Hastati Sentinels?"

Bannson cut between the two, separating them as he moved to a nearby bar stool. He silenced the woman with a commanding glance. *That* information had been worth something, and she had given it away for free, just to score points.

Well, it had worked. "The Sixth Hastati?" Rieves glowered. "We were told that New Canton would not involve itself in the affairs of Prefecture V."

"Because of some border raids being pushed on Elnath and Ohrensen?" Bannson asked. "I've heard that the Oriente Protectorate is pressuring Prefecture VI." Oriente was one of the stronger duchies left over from the fall of House Marik. "You may inform your superiors that I will have intermediaries open talks with business leaders on New Canton. Perhaps the Sixth will be recalled."

Perhaps not, he didn't add.

"If the Sixth Hastati are under the localized command of Prefect Shun Tao, that gives him breathing room on New Aragon. Can he push out at Menkar or Wei?"

A bowl of pretzels sat on the bar near his right elbow. Bannson helped himself to a few of the salty twists, considered how much to commit to this Capellan officer.

Menkar, he knew, was the key to the Confederation's push along the spinward border of Prefecture V, the so-called "Algot theater," under the joint command of Warrior Houses Dai Da Chi and Hiritsu. It was the focal point of several trade routes, and had good on-planet industry that could be pressed into service to feed the Confederation juggernaut with consumables and basic equipment. Five hundred million C-Bills's worth of expendable annual GNP, two hundred seventy-five of that currently under the control of Bannson Universal subsidiaries. Menkar was also one step off from Algot, which would be important for its working HPG.

Wei was a different case. Solidly behind the Confederation's return, the planet had become the logistics center for the antispinward front, moving supplies and troops into the fighting on Gan Singh and Shensi. Two of Bannson's Jump-Ships had been "commandeered" by Capellan forces—creating deniability—to bring that logistics network up to five transport vessels. Call it an average of two-point-three DropShips per day passing through Wei's system. That was approximately thirty thousand tons of cargo capacity. Each day. Bannson's profits on that arrangement amounted to more than five million Ls—Liao dollars converted into neutral ComStar currency at point-six per, for a yield of three million—so far.

Jacob Bannson had a head for figures. And for knowing when his interests lay in common straits with another.

"I can't tell what Prefect Tao will do," he said. Though not for lack of money being paid out on New Aragon. "He *could* move against Menkar, but he has limited transportation to ferry troops around right now, thanks to a labor strike by some peace-loving employees of one of my shipping companies. I can keep that tied up for another week."

"Two would be more useful," Rieves said, trying to dictate terms.

Which was why Bannson had forbidden Maskirovka agents

from being present. They might have been entrusted with enough authority to put real pressure on the CEO.

"One. At best. In the meantime, I will continue to make inroads into Prefecture VI, but the antitrust restrictions slapped on me by the Senate will make it difficult."

"One," Rieves said, testing the word. "One, one." Eyes half lidded, he looked inward to how that played with his own timetable. "That is not easy, but possible. *If* you can deliver us to Liao by the twentieth of next month, and guarantee a stealthy insertion."

Liao. Bannson had long since guessed that Daoshen would push for the seat of Prefecture V. Now, through Rieves, the Chancellor looked for a guarantee. He exchanged a knowing glance with Jones. This was what you paid insurance for.

"It may be possible," he said, feigning some hesitation. "I have assets in place on Liao that should help mask your arrival. Yes." He paused for effect. "He should do nicely."

"He? One man?" *Sang-shao* Rieves did not look impressed, or particularly confident. "Unless you own the Planetary Legate, what can you expect one man to do?"

Bannson shrugged. "Ask your Chancellor. The Betrayer of Liao was only one man, after all."

"And you have such a man in place?" Rieves sounded dubious, but looked hopeful.

Bannson smiled, took another pretzel and then brushed his hands clean as he left the bar stool. "Such a man?" he asked. "Yes. Something like that."

13

A Blow Struck For Freedom

The city of Opskillion is still burning. Although Lord Governor Hidic's public address puts the blame squarely on elements of the Second McCarron's, independent sources verify that a contingent of militia infantry started the blaze by firing on their own supply trucks rather than let them be taken by "the enemy."

—The Nánlù Daily Apple, 21 June 3134

Yiling (Chang-an)
Qinghai Province, Liao
Prefecture V, Republic of the Sphere
21 June 3134

Blood oozed from a gash over the student's left eye, smearing down the side of his face as he tried to staunch the flow. Ritter Michaelson handed him a patch of gauze, liberated from the ambulances that came and went from the Conservatory grounds, and showed him where to apply pressure. He glanced around. Still, fifteen . . . twenty bodies stretched out on the Conservatory's wet grass, attended by very few volunteers who were lucky to keep the two sides from each other's throats.

And hundreds more thronged around the Guardian, waiting their turn to join them.

"We deserve representation. We demand recognition." The amplified voice belted out in strident tones over the cheers and heckling. Though distorted slightly by the portable PA system, this Hahn Soom Gui had a timbre in his voice that caught your attention, held it. He paced the edge of the *Men Shen's* pedestal, using it as his impromptu stage. "We will not sit back and allow ourselves to be ignored. Capellan unity is not treason. Capellan unity *is Liao*." A long roar of approval drowned out all but the closest calls of derision.

"Damn right!" a nearby student shouted, rising up on his elbow. He was tall but not very muscular, and had blood-soaked gauze shoved up into his nostrils. "Free Liao!" he shouted.

"*Tā mā dè*!" the student with the gash over his eye shouted back, suggesting violent relations between the other cadet and his mother. "Bloody Crapellan!"

The young man with the broken nose lunged forward, and another student lying nearby tried feebly to rise as well. The anti-Capellan supporter also surged to his feet. Michaelson got tangled in their way, trying to keep them from new blows. A fist glanced off his ear which burned with pain.

Michaelson shoved the taller youth back, and when he came at the veteran again grabbed his broken nose in between two thick fingers and *squeezed*. The student sagged to his knees. As the smaller man tried to slip around Michaelson, the ex-Paladin brought him down as well with a firm kick to the side of one knee. Not enough to injure, just incapacitate.

"Get up again, I'll break it," he promised.

The furious cadet rubbed at his leg, but stayed on the ground. Michaelson backed the other student up by keeping his nose in a good grip and leading him back to the matted muddied grass where he'd been laid out before. "And you, this is your own little piece of Liao today. Plant yourself on it."

He let the youth go, stepped back and wiped the blood off on his trousers. A female student—Jenna, she'd said her name was—moved up to help him keep the two apart. She offered him a weak smile.

"*Xiè-xie*," she thanked him. Her breath misted in the cool air.

He nodded. "*Bú kè-qi*." Though he had forbidden himself the language more than two decades before, the *hàn-yǔ* courtesy rolled easily off his tongue. Maybe it was how darkly familiar this felt to his own academy years.

He had wanted to judge for himself how serious the current threat was, with the local government cracking down on anything that smacked of resistance. Well, he had seen battlefields with less fury than what greeted him now. Despite the ugly shift in weather, hundreds—maybe a thousand students and local civilians—crowded around the old *Men Shen* Battle-Mech to stage a "duly-registered protest." A few hundred vehement Republicans had shown up to disrupt things, and it hadn't helped that the local administration chose today to replace the stone arch that framed the Conservatory's main entrance. Ruined by *Ijori Dè Guāng* vandals a month before, two ConstructionMechs and a team of civilians worked to erect the new gate. What had once been the Liao Conservatory of Military Arts, later just the Liao Conservatory, was now cast as The Republic Conservatory.

Most students were not taking well to that newest change.

And not just students, either, he discovered. He knew a professional soldier when he saw one, and a few among the pro-Republic cadre were obviously military men in civilian clothes. Same with the pro-Capellans, though they had the greater numbers of a real mob on their side. Both sides thrust placards skyward, and on more than one occasion wielded them as clubs. Now law enforcement—the local *jǐng-chá* as well as some MPs—milled about on the edge of the large crowd to see what became of the rally.

Not nearly enough, though.

"Madness," he whispered to himself as campus security once again shoved their way through the crowd with orders to disperse. Into its fourth hour, the crowd swelling on both sides every minute, the rally was not going to be diffused easily. Michaelson watched as Hahn Soom Gui gave up the microphone to another demonstrator.

"The Republic blames us for their problems here," the new youth shouted. A squeal of feedback growled out through the amplifier. He was not nearly as polished, but made up for it in enthusiasm. "Maybe they're right. Maybe we *should* start working with the Confederation. Maybe they will actually *listen* to us."

He was pulled down off the Guardian's pedestal by a pair of baton-wielding security guards. Another student leapt up in his place. "*Yóng yuǎn—*"

"*Liào Sūn Zǐ*," the crowd shouted back.

"*Yóng yuǎn—*"

"*Liào Sūn Zǐ!*"

He was also pulled down and escorted away. Two other security guards grabbed a student who tried to intervene, and that left no one to interfere as Hahn Soom Gui once again took center stage and thrust both hands skyward in symbolic defiance. Michaelson nodded reluctantly as the crowd responded. They loved Hahn, they responded to him, but more than that they had seized on something deep within, and it came out in every cheer. Apparently, Sun-tzu *would* become something of an immortal.

The Republic, the way it was handling things, kept him alive.

Mai Wa had thought himself above reaction to pro-Capellan rhetoric. Six months as a guest of the Maskirovka put such empty words in perspective. Deeds. Action. Those were what were called for now. The kind of leadership as embodied by Evan Kurst, his old disciple.

But this Hahn Soom Gui, he had a gift. Mai found himself being pulled along in the furor of the moment. Evan glanced his way, once, and frowned, clearly not liking that Mai was here, involved with his friends. Well, Hahn had contacted Mai Wa, not the other way around. And anything that drew Evan back into Mai's circle of influence the elder man would use.

"We did not invite the Confederation back to Liao," Hahn said now, having once again taken the microphone. Campus security had confiscated one amplifier and a bullhorn already, but always the students seemed ready with another means of keeping the rally going. "We did not create the *Ijori Dè Guāng*." Another glance passed between Mai and Evan. "The Republic did this. They did this by ignoring for too long our simple cries for justice and equality. To help guide our own destiny. Lao-tse says that it is when rulers take action to serve their own interests, then—*then*—their people become rebellious. We are not rebellious. But we are determined!"

"*Yóng yuǎn, Liào Sūn Zi!*" The crowd no longer needed prompting to chant their refrain. They celebrated Hahn, who basked in their admiration and paraded around the feet of the giant, immobile *Men Shen*. He gestured to Mai Uhn Wa, lowering a hand to help the elder man up onto the pedestal, giving over the microphone.

"I am a traitor," he said simply. "I serve the Capellan people."

The self-damnation rose smoothly to his lips, practiced for so long under Maskirovka direction. A simple thing, to substitute *Capellan* for *Confederation*, and suddenly the crowd thought that he proclaimed his devotion to *them*, and so The Republic named him traitor.

They cheered and roiled, like a pot left too long to simmer.

"I have worked most of my life to bring the true citizens of Liao a voice. I have been a warrior in your name, in your cause. I would give my all if you could celebrate your heritage without worrying, wondering, if someone has taken notice and marked your name in their book. I would shine a light over Liao so bright that only *true* citizens would dare face it. The Light of Liao!"

"*Liào Dè Guāng, Liào Dè Guāng*," a portion of the crowd chanted, making the connection he'd wanted them to between the *Ijori Dè Guāng* and any chance for a free Liao.

"I was not here for the Night of Screams," he said, striking to the core of the crowd's emotions. Pro-Republicans stirred at the edge of the crowd again, flinging insults and a few hoarded rocks. Fists argued back. "I felt that loss deeply, I promise you. I was not here when Confederation forces landed, hoping to return some stability to your lives. It was not for me to be among you, as much as I wished, when you cried out for relief in the years of hard, brutal fighting which followed.

"I was not here," he said with patient regret, the amplifier conveying some of his shame, even through the distorted volume, "when Sun-Tzu Liao came home to you."

Even as he disavowed all participation in those dark events, he celebrated them.

"The Chancellor heard your cries, your pain, and he came here to end your suffering. And here he ascended." At the forward edge of the crowd, Evan started and glanced up at his old mentor. Something there. . . .

"It is not for me to say what happened that day. You are more likely to know." Evan pulled his mask back into place. Mai shook his head, and continued. "But I saw the results. I heard the people rise up on Liao and say, 'This is enough!' I watched as Confederation forces rallied to the memory of their great leader, struck down on a mission of peace, and forced on The Republic military another uneasy truce. And then I despaired. For once again you were robbed of your voice, disenfranchised and disregarded. And so we have been for another twenty years."

Now Hahn glanced around uneasily, Mai saw. Perhaps his empathy with the crowd noted its ugly shift. Mai had taken their energy, their fervor, and mated it with feelings of futility and their anger of abandonment. It wasn't so hard a step, really. And while they might not be ready for it, not in truth, Mai had to take a harder stance. The *Ijori Dè Guāng* had to witness him at the forefront of a new resurgence in Capellan pride, or they would forever dismiss him as the man who ran out on them.

He had to make them all see.

"Twenty years," he repeated. "What has it brought you that didn't first require drastic action and the threat of continued disobedience? Nothing." Thunder rolled overhead, threatening another shower. Mai waited for it to pass. "Even your hard-won right to resume courses in history and heritage, and to peacefully assemble as you have done today, those are rights freely handed out on other worlds, on safe worlds, on *non-Capellan* worlds."

Anger and dark bitterness boiled up into the crowd's voice as it shouted back its agreement and frustration. He had them, all right. Evan's friend had turned them over to him in a nicely wrapped package. There was more pushing and shoving, fists and kicks.

And there, coming back for another batch of the rally leaders, was the local Conservatory security force. This time, though, they had uniformed members of the local police with them. The *jǐng-chá*. Was it the crowd's growing surliness or his own presence that had warranted more force? And how could Mai Wa use that?

"*Securitat!*" someone called out a warning, voice heavy with a Slavic accent. Whit Greggor.

"Yes. Security is here. As determined as the Maskirovka to enforce their own idea of free speech." Mai cautiously tread a thin line now, invoking the name of the Confederation's feared secret police agency. Did people see that they had given up one type of oppression for another? At least the Confederation was not hypocritical about it.

A few in the crowd picked up on the idea, or something close to it. Or maybe they were just charged up enough to vent their anger at the nearest authority. Punches and kicks were thrown again, and the police used their clubs. Some uniformed infantrymen backed up the small cadre of security personnel, helping them force their way forward toward the impromptu stage in the shadow of the impotent *Men Shen.*

"That's right," Mai encouraged. "The military does not serve in spite of the people, but in support of them. Citizens . . . residents . . . they are supposed to represent the best interests of all. How many of you feel your right to free speech, to your culture and its millennia-old heritage, threatened right now? Do you welcome the appearance of soldiers, of stormtroopers? Is this the military you yourselves have worked so hard to become a part of?"

They had almost reached the pedestal. "Will it be another twenty years before I am allowed to speak to you again?"

It might. Or longer, depending on the exact laws the local authorities tried to charge him under.

Mai Wa knew a moment's hesitation as a burly sergeant grabbed the microphone cord and ripped the device from him. Hands fastened onto his legs, pulling him off the stage, down into the grasp of the authorities. Now Evan! Release your dogs now! He saw his onetime apprentice standing off to one side with the large boy named Parks, holding back Hahn who no doubt had planned to end today's rally also being led away. Where was Greggor? Where were Evan's people?

Kept out of harm's way, Mai realized. Not risked in such an open environment as this, the better to keep the cover from under which they operated. Evan had made certain to protect his organization at the risk to his old mentor. Damn him.

He had learned too well.

But then, Mai had other tools in his hands now, didn't he? He leaned his head back. "*Yóng yuăn—*"

"*Liào Sūn Zǐ*!" The crowd roared and jostled forward, shouting the name of the old Capellan Chancellor.

Mai prompted them again and again, struggling in the grip of soldiers who tried to muzzle him with their large, strong hands. They hauled him up off the ground, carrying him overhead where hundreds could see him carry on his struggle. One foot broke free and kicked a policeman in the head. A baton smashed back in response, striking him in the hip, in the arm.

A rib broke as a second baton joined the first, snapping with exquisite pain, stabbing him with every breath.

Then a solid tap struck him just over his right ear, and there wasn't much struggle left in him after that. He sagged limply in the grips of the infantrymen, the fight gone out of him . . . and placed instead into the hearts and minds of the mob.

With a wounded roar the crowd of students and civilians, soldiers and cadets, surged forward to reach the small knot of security personnel trapped in the *Men Shen's* shadow. The world swung dizzily around Mai Wa, but he knew, he knew.

Jeeps blared horns and gunned their engines as they moved from nearby streets onto the grounds themselves, coming to the aid of the besieged group. Warning shots were fired, barking into the air and adding to the chaos. More fighting broke out as the mob turned their anger on their nearest pro-Republic brother. Mai knew he was in the hands of professionals, that they would somehow get him clear of the sudden riot and that he would answer for his actions very soon, but even in his half-stunned state he felt the rise of true anti-Republic sentiment, and found hope in the madness.

The true liberation of Liao had struck its first blow.

14

Loyal Son

Prefect Tao's office confirms that elements of at least five Confederation commands are operating inside of Prefecture V, divided into two theaters. Warrior Houses and the Reserve Cavalry are driving through Menkar and Algot, while closer to home are McCarron's Armored Cavalry and the Capellan Hussars. Elements of the Citizen's Honored have moved to garrison the conquered worlds of Wei, Shipka, Palos, Foot Fall, and Foochow.
— Liao's NXLK Station 32, 21 June 3134

Yiling (Chang-an)
Qinghai Province, Liao
21 June 3134

Evan Kurst dodged away from the budding riot, sidestepping a placard swung in his direction by a Republic supporter. Evan grabbed the end of the placard and pulled the other cadet in toward him. A side-hand chop to the neck stunned his opponent. Then he grabbed both shoulders and used his full weight to throw the other man over his hip, laying the Republican straight into the side of the Guardian's pedestal. He'd wake up with one hell of a headache, but it put him out of Evan's way and out of danger from the fury of the mob.

Large groups began to break away from the riot now, looking for opportunity or mischief. Some headed toward the Conservatory entrance and the YiCha suburbs. Others moved

toward the dorms and lecture halls to spread word of the unrest. Some carried police or military weapons. Hundreds
swarmed across Evan's path as he fought his way after Mai
Wa. Hahn and David were lost in the crowd, and he hadn't
seen Jenna since she'd helped a bleeding cadet over to the
ambulances. Mark Lo disappeared right about the time all
hell broke loose—looking for Jen, probably.

That left Evan alone and trying to decide how best to help
his former mentor.

Part of him smoldered with resentment, that the freedom
fighter had used his friends so blatantly. He considered leaving the man to his captors. That was the selfish side of Evan
Kurst. The practical side spoke louder, and that side worried
about the damage Mai could cause to the *Ijori Dè Guāng* if
forced to talk.

Also, Evan did not like to waste potential resources. Whatever Mai's personal reasons for leaving and now returning to
Liao, he had connections and had proven in the past a reliable
source of information and equipment. The way things were
looking on Liao, they might need both.

"Evan!" A hand clamped down hard on his shoulder, spun
him around. He grabbed the hand, twisted, then caught himself before he broke Mark's wrist.

"Hey, easy. It's me." His friend shook life back into his arm.
"Jen's disappeared. Can you help me find her?"

"We have bigger problems," Evan said, trying to spot an open
path to chase after the knot of security. They had chosen a perfect
route, damn it, right through a large knot of Republic supporters
who gave their all to hold back the mob. "Those militiamen have
radios. We're going to see a lockdown of the campus in twenty
minutes or less. People are going to get hurt really bad." Find Mai
Wa, and stop the riot. His list was short, but daunting.

"And Jen is out there in that mess somewhere," Mark
shouted.

"Jenna can take care of herself."

"Jenna is stealing a jeep," David said, jogging up with a field
radio clamped against his ear.

Mark and Evan stared at him, at each other. "She what?"
they both asked, nearly at the same time.

"She said we need to find a way to get a handle on this fast,
before the local militia commander decides to pull a Kang."
Legate Kang. The man who had helped trigger the student up-

rising of five years before, rolling in with tanks and armored infantry. "She thought we might need some wheels."

"We may be beyond avoiding a Kang," Evan said, "but a well-commanded mob is better than an unruly one." An idea glimmered at the back of his mind. "First, we'll need something to grab their attention." He looked back the way he'd come, past the frozen profile of the *Men Shen*.

"The Guardian?" David asked. "You want to climb up there and wave your arms or something?"

"Or something," Evan said, turning back the way they'd come and pulling his friends after him. "Come on. We need to beat them to the Grand Arch."

Ritter Michaelson heard shouts of "the training grounds!" and knew that the situation was about to get a whole lot worse. There were two reasons for rioting students to storm the Conservatory's training grounds. Weapons. BattleMechs.

That was where the students had first taken control in 3128. Security was tight there, but all it took was one cadet officer with a few access codes and eventually you'd have everything hot, walking and ready to fire. Cooler heads had to prevail before then, before the students caused permanent damage that could not be forgiven. Or at least pardoned.

Grabbing together a small cadre of students and civilians, ones with enough military bearing to respond crisply to orders, he had veered around the larger mob and formed a buffer between the fury of the riot and the fleeing security detail. The gap had narrowed dangerously over the last fifty paces.

"Let them go," he suggested now, jogging up next to the policeman and two infantrymen carrying the stunned speaker. Two campus police hustled along another man, collared when he took a swing at them. "Pick them up later."

The *jǐng-chá* merely sneered. One military man half shrugged. "A little late for that now, we're thinking." He pushed along for a few more paces. "Besides. We're nearly at the Double-V."

A VV1 Ranger, not an uncommon sight on the Conservatory grounds, had been the second-closest vehicle. Closer had been a standard-issue truck with green "turtleback" shell to protect passengers sitting in the bed. It had waited, invitingly, door open and motor running.

And they had watched as the truck suddenly pulled away,

with a burst of speed that belied its fair size, an impressive powerhouse under the hood.

A fast-thinking Conservatory cadet, no doubt, at the controls.

"You and you." Michaelson tolled off two students who had some brawn to back them. "Double-time for that Ranger back there." He sent them ahead, to make certain the security force would not find themselves stranded. A rifle-toting infantryman peeled out to jog with them. Going for the Ranger meant pushing deeper through knots of rioting students, but most of cadets knew a losing fight when they saw it and veered away from the organized cadre.

One group did not.

"Free Liao!" a large man shouted, brandishing a short length of broken pine board. He dressed civilian and carried himself in a very nonmilitary slouch, but still he led seven others forward in a push to get at the two prisoners. Most of them were good-size, even the one woman among them. And all knew hand-to-hand.

Which only made the fighting that much more desperate.

"Grapple only," he shouted to his small band of followers, hoping to stave off anything worse than a strained shoulder or broken arm. He made the call automatically, leaping into the front and putting himself between the stick-wielding leader and the collared protestor. Wrestling moves ate up time. Grabs and throws did not raise a killing fever as easily as elbows and feet might.

Splintered stakes, however, were a whole different matter. The civilian did not brandish it as a club, but instead thrust the broken end at Michaelson's face. This guy was street savvy and had good weight behind him. Michaelson barely deflected the blow in time, turning a stab at his eyes into three bloody, parallel stripes down the side of his chin.

Reacting on instincts more than thought, Michaelson fell back on Ezekiel Crow's training in close-quarters combat. He wrapped an arm up and over the thug's, trapping it, then applied pressure at the elbow with his other hand. The armlock twisted the man toward the ground, and he dropped the improvised weapon from suddenly numb fingers.

But this guy wasn't without a few tricks of his own. Faking a kick at Michaelson's groin, gaining just a bit of slack, he twisted his arm enough to bend the elbow and thrust his entire weight forward. The head butt was off mark, catching

Michaelson in the side of the mouth and not the nose, but it was enough to knock him back several paces.

The two men circled each other with much greater respect for the other's skill. Other students ran by, at times cutting in between them as the main body of the riot moved dangerously close.

"Greggor, c'mon." Another street-dressed civvie ran up and pulled the larger man away by the arm. He said something else, which might have been a code word between them. It sounded like "cursed." It was enough. The tough dodged back into the crowd and most of his followers with him.

Some of Michaelson's people stretched across muddied ground, but none seemed permanently hurt. The security force gathered at the Ranger and a second truck, piling in, transferring their prisoners into the back of the Double-V. Putting a man in the turret.

"No!" Michaelson sprinted forward. He leapt up onto a sideboard just behind the passenger door as the driver threw the large machine into gear. The Ranger growled forward into a tight, tire-squealing turn. Holding on, dangling out over the blurring avenue, Michaelson reined himself in to the vehicle's side and beat on the ferroglass window.

"Get that man out of the turret," he yelled. "Do not fire on these people."

The military had greater discipline than that. The double-barreled gun swung around to threaten, but never spoke once in what would have been a deadly chatter. Even so, the effect was not lost on some of the more furious cadets who ran to other vehicles, forcing doors and shattering windows in their attempt to commandeer new resources of their own.

But they would be too late, Michaelson knew, hunkering down in the small space behind the cab, leaning his head out and squinting into the breeze as the entrance to the Conservatory grounds approached. The driver was hell bent on making good their escape, and students in between the Ranger and the arched gateway seemed to know this, and dove out of the way. They had nothing to stop them

Except for the ConstructionMech that stepped into the avenue to bar the Ranger's path.

*   *   *

Evan Kurst had recalled the work being done at the university's main gate. The new Great Arch, with its new attribution: The Republic Conservatory. A small work crew had narrowed incoming traffic to one lane while a pair of ConstructionMechs manhandled new stonework into place.

The ConstructionMechs!

He filled in David and Mark on the run across the grounds. They circled behind students and cheering civilians who crowded around the Guardian's base, holding it like some kind of military objective against all comers. That lasted until someone in the crowd spotted the fleeing security detail that carried Mai Wa and another student protestor. As if controlled by a group mind, the main body surged forward.

Evan let them go, hoping that Hahn was still free to act and that his friend could regain some control over the rabble. He had to get to the construction site ahead of any other protestors with a sudden thought for heavy augmentation.

Close enough. A few dozen people pressed in around the construction workers by the time Evan and his friends arrived, but they were more intent on stopping the work than taking a proactive stand. The workers hefted large metal tools or wielded sharp utility blades. The operational IndustrialMech fended for itself, but its driver was reluctant to step forward into the crowd. It managed a kind of guttural roar as the operator gunned his diesel engine loudly, belching thickened plumes of dirty soot into the air.

Evan ran for the second machine parked by the Conservatory's outside wall, grabbed the iron rungs, and swarmed up the side of the yellow-painted monster. A worker saw him and moved his way with a very heavy wrench. David and Mark took him down from behind, one tackling high and the other low.

The cockpit was cramped and smelled of sweat, stone dust and coffee. There was still a steaming cup in the drink holder, which Evan spilled over the floor as he slid into the seat, then slammed and locked the door behind him. No time for the safety harness, he left the buckles digging into the small of his back as he yanked on the control helmet and fired the huge machine to life. The engine coughed and growled, shaking the exoskeleton. He dried his palms against his thighs, then wrapped familiar hands around the well-worn control sticks.

It was similar to piloting a real BattleMech, but rougher.

The neurohelmet wasn't military grade, tuned to a specific brain wave pattern, but it wasn't even remotely calibrated for his use either. The ConstructionMech's arms moved in jerking fits, and his first step nearly toppled the entire machine when he failed to shift enough weight onto his right foot.

"Come on, come on!" He swung one of his vise-clamp arms out for counterbalance, centered his mass, and tried again. Small step. And another.

He was definitely top-heavy, and no wonder. The hulking arms on the ConstructionMech bent upward from the shoulder, then down again in a reverse elbow joint. Not to mention that his cockpit nest was slung low and forward of the machine's torso, riding him only three meters above the ground.

David Parks waved frantically from the street, pointing at the entrance with enthusiastic stabs. No time left, Evan decided. He pushed up the engine's throttle, thankful that the control helmet afforded him some hearing protection as the diesel coughed and roared and belched.

A larger step, leaning into the awkward turn toward the gate. Another. He found that a kind of swaggering walk worked best, as if the 'Mech was slightly bowlegged. Careful of the growing crowd, he paced the lumbering machine forward, into the gated entrance and right into the path of the escaping Ranger, which power braked into a skidding, sideways stop.

And then Evan stumbled backward as the Ranger's machine guns opened up, slamming twenty-millimeter caseless into the ConstructionMech's bulky frame.

"*Zāo gāo!*" Evan yelled, his commandeered machine shaking with palsy. Sparks jumped off the bulky arms as bullets ricocheted, scoring the industrial yellow paint with bright metal scars. Two bullets starred the safety grade ferroglass off to his left, and a third punched through to ping against a metal support to Evan's right.

"*Hùn dàn* cretinous *oubluduk!*" he cursed, mixing *hàn-yǔ*, English and Russian.

Then he pushed forward on the gearing stick, wading into the maelstrom of machine gun fire.

The controls were just awkward enough that Evan had to think about every movement. It wasn't an efficient melding of man and machine, but it was still a 'Mech and the Ranger was really a glorified military truck. He swung one of his arms in front of the yellow, glare-resistant ferroglass as a kind of shield, grateful when a fury of sparks danced around its edges. Working thumbsticks, he opened the claw into a narrow slit. Just enough to see through.

Just in time to see a turtleback jump the curb and fishtail through the muddy turf, then angle back in to sideswipe the ConstructionMech. Evan tensed for the impact, and at the last second kicked his left leg forward to meet the onrushing vehicle. His kick staved in the side of the engine compartment and shattered the left front wheelwell. The truck spun, tilted up and rolled over, smashing up against the Conservatory's inside wall.

The impact also teetered the ConstructionMech sideways, forcing Evan to stutter-step-stumble to the right, opening up a path for the Ranger. The vehicle cornered forward, straightened itself out and made a run for the Chang-an suburbs of Yiling.

Evan thrust out another arm, low, opening his claw as wide as he could. His grab for the Ranger's fender missed, and the front wheel careened off the extended claw. The driver had to brake again rather than risk hitting the overturned truck. Evan reached out again, this time managing to catch hold of a side-mounted running board. He clamped his vise-claw down on the exposed metal, binding himself to the armored vehicle.

A shallow victory. The Ranger might be held fast, but it still had a lethal bite. The turret weapon swung around again, tracking to the left and in Evan's direction.

Sparks jumped off of the turret. Off to Evan's right, a cadet had appropriated an infantryman's rifle. He opened fire, trying to add some meager support for the industrial machine. Behind him came a large crowd of demonstrators-turned-mutineers. Evan wasn't certain he saw it right, but as the turret gun tracked past him toward this new threat, and also into the people behind, he thought he saw a man leap from the opposite side of the Ranger and make a wild dash at the rifleman, arms waving madly.

He didn't make it. New fire licked long fingers of flame out of the turret barrels, and lethal metal stitched small furrows into the ground at the rifleman's feet. The bullets tracked upward, shattering legs into bloody ruin and then pitching the body up and back. A few people farther back dropped as well, catching pass-through fire.

Enough!

Evan extended the legs on his machine, standing it as tall as he could and dragging the Ranger up at an angle. Working the controls, he levered up his bulky right arm, extended it over the back of the Ranger, and then brought it down on the turret, smashing, bending the barrels, crushing armor and caving in the roof as he struck again and again and again.

A muted knocking at Evan's left ear and a gesture of movement caught his attention. He glanced over, then did a double take as his brain registered the threat. The same man who had run from the Ranger had picked up the fallen rifle. He crouched outside of the cockpit, perched awkwardly on the cowling that covered the ConstructionMech's left knee, holding the rifle in a sideways firing position and tapping the barrel against the ferroglass. He dressed civilian, but had hard eyes and burn scars eating up one side of his face. The easy way he handled the assault rifle proclaimed him a veteran.

Before Evan could respond, violently or otherwise, the man simply shook his head and gestured toward the Ranger. He swung down using the nearby rungs for support, landing on the ground and walking out from beneath Evan's cockpit nest with rifle held ready and pointed right into the Ranger's forward window. Over the roar of the competing diesel engines and through their own armored window, Evan doubted the soldiers inside could hear much of what the man was saying, but there was no mistaking his gestures, demanding their surrender.

More people surged forward now, creating a living wall around the besieged Ranger. They had nowhere to go. The Ranger shut down and a door popped open. Raised hands were the first thing to appear as one by one the occupants surrendered.

Then a cheer swept through the assembled people as Mai Uhn Wa appeared, a bit unsteady on his feet, but well enough. He was carried up onto the shoulders of a few larger men, hands all around him grasping, slapping his sides and arms, wanting to touch the man who had sparked the uprising.

Mai Wa was not accepting accolades alone. Students also clambered up the sides of the ConstructionMech, slapping at its metal carapace. They raised fists into the air in celebration. Evan saw Mai Wa reach into the audience, pulling and prodding until Hahn Soom Gui also rode high atop shoulders.

Evan's relief at seeing his friend in one piece was short lived, however, as Hahn leaned in to clasp warm hands with Mai Wa. Shouts of *Liào Sūn Zǐ* and *Liào Dè Guāng* mixed together, loud enough for Evan to hear even over the 'Mech's engine noise. Then Mai began to order the crowd into small, organized groups, which was when Evan realized, regardless of best intentions or who fired first, the end result was all that mattered. The end result was that Hahn, Evan, and some Republic-fanatic infantrymen had put the full fury of the uprising into Mai Wa's hands.

Evan had wanted to instill a measure of control over the riot, and he had helped do so.

And were things now better, or worse?

PART TWO

The Marches of Chaos

15

Council of Fear

In a stunning announcement, the world of Styk de-
clared its independence from The Republic of the
Sphere. Lord Governor Hidic is calling home Sena-
tors Jiu Soon Lah and Tiberius Denton to deal with
this latest crisis, hoping that the return of our senior
diplomats will bolster his position and help bring
Styk back into the fold.
   —Governor Mikhail Cherenko, Genoa, 25 June 3134

Sovetskaya
Lower Nánlù, Liao
26 June 3134

Lord Governor Marion Hidic's refuge near Sovetskaya was opulent, well guarded, and, in Viktor Ruskoff's opinion, a completely inappropriate setting for the high-level meeting.

A roaring fire burned at one end of the study, putting out far too much heat for the medium-size room. Scented logs snapped and popped. A gold, wire-mesh screen saved the thick pile carpet that swept around the hearth like a malachite ocean breaking against redbrick sand. Bookcases framed two sides of the study; history and law on one wall and an impressive set of classics on the other. The Lord Governor had already shown off the prize of his collection, encased under glass and held in a nitrogen atmosphere: a copy of the world charter, granted by the ancient Terran Hegemony and referring to Liao by its original name of Cynthiana.

Interesting, but hardly worth pulling Viktor away from the troubles plaguing modern-day Liao. Not when he had Confederation forces on-planet and a student uprising in control of the Conservatory. His plate was full.

Lord Governor Hidic didn't mind. He paced the room, promising the head of Styk's world governor on a platter. Leon Beresk, his staff section chief, looked as if he'd like to do the Governor's pacing for him, shifting uncomfortably on the overstuffed leather sofa. Even Gerald Tsung looked uneasy. Elbows on his chair's armrests, Tsung repeatedly tapped his fingers together. Only Knight-Errant Eve Kincaid, recently arrived on Liao and the other professional soldier in the room, exhibited some reserve. She asked intelligent questions, and gave succinct, useful answers when she spoke at all.

Ruskoff stood at the window, avoiding the small group. Outside, snowy drifts piled up near braces of tall evergreen. A venerable *Raven* BattleMech strutted by with its birdlike gait. The dropping nose, so much like a bird's beak, contained an impressive sensor package that rivaled anything The Republic produced today. A good, solid *Capellan* design. Leaving out the fact that Hidic had federalized local troops for his own protection, a move that undercut Ruskoff's authority, there was no reason other than power politics that demanded this meeting be held in Nánlù and not in Chang-an. He'd debated saying so, then realized that he'd only be telling one other person in the room something they didn't already know.

Maybe not her either.

"Are you determined not to join us, Viktor?" Hidic had paused for breath, noticed that he did not have the room's full attention. He took a seat next to his aide.

Ruskoff let the heavily brocaded draperies fall back over the window, shutting out Nánlù's winter. Crossing the carpeted floor in half a dozen easy strides, he stood at one end of the small congregation with hands clasped behind his back in a semblance of parade rest. He felt no desire to sit. In fact, he felt a subtle push to remain slightly removed from the council. "At your service, Lord Governor."

Marion Hidic was a square-jawed man of medium height but good build. He wore his conservative suit quite well, with the SuDa University tie tack polished to a golden shine. His family had earned citizenship supporting Devlin Stone's formation of The Republic. He would likely quote The Republic's motto on his deathbed: *Ad Securitas Per Unitas.*

Liberty through unity.

"What I'd like to know," the Lord Governor asked, "is your impression of Legate Heivilin. Is she likely to have gone over with Governor Lusebrink?"

He spoke of Legate Daria Heivilin, Styk's senior military official.

"There is no way to say, sir." He paused, then, "If I were you, I'd hope that Daria was not party to the idea of secession."

"Why is that?" Gerald Tsung asked. Governor Lu Pohl had sent her aide in her stead, a decision which did not sit well with Hidic. But it was a good question regardless. The Lord Governor backed it with a grunt and a nod.

"Because if Daria supported this move, she did so in such a way to organize it bloodlessly and keep a sound command structure within the local military organization. She will be ready to meet any challenge of force." Lady Kincaid nodded her agreement.

"What makes you so certain?" Hidic asked.

"That is what I would do."

Which also did not sit well with the Lord Governor. If Hidic was looking for reassurance, the man had summoned the wrong person to his State-supported retreat.

Leon Beresk sat forward with a creak of leather and old knee joints. His sharp blue eyes promised strength for a man who had only thinning snow on the roof. "Look, Styk will take care of itself. We've sent to Terra for Senator Jiu Soon Lah, haven't we?" He waited for Hidic's nod, which came short and curt. "Then we wait for her to get back. She may be Decentralist Party, but she's still Republic. And she's respected on Styk."

Tsung shrugged. "That's Styk. Governor Lu Pohl will want to know what we will do about Liao."

"That should be our question for her," Beresk said, then took a sip from his sweating water glass before replacing it on the redwood coffee table. *Our* seemed to include only himself and the Lord Governor.

Ruskoff rubbed at his jaw, feeling stubble as his afternoon shadow filled in. Politics, he reminded himself, was the art of asking for one thing in order to get another. "What we could use," he began slowly, "are the Sixth Hastati Sentinels being employed on Gan Singh."

Eve Kincaid looked him over coolly, her winter blue eyes betraying neither insult nor injury. "Are you implying that we cannot handle the local problem ourselves?" she asked, her voice tightly controlled.

Her uniform decorations rated her at twelve years of service with numerous awards for bravery and accomplishment. She had been working with a small cadre of Republic Knights and Prefect Shun Tao on New Aragon, but with McCarron's Armored Cavalry slipping forces onto Liao she was ordered to investigate and assist, bringing with her a mixed company from the veteran Principes Guard.

Ruskoff also suspected that she acted as Prefect Tao's local eyes on Ruskoff. With the current state of chaos gripping Prefecture V, unsure whom your allies might be from one day to the next, Ruskoff couldn't blame the Prefect.

"My assessment is that we should lock down Liao, now, rather than delay and fight any kind of lengthy campaign."

"Lock it down?" Hidic waved off the idea. "We have two isolated incidents and a small enemy force running around on planet. Handle it."

Isolated? "Lord Governor, the incidents are not separate at their root cause. In Shanto, the small garrison post self-destructed over whether or not to take control of the local preparatory school when students acted out in support of the Conservatory uprising. Shots were exchanged. Men were killed. Sir."

Leon Beresk placed a cautionary hand on Hidic's leg, keeping the noble from making any statement that might be used against him later. "The Lord Governor does not impugn the tragic loss of these sons of Liao," he said. "What he meant is . . . there are no organized ties between the two events."

"Are there?" Lady Kincaid asked directly of the Legate.

"Not that we have discovered," Ruskoff admitted. "But we are seeing more cases of insubordination and even outright revolt. With the Second McCarron's running free on Liao, we spend too much time worrying our own ranks to discover whom we can trust. Administration policy to confine pro-Capellan troops to Liao is working against us."

"There is no such policy," Hidic said, managing to sound accused and self-righteous all at once.

"We can argue that there is or there isn't, Lord Governor." Ruskoff walked his career into dangerous ground. "Prefect

Tao will certainly confirm that our official policy is one of enlightened liberalism. That does not explain why some top-drawer grads from the Conservatory, as well as Bulics and Renfield academies, were not accepted to postings in the Triarii and Principes and lesser candidates were."

Lady Kincaid blinked slowly, digesting this idea. "You are worried that any show of less than complete control will encourage further episodes."

"I have eleven men and women, three of them officers, absent without leave. I cannot prove they have gone over to the Second McCarron's, or to the *Ijori Dè Guāng*, but there is that chance."

"Eleven." Leon Beresk shrugged. "Hardly a drop in the bucket."

"Legate Ruskoff," the Knight-Errant spoke up again, "how many soldiers have you lost to underground activity in the past four years. Prior to the invasion?"

"Three."

"That is an increase of nearly four hundred percent."

"You aren't buying into this?" Hidic asked. The Lord Governor went to a side bar to splash a small stream of bourbon over ice. "We're talking eleven people who may simply be scared their first time facing live fire. We don't know."

"No, we don't." Gerald Tsung plucked at the sleeve of his shirt where it peeked out of his suit jacket. "But we've also had two local diems and the city magistrate of Duan question Republic policies in official forums of late. Their stand mirrors the Cult of Liao platform. Not a lot, in and of itself, but ... suggestive."

"Suggestive. A politician's word for needing more polling data." Hidic nearly smiled. "Anna worried about the next elections?"

"Why should she be?" Tsung asked breezily. "She ran on a People's Choice platform. At this rate she'll be looking at a landslide."

The discussion was getting far afield from where Ruskoff intended. He dialed back the rhetoric. "I'm not saying that we're looking at open rebellion in the streets," he said, conceding the point, "but I'd like to show a decisive move. Now."

"Then deal with McCarron's Armored Cavalry," Hidic ordered. "You've let that wound fester too long."

He nodded. "Tell me where they are, and I will destroy

them." He waited. "That is our problem. The Armored Cavalry moves too swiftly, striking only when it suits them. They are quite obviously getting support from the local population as well."

The Lord Governor frowned. "What do you propose?"

Knowing he was about to make a political enemy, Ruskoff said, "First, we retake the Liao Conservatory. The longer we leave students in control, the more we legitimize their position. And I don't want that dagger held at my back if we *do* get a line on the Armored Cavalry."

"You've given them five days," Lady Kincaid noted. "Why haven't you handled this already?"

Tsung cleared his throat. "That was the Governor's call. We have two dead students riddled with machine gun fire, several more wounded . . . a lot of fence-sitters went over to the demonstrators after that. The Conservatory also has popular support from the suburbs of YiCha and Suri. The Governor hopes to avoid further loss of life and try diplomatic means. It worked once before."

"But not permanently," Beresk noted. "Another black mark against Ezekiel Crow. That man must've had the devil's own touch." A look of disgust passed over Lady Kincaid's face at the mention of the Black Paladin. No one liked to think of Paladins and Knights of the Sphere as corruptible.

Ruskoff had an agenda beyond discussing Ezekiel Crow. "We have no time for diplomacy in this case. I respectfully suggest using my Triarii and the Principes Guard to retake the Conservatory. Then we bottle up the Armored Cavalry best we can while waiting for whatever reinforcements the Sixth Hastati can spare."

Hidic tossed down the rest of his drink, and set his glass back to the sideboard with a rattle of ice. "Unacceptable," he finally declared. "First of all, there will be no reinforcements, Viktor. Prefect Tao is stretched thin as it is. Second, *second*—" he held off an interruption with a raised hand "—allowing the Confederation to contest Liao is a show of weakness that undermines the entire Prefecture. You said it yourself; we must be decisive."

"You're telling me what you want, Lord Governor. I'm telling you what we can *accomplish*." Tension tightened Ruskoff's shoulders. "If we cannot call in the Sixth Hastati, why not bring up more of the Principes Guard?"

But Legate Ruskoff was not fully briefed on off-world movements.

"The Principes Guard is on Gan Singh," Eve Kincaid told him now, "replacing the Sixth Hastati, which are being pulled back. Prefecture VI is having more border trouble with the Oriente Protectorate."

This wasn't news to Hidic or Beresk, who glanced nervously at each other. Gerald Tsung collapsed back into his chair, momentarily stunned.

Tsung found his voice before Ruskoff. "What of our arrangement with New Canton?" he asked, his polished voice showing a bit of tarnish for once. The Lord Governor had promised to coordinate with his counterpart in Prefecture VI for their mutual defense.

"Suspended, for the time being."

Ruskoff distanced himself from Tsung, paced a tight box around the room, thinking. With the exception of Lady Kincaid, everyone seemed too wrapped up in their own fears to focus on anything he had to say. "So we can rely on no new resources?" he finally asked.

"Minor," Lady Kincaid answered for the Lord Governor. Or, more likely, for Prefect Tao. "Our hope is to delay the Confederation advance, reorganize our defense, and then break their thrust off at the base."

Extend and amputate. Ruskoff nodded, knowing what the Knight-Errant had just given him. She *was* a second link to Prefect Tao, and they were planning to strike back at Daoshen on his staging worlds inside The Republic or actually over the border into Confederation space. That would likely be determined by the level of reinforcements—any reinforcements—that Shun Tao could draw from other sources.

"In that case," Ruskoff said, "we simply cannot run the Armored Cavalry to ground. Not without calling up militia units, which risks more defections and the real possibility of open mutiny."

Marion Hidic wasn't hearing it. "I don't want excuses, Legate. I want results." He drew a measure of strength from nods by Beresk and Tsung. "You may handle the students politically or you can ignore them, but get that blasted Confederation force off my world."

"At your service," Ruskoff promised, then cut a military turn for the study door. He'd had enough of this room and quite enough of this council. Liao was more Governor Lu Pohl's world, more *his* world, but the Legate knew when to accept a tactical retreat. Viktor Ruskoff was still a soldier. And he had his marching orders.

16

The Bitter Taste of Diplomacy

Mercenary forces in the employ of the Chancellor Daoshen Liao, held in reserve until now, have spearheaded new Confederation drives with assaults on Algot and Tsitsang. With these worlds in contention, the two operating theaters begin to close and Prefect Tao on New Aragon is surrounded on all sides by hostile forces.
—Cassandra Clarke, reporting from New Aragon, 27 June 3134

Yiling (Chang-an)
Qinghai Province, Liao
29 June 3134

A *Rifleman* BattleMech stomped across the street, paused to track the open jeep, and then continued on its way. It passed close to the *Men Shen* Guardian, where evidence of the uprising's beginning was now limited to muddy scars in the grass. Armored vehicles lined the Conservatory's main avenue: one lance of Condor multipurpose vehicles to one side, a mixed unit of Jousts and JES II Strategic Missile Carriers to the other. Armed riflemen and armored infantry wearing Infiltrator and Purifier battlesuits patrolled the walls and grounds.

Sitting in the front passenger seat of the jeep, Evan Kurst nodded his approval of how Colonel Feldspar set the Conservatory's defenses. There weren't many senior instructors the students trusted, but Feldspar had stepped up on the day of the uprising to take control around the training grounds, organize the cadet corps and set an immediate defensive perimeter. Feldspar's efforts, Evan felt certain, were not lost on the two officers sitting behind him.

"An impressive display," Legate Ruskoff said with bland interest. "Since you don't expect an attack while I am in your company, you've shifted . . . what? Half your active forces to the formal grounds?"

Less than that. Only about a third. Under the cover of night, Whit Greggor had brought in all military equipment appropriated by the *Ijori Dè Guāng*.

"Something like that," was all Evan said. He didn't mind the Legate underestimating the students' strength. "We're taking nothing for granted, though."

"In your position, no, you can't."

Evan glanced back, but the Planetary Legate let his comment stand. Ruskoff's gaze roamed, constantly on the move, studying the defensive posture.

"We heard that a Knight made planetfall," Evan said.

"Did you?"

They did. Information leaked out of the regular military faster than ever these days. "We half expected to see her with you." Instead, Ruskoff's aide was a lieutenant not much older than Evan, with a stiff spine and nervous eyes.

"Believe it or not, Cadet, there are other issues confronting Liao at the moment."

Yet Ruskoff was still here. Did that say the Conservatory uprising was more important to the Legate, or less important to the Knight?

It was something for Evan to think on as the jeep turned in between a pair of administration buildings with white stone facades. The avenue split two lanes off into large parking lots, then narrowed into a circular drive around the Conservatory's monument to the Jihad. A *Yu Huang*, created in dark steel and red enamel, stood at one-third scale. A dozen sculpted people crowded the impressive machine, touching it, standing on its feet to raise fists in victory. More figures carried clubs, farm tools or liberated rifles, swarming a fallen machine laid out before the *Yu Huang*. There was no way to tell what that machine once was, as the people of Liao ripped it apart with their bare hands. Only the artist had known.

"Did you know the Conservatory's original monument actually survived the Jihad?" Evan asked.

The lieutenant glanced away. Ruskoff paid Evan the basic courtesy of meeting his gaze.

"It commemorated the retaking of Liao during the Offensive of 3057. A *Ti Ts'ang*, a *Vindicator*, and half a dozen Fa Shih troopers making planetfall, suspended above a cheering throng of people. Each large piece displayed a different emblem of the Capellan Warrior Houses. It was buried in the rubble of the old Conservatory. After being excavated, it was cut apart and scrapped."

Ruskoff held his ground, stone-faced and calm. "Lots of things changed after the Word's defeat," he said simply.

Evan pressed. "Did you know that work to restore the Conservatory was halted for two weeks as alumni staged a sit-in demonstration?"

Was that a flicker of surprise twitching Ruskoff's brow? "No, I didn't."

"It was our first student protest of Liao's occupation. Each member of that demonstration was arrested, and all were cashiered out of service within the next five years."

The Legate adjusted his uniform. "All militaries downsized after the Jihad, Cadet Kurst. Coincidence."

"I don't think you believe that any more than I do."

"Where did you learn this?"

From Mai Wa, and some treasured documents that survived among various underground movements. Evan smiled tightly. "I went to school," he said.

The jeep pulled up in front of a bunker-style building, all gray concrete and narrow windows. The vehicle rocked to a halt as Evan's driver applied the brakes with gusto. Jenna and Hahn stood in front of a small crowd. Hahn wore a heavy sidearm at his hip. Evan also spied Major Ritter Michaelson, who had offered to remain on campus. David Parks led a patrol on the south side of the university grounds, and Mark had refused to take part in this meeting. Mai Wa. . . .

Evan actually wished his mentor luck in what he was about today.

"I have to ask," Ruskoff said as the troop moved indoors, shuffling down a wide, tiled hall. "What is the status of your detainees?"

Ignoring the question, Evan stepped through a door. "In here," he said.

It was a conference room normally reserved for meetings among the university's staff. A citrus-polished table glowed under the room's bright light, crowded by twice the usual number of chairs. An infantry cadet with David Parks's personal endorsement stood near the door with the only rifle, though several students besides Hahn carried pistols.

Evan took a seat at one end of the table. Surprisingly, Legate Ruskoff chose a seat right next to Evan, and the lieutenant stood behind his master. An intimate chat, then. Ruskoff would not start off with ultimatums or threats.

"The students and teachers you have detained?" he asked again, very patiently.

Evan spread his hands, then placed them flat on the table's smooth polished top. "There are none left to worry about."

"You . . . ?" The Legate nearly rose to the bait, but decided that Evan spoke more literally than with malice. "You freed them all?"

"Days ago. The staff who did not wish to stay, the nonmilitary students, pro-Republic cadets. All of them were made free to leave."

The Legate frowned, studying faces around the room. Very few showed anything but hostility. "We've only accounted for sixty percent of the staff and thirty-five percent of the student body."

"Most of them chose not to leave. I guess your screening techniques weren't quite as good as you had hoped." Two very public funerals had also helped sway some hearts and minds.

"All of them are pro-Confederation?" The lieutenant spoke out of turn. "Impossible."

"We are only as pro-Confederation as you wish to make us," Jenna bit back, seated only a few chairs away from Evan. Her surgically altered eyes narrowed into dramatic slits. "That has been the problem all along, treating those of us who respect our heritage as the enemy."

Ritter Michaelson stood against the wall, holding himself slightly apart. He faced directly across at Ruskoff. "Regardless of their politics, a fair percentage of the cadets and students admit there is a Republic bias. They wish to be heard. You know they have a legitimate concern or you wouldn't have agreed to this meeting."

Especially in person. Legate Ruskoff had obviously felt secure enough accepting the students' guarantee of safe conduct.

"And your place in this, *Major* Michaelson?" He peered intently at the other man.

Michaelson broke his gaze away, turning the ruined side of his face toward Ruskoff. "Trying to save lives, Legate Ruskoff. I believe that's still my sworn duty."

"Damn strange way to show it," Ruskoff offered.

"I was there when your man gunned down two students, Legate. Damn strange way to protect the people of Liao."

Hahn Soom Gui had also remained standing. "The sooner you recognize The Republic shares in the blame for this incident, the sooner we can meet on equal ground to diffuse it." He rested one hand on his side arm in a pose for strength. "Until then, we will hold the Conservatory as a refuge for any resident, citizen or soldier who wants to join us for a free Liao."

"What does that mean," Ruskoff asked, "a *free* Liao?"

Hahn rose flawlessly to the occasion. "We want a forum to address our grievances, with assurances from Governor Lu Pohl that we will not be saddled with pro-Republic judges. Anyone who wishes should have a say in the selection of such overseers . . . not just Republic citizens, but *all* residents of Liao. The discrimination may not end, but we'll bring it into the open where it belongs. It is time to acknowledge that Liao is Capellan first, and Republic second."

Worship spread over the faces of many assembled cadets. Ruskoff shook his head, and Evan heard the sound of the man's mind closing. "I cannot approve of those demands," he said flatly.

"You do not have to approve," Michaelson said softly. "Only Governor Lu Pohl does."

"Anna Lu Pohl must answer to Lord Governor Hidic. He is not going to allow terms to be dictated in this manner. What if other worlds took it upon themselves to challenge The Republic's leadership this way. What would we have then?"

"Equality!" Evan said, surprising himself. Cheers and a smattering of applause greeted his outburst.

"There are other ways to accomplish this. Some of you have already earned your citizenship. Others are working in that direction. If you truly support the Governor's example, you should work within the system."

"Where you will continue to stack the deck against us," another cadet said, her voice breaking.

Michaelson stepped forward and placed a comforting hand on her arm. "Legate," he spoke carefully, choosing each word with great care, "I have . . . suffered through a great deal in service to The Republic. I have fought and bled for it, and I've made my share of mistakes. I have also seen for myself the trials Liao has endured over the past twenty-two years. These people are frustrated. They are simply asking for a forum. How can this be a bad thing?"

Ruskoff visibly winced at the mention of mistakes made in service to The Republic. Perhaps the Legate was not so immune to the overbearing weight often brought against Liao. He recovered quickly. "Perhaps if Governor Lu Pohl were to introduce measures during the next world campaign. . . ."

"No!" Evan banged his hand down on the table. Michaelson started to speak, but Evan silenced him with a gesture. The veteran's calm words were not what they needed. "No more promises, no more delays. We're tired of feeling afraid on our world, in our towns and around our campus."

Everyone stared at him. After two years of working in the dark, attention was hard for him to bear. He took a calming breath.

"It is time for The Republic to step back and exercise a measure of the grand tolerance it preaches. Devlin Stone is watching us: that's what the politicians throw in our faces. Do you realize how much that sounds like a threat? Well, Stone is gone. He left. It's The Republic's eye always on us to decide if we'll toe the line. Well, we won't. I won't." More cheers, many with a bright edge that could cut if he was not very, very careful.

"You don't have a choice." Ruskoff appealed to the assembled group. He found only Michaelson. "Major, help them understand. This solves nothing."

"And walking away now?" Evan asked. "That's in our best interest?" He shook his head. "We know that our military careers are over, Legate. We realized that the next day, and we accepted it. You'll never trust us with troops. You'll never give us a voice. And you know what? Most of us have embraced the idea, and so have troops from under your own command, who are on campus to support our position. We also have a fairly large and growing tent city of local civilians presenting themselves for service. Because this is our time. Now."

Evan pulled his appointment of citizenship out of a pocket. "My citizenship, finally offered when The Republic is desperate enough to need me." Evan held it up. Some cadets watched with admiration, some envy and then shock. Jenna stared at Evan with sadness welling in her eyes as he ripped the appointment in half, lengthwise, slowly, so that the sound of tearing paper filled the room for several long and painful heartbeats. "It's too late, Legate. It was too late when I came to this school."

He tore another stripe. "It was too late when I joined the *Ijori Dè Guāng.*"

Another. "It was too late the day I was born."

He laid the scraps of his citizenship onto the table. "Take this back to Lord Governor Hidic, with my compliments."

Ruskoff stood. He nodded to his lieutenant who moved for the door, opened it, and stood aside for the senior officer. The Legate leaned in toward Evan, speaking very calmly. "You are going to force me into doing something that I truly do not want to do, Evan Kurst. You and all of your comrades. This may be the only round of diplomacy you get. Eventually, I will have to come back. And if I have to pull this school apart again, stone by stone, I will. Who wins then, Evan?"

Ruskoff left on that, striding for the door and out into the hall. Michaelson followed, and Hahn. Others filed out after them with a few pausing to place a hand on Evan's shoulder and giving him a reassuring squeeze. They left him there, alone with his thoughts and with their silent approval.

Jenna was last to leave.

"You did not have to do that," she said.

"But I did, Jen Lynn Tang. I did. For me, if for no one else." He stared at the shredded page, where Ruskoff had left it. "Either I believe in what we do here, or. . . ." Or else he accepted that Liao would never be free. "Or, I do not."

She bent down, and kissed him on the brow. His skin burned where her lips brushed him. Then she, too, left.

Evan glanced around the empty room. Some cadets and students would slip away tonight, he knew. More, he hoped, would steel themselves for the trials yet to come. How many would be left, he wondered, to be remembered as heroes or tried as traitors?

Who wins?

"The people," he whispered to the departed Legate. "The people win."

And he truly believed it.

17

Convergence

Heavy fighting continues on Algot and Menkar, on Shensi and Gan Singh. Tsitsang has been abandoned to the Confederation, while Hunan and St. Andre remain heavily garrisoned against attack. And as The Republic Armed Forces rotate through New Aragon, refitted to be thrown back into the fight as soon as possible, one wonders what Prefect Tao hopes to accomplish against such a determined foe.
  —Jacquie Blitzer, battlecorps.org/blitzer/, 27 June 3134

Xiapu
Huáng-yù Province, Liao
30 June 3134

A Triarii company had thrown itself into the path of McCarron's Armored Cavalry. The battlefield was less than three hours old when the Zahn Heavy Transport lumbered over a small rise, the truck rocking wildly back and forth as it powered its way over a rare patch of pristine field. Its massive wheels crushed down the tall grasses and dug twin furrows into the wet soil.

Mai Uhn Wa sat in the front cabin, holding himself back into his seat with arms braced on the forward panel. He stared out through wiper-streaked ferroglass. When the truck braked to a muddy halt he shouldered open the door, leaving the vehicle and its reckless driver behind. Whit Greggor and another resistance fighter clambered out of the

Zahn's back. Even the burly tough looked a bit pale after the ride.

An icy drizzle pattered down, dousing a few stubborn fires, washing the haze and smoke from the air into oily ground cover. Rainbow puddles stood inside of giant footprints and half-track scars. The cordite smell of burnt gunpowder and solid-fuel missile exhaust lingered over everything. Mai Wa heard the distant chop of rotors, scanned the heavens, and counted five VTOLs thundering their way southeast toward the nearby city of Xiapu. Smoke-contaminated rain trickled down his brow, stung his eyes.

Mai grabbed the longer strands of his graying hair back into a loose horsetail, and then tugged a service cap over his head to hold it away from his face. The older man stood in his basic camouflage fatigues, surveying the wreckage laid out over the golden range.

The corpses of two BattleMechs lay facedown on a gentle slope nearly a kilometer distant, one of them obviously a *Firestarter* from the shoulder profile that stuck up above the rise. It explained a large swath of burnt grasses that stretched a black, smoldering hand over several square kilometers to the east. Closer up were the gutted shells of a Scimitar, a MASH vehicle. An overturned Regulator II, which might see combat again, and a Po II, which had thrown a track, but otherwise looked fine. The Po was painted in dark metallic blue, trimmed in green, and proudly bore a dark knight emblem crested with a red plume, the crest of McCarron's Armored Cavalry.

"*Sao-shao* McCarron will be over this way," the noncom *san-ben-bing* said, catching up with Mai Wa and nodding toward the Po.

Mai Wa nodded to Greggor. "Wait for me," he said. Greggor had a loose guard on his tongue, and Mai did not need him making this any harder. He followed after the driver.

A small group of men stood near the tank, walking around the sixty-ton machine and pointing out more damage. The *san-ben-bing* jogged on ahead, approached the smaller man who wore simple tank crew togs of green, padded fatigues with tight cuffs and a high collar, a beige, armored bodyshell vest, and a metal-reinforced forage cap. The serviceman pointed back toward Mai Wa, who walked forward at a more sedate pace.

Rather than wait, Terrence McCarron walked out to meet him with a cautious, appraising glance and a hard-muscled handshake. He wasn't as small as Mai had thought, actually. He'd merely been standing among some very large men who now trailed protectively in his wake. Infantry, only recently stripped out of their battle armor.

"*Nǐ shì* Mai Uhn Wa?" the armor commander asked. "*Néng rèn-shi ni.*"

"*Shí-fēn gǎn-xiè,*" Mai said, surprised, thanking the man for his courtesy. He had expected a more hostile reception. His name was not exactly in clear air. "You were told to expect me?"

"By our Maskirovka liaison, yes." He glanced in the direction of the departed VTOLs. "He is thankfully overseeing our provisioning needs in Xiapu."

Which could be interpreted in more than one way. Mai looked over the on-world senior Confederation officer, heir to the Cavalry after an older brother. Terrence McCarron was in his early thirties, perhaps late twenties. He wore his reddish hair shorn tight and a nonregulation earring in his left ear. A gold hoop. He radiated both youthful arrogance and a veteran's seasoned strength, the perfect commander for an advance force that would be operating without support for some time. The kind of man others followed without question.

Mai nodded at the damaged Po II. "Yours?" he asked.

"Mine. Not the most unique design out of Ceres Metals, but she is a tough old bitch."

"I was made to understand that you had BattleMech forces at your command."

"Nothing more than a lance, and I sent them down to Nánlù where the local factories turn out good armor and not half bad electronics. That's the kind of salvage they can live off. Better than the sleeping orchards and skittish livestock around here." If the Confederation "captain" found it odd to be questioned by an old warrior without unit or rank, he didn't show it.

No local BattleMech support, and a tank commander by choice, McCarron had steel wrapped around that spine. A pity he looked so comfortable in this command. "From what I have read in Chang-an headlines, you are doing more than knocking down naranji trees and frightening horses."

"I should hope so. The local militia, they make it easy. Garrison posts spread too thin. Supply convoys underguarded. MechJocks." He dismissed them with a casual wave. "They always underestimate the value of good armor and solid men."

"And it helps that most locals aren't really interested in reporting your location."

"That it does. There are also the ones who come out after my people in old farm trucks, carrying shotguns." A sharp gust blew rain into his face. He wiped it away with a calloused hand. "Sometimes it seems like we can tell which district we are in by how the people react. Of course, that is why we are here, after all. To disrupt military operations and gather intelligence for the Dynasty Guard."

"Who will arrive when?" Mai asked, perhaps a touch too eagerly.

McCarron seemed an agreeable fellow, but he was not so open as he acted. "When they do," he answered cagily. "I understand they are supposed to deliver to you a good deal of equipment?"

Mai Wa counted under his breath, stilling his anger. "They are. And it would be of service if I could find out when to expect it. We have encountered . . . a situation."

"You have taken control of the Liao Conservatory," Terrence McCarron said, proving that his own intelligence gathering had indeed kept up with current events. "A mistake, to trap yourself where the enemy can find you."

Shrugging a falsified indifference, Mai shook the water from his service cap and then replaced it on his head. He was trying not to think about what was going on at the Conservatory without him. Evan had very clearly not wanted him present for the meeting with Legate Ruskoff, and had put Mai in touch with resistance cells outside of Chang-an as a way to sidetrack him. Except that by doing so, he'd given Mai some bargaining power where it might really matter.

"No plan survives contact with the enemy," he said, and shivered. The rain grew heavier, tapping heavy fingers on the brim of his cap, and the wind was picking up. He felt the cold in his joints. "We improvise, and we adapt. Which is why I have come here." The older man clasped hands behind his back, wanting not the smallest tremor to give away his very desperate need. "What if we could help each other?"

Terrence McCarron glanced at his two nearby bodyguards.

One of them, a very large woman with a shaved head and flat features, raised an eyebrow. Mai caught the exchange, and wondered: a confidante, or advisor? The other had dark skin and a fiery look in his eyes. McCarron nodded something reassuring and, with a pointed look, dismissed the two. Both left with obvious regret. Now it was just him and Mai Wa.

"Jeremy is one of my infantry commanders, and he is too close to our Maskirovka *friends*. You understand?"

Mai nodded. Mask agents were a fact of life, though usually you had nothing to fear unless you acted against the Confederation's better interests. "I am a traitor," he said with heavy reservation. "I serve the Confederation."

"Just so." McCarron nodded as if Mai had just given the best endorsement. He walked over toward his Po II. "Things happen, things that have no direct bearing on men in the field. *Nǐ dǒng ma*?" he asked, again wanting to know if Mai Wa understood.

In *hàn-yǔ*, there was less room for error. You did not hedge by words, only in tone. "*Wǒ dǒng le.*" Mai made certain that he sounded very, very sure.

McCarron squatted down to take a closer look at the ruined tread. It looked to Mai as if a main hub had taken accurate laserfire. Or a very lucky shot. "Good," the younger officer finally said. "Now what can you offer?"

"Not as much as I'd hoped." But then, if Mai Uhn Wa had discovered as much support among the resistance cells as he'd *hoped*, he wouldn't have needed McCarron at all. "I'm tied in to the *Ijori Dè Guāng* and the Conservatory's network now. There are also some tentative reaches into this so-called Cult of Liao." Evan hadn't volunteered anything on the Cult, but it was apparent there were crossover ties in the two organizations.

"Right." The other man nodded. "Sun-Tzu, the Immortal One. They are the ones who claim to have sightings of the Chancellor. What can they do for us?"

"They can supplement whatever other intelligence assets you've developed," Mai offered. "And they would be willing native guides, the *Ijori Dè Guāng* especially. They have been skulking around Liao for the better side of two years now. Convoy schedules. Back roads. They have a great deal to offer. We can also coordinate efforts in planning and support from the Conservatory, for as long as we hold it."

McCarron stood, looked down on Mai. "So it would be in our better interests to help you hold the Conservatory, then. Troops and armor?"

"I'll settle for surplus equipment and sharing intelligence," Mai countered, sensing the other man's hesitation. "And I'll ask for nothing that can't be repaid after the arrival of the Dynasty Guard. You'll share in whatever they bring us. Of course, you'll have a better idea of when that will be."

"Soon," McCarron promised, still seeing no need to share such strategic information. He squinted up into the heavily laden skies, as if searching for their DropShip already. Rain washed his face with icy fingers. "All right. We feed at the trough first, but you're welcome to whatever we don't eat."

Mai Wa smiled. Spoken like a true workhorse regiment. "With so much of Liao left to be harvested," he said, "there should be enough for us all." Even a return of Warrior House Ijori.

=== 18 ===

Suiting Up

No, I do not believe that Prefect Tao completely respects our situation on Liao. He is a soldier, and we need good soldiers. But all he sees is the Confederation come again, when quite obviously it has never truly left us.
—Governor Lu Pohl, Liao, 2 July 3134

Yiling (Chang-an)
Qinghai Province, Liao
2 July 3134

Evan Kurst hung on to the back of the hoverbike, feet braced and arms aching as he pulled his chest into the back of David's seat. The small, military vehicle was built for one, but a passenger could hitch if the driver was very careful. David Parks was borderline. Air blasted out from under the metal skirting as they cruised over the Grinder and David opened the throttles. Evan clenched his eyes shut and pictured the checkpoint gate as it sped blessedly closer.

The Liao Conservatory's campus had an hourglass shape to it, with its administration and educational campus squeezing into the YiCha suburbs. The training grounds opened up from the southern edge of the city proper where commercial districts leaned in from east and west to form the narrow waist. The Grinder, a wide expanse of rough-topped ferrocrete where cadets marched parades, divided the campus's manicured lawns and cobblestone walkways from a long fence line of chain-link and razor-tipped wire. Beyond the fence line was a small military post complete with garages, service depots, an armory and BattleMech hangars.

The lift fans calmed down to a mere growl as David slid the vehicle up to one of the gates and reversed exhaust to power bake. Evan opened his eyes. Two infantrymen stood watch in Infiltrator battlesuits, looming over Evan and David. Identification was hardly needed, as Evan had become one of the best known cadets on campus. His stunt with the ConstructionMech had been a good start.

Coming out and finally admitting his involvement with the *Ijori Dè Guāng*, that had been a much larger boost.

Still, he dug out his badge. The Full Access Pass was a new design, and handed out very carefully. It gave Evan's small coterie and perhaps a dozen others the right to move anywhere on the tightly controlled Conservatory grounds.

The Infiltrator infantry saluted and waved them through, raising the gate.

David gunned the hoverbike's engine, powering forward. Evan had to duck to clear the lifting bar.

"I can't pilot a 'Mech with brain damage," he shouted in his friend's ear.

David barely turned his head to shout back. "So how did you get in the program to begin with?"

He'd pay for that. Evan wasn't completely certain when or how, but Parks would pay.

Through the gate, the pretenses of a prestigious university disappeared. Reinforced roads, good for marching Battle-Mechs, cut between plots of scrub grass and tangled brush. This was the business side of the campus, where cadets trained in hands-on lessons. There were no barracks or clubs. This wasn't a true garrison post, after all. Cadets came here to grab equipment and take to the field for parade, maneuvers, and live-fire ranges.

And now, to report for patrols and scouting assignments that put them into harm's way.

A pair of DI Schmitts rolled along one side of a wide avenue, heading in for maintenance. A squad of Purifiers crossed the road behind them, disappearing with a chameleon's grace into the brush. Evan tried to follow the blur of color, but lost them as their mimetic armor adapted.

David lifted one arm from the hoverbike's controls and stabbed his hand at ten o'clock. From behind a stand of tall alder a *Tian-zong* stomped into view, swept the area with sensors, and then lumbered off to the southeast.

This is what Evan's actions had wrought: cadets worried for an attack by their own military. Legate Ruskoff would not back down easily. Fortunately, Mai Wa had brokered a deal with McCarron's Second, one which Evan honored through the *Ijori Dè Guāng* in order to procure more military equipment for the campus standoff. No one looked too closely at where the new materials came from.

Sound military policy: don't ask, don't tell.

The five-story hangar rivaled campus buildings for its massive size, dark gray, steel-reinforced ferrocrete, bunker-style construction, no windows. Just a set of massive doors that rose sixteen meters above the local tarmac.

"Door number one," David called out as he drifted the hoverbike into a coasting glide. The engine cooled down into a whispering purr, generating just enough lift to keep the skirting from digging into the paved road. "Techs, 'Mechs, and ladies' lingerie."

"What you infantry wear under your battle armor is your own business," Evan shot back, stepping down from the skirt and flexing some life back into his arms.

David goosed a one-eighty and the hoverbike grounded almost perfectly between the yellow stripes of a parking space, nose pointed back out. He powered down the engine, then pulled out the activation chip, but left it dangling on one of the control sticks. "Do your aerobics later. Get in there and meet your ride."

Evan *was* delaying. He nodded, and led his friend around the corner, into the cavernous bay.

It was like stepping into a fabled chamber, where suddenly you were Jack serving the Giants' table. The smell of oil, grease, and hot metal assaulted Evan. Technicians wheeled around handcarts and drove bright yellow forklifts and, in the darker recesses of the hangar, someone stomped around in a LoaderMech with a massive crate clenched in viselike hands.

IndustrialMechs were racked into bays on either side of the massive doors. A ForestryMech, and a modified Construction machine with one arm replaced by an autocannon and the second arm being worked on. Evan quickly dismissed them for the machine facing him from across the expanse of stained ferrocrete. A *Ti Ts'ang*, brought in by an officer defecting from the Triarii. Named for the King of the Earth's Womb in Han mythology the ten-meter-tall 'Mech sported an obviously Capellan-influenced design. The head was fashioned after a helmet of ancient Chinese armor. Angled shoulder-plates resembled a mantle similar to those worn by Capellan nobles. It also carried a double-bladed ax in the right hand, although no Mongol barbarian had ever carried such a weapon with its laser-sharpened titanium blade.

Evan was one of the three MechWarriors now authorized to pilot the sixty-ton avatar.

"Go on," David said, rocking Evan forward with a shove. "I'll meet you outside."

"You aren't heading back?"

David laughed and nodded toward a small team of technicians making final adjustments to a set of Fa Shih battle armor, a gift from the Second McCarron's. "Are you kidding? I've waited days to get checked out on that gear."

"Ready in ten," Evan told him.

"I'll be gone in five." David sketched a casual salute, then jogged over to the waiting techs. It was still a game to the larger man, but finally he'd found the chance he'd always wanted.

A 'Mech-rated technician waited for Evan at the foot of the *Ti Ts'ang*. She wore a red-stained jumpsuit that looked as if its arms had been soaked in blood. Packing grease, actually, the kind that protected fresh myomer.

"Problem with the myomer?" He read the name tag embroidered onto her work clothes: Brett Spore, Tech Sergeant.

"Right leg was twitchy," she said, her voice a bit high-strung, but confident. "I added some new thigh roping." Myomer acted like muscles, expanding and contracting when electrical current passed through it. It made the upright machines possible. "Also replaced two heat sinks and tightened up the right arm actuator, so expect your swing to be a little stiff."

Evan let his gaze wander up the massive machine, from the bell-bottom flare of its jump jets to the dark visor of ferroglass. "I'm not taking her into battle today," he promised. "Just a short patrol."

"You don't know that, sir. Just try to bring her back in one piece." Tech Sergeant Spore walked over to a gantry and powered up its cradle.

She was right, he didn't know. No one did. He nodded his thanks, climbed into the cradle and gripped the steel rail with both hands as she lifted him to the level of the BattleMech's head. Dogging the hatch shut behind him, Evan quickly stripped down to a pair of tight-fitting shorts and field boots. He stored his clothes in a locker built into the back of his command chair, trading them for a cooling vest. He buckled on the vest and slid around, into the chair.

A series of toggles warmed up the fusion engine and all control musculature. A coolant line fed out of the base of his chair, and Evan inserted it into the snap-lock fitted at the lower edge of his vest. From an overhead shelf, he pulled down a neurohelmet, made certain it was his, and then snugged it on for a good fit.

A cable spooled down near his feet. Evan picked it up, checked for tangles, and threaded it into the restraining loops on the front of his vest. The cable's plug locked into a helmet socket just beneath his chin. It was the last link of the neurofeedback system that fed his own equilibrium into the massive gyroscope. He flipped one final set of toggles, and the fusion engine thrummed to life with a deep, muted roar that vibrated up through the deckplates.

"Startup sequence complete," the computer's synthesized voice whispered through the gear built into his neurohelmet. The voice was asexual, though Evan thought he detected just a hint of feminine current running beneath the surface. A cadence like Jenna's lilting tone. "Proceed with primary security protocol."

"Kurst, Evan. Cadet. Identification: LCMA-77-EK." He waited while the computer checked its security logs, compared his identification and voiceprint and mental signature to the record physically stored on a circuit board.

"Identification confirmed. Proceed with secondary protocol."

Because voiceprints and even brain wave signatures could be faked with the right equipment, BattleMechs were coded with a verbal key that only the MechWarrior knew. Some cadets strung together a list of nonsense syllables—fa-la-do-do-ray-ti-la and so on—since stealing another's simulator code (and then using it to crash sim-grade averages) was just one more game played among the student body. Evan had memorized a passage from Lao Tse's *Tao Teh Ching*.

Wú yán shèn yì zhī, shèn yì xíng.
Tiān xià mò néng zhī, mò néng xíng.

"Authorization confirmed. Full access granted."

Throttling into his first heavy steps, rocking with the wide-legged gait of the *Ti Ts'ang*, Evan strode for the open bay doors even as he whispered the translation of the key back to himself. "My words are easy to understand. And my actions are easy to perform. Yet no other can understand or perform them."

Verse seventy, on Individuality.

"Now let's see what there is to see," he said in a stronger voice as he broke out into the Liao sunlight. A blue speck brightened on his head's-up display, and the BattleMech bumped forward as if it had been tapped on its right shoulder by a heavy hand.

"Mind if I tag along?"

David. Evan glanced out of the ferroglass shield at his right side, saw the Fa Shih battlesuit perched on his right shoulder-guard with magnetic locks sealing it to the 'Mech. "I guess I don't have much choice," he said, voice-activated mic picking up his words and broadcasting them on a secure band. He steered straight south, intending to take a run along the lower picket line. "Not unless I want to scrape you off with my hatchet."

At least the infantryman glanced up at the four-ton hatchet. "That would not be cool. Especially since I was kind enough to give you a lift earlier. You're just returning the favor."

"So I am," Evan said, remembering the breakneck pace at which David had pushed the hoverbike. He throttled into a run, pushing the *Ti Ts'ang* forward at better than ninety kilometers per hour. Metal-shod feet pounded the ground with earthshaking force.

Outside, David hunched down to strengthen his magnetic grip. "Can't you smooth it out a bit?" he asked, voice vibrating.

"Sure can."

And Evan stomped down on his pedals, cutting in jump jets and hurtling sixty tons of BattleMech and two passengers sky-ward on jets of fiery plasma. David's yell was mostly exhila-ration.

But not all of it.

19

Paths Into Future Glory

"We have heard our brothers, our sisters, calling out for a return to Capellan ways. For too long we have denied them. For too long we have capitulated to a government created by treachery, by threats, and by force of arms, which sits in stewardship of Liao, one of our most blessed worlds. Father, we return for you.
— Chancellor Daoshen Liao, Public address, Sian,
1 July 3134

Celestial Palace
Zi-jin Chéng (Forbidden City), Sian
Sian Commonality, Capellan Confederation
3 July 3134

On one of the Celestial Palace's restricted floors, Agent Michael Yung-Te paused just outside a darkened doorway, bowing his head as if in prayer. His dark eyes remained open, though, as he searched with every sense for warnings, for danger.

The supports on either side of the door were thick, red-grained and exquisitely carved with the semblance of a sleek tiger clawing its way up toward the top. The tiger's stripes were detailed in gold and, when looking closely enough, one saw that each small crescent was actually a *dadao* sword—some rough edged, some with fresh blades. He couldn't see the heavy teak lintel up at the top. Didn't need to. Everyone knew what was carved there.

Liào Sūn Zǐ. Yì Guó Zhī Fù.

Sun-Tzu Liao. Father of the State.

The corridor's blue-tinted light fell into the room, framing an irregular rectangle on the hardwood floors, but adding very little in the way of illumination. Darkness held sway here, pushing back against prying eyes. Not a sound came from within. Michael would have to step into the doorway, but he hesitated. Being summoned into the Chancellor's presence provoked uncertainty enough in anyone, even an agent of the Maskirovka. Sent to summon Him, to remind the Chancellor of an audience he should be giving, that was for court functionaries who were better suited to gauge the Chancellor's moods and risk his wrath. Daoshen the Inscrutable, His Celestial Wisdom, God-Incarnate of Sian, kept his own counsel. He was not a man to be hurried along.

Some believed he was not a mortal man at all.

Michael did not know what to believe. He'd heard many of the whispered legends. Assassins plucked out of closets by the Chancellor's own hand, left broken and dying. A farmer on estates bordering one of the Chancellor's rural retreats, trapped under an overturned combine; Daoshen Liao freed him with a demonstration of superhuman strength. Divining the future, the reading of minds, a channeling of his father's spirit . . . nothing was left unattributed to the Great Soul of the Confederation.

Michael Yung-Te had already languished in the shadow of the Chancellor's disfavor for eight long months, for no other reason than his assignment to oversee the interrogation and confession of the traitor, Mai Uhn Wa. And now he was being asked to put his face before the Chancellor again?

As if his question had been spoken aloud, the whisk of sandal against wood shuffled out of the darkened room. Michael tensed. The God-Incarnate of Sian was indeed spending time in his father's old office, one of several rooms preserved in the memory of the great Sun-Tzu Liao.

"You were sent for me." Daoshen's voice drifted out on a harsh whisper, rough edged and violent.

How the Chancellor knew of Michael's presence the Maskirovka agent could not tell. He cast no shadow into the room, and his approach had been as quiet as only a trained agent moved. "I was sent, Omnipotent One." Truly divine or

merely godlike in his authority, one always—always!—
awarded the Chancellor his due honors. "I do not mean to dis-
turb your meditation."

"The representative from Jacob Bannson. The ambassador
from the Oriente Protectorate. They await audience." It was
not a question. "They are in the antechamber to my parlor, together?" They were.

"So it is my understanding, Heavenly Patience. They do
wait together."

"Step inside, Michael Yung-Te."

Maskirovka agents were disciplined and very well trained.
There were not many polygraph devices that they could not
subvert. There were not many secrets they could not learn . . .
and keep to themselves until demanded of them. Still,
Michael felt naked as he stepped past the threshold and into
the room, shuffling immediately to one side, out of the light.

The shadows had a clammy touch. He smelled perfumed
oils and a touch of dust common to unused rooms. His eyes
adjusted, and he saw a desk, a terrarium, a display curio filled
with treasures collected by the Ascendant Sun-Tzu Liao.
Michael found his eyes drawn back to the desk, where
Daoshen's father once sat and planned such events as the Xin
Sheng movement of 3062, and his retreat from Sian during the
Jihad. It was here that he made his decision to return to Liao
after the Night of Screams. The trip where, according to all belief, he ascended to a godhood of his own.

But where was the Chancellor? The room stood empty. Or
did it?

"You fall back into the shadows, Agent Yung-Te." Daoshen
shuffled forward from near the curio, as if materializing in the
room. Like a dark spider spinning its gossamer web, Daoshen
Liao remained just this side of invisible. As if the light dared
not approach him. "That is a good skill for one of the Mask.
But it does not hide you from my eyes."

"Nothing is hidden from your eyes, Celestial Spirit." The
Maskirovka helped make that so, but Michael still wondered.
"This unworthy one meant no insult."

"You have read reports of the fighting?" Daoshen asked.

Did he know that Michael was one of a dozen agents that
helped prepare the Mask's Daily Report, assigning levels of
risk to the State in each of a hundred different ventures and
events? The report was not so timely without working HPGs,

but a command circuit of JumpShips ferrying news from the front put Sian only a few days behind any major advance or setback.

"I have read reports," Michael agreed. Straight from the hand of Strategic Director Isabelle Fisk. But he sensed that the Chancellor was looking for more than mere affirmation. "We proceed well along the Algot front, especially where we rely more heavily on our own supply lines and have no worries with regard to a bordering Prefecture." Along that border, The Republic of the Sphere fetched up against a small piece of Confederation space and then a protruding thumb of the mighty and much despised Federated Suns. "The fighting on Menkar has turned particularly desperate for The Republic."

"Signs, Michael. Read the signs. Desperation is a judgment. Why Algot? Why Menkar?"

"That is where our forces are strongest. That is where Prefect Tao comes to find us." Shun Tao. Michael had been responsible for a biography and threat assessment of the man only a year ago, before he was assigned to the traitor. Before he lost Daoshen Liao's favor.

"What is of supreme importance in war is to attack the enemy's strategy. Next best is to disrupt his alliances. Afterward, to attack his army."

It took Michael a moment to realize the Chancellor was quoting. "Li Ch'uan?" he asked.

"Much older. The Art of War, by Sun Tzu. *His* namesake."

His gaze flicked to the desk. In a way, there were three people in the room. Was Daoshen Liao seeking approval? Was Michael?

"So, has the enemy attacked our strategy?" the Chancellor asked.

"No. They engage our troops. Both there, and on the Liao front." Of course, Republic news still referred to it as the Gan Singh theater, as if the small force landed on Liao did not constitute a real threat.

"And our alliances?"

Bannson. Michael was not privy to all dealings, but he knew enough to realize the Chancellor had struck a deal with the industrial giant. "As yet, they seem to be unaware of our connection with Jacob Bannson. Of course, he operates very carefully, which has led to our slowed advance on Liao. We depend on him too much."

Michael immediately wished he could recall those words. His role was to report, not to counsel. Daoshen Liao let a long silence speak for him. Then, "Bannson's caution *may* hurt us," he agreed. "Imagine what would happen should the Dynasty Guard and McCarron's Second be isolated on Liao for any length of time."

"They would take heavy losses. The Hussars and the Armored Cavalry would demand blood." A dark thrill shook Michael as he was allowed to glimpse a piece of the political machinery working so far behind the scenes.

"And the Warrior Houses," the Chancellor whispered. "After all, the stillborn rebirth of House Ijori could hardly go unnoticed."

The traitor again. The Maskirovka agent had learned of Mai's divine goal to raise up one of the fallen Warrior Houses. His quest for that boon had led to a direct betrayal of the State, a failure in policy and a refusal to answer for it. Either should have cost the man his life. Michael's mood darkened. Instead, Mai Wa had been freed to pursue his dream again, sent back to Liao where his—

Sent back to Liao.

A cold pit opened up in Michael's stomach. This was more than a glimpse. He knew then that the Chancellor had indeed summoned him here today, now, for a reason. Daoshen Liao pulled back a corner of the curtain, allowing him see the plans within plans and the machinations that fueled them. Soon the Confederation would have tokens in place on Liao representing three of the strongest Capellan military forces. Should they be threatened, wounded—destroyed!—Bannson could be held accountable, put fully in the Chancellor's power, and the following bloodlust would make the Confederation all but unstoppable. *Then* Liao could be retaken. No quarter accepted or offered, the Confederation armed forces would sweep through Prefecture V.

And beyond?

Next best is to disrupt his alliances.

Right now a representative from the Oriente Protectorate was sitting in a room, unattended, with Bannson's man. Bannson—Daoshen—the world of Liao. Bannson—the Oriente—New Canton and Prefecture VI. Two interlocking circles. How far did the Chancellor's reach extend? Michael trembled with a thrill of power. What was truly beyond the God-Incarnate of Sian?

"The signs are all favorable," Daoshen intoned in a deep whisper, as if reading the other man's mind. "I know that Liao will be ours again. I know that my father watches over all to ensure this will happen. And you, Michael Yung-Te, will carry my messages forward to put the final pieces in place."

Even the gods, at times, required mortal servants. Michael bowed, then sank to his knees and fully prostrated himself before his Chancellor. "I am not worthy of this honor. I serve the Confederation."

"See that you do," Daoshen Liao said, dismissing the agent, His messenger, with a final command. "Your full orders await you on the *Celestial Walker*. Take them forward."

Michael rose and stepped into the spilled light, then backed his way from the room. His mind was already on the Confederation's eventual victory, wrapped about his return to the graces of the Chancellor's service. He had not lost favor in those months as Mai Wa's minder. He had never been forgotten. His was a powerful future, following one of the Chancellor's many divined paths. And in the end, he would see justice done.

Mai Uhn Wa would not be allowed to succeed. He would die in one last service to the State.

Michael Yung-Te now *believed*.

20

Vanguard

Even though Wei's lunar New Year is a month past, the people are just now beginning their festivities. Parades and nightly displays of fireworks thrill the crowds. Cargo DropShips filled with Confederation delicacies arrive alongside military transports and logistics vessels. It is a world celebrating its relief.
—Authorized Press Release, Governor Fowkes,
Wei, 9 July 3134

Overland Orchards
Paragon Province, Liao
Prefecture V, The Republic
10 July 3134

Wading through a bramble of spike-topped trees, Viktor Ruskoff slammed his throttle forward against the upper stop. His *Zeus* limped onward, eating up six meters in every stride as it pushed for speeds nearing sixty kilometers per hour. Naranji tree limbs snapped off as the eighty-ton BattleMech brushed past row after row, leaving smears of greenstick splinters down its legs. His machine's left arm, amputated at the elbow, swung just above the dead canopy. Scattered machine gun fire pecked and prodded from thicker parts of the orchard, which the Legate ignored.

The *Zeus* broke through to a dirt road, passing between orchard stands, and Viktor throttled back as a new threat icon popped on his HUD. Half a klick along the road a Po II heavy tank crawled forward on chevron treads. A flash of electrical storm and a dark blur, and a Gauss slug shattered armor across the *Zeus's* right leg. Then the Po spun and powered into the next orchard, hiding from the assault 'Mech's return fire and no doubt calling in support on its position.

Wrong again. The Po II immediately backed out, turret wheeled over, and struck at him a second time. A new Gauss round hammered into the assault 'Mech's left side, raining shards of fractured armor around its feet.

The number of Viktor's guesses being proven wrong were beginning to mount up. He'd guessed that he could move forces and supplies up to Qinghai from Paragon Province without alerting the Second McCarron's Armored Cavalry. And then he'd gambled that a pair of BattleMechs and a mechanized infantry company would be enough to run vanguard on the convoy.

Now he was second-guessing Terrence McCarron himself, and paying dearly each time he underestimated his opponent.

Dropping his crosshairs over the Po's blocky profile, Viktor reached out with large laser and missiles in an attempt to smash the cocky bastard before he dodged back into the orchard. McCarron hammered into a reverse-right tanker's turn, taking the laser against his stronger front armor and letting the flight of missiles chew up nothing worse than the soft, black earth.

Staying into the turn through an entire one-eighty, the Po finally backed itself into the orchard and out of sight.

Rather than chase along the open road after McCarron, Viktor crossed the shoulder to wade once more into the sleeping orchard. Like flushing pheasant, a pocket of Achileus and Infiltrators popped up on jets, scattering in three different directions. The Legate ignored them, turned his *Zeus* eastward, chasing after the Po II and the leader of McCarron's Second.

"Alpha, Bravo," Ruskoff barked into his mic. "Report."

"Alpha, NOC."

No official change. Which meant the 122nd Pathfinders were still down one transport and three men, and had yet to claim an enemy kill.

"Bravo. Lose one Harraser." Both VTOLs down now. "Cripple one Demon and score a squad of Infiltrators on the belly flop."

So the VTOL had spoil-sported and crashed itself into a McCarron's armored infantry squad. A waste of damn fine infantry, in Viktor's opinion, but better a waste of their infantry than his.

"Alpha," he checked his HUD in a practiced glance, backed it up with a scan through his ferroglass shield. He picked up only one hundred twenty degrees of the horizon, but sometimes it helped him keep the pieces straight in his mind. Like playing chess and looking at only half the board, playing the rest from memory.

"Alpha, start drawing them nor' nor'west. If you can't scratch their paint, at least leave your trail of bodies to lead them toward Reggat's Canyon."

Reggat's Canyon might let Alpha eventually circle back toward the convoy. If not—if McCarron's forces proved too bullheaded to let them run—he could save lives as his men worked their way into the Reggat's Canyon caves. By the position of their VTOLs, dipping and hovering over trees to the far north, they had at least ten rough minutes ahead of them.

Bravo had lost both of its attack choppers, but there was no mistaking the swarming attacks of McCarron's VTOL formation just a few kilometers to the east. The other side of Terrence McCarron's position.

"Bravo, I want you to hold. You'll see armored infantry and maybe some assault tanks pushing back your way, but stand fast."

They could do it. They still had antiaircraft Partisans to worry the VTOLs.

One unit in flight, one to hold fast as a wall against which he pushed the enemy. That was never an easy call, deciding who lived and who risked death. The difference this time was that he was in a position to work with only one of the demi-companies, and if he had to leave one unsupported, he'd at least give them the chance to extend and escape.

Military talk for run like hell.

McCarron wasn't through throwing little twists into the Legate's plans, though. Threat alarms wailed for his attention as Infiltrators and Achileus battle armor took turns popping up above the trees on their small jets to snipe at the assault 'Mech. The *Zeus* did not have great antiinfantry weapons, but Viktor managed to swat one Infiltrator from the sky with a pulse laser. Then a JES II tactical carrier broke cover, slalomed between trees and traded flight after flight of short-range missiles for nothing worse than a few red-tinged scars from Viktor's laser.

He wished again for his particle projector cannon, lost with his left arm in earlier exchanges of firepower. Standing a full story higher than the trees around him, the Legate had a commanding view. If he'd wanted, he could have pointed out each heavy encounter, places where oily smoke seeped up above the canopy, or where fires burned in the local orchards.

Ten kilometers back, for example, when the Armored Cavalry had struck with such numbing force that his small vanguard had shattered.

Five klicks: a full-fledged forest fire marked where Sergeant Ho gave his life for two infantry carriers and a Regulator. A Confederation head-hunter team broke the seal on his cockpit and smeared him over the inside of the cockpit shield. Hardly equitable, trading away an experienced veteran and his *Phoenix Hawk*. The *Zeus* was too heavily armored. Too slow. Ruskoff had been unable to rendezvous in time.

Three klicks, then one: Places where units lay dead or crippled or where the *Zeus* had been delayed by McCarron's wheel-and-flank tactics.

"Contact!" Bravo's commander, Sergeant Jason Lee, let worry tell in his volume. "Four . . . five! Five armored vehicles closing. Battle armor everywhere."

Ahead Viktor saw an explosion in the tree canopy where a Gauss rifle punched through from below. Enemy VTOLs swarmed down toward the break, searching for prey. Spot fires began to show in the branches, and smoke rose in a haze as ground support vehicles battled unseen.

"We're in thick soup here, Commander."

The *Jessie* swerved into a new row, tracked by his sensors, but lost from his immediate sight as it tempted him into chasing. Not this time. Viktor pushed ahead, slowed by the orchard's grasp, but always with one eye on his HUD for distance against the hovering VTOLs. Sixty seconds, he guessed.

He got only six before a new problem opened up.

"Vanguard, vanguard. Convoy has hit a minefield on the Paragon Thruway. We're seeing Fa Shih infantry. 'Mechs! Two of them! Forestry . . . *Ti Ts'ang*! Tanks. Two . . . four, five. . . ." The count disappeared in a wave of static as local jamming overrode the transmission.

"Convoy." Ruskoff toggled for his secure line. "Major Demmens!" A few nonsensical syllables crackled through. Nothing the Legate's communications gear could latch onto. A quick mental tabulation—the convoy was protected by two more BattleMechs and a small collection of support vehicles. They had a slim chance, if Demmens held up.

The Legate glanced out over the orchard's canopy, knowing the destructive firepower already lurking below. Where was McCarron drawing up extra forces now?

At extreme range, he levered his right arm forward, gained a partial lock on one of the VTOLs and spent two missile flights against the darting craft. His first salvo fell short, hammering down into the branches, starting a new fire. His second swarm arced in on one of McCarron's Balac Strike VTOLs, pummeling the fragile craft with blossoms of orange fire. Smoke belched out of a crippled engine. The helicopter attempted to bank away, but it was too low and falling fast. Landing skids snagged the top of one naranji tree, tipping the craft over until its rotors caught into the branches as well.

It disappeared in a shatter of tree limbs and finely balanced blades. To Ruskoff, it looked as if the orchard's stark limbs had reached out to swallow the wounded craft, belching up a small burst of fire and smoke afterward.

The other VTOLs spun around and broke for three different points on the compass. Ruskoff's laser slashed a ruby lance at one of them, scoring the body. Another dozen paces, the *Zeus* powered its way forward into a haze of smoke and burning trees and a close-quarter battle between heavy armor and infantry.

Partisan antiaircraft tanks and a double handful of Cavalier battlesuit infantry would not normally be a good match against Regulators and *Jessies* and a trio of Demons, especially those supported by superior battle armor assets. Sergeant Lee had set his line well. Overlapping the Partisans' fields of fire, he had created a killing zone that shaved armor from the tanks as easily as the multiple autocannon shredded bark and leaves from orchard trees. Any battlesuit infantry braving the storm of flechettes now lay dead or dying on the soft ground. Jason Lee had held his own infantry back to harass the tanks, pin them in place, and hold them for Ruskoff's arrival.

He was a bear suddenly loosed among savage dogs. Missiles

fell in a hard rain of destructive power as the Legate dumped flight after flight over the killing ground, hammering into Mc-Carron's armor. His laser stabbed out in short, powerful lances, slashing away armor and boring into the crew compartment of one Demon, which ran full force into the thick bole of a large tree. He stove in the side of a Regulator with a hard-swinging kick, and then chased after it with emerald darts from his pulse laser. All the while he searched in vain for McCarron's tank.

Infantry tried twice to swarm his legs, but Bravo's sergeant sent Cavalier troopers forward to grapple hand-to-hand against the lighter-armored Achileus infantry. Viktor heard metallic scratching outside of his access hatch, ignored it as he finished off the Regulator with a flurry of missiles. They erupted inside the lift fans. The hovercraft flipped over onto its side, coming to a tilting halt against a nearby tree. Still alive and in control of his BattleMech a moment later, he assumed that some of his own infantry had dealt with the problem.

"They're through our line," Lee called out a few seconds later. "They're running."

Not all of them. A wounded Demon parked itself between a Cavalier squad and the fleeing Confederation force. The remaining Regulator II led the Capellan retreat, with Achileus and Infiltrators attempting to pile onto the JES tactical carriers or simply fleeing deeper into the orchard. The Demon lasted only as long as it took a Cavalier infantryman to rip open one of the hatches and shove a laser into the crew compartment. Then it fell deadly still as well.

"Sir, do we pursue?"

Viktor turned his *Zeus* in place, shuffle stepping around the ruined Regulator and leaning out of the worst of the smoke. He tasted the acrid bite of burning fuel, and knew then that his own cockpit had been breached. The swarming Achileus troopers had come closer than he'd thought. A trigger's pull away from losing his life.

"Sir, do we—"

"We do not," Ruskoff said, cutting off his sergeant. Not today.

Farther south, McCarron's remaining VTOLs swarmed back together, giving Ruskoff an idea about where the Armored Cavalry commander had slipped away. The Capellan officer would quickly rendezvous with his remaining forces, and might arrange a counterthrust. The very real fact was that

McCarron had somehow summoned superior firepower both here and, from the sounds of it, back at the convoy, too.

"No. We've made the Cavalry earn their pay today, and that's good enough. We need to pull back to the west and try to hit the convoy's trail." He toggled for a secure line to Major Demmens, then switched back away from the wash of static. "See what pieces are left to pick up." But he knew, he knew.

Not many.

Not for the first time Legate Viktor Ruskoff wondered if anyone—Prefect Shun Tao and himself included—truly appreciated the local threat to Liao.

21

Light of Ijori

In a bold move this week, Prefect Tao threw elements of the Fifth Triarii and the Eridani Light Horse at entrenched Confederation positions on Gan Singh. The Voranish DropPort was retaken, and families of the local nobility escaped on MedCross vessels originally sent to aid in humanitarian efforts. World Governor Littlefield defended this decision, worried that such important families might be taken hostage by Confederation forces.
      —Cassandra Clarke, New Aragon, 8 July 3134

Paragon Thruway
Paragon Province, Liao
10 July 3134

With its vanguard under attack by McCarron's Armored Cavalry, the convoy ran full speed for Qinghai Province. Right into the ambush set by Evan Kurst and Mai Uhn Wa. Ten minutes turned the Paragon Thruway into a haze-shrouded battlefield. Missiles arced and fell along the six-lane highway. Lasers splashed back and forth, jewel-toned darts and spears that flashed briefly and were gone. Armor fractured, splintered, melted and dripped smoking, black-husked coals onto the road and the hillsides of the Methow Narrows.

Sweat tickled Evan's brow as he ducked over his controls. Bending his *Ti Ts'ang* at the waist, he hunched under a militia *Legionnaire's* long stream of autocannon fire. Tail-end bullets scored and pitted his armor. He backpedaled onto the highway's cinder-strewn shoulder, firing all the way, then turned his weapons against a nearby Giggins APC. A blistering salvo of lasers silenced the APC's machine guns. His hatchet rose and fell, rose and fell, sheering through the forward wheelbase.

Two APCs down. The first had fishtailed through a minefield laid out by David Parks and his Fa Shih comrades. Both had dumped full loads of Cavalier battle armor, and the remaining infantry pressed forward in the *Legionnaire's* shadow.

Regrouping. Not what Evan wanted to see.

"We need backup," he demanded. They needed something.

The pro-Capellan force had been thrown together at the last minute, mixing Conservatory cadets among *Ijori Dè Guāng* irregulars and resources begged from the Armored Cavalry. Barely enough to get the job done. Two JES II strategic carriers and a modified ForestryMech held the Narrow's gap, stalling the long column, while Evan pressed in from the front. *Ijori Dè Guāng* irregulars, armed with nothing more than rifles and a great deal of courage, converged on the convoy from both wooded slopes. They mixed among Fa Shih troopers and a few Saxon APCs. A mixed unit of hoverbikes and minigun cycles attacked from behind.

Two Jousts lay overturned and burning, victims of The Republic forces that jealously guarded the convoy.

Most of The Republic troops were militia forces: the *Legionnaire*, Cavalier infantry, and a squad of Pegasus hovercraft. A *Thunderbolt* added supporting fire, painted the same colors as the SM1 Destroyer and Elemental infantry making up the convoy's rear guard.

White and gold.

Fifth Principes Guards.

Evan pushed forward across the blacktop. The Battle-Mech's feet crushed through the thin surface, leaving behind cracked footprints. He swerved around a small pileup of civilian vehicles. The *Legionnaire* advanced a few more steps, trading another long burst of autocannon fire against Evan's lasers. The *Ti Ts'ang* shook under hammering blows.

"Help is on the way," Mai Wa finally promised.

Evan checked his rearward monitor. The ForestryMech slowly dismantled a militia Pegasus, using its diamond-toothed saw to hack off large chunks of engine cowling. A

hundred meters behind it, the JES II carriers disappeared behind a curtain of gray exhaust as they spread scores of missiles
into the air.

A firestorm erupted around the *Legionnaire* as the missiles
rained overhead. Still, the fifty-ton machine trudged forward,
shrugging off the damage. The *Thunderbolt* turned toward the
rear of the stalled convoy, lending its own missiles and a
deadly laser to the Destroyer's aid.

"They're splitting!" Evan could hardly believe it, even
though Mai Wa had assured him. Militia and Republic regu-
lars weren't prepared to fight as a unit.

Then again, neither were the various pro-Capellan factions.

"I'm on him," David Parks called, voice trembling as he
leapt his Fa Shih battlesuit into a short arc. He dropped
nearer the *Thunderbolt* than anyone should get.

Another student followed, as did a ragged squad of *Ijori Dè
Guāng* infantry.

"Get out of there, David. Infantry fall back. We *want* them
to separate."

Too late. The Principes Guardsman raised a massive foot
and brought it down on one of the Fa Shih. Missiles slammed
around the remaining infantry, geysered scorched dirt and asphalt into the air, along with whole bodies and parts.

Evan never had time to see if his friend had been the one
pulverized under the *Thunderbolt's* foot or, if he hadn't, then
escaped death by missile fire. Smoke curled around the entire
area, his HUD was a tangled mess of icons and threats, and
that was when the *Legionnaire* opened up into his back.

Nearly as fast as a *Pack Hunter*, the fifty-two-ton 'Mech
sprinted forward to slip into Evan's rear quarter. A long pull
of autocannon fire walked over Evan's left hip and pounded
into the thin armor protecting his back, chewing through, pitting supports and clawing at the massive gyroscope. His cockpit shook violently and the *Ti Ts'ang* pitched forward. It
sprawled into the blacktop, plowing up a small pile of debris.

Another hail of hot metal spanged into his armor, but failed
to do more than chip away fresh composite. Evan shook his
head clear, fought the sixty-ton BattleMech back to its feet.

"*Sa-bing* Presci," Mai Wa ordered very cordially, "at your
convenience. Minus seventy meters."

Mai Wa was early! Evan punched a hot button, transferring
to a general frequency. His parched throat ached as he dry

swallowed life back into his voice. "Hoverbikes and infantry, break and run now, now, now!"

The pro-Capellan force turned and ran for the wooded slopes. Only a pair of hoverbikes remained, crowding the Destroyer to push it into a tangle of convoy trucks. The Destroyer's autocannon spit fire and metal into one hoverbike's engine. It erupted into a fireball that threw the entire machine over the Thruway's wide shoulder and into the base of the valley slope.

Then, as if in retribution, a convoy truck at the end of the stalled column jumped into the air as the ground around it erupted in a violent geyser of fire and shrapnel. The artillery blast also caught a full squad of Elementals, tossing them aside like rag dolls. One crushed infantryman slammed into the side of the nearby *Thunderbolt*.

Farther along the Thruway, a single Danai support vehicle was reloading, adjusting its trajectory by a fraction. Evan had to push now! He throttled into a flat-out run at the *Legionnaire*, braving its screen of Cavalier and a flanking pass by one Pegasus. He fired his lasers again and again. His heat scale climbed quickly through the yellow band, edging into the red. Right where Evan wanted it.

Ti Ts'angs used a type of myomer different from most BattleMechs. Its special properties made it work *better* under high heat conditions rather than worse. Muscles stretched a bit farther, allowing longer strides, and retracted a bit faster, increasing overall speed up toward one hundred and twenty kilometers per hour.

It also leant power to the arms. As Evan swung up his right arm and slashed back down, he gathered twice as much raw kinetic force behind the edge of his titanium hatchet.

The blade bit into the *Legionnaire*'s left side, caving in armor and cutting deep into the internal skeleton. One severed strut punched through the targeting computer and skewered the physical shielding surrounding the 'Mech's fusion engine. Sparks and flame mingled together in the wound as Evan again raised the hatchet overhead.

Ax-wielding BattleMechs were dangerous, and the militia pilot wasn't about to stand up against a machine that could decapitate it with one lucky blow. He broke away quickly, with Evan right behind, racing for the aid of the *Thunderbolt*.

Both 'Mechs faced back down the Narrows when the second artillery round smashed into the ground next to the *Thunderbolt*, toppling the sixty-five-ton machine with a violent shove.

Fa Shih and unarmored *Ijori Dè Guāng* fighters swarmed back en masse, racing for the fallen machine as Mai Wa calmly directed the artillery fire in a ground-pounding walk back down the valley highway. A follow-up round punched through the armor of the SM1 Destroyer before detonating. Another caught one of the hoverbikes, rolling the light hovercraft into a tumbling wreck.

Evan heard metallic claws scrabbling at his *Ti Ts'ang's* armored carapace, and knew he was in danger of being pulled bodily from the cockpit, tossed aside. But with nothing more to lose, the *Legionnaire* had turned to fight. Evan could have dropped to the ground for a flailing attack, tried to shake off the biting ants. Instead, he blistered the *Legionnaire's* armor with his lasers and struck again with his hatchet.

And again.

The *Ti Ts'ang* shook again as more infantry landed on its back and shoulders, and Evan saw a Cavalier tumble past his cockpit shield. Then he poured his lasers into the earlier hatchet wound that had caved through the *Legionnaire's* chest, pumping megajoules of deadly power into the smoking crevice. The *Legionnaire* trembled, and its head split open as escape charges blew away the canopy. The militiaman rode his command seat upward on ejection rockets, abandoning his 'Mech and the battle.

But MechWarriors did not simply punch out in token surrender. They did it as a last resort. Evan overrode the *Ti Tsang's* heat alarms and cut in his jump jets. Leaning back, he rocketed away from the fireball of plasma that blossomed at the *Legionnaire's* heart. One of his lasers had cored through the reactor shielding, disrupting the fusion reactor. Golden fire bled out of the various hatchet wounds, filled what was left of the cockpit, and finally bulged out of every seam, vent and rivet as the reaction expanded out of control.

The explosive shockwave caught Evan in the air and nearly tumbled his damaged gyro beyond help. He crouched forward, balancing himself for landing. It almost worked. He came down on his feet, always a helpful beginning, and managed to fight against a sprawling fall. The *Ti Ts'ang* ended up on one knee, hatchet pressed against the ground in a steady, three-point crouch.

Evan closed his eyes and drew in a shallow breath. Reports of militia and Principes surrenders bled over one another as the loss of their two leviathans demoralized the convoy's protectors. He let his breath whistle out through his teeth, as if straining what little oxygen he could from the scorched air, and then opened his eyes.

A Cavalier infantryman stood on his cockpit "cheek," claw arm fastened to the *Ti Ts'ang's* brow and a laser barrel pointed straight into the ferroglass shield. Right at Evan.

He didn't remember the bore of those small, hand-mounted lasers ever looking quite so large, or so deadly.

The battlesuit trooper cocked his head to one side, as if listening to the mist of molten ceramic composite that exploded next to his temple. Then he released his grip and tumbled backward. Evan heard metallic scratches at his left shoulder and glanced out to the side. A Fa Shih trooper clung there, laser still extended toward the front of the *Ti Ts'ang's* face.

"You looked like you could use one last helping hand," David said, voice shaky, but strong.

"Yeah." Evan levered the *Ti Ts'ang* back to a standing position, careful not to dislodge his friend's tenuous grip. "Always good to see a friendly face." Even though he couldn't, not through the Fa Shih's reflective faceplate.

And the way David turned away, hiding himself from Evan's gaze, Evan was not to certain that he truly wanted to.

The Conservatory's BattleMech hangar was alive with lights, activity, victorious cheers and some silent crying. A few of the new veterans held court, relating their version of what had happened. Meanwhile, technicians worked feverishly to unload the convoy trucks, assisted by student and civilian volunteers. Other volunteers, including Evan, helped triage the walking wounded. Desperate cases were sent directly to the small field hospital. Several yards away, somber hands carried body bags and arranged them in a respectful line.

Evan saw Ritter Michaelson waiting for him near the ambulance. The major had a bloody smear on the sleeve of his chambray work shirt and a haunted look in his eyes.

As always, Michaelson held himself apart from the students, participating in neither the celebration of the Conservatory's first military victory nor in the efforts to sort through and organize the salvage left behind by McCarron's Armored Cavalry. Despite a heavy cost, the pro-Capellan forces had captured the damaged *Thunderbolt* and several vehicles, as well as ten cargo trucks loaded with supplies, munitions and spare parts. It was a stunning success.

Michaelson didn't seem to think so.

"No prisoners?" he asked.

Evan slowed, stopped. "No one worth the trouble. Better to let them go back to their units. Or, preferably, their homes." Evan was bruised and battle weary. He wasn't up for another argument with Michaelson. "We won't force them to change their lives. We're simply asking for the same courtesy."

"Very enlightened of you."

"I'm not a monster."

"You don't have to try to become one, Evan. Believe me. The road to hell is paved with the best of intentions."

Evan massaged his temples. "That's nice, Major. Do you have more platitudes for me now, or can we save this for later?"

"Will there be a later? Ever since Legate Ruskoff's visit, you've pushed your way forward like a driven man. Do you truly understand what you are doing?"

More than ever. In fact, Evan felt exposed by the light of his own making. *Ijori Dè Guāng.* The *Light of Ijori.* Now that he had outed himself, that light shone brightly on the consequences of every decision, every action. It settled a huge weight on his shoulders. One that he might not be ready for. Evan found himself worried for his friends, fellow students and even for The Republic soldiers on the other side. They were also sons and daughters of Liao.

Several were now wounded, dying or dead.

That's when Evan noticed that the ambulance was too quiet. No running engine. No medics. "Cadet-Sergeant Taylor?" he asked.

Michaelson shook his head. "Internal bleeding. No one caught it in time."

A hollow feeling wrenched at Evan's guts. "I was just coming to see him off. To—" To thank him. When the Destroyer needed slowing down, Taylor had been one of the hoverbike drivers to help pin it in place. He'd been thrown, caught by the force of an artillery strike, but insisted he was all right. He'd kept pushing other wounded men into the triage line ahead of him. Damn.

"I saw him off," Michaelson said, though the meaning changed when he said it. "He wasn't alone."

"Thank you," was all Evan could think to say.

"You want to thank me, Evan, then come meet with Governor's Aide Tsung. He's an important man and he has the Governor's ear. It has to be kept quiet, but I'll make all the arrangements."

Evan shrugged. He began to turn away, heading back to the triage. "Bring him here."

"That's not the way it works. If Governor Lu Pohl were to send her top aide to meet with you after the way you treated with Ruskoff, it might—"

"What?" Evan interrupted, rounding back on Michaelson. "Might confer some extra legitimacy? Don't you see, Major, that's what we need. Without it, we'll be shuffled aside again."

The other man blew out an exasperated sigh. He rubbed one hand over his face, let it slide across the angry scars he'd earned on Terra. "There are worse things than falling back into insignificance, Evan. I wish I could make you understand. You make even a simple mistake now," he said, glancing at the side of the ambulance, "and people die. It doesn't have to be that way. Talk this out, Evan. Don't let it go any further."

"Major, I know you mean well. But you're living in the wrong age. This isn't 3128 and you're not Ezekiel Crow." Michaelson recoiled as if he'd been slapped. "This one does not get solved by a political deal. It's gone too far. We've made certain of that. Capellan or Republic—*Confederation* or Republic—it's time for people to decide."

"You have no idea the kind of trouble you are asking for." His voice was a whisper.

"Maybe I don't," Evan admitted. "But it seems like you're too willing to back away from the hard choice, Major. I didn't give myself that option." Or perhaps Evan had simply made his decision years before, when Mai Uhn Wa first approached him. And if that was the case . . .

"Maybe I thought there was another choice, once, but I discovered the truth of that today when I pulled the trigger." He shook his head. "You're talking to the wrong man. There's no going back now."

Evan left Michaelson next to the ambulance. He felt the other man's disappointment, and his very real fear. Whatever was behind either feeling, it was his to work out, not Evan's. Evan had his own worries to consider.

No, there was no going back now. There was only deciding how he would go forward.

22

New Orders

*Lady Eve Kincaid, taking local command of Nánlù
forces at the request of Lord Governor Hidic,
handed McCarron's Armored Cavalry a Pyrrhic victory today. A Cavalry Hatchetman was destroyed
and several vehicles crippled during McCarron's raid
against the Mau-ti Supply Depot. The depot was also
destroyed.*

—The Nánlù Daily Apple, 14 July 3134

Chang-an
Qinghai Province, Liao
14 July 3134

Ritter Michaelson shifted uncomfortably in the straight-
backed chair, feeling trapped by his own best intentions. It
was certainly not a new sensation. He kept the left side of his
face turned toward Gerald Tsung, hiding behind his scars
while Hahn Soom Gui presented the Conservatory's case to
Governor Pohl's aide.

Tsung's working office certainly fit the man's conservative
style. Spartan. No photos of the family, no diplomas. No letter
of appointment. Golden oak paneling added some character
to the room, but no other art or decorations accented the
space except a simple picture of Governor Anna Lu Pohl
hanging next to the door. It was a room designed not to step
on toes, Michaelson realized. Nothing existed except a
demonstrated loyalty to the Governor herself.

He could appreciate that. This kind of severe existence was how Ezekiel Crow had lived his life. No encumbrances. No reminders of his past, or what he currently risked whenever heading out for battle. Ezekiel Crow had owed his life to The Republic. Anything else—anyone else—was a dream.

And as Ritter Michaelson? Did he owe any less of a debt?

Hahn had been talking about the systematic discrimination used to influence the Conservatory's martial programs. Now he presented the last of his papers, documents rescued from the administration offices. "Here's the proof," the budding politician offered, slapping the pages down on the corner of Tsung's desk like a lawyer might produce damning evidence.

Michaelson had already seen the documents—had helped compile them—and suggested to Hahn that they be the last evidence offered to Tsung. They contained personnel files on every student who applied for permits to hold on-campus demonstrations—Hahn's name near the top of that list—and those who took Capellan History and Culture. Also *loyalty assessments* of any cadet on the aforementioned lists, and cadets who had simply been unfortunate enough to be born to residents and not Republic citizens.

In short, the students had been right in their paranoia.

Evan Kurst had been right, but he was still bound to self-destruct if he continued to take everything upon himself to decide. Michaelson saw so much of his younger self in Evan, so much of what had ruined Daniel Peterson. Maybe that's why it bothered him that he had been unable to reach the younger man.

Tsung gathered the pages up carefully, ordered them into a neat stack in the middle of his desk. Hahn handed over computer records on three data crystals, which Tsung set carefully atop the printouts.

"Governor Pohl will be very interested in these."

Hahn smiled thinly. "As will Legate Ruskoff, I'm sure." The accusation was easy to read in his tone.

Michaelson hedged. "Nothing in those reports, or any, proves a tie to the Legate's office. This looks more like a concerted effort on behalf of mid-ranking officers and a few Conservatory officials to 'purify' the military by controlling recruitment and academic training."

"Still," Hahn intervened, "you can see why we do not trust

Legate Ruskoff to look after our interests. This requires civilian oversight. We need the Governor's personal attention."

Smearing Viktor Ruskoff's reputation accomplished nothing. Michaelson had pointed this out to Hahn, who at least had been willing to listen after the disappointing interview with Evan Kurst. But Hahn was proving just as headstrong. Like Eridani horses taking the bits in their teeth, he and Evan charged forward, each along his own path. Over the last few weeks, Michaelson had watched Hahn fall into a one-sided rivalry with Evan, but hadn't realized how damaging that rivalry could be. Now Hahn seemed determined to open a rift between the Governor and her Planetary Legate in a game of one-upsmanship, if for no other reason. And that was not going to help matters, Michaelson knew very well. It was one of the tactics he himself had used six years before.

3128, when Legate Kang pushed cadets so hard to conform to The Republic mold that Confederation agents had managed to gain a stranglehold on the student body. Kang's knee-jerk reaction cost two students their lives, and eventually cost him his position. Ezekiel Crow prevented a full assault on the Conservatory only by withholding proof of Confederation complicity, and undermining the Legate's authority. It bought time for a political solution. A peaceful solution.

Except that it hadn't worked.

As Crow, all he had truly accomplished was to further alienate the students. Giving them hope, but setting them up to fail.

Best intentions. The paved surface to hell.

And here he was, at it again. Trying to form a new bridge between the students and local government, trapped by his feeling of responsibility.

Gerald Tsung stood, leaning against his desk. "I can assure you," he promised Hahn, Michaelson, "the Governor will give this due attention. What she can do to strengthen your case. . . ." The shrug was heard in his voice.

Hahn stood, shook hands with the Governor's Aide. Michaelson stood as well.

"Thank you for arranging this meeting, Major." Tsung offered another handshake.

Ritter Michaelson accepted it with a nod, and escorted Hahn from the Governor's Palace without a word spoken until they reached the front steps. From the upper balustrade, they looked out over a wide avenue. People crossed between the palace and other buildings of the White Tower District. Everyone hurried, which was due more to the cold winter day than any burning desire to see bureaucracy done. Sections of the wall that cut the governing sector out of the heart of Chang-an could be glimpsed in between tall hedge trees.

Hahn glanced back, taking in the Han-inspired architecture with a satisfied look. "I think we made progress."

"I warned you against that last bit. Legate Ruskoff is a good man."

"Maybe," Hahn admitted carefully. He buttoned up his jacket, slipped on a set of red-tinted aviator glasses. Leading the way down the polished stone steps, he waved for a nearby rickshaw. No civilian cars were allowed inside the walled area, only a few military and government-registered vehicles. Cabs waited for visitors outside the gated entrance. "Maybe," he said again. Then he lapsed into a determined silence, which Michaelson had no intention of breaking into until they were back at the Conservatory.

He himself was never going to get there.

The rickshaw driver was short and stocky. He delivered the two men to the line of cabs, turned, and raced for the corner where a dark sedan waited. Hahn had not been paying attention, but Michaelson was. He climbed out of the rickshaw, tense, and was not reassured in the slightest when the sedan's window hummed down and Jack Farrell nodded a curt greeting.

"Ditch the kid," Farrell said. It was not a request.

The rickshaw driver was gone, having been paid his money earlier and smart enough to know when his presence was not wanted. Hahn bristled at the rude dismissal, but Michaelson laid a hand on the younger man's arm. "It's all right. Take a cab and I'll meet you at the Conservatory."

The sedan smelled of thick cigar smoke. At least it was heated. Michaelson pulled the door closed, but kept one hand on the handle.

"You're a hard man to follow." Farrell put the car in gear and eased away from the curb. Traffic was fairly heavy and they crawled along at the pace of a brisk walk. "Xiapu to Chang-an, all in a few short weeks." He turned far enough to see Michaelson with his one good eye. "You just can't keep your head down, can you?"

Michaelson considered remaining mute, then realized that it would keep him that much longer in the raider's company.

"What do you want, Jack?"

"Time to repay some of Bannson's goodwill," Farrell said. "Not that you've got a choice. Since you're all buddy-buddy with the authorities, you can make certain that a particular DropShip lands unmolested. Just one DropShip. That's it."

One DropShip. Daniel Peterson looked out from the back of Michaelson's mind and shuddered, and refused to shut the door after him. Screams echoed up from the darker recesses of his memory. Screams of terror, and of bloodlust.

And his own screams, as he lifted the bodies of his parents back onto the bed, covered them with a heavy blanket.

"One DropShip?" His voice broke. "More Confederation forces?"

"The Second McCarron's aren't going to take the world by themselves, are they? This is right up your alley. You've even got experience."

"I'm in no position to make that happen. And I wouldn't. Not again."

Farrell glanced over, taking his eye off of traffic for several long seconds. Then he whipped the wheel over and jammed the sedan into some open curbside. Loading Zone, it said. The raider certainly didn't care. He pulled a cigar out and lit it up, taking his time about it. Violence burned not too deeply beneath his calm exterior, Michaelson knew.

"Then you get yourself into a position to make that happen. This is not a request, *Daniel*. It's an order. Straight from the top."

His teeth clenched hard enough to grind enamel. Michaelson—*Michaelson!*—shook his head. "I can't get that close to the action again, Jack. Tell Bannson that. I wouldn't be any good to you if I tried."

The other man snorted. "You're no good to us now. No good to anyone except maybe those kids back at the Conservatory. G'head. Let the locals find out who you are, and watch 'em pull that entire university apart brick by brick. Not even the most die-hard Capellan-lover would stand up to protect you."

Michaelson clenched his eyes shut. He heard traffic coughing by on the street, the stream of citizens and residents who shuffled along the walk with their chatter and packages and errands to perform, and pushed them away as well. He had forfeited his rights to be a part of that world long, long ago. He couldn't even stand for The Republic anymore. Not after Northwind, and Terra. All he had left now was himself.

And Jacob Bannson was collecting the mortgage on that, too.

"Which and when?" he asked, voice no more than a whisper.

Farrell didn't bother to hide the smile in his voice. "July twenty-fourth. By local reckoning, that should be the lunar New Year." The first new moon of Liao's spring. "The ship's an *Overlord* conversion, part of the regular Bannson fleet on loan to MedCross. The *Astral Prize*. Take good care of it."

Michaelson grabbed at the handle, jacked it open and threw his shoulder into the door. "Yeah. I'll take care of it," he promised in a dead voice. He didn't look back at Farrell, not wanting to see that gloating face. He threaded his way through the crowd, hands thrust into his jacket pockets and face pulled tight into a mask.

One DropShip. That's where it had started. It had ended with millions dead, bodies carried in refuse haulers and shoveled into mass graves. The first war of the new century. The death of a golden era.

It had ended with the "suicide" of Daniel Peterson, and the birth of Ezekiel Crow.

Could he do it again? Was it still within him to make that call? And would it be the right choice this time?

His questions led him right back to the White Towers District. His faked military identification got him through the gate and up the long block of administration buildings. His assumed name, still on the list to see Gerald Tsung, bought him a new escort to take him into the palace halls, moving along with a flow of robed nobles with their wide-shouldered mantles and conservative politicians in their suits and long skirts.

Back into Tsung's office, where Tsung was busy reading through every document left by Hahn Soom Gui and marking his own notes into a small noteputer.

Lieutenant Daniel Peterson stood before the Governor's Aide, doing his best to bury both Crow and Michaelson in the back of his mind. Twenty years of doubts and recriminations sloughed away, leaving him with a certainty he hadn't felt in far, far too long.

"I'd like you to get me an interview with Legate Ruskoff," he said with tight, clipped words. "Today."

"May I ask why?"

Daniel pulled himself to attention. "It may be time for me to reenlist."

23

The Dynasty Guard

Citing "Manifest Domain," Prefect Tao landed military forces on Styk to seize control of BattleMech production facilities and a local DropPort. The local militia, under the command of Legate Heivilin, moved to contain the limited occupation, but not challenge it. At this time.
—In the News!, New Aragon Free Press,
14 July 3134

DropShip Grand Sire
Huáng-yù Province, Liao
17 July 3134

The Du-jin Mountains were one of perhaps five places where the *Overlord*-class *Grand Sire* could hide itself. One hundred thirty meters high and nearly ten thousand tons, it seemed to Evan as if someone had dropped a thirty-five-story skyscraper into one of the most remote regions on Liao's northern continent. A gray-painted, egg-shaped *military* skyscraper, proudly bearing the gauntlet-and-sword crest of the Capellan Confederation.

Standing in the pelting sleet, Evan and Mai Uhn Wa had watched the leviathan make planetfall that afternoon. Dropping in tandem with a *Mule* cargo ship to hide in its sensor shadow, the *Overlord* simply split away several dozen kilometers over Huáng-yù Province for its new mountain nesting grounds. It landed on a bright pillar of fusion-driven flame, painful to stare at, burning acres of forest into ash and instantly jumping the local humidity as rain-soaked ground baked under the driveflame kiln.

"This is what you have been waiting for?" Evan had asked then.

Tugging at his wispy beard, Mai Wa nodded slowly. "One of the things I was promised. Perhaps we are favored after all." He would explain no more than that.

Remembering the last time Evan had relied on the elder freedom fighter for much-needed supplies, he accepted the arrival of the Dynasty Guard at face value. They were here, not delayed in some other system, never to arrive. It was a good sign.

Such optimism lasted only until the two men met with the Guard's commander.

Five hours later, the scent of wood smoke and charred greensward still lingered in the humid air. It competed with choking exhaust from diesel-powered vehicles and aviation fuel from the constant VTOL runs to haul supplies and equipment quickly out of the valley. Evan lumbered along in a LoaderMech, a modified construction machine that used viselike grips to move cargo in special cradles affixed with steel flanges. *Sang-shao* Carson Rieves had ordered Evan to work, and one didn't argue with a man who had an elite combined-arms battalion to back him up. Evan relieved one of the Loader drivers and spent two hours walking cargo from DropShip bay to VTOL, staring out through water-beaded ferroglass, biting down on the inside of his cheeks until blood teased his tongue.

He didn't notice Mai Uhn Wa. Not until the man bounced a rock off the yellow-tinted canopy, startling Evan on his return trip to the *Grand Sire*.

"Evan!" Mai called and waved to him, barely able to compete with the LoaderMech's throaty engine noise. He stood next to an enlisted man, gesturing for Evan to cut the motor. To dismount.

Evan set his machine into a wide-legged stance, then throttled down to a coughing idle. Jacking the latch and swinging the door up into the still steady rainfall, he formed a small overhang that allowed him to climb down and stand in relative dryness. The Confederation recruit—a *san-ben-bing*— shoved forward, grabbed hold of the steel rungs, and climbed up into the Loader's cab.

Evan stumbled out from under the large machine before being crushed underfoot. "I guess that means I'm relieved?" he asked Mai.

Mai Uhn Wa's leathery face was wrinkled in distaste. He gestured back to the DropShip, started the damp walk toward the ramp that had been extended down from the *Overlord*'s main cargo bay. "It means we are dismissed. *Sang-shao* Rieves has tired of my constant arguments."

They waited as a new BattleMech—a *Targe* this time— filled the ramp's entrance and then stomped its way down. Painted a deep maroon, the Dynasty Guard 'Mech was trimmed in greenish gold and black. It also bore the Confederation crest proudly on its right breast. A muddied path chewed up by the heavily shod feet of seven 'Mechs before it made an easy course to follow. It throttled into an easy walk, eating five meters in a stride.

"No swaying him?" Evan asked.

He had to repeat himself, louder, as a pair of Garrot Super-Heavy Transports thundered over a nearby rise. A Garrot wasn't much more than a flying cradle with pairs of crablike arms extending down from three points along its body. Mai and Evan watched as the VTOLs each picked out a parked vehicle and then hunkered down over it, getting a thumbs-up from ground crew and clamping down with the cradle arms to secure the tank. A great roar of raw power and the sky-cranes lifted off with their burdens, ferrying the armored vehicles in the same direction taken by the *Targe*.

"Not yet," Mai finally answered when they could hear themselves think again. "He seems to be holding us responsible for the damage his unit took on Gan Singh. He will release nothing until his unit is up to full operational strength, with on-planet resources confirmed."

"Then why not just let us leave?" Evan glanced back at their Lamprey transport, grounded just beyond the active loading zone, looking very weak and small compared to the Garrot VTOLs.

"Operational security, perhaps. Didn't want to let us fly out of the mountains too soon, in case we were spotted and backtracked." Mai glanced around. "Also I believe he was waiting for someone to arrive on that *Sprint* that came in. I missed their meeting, but not the enlisted men's free talk. Someone who was on the *Mule* they followed down. Helping to coordinate."

Evan rubbed his hands against his damp fatigues, letting his interest in the landing maneuver overshadow his desire to simply be away. Far away. "Anything more on the *Mule*?" Whoever it was in the civilian cargo vessel, they were certainly more than closet supporters of the Confederation. Both Evan and Mai Uhn Wa evidenced interest in finding out who, and whether or not they were an asset that could benefit the local pro-Capellan struggle.

"No. *Sang-shao* Rieves is being most obstinate." Mai glanced over at his former student, now his partner in the unsteady alliance between rebels and cadets, and McCarron's Second. "I am sorry for this, Evan. I know how badly the Conservatory needed these supplies."

Evan could not justly refuse the elder man something. "Not as badly as we would need them if you had not struck a deal with the Armored Cavalry," he offered. As bridges went, it wasn't the most steady, but it was a start. He had known even before his conversation with Ritter Michaelson that his destiny and Mai's were inexorably tied together. The major, without meaning to, had merely pushed Evan into accepting it a little faster.

Until Mai Uhn Wa and the *Ijori Dè Guāng*, he had never truly felt at home.

They set foot on the ramp's nonskid, leaning into the five-story climb to its top. *Sang-shao* Carson Rieves waited at the head of the ramp. He still cut quite the figure. In his Confederation uniform, blue gray trousers and a mandarin-collared tunic trimmed in Capellan green, a *dao* sword slung down by his left hip, he stood arrogantly with one foot up on the ramp's lower rail. His Han-influenced helmet shed the rain onto his shoulders. Beneath the brim, his eyes were two black pits, supervising all in his domain. Evan felt the back of his neck warm with a guilty flush, and dried his palms again.

Mai Uhn Wa bowed politely. "We salute the Dynasty Guard's strength, *Sang-shao* Rieves. If you are determined to refuse us the Chancellor's promise, then we must soon depart. We will have a great deal more work to accomplish."

"Waving placards and painting graffiti." Carson Rieves's smile was not a pleasant one. "If you can distract the garrison at LianChang with your rabble-rousing, you will have done the Confederation a mild service, Wa."

Evan tensed. "We do what we can." Belatedly, prompted by Mai's glance, he added, "Sir."

"Well, your work has been adequate this day at least." The commander's gaze followed a Loader down the ramp, the machine carrying boxes of munitions and mines to the loading area. Evan steeled himself for any following accusation, and the consequences. "I will allow you to select a crate of weapons and another of ammunition."

And by his standards, no doubt considered himself generous. Evan bit off a hot reply. Angering the senior Confederation officer on Liao any further would not be wise.

"It is our hope to work with you again, *Sang-shao* Rieves." Mai was not ready to give up, especially spying a potential crack in the other man's armor. "As we have proved with the Armored Cavalry, our network of informants and guides, and the military forces controlled by the students as well, can be a welcome addition to any order of battle." He hesitated. "The Light of Ijori grows ever stronger."

The commander glanced back into the DropShip. "Yes. I have been made aware of your ambitions. But I do not see a Warrior House yet, Chancellor's word or no. If I have use for local support, I will demand it as needed. And you shall provide it. That is the way of things, is it not?"

Mai Uhn Wa stiffened, but the gray bearded man nodded nonetheless. "I am a traitor," he intoned with obvious disgrace. "I serve the Confederation."

"We will see that you do."

Evan was faster than his *sifu*. "We?" *Sang-shao* Rieves did not seem the type to use the royal possessive. Confederation nobles might take exception to a military officer putting on airs.

The officer nodded. "Certainly. I am not sending you away with merely a few assault weapons. I have one further delivery to make." He glanced into the bay again. "I believe you know each other?"

Evan saw Mai hesitate, shoulders slumping every so slightly as if he suddenly carried a much heavier burden. He knew. Even before he turned, Evan knew.

"Mai Uhn Wa." The man's greeting was cold and empty. Beneath his robed mantle he wore a basic gray uniform, the mandarin collar closed with a silver clasp in the form of the Capellan Confederation's crest. His eyes were grayish blue, and stared ahead without blinking.

Even though he had never known one before, Evan did not

need a uniform patch or identification to know a Maskirovka agent.

"*Nĭ-hăo*, Michael Yung-Te." Mai Uhn Wa's greeting was formal, but hardly any warmer.

"You do not ask my purpose?"

"I do not believe in coincidence. I assume you are here to check up on me."

Evan could only grab at the unspoken conversation occurring between these two men, and it left him feeling more nervous than before. A Mask agent sniffing around. The only thing worse—

"I am assigned to you," Yung-Te said. "To you, and your motley, paramilitary group. For the good of the State, Mai Uhn Wa."

Sang-shao Rieves smiled thin and hard. "Welcome home."

An enlisted man carried Agent Yung-Te's gear, stored in a proper military duffel, and others were quickly sent by *Sang-shao* Rieves to load his gift of two crates. Mai deferred to Evan, who knew the needs of the Conservatory better, and Evan chose infantry SRM launchers and inferno rounds. The men were sent on ahead to properly store the crates inside the Lamprey's transport area.

Dismissed from Carson Rieves's presence, they had only a short hike back down the ramp and across the muddy fields. Evan did not wait long, barely away from the DropShip ramp before he asked, "Warrior House?"

"We can discuss that later, Evan."

Evan stopped walking, ignoring the frustration of Yung-Te who clearly wanted to hurry to the Lamprey, but was not about to leave the two alone for a private conversation. "More secrets, Mai Uhn Wa? You wanted me to trust you again."

The elder warrior nodded. "Yes, and I have withheld nothing that would have meant anything to you." He took his former student by the arm and pulled him along. "There *was* more to my forming the *Ijori Dè Guāng* than a simple resistance organization," he admitted. "And you would have been informed of those plans, *in time*."

The Lamprey was only a few dozen meters away. Evan saw that one of the munitions crates had yet to be loaded. He stopped again. "We are not always given time, Mai Uhn Wa. Perhaps you should tell me now."

"On the flight, Evan." The elder man glanced up into the freezing rain. "Where we can at least be dry, *qǐng*?"

"And fiction often helps pass the time," Yung-Te said sourly.

Michael Yung-Te would obviously take some getting used to. Evan wrestled with his feelings about having a Confederation agent always looking over his shoulder, and the potential difficulties it raised in his own plans. Maskirovka were trained to ferret out secrets. Evan still had several.

Some more pressing than others.

But he had dragged his feet long enough. His obvious hesitation was beginning to draw confused looks from Mai Uhn Wa and irritation from the Mask. Irritation that quickly turned to concern, seeing the full VTOL payload with hardly any room for the passengers to squeeze inside.

"Where?" Yung-Te began, holding them up outside the main door. Then his cold eyes fell on Evan. "You stole these supplies."

Evan slapped the side of the forward cabin, twirled one hand in the air as he gestured to the pilot to crank up the rotors and get them airborne quickly. "I was ordered to assist in loading cargo carriers. No one told me to restrict that to the Guards' VTOLs."

The Lamprey's engine coughed to life, rolled over, and began a staccato rattle that quickly smoothed into a deep thunder. Mai Uhn Wa stared at his student with an expression caught between respect and concern for Evan's safety. But so far as Evan was concerned, the only thing worse than ruffling the Maskirovka's feathers would be to stand up under a militia assault without enough equipment.

"Missiles. Actuators. Fa Shih battlesuits." Yung-Te inventoried the crate stencils he could easily read. "You took Fa Shih suits? *Sang-shao* Rieves will not look kindly on this theft."

"Maybe not," Evan admitted. He had to shout to make himself heard over the choppy rotor blast. He slipped past the Mask agent, climbed into the VTOL and crouched at the edge of the sliding door. "Would you like to go tell him? I'm certain you can catch the next transport Rieves sends to Chang-an."

Mai Uhn Wa looked to the agent, shrugged, and climbed into the helicopter transport as well. He coughed long and hard, and then said quickly behind his cupped hand, "You play a dangerous game, Evan. Do not underestimate this man." He then distanced himself from the Conservatory cadet, as if Evan's minor theft did not touch upon him as well.

Evan licked his lips, returned the agent's distracted gaze with one of his own. "In or out, sir. We can't wait much longer."

Michael Yung-Te smiled. It wasn't exactly a gesture of respect, but close. A gamesman's smile, conceding the coin toss, if not an opening move well played. "We are not through, you and I," he promised. With a final look of apprehension at the secured barrels and crates, he jumped up as the VTOL lifted off the ground.

Evan simply rolled the heavy door shut.

"Welcome to Liao."

24

Dropped Ship

Mercenary forces in Capellan employ have struck at Buchlau and are being used to support "Styk Independence" as well as several other world campaigns. We consider this a positive sign that the Confederation may be running short on troops. If this is so, it should not take much more to dislodge them.
—Lord Governor Marion Hidic, Liao, 20 July 3134

LianChang Military Reserve
Qinghai Province, Liao
24 July 3134

His name was Daniel Peterson.

He was born October 7, 3089 in the Chang-an suburb of SuiCha to proud citizens Michael and Celia Peterson. His entire life, Daniel studied the confusion around him as Capellan residents and Republic citizens struggled with who they were—and to whom the world of Liao truly belonged—with either side rarely at peace. It was a question with no answer, or so Daniel thought then.

He attended the Conservatory for his academy years, courting a local girl during his senior year, though they decided not to marry before graduation. His appointment as a lieutenant serving the Liao militia kept him home and gave them a chance to proceed slowly.

Then an alumni of his alma mater, Conservatory Class of

3097, approached him on "a delicate matter." And going slowly was no longer an option.

Now Daniel Peterson had returned to the LianChang Military Reserve—still in his guise as Major Ritter Michaelson—to watch history repeat itself. Legate Ruskoff had appointed him a senior aide for the intelligence he'd volunteered on the Bannson Universal vessel and for his supposed experience as a major in the Hastati Sentinels.

A nervous cup of coffee held in a trembling hand, Daniel sipped the hot beverage without tasting it as he followed in the Legate's wake. Ruskoff was always moving, always checking and rechecking what workstation computers and on-duty personnel told him. The Planetary Defense Center was located two levels underground beneath a low, bunker-style building of gray ferrocrete. Daniel doubted the PDC, normally manned with a skeleton crew, had seen anything less than full duty schedules over the past month.

Tonight was even worse as Ruskoff ordered backups to stand ready and admitted several political liaisons, most of whom crowded the back wall and tried to stay out of the way. Lady Eve Kincaid waited among them, present for her own purposes as well as to represent Lord Governor Hidic at his direct request.

There was also Gerald Tsung, always ready with another question. "The *Astral Prize*. It is still off course and refusing communication?"

Daniel shuffled aside as the Legate's junior aide, Lieutenant Nguyen, brought Ruskoff a noteputer with the latest reports from the Lianyungang DropPort Authority. The Legate looked a question at his aide, who shook his head. "Nothing," the lieutenant said. "No expected arrival. No JumpShip passage."

"Tracking?" Ruskoff growled.

"Sir." A captain at a nearby console. "The *Astral Prize* is still over the western oceans at six kilometers elevation. They will be over Beilù in five minutes on final approach, passing directly over Chang-an and then the Reserve fifteen minutes later. It looks like they're heading for the eastern DropPort of Hussan, and that will still take a serious course correction."

"There is your answer, Mr. Tsung. Chang-an is restricted airspace and we do not allow civilian flights over LianChang either. All indications are that this is an attack run."

"From six kilometers up?"

Lady Kincaid volunteered that answer. "If you are launching aerospace fighters and BattleMechs in drop packs, yes."

A different approach this time. Daniel Peterson thought back to 3111, when the *Overlord* had landed. One DropShip. That was what the cabal had promised. Look the other way for five minutes. Daniel had envisioned a single battalion landing to honorably challenge the standing militia. The citizens and Capellan residents would finally know to whom Liao belonged.

But the Capellans had double berthed—maybe even triple berthed—the vessel. Confederation troops came marching out, rank upon rank, forming up into organized death squads and moving on Chang-an. So many. . . . There would be no even matching of forces, no cathartic moment for Liao. The Confederation brought more than enough to smash the local militia. Then everything fell apart as the fires spread and the death toll rose.

The cabal had been "most pleased" with Daniel Peterson. They had paid him a bonus of one Republic bill for every dead citizen.

"One DropShip," Daniel whispered aloud. "That is where it starts."

He hadn't meant to be overheard, but Lady Kincaid caught it. "And you are certain that this is the one?"

Daniel nodded vacantly, his eyes on a nearby panel that showed the incoming DropShip as a small, green blip on the screen. "Bannson Universal. January Twenty-fourth. *Astral Prize*." He recited the data mechanically.

"But how do *you* know?" Tsung asked.

Careful. "Because the Second McCarron's Armored Cavalry knows, the *Ijori Dè Guāng* knows, and the student militia at the Conservatory knows. They are expecting the Dynasty Guard to support the Confederation's drive to take Liao." That much was true. He turned the ruined side of his face toward Tsung. "This is the vessel I was warned about." Also true, if from another source.

A comms technician interrupted with a stuttering, "Sir . . . sir! Our pilots are about to make another high-speed pass."

Aerospace fighters. TR-10 *Transits*. Ruskoff had dispatched a full wing of the fighters—Beilù's full contingent. Their first pass moments before had been at supersonic speeds, shaking the DropShip with their sonic wake. No response.

"Tell them to proceed," Ruskoff ordered, voice tight.

Another technician waved Lieutenant Nguyen over, quickly handing him a headset. Daniel watched with growing apprehension, waiting for the chaos always certain in a military operation to erupt. Nguyen turned to Ruskoff. "Drop-Ship *Astral Prize* is contacting Lianyungang! Civilian frequencies. Sporadic contact. They report minor electronics failure due to damage, and say they are being chased by Confederation fighter craft."

"Our fighters," Daniel voiced first. "They are talking about our fighters. Trying to buy time."

Ruskoff wasn't playing. "Find that frequency and order them back into orbit, and prepare to be boarded for inspection. Or get them on our channels. Partial comms failure, my ass."

"They are ignoring our calls," a tech reported seconds later, "or cannot receive them."

"If they can reach Lianyungang, they can hear us." Ruskoff glanced over at Daniel. "Major. Is all this keeping with what you expected?"

Play by play, so similar to the night of the Massacre. The Night of Screams. "Only the beginning," Daniel said, just as the Tracking Station reported that the DropShip was now off the ocean and over Beilù's coastal range. Elevation, four kilometers. Time to Chang-an, fifteen minutes.

Tsung still looked unconvinced. "This *is* one of the vessels on the list of those lent to MedCross activities on Gan Singh."

Ruskoff backed up his new aide. "Then it should be on Gan Singh, not sneaking into the Liao system from a nonstandard jump point under communications blackout. The *Astral Prize* is a merchant-converted *Fortress*. Six thousand tons, and originally capable of transporting a mixed-arms battalion. I will *not* allow that vessel to overfly Chang-an or LianChang."

"God help you if you're wrong," Tsung argued back.

The Governor's Aide almost did not get to finish his statement, though, as several workstations erupted in a buzz of excited conversation. "Legate. Aerospace fighters report taking fire from the DropShip. *Astral Prize* has opened up with weapons."

"Legate Ruskoff! Liao Defense Wing requesting permission to go weapons-free."

"Legate. Legate!" Lieutenant Nguyen, now taking over the workstation that kept LianChang in touch with local Drop-Port Authority. "DropShip *Astral Prize* reports that it has opened fire on Confederation fighter craft. They are pleading for help . . . on civilian channels."

"We just . . . *Zāo gāo!* We just lost two fighters. Two down, that's *two* down."

So fast? Even if the merchant-converted DropShip had re-mounted many of its old weapons, Daniel would have expected a longer fight out of the *Transits*. But aerospace control answered that in the next breath.

"One may have clipped the second, sir. Midair collision. Other four are outside of the *Fortress's* reach now, but circling back around."

"Position unchanged. DropShip, twelve minutes—one, two—from Chang-an."

Legate Ruskoff glanced at Tsung and then Kincaid. So did Daniel. He read a similar conviction on both faces. The Legate nodded. "Weapons-free," he ordered calmly. "Force down that DropShip. And get me comms on that civilian channel and our fighters' channel both."

It took only a few seconds for a tech to route the different frequencies into a common broadcast, with the aerospace pilot chatter bleeding through first in a wash of static.

"Bravo-one, I have good tone. Firing."

"DropShip continues to track us with lasers. Some are firing blindly as if—"

"Lifeboat! Lifeboat! One lifeboat away, dropping fast at four o'clock low."

The *Astral Prize's* broadcast was much fainter, but full of desperation. "Lianyungang, please respond. We are taking heavy fire, power systems failing, guidance . . . we are ordering passengers and crew to abandon this vessel. Please respond. We are suffering under heavy attack. . . ." The message repeated itself in a variety of different ways. DropPort Authority tried several times to interrupt their pleading, but the *Astral Prize* could not—or would not—acknowledge.

And then, suddenly, a burst of white static and silence. Daniel counted six heartbeats pounding at the wall of his chest.

"DropShip is tumbling," one of the fighter pilots finally broke back in. Her voice was soft, almost casual. "DropShip is out of control, heading down. Breaking off attack runs." No one inside the PDC spoke, everyone straining to hear the next report. "DropShip has impacted. Minimal fire. Survivors possible . . . but not probable. Two lifeboats on course toward Chang-an, we are riding guard."

Ruskoff nodded at the tech, and cut a hand over his throat. Comms were silenced and an adrenaline slump washed over the entire room. Daniel tried to imagine what a *Fortress*-class vessel looked like, broken and scattered over however many kilometers. How many crew? How many military? Better this way than striking at Chang-an.

"Get our security squads on site," the Legate ordered. "Lieutenant Nguyen, bring me news once we have on-site verification that no military forces managed to deploy. Mr. Tsung. Lady Kincaid." He gathered Michaelson in with a nod, and the four of them left the room as a team, a sense of solidarity between military and government that lasted four paces into the brightly lit and empty corridor.

"Governor Lu Pohl expects me to call in with a report," Tsung said then. "I will use your adjutant's office."

"I should inform the Lord Governor as well," Kincaid agreed.

Ruskoff shrugged. "Join us when you can." He led Daniel farther along the tiled hall, into his private retreat at the PDC. A well-appointed office, cold and indifferent with lack of use, but Daniel knew that would change as the Confederation pushed harder for Liao.

The Legate did not ask and forgot Daniel's aversion to drinking, pouring them brandies at a small cupboard bar kept to the left of his desk. He set one on the desk corner, next to a visitor's chair. He cradled his own in a large hand, swirled it around, and then sipped at the smoky liquid. "They truly thought they could run that play again. They think we do not learn from our mistakes?"

Daniel sat stiffly in the offered chair. He didn't so much as sniff the elegant liquor. The thought of the cabal's laughter still haunted him. *To the Betrayer of Liao. . . .*

"Some of us do not learn," he spoke without meaning to, thinking of his own mistakes.

"Speaking from personal experience?" Ruskoff asked, settling back into his high-back executive chair with a creak of leather and a sigh of pleasure as the brandy burned down his throat. "Well, I hope that I do. The only thing worse than suffering the consequences of the same mistake twice . . . is when others suffer in your place."

Startled, Daniel nearly elbowed the brandy glass off the corner of Ruskoff's desk. "Officers are often put in that position," he said, speaking through a tight throat and a tongue suddenly grown thick. "Now it sounds like you are speaking from personal experience."

"I don't think you were on planet," Ruskoff glanced around his empty desk, as if he'd just mislaid Ritter Michaelson's service record. "I was Senior Colonel for Beilù, and you must have been with the Tenth Hastati four . . . no, five years ago." Daniel said nothing. "That was when the Conservatory had its first uprising."

"Second."

Ruskoff blinked. "Sorry, Major?"

Daniel pushed the brandy snifter away from him. "My apologies, Legate. I did not mean to interrupt. I only recently learned that 3128 was the Conservatory's second student uprising." And he told Ruskoff the same story Evan Kurst had relayed to him. Daniel wasn't sure why he did, but it seemed that the Legate would benefit from knowing. It also prevented him from lying again, as he *had* been here for the student troubles in 3128. Or, at least, Ezekiel Crow had.

"Is that true?"

"I looked it up. Wasn't easy," Daniel admitted, "but the event is documented if you know where to look."

"We haven't done well here on Liao. Not as well as Devlin Stone would hope." Viktor Ruskoff finished his brandy, set the glass on his desk. "I've been wondering if it's too late to fix things. Wondering if I'm going to end up like Kang Lo Den."

Legate Kang. The man had suffered every commander's nightmare during the uprising of 3128, bringing force against a civilian target. But he let the situation get out of hand, applying a military solution before diplomatic possibilities were exhausted. During a "show of force," a cadet crew rammed their Pegasus into a militia Joust, trying to keep it from breaking through the wall onto Conservatory grounds. A Schmitt went weapons-free and blasted the smaller vehicle into burning scrap.

The affair played so badly in The Republic media, in no small part because Daniel (as Ezekiel Crow) withheld evidence of Confederation involvement, that Kang was later "encouraged" to resign. That was the price of peace. And Kang *had* acted with inappropriate force. Daniel said so out loud.

Ruskoff winced. "Except Kang never did give an order to use force against the Conservatory."

"How do you know that?"

"Because I talked him out of it. Kang wanted to use quick and decisive force, and I suggested a token display of strength to give the students something to think on. I didn't think their heart was truly up for a fight. They acted out under pressure, not out of malicious intent."

Do not be so certain of that, Daniel wanted to say, but didn't. There was definitely Confederation involvement, though never enough to convict, only to convince. Maybe he should have brought it all out into the open. Maybe *that* was the time for an open and frank confrontation between Republic and Capellan interests.

"So Kang was innocent?" he asked.

"No, he was guilty of the charges admitted to. Kang's only error was trusting the show of strength to Major Thom Greggs, a die-hard citizen who reviled Capellan ways. Thom was court-martialed for disobeying orders and using excessive force. I believe he was allowed to resign without pension rather than face imprisonment."

Daniel cast back for the final decision on Legate Kang. Crow had already left Liao, moving on to a new assignment, but, "Kang admitted to authorizing the use of force," he said, thinking aloud. Then, "No. He took responsibility for the men under his command and their actions." That wasn't quite the same thing, though it had played so in the public spotlight. Amazing what a simple turn of phrase could do to you, and to your memory of events.

Ruskoff nodded. "He took the brunt of responsibility. My name never came up in the scandal, and I was confirmed as the new Legate six months later."

And had worried ever since that his inaction, his counsel for caution, was a root cause of the entire conflagration. Daniel wanted to tell him that it wasn't. But he couldn't. Ezekiel Crow was dead, and that was where the Black Paladin had to remain.

It was a decision barely made when a sharp knock rattled

the office door and both Lieutenant Nguyen and Gerald
Tsung entered behind it. Tsung looked ashen faced, walking
with his arms held stiffly down at his sides as if he did not
know what to do with them. Nguyen carried his noteputer in
two hands, almost afraid he would drop it. Ruskoff sat forward sharply, as concern took over.

"What? Did the Dynasty Guard land forces before the
crash?" He sounded prepared to mobilize the entire military
reserve on a moment's notice, ready to defend Chang-an.

"No, sir." Nguyen hovered between door and desk, then
stepped forward to place the noteputer in Ruskoff's outstretched hand. "No Dynasty Guard forces."

"Well, who then?" Ruskoff snapped out, pressing his thumb
over the verifax reader and opening the report. His eyes remained on his junior aide who obviously had the news already.

"No one. Legate, it's already on the news channels. Video
journalists arrived at the same time as our security team, and
the lifeboat occupants are in Chang-an under MedCross protection." He was beginning to ramble off topic.

Tsung stepped in. "There were no military forces," he said.
"It *was* a MedCross vessel, Legate. We downed a civilian craft,
bringing refugees from Gan Singh. Capellan refugees. Displaced *residents*."

No one in the office spoke. Daniel tried, several times, but
always fell back into a downward spiral of chasing thoughts,
trying to see how his information could have been so off-
target. No! This could . . . not . . . be.

He must have whispered it aloud. Tsung nodded. "It is, and
worse," the Governor's Aide promised. "People are storming
the capital's streets." He looked sick.

"Chang-an is in flames."

Pelago Estates
St. Andre
Prefecture V, Republic of the Sphere

Sitting in his library, the lights dimmed so that only the spot
pointed at his desk provided any real illumination, Jacob
Bannson watched the clock tick down toward the bottom half
of the hour—the final moment, when not even Republic caution could save the doomed *Astral Prize*. If she wasn't dead al-

ready, scuttling charges would blow. Enough prefabricated evidence would be left behind to point at The Republic militia.
Ritter Michaelson's report, made to the local authorities days
before, sealed the verdict. It never truly mattered what *was*,
but only what the public believed.

Perception was a tool of the mind. And Jacob Bannson was
a master in wielding it.

Three . . . two . . . one . . . time.

Bannson raised his glass, wine glowing red as blood inside
perfect crystal, and toasted the memory of Ezekiel Crow with
a satisfied laugh. "*Ad infinitum, perdere travus.*"

Through infinity, walk in perdition.

25

New Year Resolution

*One of the dedicated JumpShip couriers that links
Genoa and Liao took weapons fire this morning. The
vessel was forced to flee the Liao system by hot-loading
its drive. Damage to the vessel is described as "minimal." There is no official word yet as to what prompted
pro-Capellan nationals to seize the local Recharge Station. Genoa's Legate Gryzick has suspended civilian
traffic to Liao until a root cause is determined.*
—The Republic Voice, Morning Issue, Genoa,
25 July 3134

Chang-an
Qinghai Province, Liao
25 July 3134

And so began the New Year's Riot.

Shouts and the distant wail of sirens hung over Chang-an
like a roar of bloodthirsty approval celebrating ancient blood
sport games. A pall of dark, sooty smoke ruined the morning's
blue sky, and gray ash continued to drift down into the streets
from fires started the night before in another commercial district. Ash scattered into the gutter, forming small drifts that
people kicked through as they stormed the streets, looking for
vengeance, for justice, or just for opportunity.

Mai Uhn Wa waved his Hahnstock gyrojet pistol in the air,
signaling a cadre of freedom fighters toward another nearby
delivery van—this one with flat tires and a smashed-in wind-

shield. *Ijori Dè Guāng* members jostled through a stream of looters more worried about carting video equipment from a nearby appliance store than they were of heavily armed men on the streets. A few local thugs were dragooned at gunpoint. Two men with SRM shoulder launchers stayed on guard while rifles were slung and pistols holstered. Two dozen hands seized the vehicle, rocking it back and forth, building momentum for the huge *push* that rolled it over with a metallic crash and more broken glass.

"Get it into the intersection, up against the first one," Mai commanded. "*Xiàn-zài.* Now." Staccato reports echoing in the distance might be automatic weapons fire, might be simple strings of firecrackers. He would take no chances.

Metal slid easily against the blacktop. They jockeyed the van into position to form one half of a two-vehicle roadblock. Nothing that would hold against rioting crowds, but enough to provide the irregulars cover against any of the urban assault vehicles that cruised through the city.

What began as a gut reaction to the *Astral Prize* incident—Capellan residents striking out in fury over the loss of so many innocent lives—had escalated quickly when police and local militia attempted to enforce order. These were people already under a great deal of stress. Once the lid came off, years of resentment boiled forth like water from a bursting dam. Within hours of the DropShip crash, most of Chang-an had fallen into the hands of a mob.

Mai Wa had been quick to take advantage of the chaos, and the militia's lack of preparation. In this environment, a small force could accomplish a great deal of damage. Several streets back along their route a pair of Ranger VV1's burned, the result of an ambush staged out of doorways and storefront windows. Inferno rounds layered them in fiery gelatin, melting tires and cooking off the ammo. A Demon had lasted only long enough for an *Ijori Dè Guāng* member to get close with a sticky-bomb—a stick of tetraglycerin in a small burlap bag, slathered in axle grease and a twenty-second fuse burning in one end. Slapped against the forward cab, it caved in the entire side.

One more vehicle taken for the cause.

Whit Greggor jogged over, SRM launcher cradled against his shoulder and balanced with only one arm. "Runners say something's heading our way," the large man told him.

"Something." Mai Wa shook his head, adjusted his armored vest. The body armor already felt heavy. "That is informative."

But what could he expect from civilian conscripts? Mai Wa's organized assault on the Rangers had gathered him an instant army as rioters flocked toward anything that smacked of organized resistance. These people spent freely of their frustration, banked during their years of outrage and shame. Not interested in looting for their own gain, but ready—finally—to take back some pride, and their world. Such fury burned itself out quickly, though. Two days. Maybe three.

Longer, if Mai Wa kept the level of fury escalated through attacks such as these.

More runners from the west—people Mai had spread out to warn him of incoming trouble. All had the same thing to say: a vehicle, moving fast, returning fire only when challenged directly. This trickle of manpower and some rioters gathering behind the makeshift barrier gave Mai resources to work with.

"Greggor, set up behind the blockade. You and Phelps, standard loads, no inferno." Too many people running loose here. He didn't need to start a crematorium and turn the crowd against *him*. He tolled off a handful of civilians, sent them to gather others and keep the two nearby streets plugged up with live bodies, making a dead-end courtyard out of the intersection. "The militia won't power through." He was guessing. "They'll turn and run first."

And it was all he had time for, as a shout of "Tank!" and "Pegasus!" warned him of the hovercraft's arrival.

"I want it taken," Mai shouted for the benefit of his people. He coughed, clearing the taste of ash that clawed at the back of his throat. "When it brakes for the turn, swarm round it!"

The armored scout craft was painted white and gold, and bore the Roman profile crest common to the Principes Guards. Racing into the intersection from the western street, it turned a tight one-eighty spin and used its drive fan to powerstop rather than mow through the rioters and looters. People in the east-facing street were blown off their feet by the sudden zephyr.

The Pegasus would be vulnerable only for a few seconds. "Now, now, now!" Mai shouted. "*Xiàn-zài! Xiàn-zài!*" His small military team raced forward under the cover of rioters who threw paving stones and bottles—some filled with gasoline, bursting into a spread of flames that might scorch the hovercraft's paint, but could do no lasting damage.

Showing disciplined restraint, the Pegasus crew did not use its twin SRM launchers to drive the crowd back. Such carnage would only fuel the mob. The gunner used the nose-mounted laser to spray a few warning swarms of emerald fire at the feet of the onrushing crowd. One of the rifle-toting irregulars went down with a savaged knee joint—more by accident than any clear intention of the gunner. Someone picked up the rifle and began firing it at the ferroglass cockpit, popping off small bursts of two or three rounds at a time.

The crew had had enough, and the Pegasus fishtailed around in search of an escape path. It pushed forward, driving over two civilians who stood in the way. With a buzzing growl like a lawnmower running over a stick hidden in tall grass, the Pegasus's lift fans sucked the bodies into their blades and chewed them into grisly pieces. A spray of red splashed over the black asphalt.

But the *Ijori Dè Guāng* crew, coming in from the sides as they'd been taught—taught well, Mai noticed with no small amount of personal pride in Evan's accomplishment—grabbed at vents and grills or leapt up for a full-body grab on the vehicle's sloped side. The Pegasus spun madly, throwing several of them back off as it cookie-cut a path closer and closer to the impromptu barricade.

Greggor stepped around one side, took aim and waited for the launcher he held to acquire lock. Thumbing the activation stud, he sent one missile directly into the back of the hover-craft, damaging the steering vanes.

The Pegasus looped into a wide curve, slammed nose first against the side of the barricade, and stalled for several painful seconds.

Enough time for a freedom fighter to plant a small sticky-bomb on the crew hatch, light it and scurry back behind the swinging turret. Mai heard the loud *pop*. Two men wrestled the hatch open and another sprayed the inside with flechettes from a needler. The *Ijori Dè Guāng* began pulling wounded men from the vehicle, passing them to waiting hands.

Several rebels had vehicle training. Mai pointed out two of them. "Get that hovercraft back to the Conservatory. Watch yourselves at the gate. Go."

He readjusted his armored vest again, appointed another

man to command the intersection, and then led his diminishing team further into Chang-an. A new street. New recruits. More mayhem to spread on the back of the mob's rage.

Eventually, Legate Ruskoff would order in BattleMechs and massed infantry to quell the disturbances. Most of the in-city forces were currently gathered around the capital buildings, but they would be released when the Governor assured herself that no organized force threatened her position. Mai certainly planned to avoid the White Towers District. He recognized the limitations of what he had to work with.

"Yet look at what we have accomplished," he said aloud, then coughed again. It made him wonder. How much more would the Confederation regiments on Liao gain this day? The next?

"And how long before the militia comes for us?"

Because they would have to, Mai knew. The Conservatory could not be allowed to stand in rebellion for much longer. Not after this day.

The sky darkened, dusk turned to artificial twilight as a gray haze thickened over the suburbs of Yiling. Still dressed in MechWarrior togs, Evan Kurst pulled the motorpool jeep over the curb and parked on the grass outside of Bartoe Hall, Jenna's dormitory. His joints were stiff and muscles tired from several hours in the hot seat, patrolling the southern approaches in case Legate Ruskoff took it upon himself to bring the Conservatory to heel under the cover of today's confusion. But he'd seen nothing more threatening than a Joust, and that was a defecting crew coming in to add their support to the students' local resistance.

On-campus defenders had been kept far busier. From the front of the dormitory Evan looked between an administration wing and one of the lecture halls, out toward the western gate. An M1 Marksman had forced its way through, deciding that the unrest in Yiling was especially brutal because of the Conservatory's closeness. Calling on other Republic loyalists to rally, it made the first attempt to penetrate the grounds.

Its corpse continued to smoke, even now. The taste of burnt fuel oil hung heavy in the air, and left a slick grime coating Evan's teeth and tongue. Two sharp reports made him glance into the sky, thinking of artillery fire. Colorful red and blue chrysanthemums blossomed and melted over Yiling.

New Year's fireworks. That was all.

Evan took the inside stairwell three steps at a time, pushing his tired muscles as he forced his way up to the fourth floor. Jenna had a north-facing room at the end of the building, the better to accommodate a late sleeper. Other female cadets sat outside their rooms, talking about the riots, the resistance. Most wore infantry and tank crew fatigues. Evan traded sketchy salutes with Tori Yngstram, another MechWarrior cadet.

Tori glanced down the hall and nodded at an open door. "She's there."

Evan slowed his pace, a load of worries dropping away. One of the reports he'd picked up was that Jen Lynn Tang had not appeared for her patrol, and her backup had been called in to take her place in the *Locust*. With sporadic fighting on the grounds, the chance that she'd gotten caught off-campus by the riots, or the very real possibility that, like Mark Lo, she had finally opted out of the fight, Evan had not known what to believe. But she was here. She was safe.

She was standing at her window, drapes ripped away and left in a pile against the wall. Jenna wore regular fatigue pants and a sports bra. A padded jacket lay draped over the chair at her desk, stained and grimy and crusted along one sleeve with dried blood. She heard Evan enter the room, but did not look back.

"Franklin Delaray," she said, catching Evan rubbing flakes of dried blood between his fingers. He had picked it off the jacket sleeve. "I was coming back inside the walls—went out to check our forward posts—and a pair of Condors hit the main entrance right behind me. Franklin was in a Regulator II. It took a savage beating, but he refused to back off. A *Pack Hunter* showed up, then a *Jessie*. They drove the Condors off."

Evan said nothing. Waiting her out.

"Franklin was hurt," Jenna continued. Finally, she turned away from the window, stepped to one side of the glass and leaned against the wall. "Missile shrapnel penetrated the Regulator's hatch. We pulled him out and sent him to the infirmary. They needed a gunner, so I pulled on his jacket and helped out."

"That's where you were needed," Evan said. He rubbed a hand up over his head, pushing back tangles of sweat-matted hair. "So you saw the main push?"

"Wasn't much of one." Jenna brushed it off with a shrug. "Condor. Couple of Double-V Rangers. One *Koshi*. Our hoverbikes pinned the armor against the wall, and we drove the *Koshi* back out with the *Pack Hunter* supported by armor and some late-arriving Infiltrators. After the Condor went up in flames, the Rangers surrendered."

She rocked herself forward, stepped back to the window. She left enough room for Evan to join her, which he did. "He's out there, isn't he?"

From her room, Evan stared out over the lower buildings and the north grounds. Salvage crews were busy removing the burned-out shells of ruined vehicles and loading up anything worth saving on JI 100 recovery vehicles. "Yeah, Mark is out there somewhere."

"Mark? Mark is back on campus. He brought in about a hundred displaced residents from Chang-an." She must have sensed his surprise. "They headed our way only because they didn't know where else to go. Mark told them we'd get them food and a place to sleep. I was talking about Mai Uhn Wa. I heard that he's been gone since early this morning."

Ah, Mai. "Mai is out there somewhere, yes." Evan stared at the distant rooftops and higher buildings in the YiCha suburbs. A three-story building burned about two kilometers away, but it looked like it might be under control. No heavy fires had been set locally, for which he was thankful. Distant Chang-an was not quite so fortunate by all reports, suffering widespread damage in several commercial and industrial districts. Was that where Mai had disappeared to? Taking some of the *Ijori Dè Guāng* cells to join in the madness? Testing, and training, his future Warrior House.

"I'm glad Mark's all right," he offered her. And he was. Above all else, Mark was still Evan's friend. It would have been much easier if Evan could hate him.

Jenna nodded. "Me, too. And I'm glad you made it back in. But now David and Hahn are out there, and who knows what will happen?"

She stepped into him then, resting her head back against his shoulder. Her braided hair smelled of sweat and smoke. The heat of her skin burned against his arm. It was nothing meaningful, Evan told himself, just a friend needing someone to lean against, but suddenly the room seemed a whole lot smaller. He drew an arm around her, offering her comfort.

"Evan, when we began this . . . when you began this . . . did you expect this? All of this?"

He looked at the orange flames licking up into a dusky gray sky, smoke feeding the haze. Another skyrocket burst over Yiling—green sparks that glittered like emeralds. He saw their *Pack Hunter* jog across the open grounds to the north, chewing up turf and cracking walks as it passed near the Guardian. A pair of Saxon APCs followed. A new patrol.

"No," he said truthfully. "I didn't." In fact, Evan still expected much worse.

As if reading his unspoken thoughts, Jenna nodded. "How much longer?"

"A couple of days," he said automatically. "After their attempts today, they'll wait until some kind of order is restored."

Which gave him enough time, he hoped, to work something of his own out with Mai Uhn Wa. There was still so much between them, good and bad. One of them had to bend. After hearing Mai's plans for the resurrection of House Ijori, Evan had known who that must be. And maybe he had what Mai needed to bring it off.

Or, more to the point, the Cult of Liao did.

At another window, across Yiling and the sprawling suburbs of Chang-an, two others also stood at a window. They looked out over the desperation and anger that had seized the capital city and, to a lesser extent, the entire world of Liao.

Anna Lu Pohl's private residence took up the entire third floor in the east wing of the Governor's Palace. She had rooms for all occasions, from solitary meals and casual meetings to banquets and balls. Her private office had hardwood floors covered in Persian-style rugs, a golden teak desk, and a wall-size curio-filled with a jade collection owned by the Liao people, but conveniently displayed for their Governor when not on tour. A gas fire glowed behind ceramic logs in the fireplace, warming the room.

Having retired from twenty straight hours on her feet, the Governor had long since kicked her shoes into the corner and loosened the robes that hung down from her mantle. Underneath she wore a smart but comfortable dress suit, rumpled and dark with sweat stains under the arms.

"One hell of a way to start the New Year," she said to Gerald Tsung as more fireworks bled across the night sky. She toasted the display, downed the last of her plum wine and set the glass on the windowsill.

Tsung continued to look over the two-story-high walls and into some distant streets of Chang-an. Governor Pohl left him there, having seen enough. The riots showed no sign of burning themselves out. Riots. Plural. Chang-an was not a homogenous city. Chang-an was a walled-off palace and several forums buildings. Chang-an was the rural stretch to the east, where single-family farms competed with larger combines, and then the suburb of Erisa beyond that. Chang-an was Yi-ling and Sua and the industrial sector of Gahn where the fires were under control now, though sixty percent of the factories were little better than gutted husks and charred grounds. Chang-an was the military reserve near Lianyungang, it was the gem of Beilù, and it was the voice of Liao.

And Chang-an was dying.

"Nothing more from Hunnan or Thei?" she asked, naming the next two largest cities on Liao's northern continent.

"Mandrinn Klein has moved no forces in response to your request. Lord Governor Hidic also sent Mandrissa Erin Ji orders, and she has refused to answer either until 'the competing Governors of Liao reach some level of accord.' " He reported as if on automatic pilot, coloring nothing with his own feelings or opinions.

"And what do you think?"

With a direct request, "Klein is scared. Erin Ji, I'm certain, has thrown in with the Cult of Liao. She has never been very stable."

Anna bypassed her desk for a red velvet sofa, easing onto the overstuffed cushion and pulling her legs up for comfort. All of the district nobles were holding fast and stubborn. They did not want the madness infecting Chang-an to spread into their own cities—not any worse than was already happening. So Qinghai and its surrounding provinces were on their own.

"Maybe they are right to do so," she said out loud.

"You are, Governor," Tsung said simply, as if that explained all. "They have no right to refuse you."

"Thank you, Gerald. Let us hope they see that as well, and soon." She dismissed him with a tight smile that never reached her eyes. "I will not be sleeping tonight. Come for me if you hear any news." Her aide bowed his way from the room, leaving her to solitude and her own thoughts.

And again, they returned to the idea that her insubordinate nobles might have the right of it. The nobility derived its power from the people, much as her own office did. Without land, without the fealty of those who worked it, they had no more authority than a man who stood on a wooden crate at the corner and preached his cause.

What did the people truly want? What was best for them? For the first time in her career, Anna Lu Pohl was not certain. She had come to power on Liao courting the populace's indecision, supporting The Republic and at the same time encouraging a resident's right to value his or her Capellan heritage. Like any good politician, she managed to walk that line found between any two opposing camps. What had surprised her, then, was how wide that divide stretched. So many people were not at all certain whom they should be or what they wanted.

Well, that wasn't quite true. They wanted it all, Capellan and Republic and citizen and patriot. Now they were learning that the cost of such desires ran high, very high.

They were also making up their minds. Anna could sense that. She had felt the shift in Capellan sympathies growing stronger, and with the Conservatory revolt she had sensed the problem coming to a head. People were waking up. They were scratching their heads and their numb asses, and they were beginning to wonder if they had surrendered too much for The Republic.

"When the people question their government, that government deserves to be questioned. And when the government is more concerned with maintaining itself at any cost to its people, the people will no longer fear. They will rebel."

So said Lao-Tzu. Many had made the conscious choice, for one side or the other. The balance swayed. Could it be brought back under control? Possibly. But it wouldn't take much to tip everything against The Republic. If that happened. . . .

When that happened, Governor Anna Lu Pohl would have everything in place. For the good of Liao, for the good of her people, she would ready herself for anything.

Even in welcoming home the Confederation.

PART THREE

The Spoils of Treachery

26

The Cult of Liao

Republic forces were strengthened on Gan Singh and Menkar this week as Prefect Tao continued efforts to recall discharged veterans and push new cadets into the field to meet the growing Capellan menace. The New Aragon Field Academy has graduated seventy-five percent of the senior class ahead of schedule, earning a new generation of soldiers early citizenship for their valiant efforts in this time of severe national crisis.
　　—In the News!, New Aragon Free Press, 26 July 3134

Beilù Northern Ranges
Sarrin Province, Liao
29 July 3134

The VTOL trio flew a tight formation, a Sprint scout helicopter leading the way and two Balac Strike VTOLs flanking. Rotors thumped hard overhead as the craft banked just above treetop level and ran hard for the approaching Northern Ranges.

Mai Uhn Wa saw no tactical or strategic reason why Evan would want him to see this remote area of Beilù. His former protégé was most secretive about the whole episode, which both pleased and irritated the elder warrior. He had taught Evan well the value of closely held information. Now *he* was the student. Mai glanced into the rear passenger compartment, where Evan sat with stoic calm, then turned back to gaze out of the forward canopy.

Two hundred kilometers northeast of Chang-an, only blue green evergreens thrived in winter's final grip. There were towns, occasionally, and small farms. Cattle, hardy sheep and goats fled from the noise of the passing VTOLs. Not even the Dynasty Guard, striking west from the Du-jín, had seen the need to press forces this far north.

"Not much longer," Evan promised, leaning forward to make himself heard over the deafening rotors. He tapped the VTOL pilot on the shoulder, made a slashing motion across his throat and then pointed out the Balac Strike 'copters that flew as escorts. The pilot nodded, and pinched closed his throat mic.

Mai wore the copilot's helmet for its sound-deadening properties as much as any need to stay plugged into the chatter. Still, he raised an eyebrow when their pilot ordered the Balacs to find themselves a good nest and wait for the Sprint's return. The Strike VTOLs were a loan from McCarron's Armored Cavalry, requested through Mai Uhn Wa. They had no way of knowing the command did not come from him, and Mai saw no need to fight with Evan now, after coming so far, over who controlled them. He let them go.

Evan would not risk their lives foolishly. Or, at least, without need.

The Sprint dodged over a few more foothills and found a small valley farm that looked no different from any other except for its hillside barn. Mai spared it a single glance, but slapped his gaze back to the control panel as alarms wailed from sensor lock. Someone was tracking them with military targeting systems! Multiple systems, in fact, though Mai saw no movement from the barn, farmhouse or hillsides.

Evan reached forward and grabbed the pilot's arm with steadying strength, pointed out a cleared area of land near the strangely placed barn. The pilot drifted down carefully, making no threatening maneuvers, bumping the landing skids against a tan-colored pad of ferrocrete painted expertly to blend into the hillside grasses and open scrabbles of hard dirt and rock.

"A strange area for an *Ijori Dè Guāng* cell," was Mai's only comment as he released his own harness and left the helmet sitting on his seat. "See a lot of military activity out this way?"

Evan followed him out through the VTOL's passenger door, both of them bending down to run out from under the still spinning blades. "Not *Ijori Dè Guāng*," Evan said. "This is the Cult of Liao stronghold."

Mai had a moment to ponder that as the two men walked toward the aged gray barn. Cult of Liao. The political faction that supported the Confederation's return. Evan was obviously involved with them, able to lead a military chopper into this protected valley. But had he chosen his words carefully when he said this was *the* stronghold? One? Mai Uhn Wa had always envisioned a cell system much like the one he had worked to establish for the *Light of Ijori*. In military terms, it made sense. So, "They are not a paramilitary order."

"Not exactly," Evan admitted.

"How involved are you with the Cult?"

"As deeply as one can be." Evan hesitated, then, "I would have told you that night."

No need explaining to which night Evan referred. The night Mai Uhn Wa had turned his back on Evan, Greggor and the entire organization. The night he had left Liao to answer for his crimes against the State.

Mai Uhn Wa felt a touch of sadness and, in a way, disappointment. When he'd first met Evan, the young student had been searching for something to fill the void hollowed out of his life. His parents killed shortly after the Night of Screams. Raised as a ward of the state. Mai had sensed the longing inside him to connect with something larger, and also recognized Evan's incredible natural talents. A future leader. He had planned to nurture Evan into that role himself, and had been just as proud to learn Evan had gone on without him.

But a cult? Mai had thought Evan destined for leadership, not servitude.

"A civilian organization," Mai asked, betraying none of his thoughts. "They are worth our time now?"

"He is worth it," Evan promised. *He*. Mai was to meet with the leader of the Cult.

They were nearly at the barn. From the ground it looked more wrong than it had from the air. Built partly into the hillside, as a mining shaft might be, the barn was *painted* gray with darker streaks added to make it look like naturally aged wood. One of the larger doors stood open, swinging neglected in the chill winds that gusted through the short valley. Mai pictured a barren floor with a rickety table and no chairs, around which a few fanatics met with a candle for light to whisper of government insurrection. And built into the hillside? A bolt-hole for safety.

Might take a military force all of twenty minutes to dig them out.

Mai followed Evan into the barn, built on a ferrocrete pad, and stood in awe of the bunker-quality doors recessed into the hillside. Twenty hours, he quickly amended his first estimate.

"There are petragylcerin charges built into the pad, ready to take off the entire side of the hill. The doors are also primed with charges, and we can bring down fifty meters of corridor inside, sealing off the primary access."

He used a palm-scanner to key open the bunker, rolling back blast doors that would have made an *Overlord*-class DropShip proud. A large number of barrels pointed into their faces. These were the first people Mai had seen, and they all were on the wrong end of assault rifles. Meaning the trigger end.

"He sleeps for us," Evan said carefully, though certainly the Cult members recognized one of their own with access to such a vault.

Like water flowing into a series of drains, the guards melted into side passages, leaving the main chamber open. Dimly lit by overhead spots, Mai saw that it ran far back into the hillside. Twenty *days*, he decided. Weeks to dig out this bunker if the fanatics caved in the ceiling behind them. Leaving those trapped inside free to do . . . what? Slip out by an alternate tunnel? And with what treasure? A bunker like this wasn't built as a bolt-hole. It was built to protect something. Or someone. What kind of man led this Cult?

"What does he want from the *Ijori Dè Guāng*?" Mai asked. "Or is it from the Armored Cavalry?"

Evan hesitated. "He wants for nothing," he finally said. The two walked along the long, narrow corridor, following ventilation ductwork and cable runs, alone with each other's company. "This is about what we need, Mai Uhn Wa. You and I. I do not bring you here lightly." They traipsed down a short flight of stairs, hewn into the surrounding rock. "I found something within the Cult that I needed. Something I have never been able to duplicate within the *Ijori Dè Guāng*. Now I realize that I was never the right person to do so.

"I kept the *Light of Ijori* burning, but I cannot bring illumination."

And the Cult leader could? Was that what Evan tried to say? A room opened up at the end of the corridor, full of bright light and the hum of large machinery. The elder man decided to withhold final judgment for a few moments more. If he trusted Evan was the man he had always believed, he had to trust that Evan had seen something in this Cult leader worth following.

Evan had. And so did Mai Uhn Wa when he stepped across the threshold of the underground shrine.

There was no better description of the room, even though it was packed along three walls with power relay systems and a collection of chemical tanks. A high-tech shrine, devoted to a single person. Mai stared at the coffinlike encasement mounted to the fourth wall, through frost-tinted ferroglass that dimmed, but did not hide, the figure inside. A God to many Capellans.

It wasn't the Cult of Liao, the world.

It was the Cult of Liao, the *man*.

Sun-Tzu Liao slept peacefully in the cryogenic chamber, body surrounded by a swirl of frozen gasses. Age lined his slackened face. Gray hair, streaked with poor remnants of youthful black, swept over his mantled shoulders. Golden robes cloaked Liao's Eternal Father, and helped to hide the various medical leads and tubes, which snaked along at the back of the chamber.

Mai stepped forward, slowly, and brought up one hand to touch the coffin with the tips of his fingers.

"He is a man, Mai Uhn Wa." Still, Evan whispered. "And he is dead."

"You withheld this from me? Even that night?"

He could not see Evan's shrug, but heard the bitter memory in his words. "You turned away from us. Why would I trust you with anything so important?" He stepped closer. "And I was still in shock at the revelation."

Mai was still reeling himself. The room swayed uncertainly around him. "Dead," he repeated. "He is not preserved?"

"Chancellor Liao is preserved, but not in life." Evan checked a readout panel on the side of the chamber. "He came back to Liao to die, *Shiao-zhang* Mai. His body was failing, and he performed one last act to strengthen the Confederation at a time when it wavered before the Republic. He 'ascended.' He let his disappearance rally his people, and Daoshen was eventually able to broker a new peace." Evan almost left his explanation there, but then continued. "Even if he could be helped medically now, we are not certain about the cryogenic technology. It is old. Many people who've tried to use such devices suffered irreversible brain damage."

Which explained why no one had ever tried to revive the Chancellor. That, and the fact that Daoshen Liao might not appreciate the idea of his father—the Divine One—as a mere mortal held permanently at death's door. And so the religion had begun. The great secret, holding Sun-Tzu's body in trust for the people of Liao.

With so many thoughts, plans and their repercussions running through his head, Mai Uhn Wa did not notice for several minutes the title Evan Kurst had awarded him. "You spoke to me as—"

"*Shiao-zhang*," Evan said again. The honorific rank of a Warrior House Leader. "We need each other, Master Mai Uhn Wa. So much of what I am is because of your influence and vision. So much of what you want to accomplish, I can help make real."

Evan had not been talking of the Cult leader earlier, but of Mai Uhn Wa! And by commending this secret into Mai's hands, Evan relinquished himself as well. But, "This is too big for us, Evan. You don't even begin to understand what this could do to the Confederation."

"I think I do. I've labored with this for nearly two years, keeping a lid on the Cult of Liao even at times they thought to go public. Even when it might have helped the *Ijori Dè Guāng*, or the Conservatory. If it is to happen, it has to happen under our control."

"I don't know." But he did know. He did.

"What will you do then? Turn your back on this, on us, again?" He did not sound angry this time, but accepting. "I will not stop you from walking out of here, Mai Uhn Wa. You have my pledge, and I will keep it no matter what you decide. But decide now."

Mai bristled at the calm ultimatum, delivered by the same man who only moments ago acknowledged him as Master. Then the elder warrior relented, realizing the large pressures Evan had been living with, alone, for too long.

"I am not walking out of here without you, Evan. You are first among warriors, and I would have it no other way." He offered his hand, and Evan clasped it with both of his own and bowed. "We will keep this secret, together, you and I."

But Mai Uhn Wa knew he planned to immediately betray that promise, and this time Evan might not ever be able to forgive. Which would be unfortunate. Mai truly did not want to kill his first son of House Ijori.

27

Truths Be Told

An anonymous report, forwarded to our offices, promises to shake Liao to its very core. To find that we have welcomed home the Black Paladin, the Betrayer whose treachery caused so many needless deaths on the Night of Screams, seemed too great a lie. But it is not. Our investigation has confirmed it. Daniel Peterson, Ezekiel Crow: they are alive and well. And they are Legate Ruskoff's new aide, Major Ritter Michaelson.
—The Nánlù Daily Apple, Exclusive Media Broadcast, Liao, 30 July 3134

LianChang Military Reserve
Qinghai Province, Liao
1 August 3134

Pulling off the highway in his motorpool sedan, Daniel Peterson tightened his grip on the wheel. A large sign next to the access road reminded him of his destination. LianChang Military Reserve. A tight flutter twisted in his stomach. Major Ritter Michaelson had been brought here the first time against his wishes, but had handled it with stiff military bearing. Daniel returned voluntarily, tired of running. After two days of no sleep and very little to eat, he hoped to face the truth half as well.

The guards at the base entrance worked with their usual efficiency, checking identification, waving through jeeps, cars and trucks. A fresh-faced corporal glanced first at the sedan's window decal, giving the driver priority access, and had already raised the gate before Daniel coasted to a stop to hand over Ritter Michaelson's fake ID.

"Lieutenant Daniel Peterson to see Legate Ruskoff," he said calmly.

Corporal Paullat didn't bother to open the wallet. His eyes widened with recognition. In the last two days, the media had made Daniel's face instantly recognizable to the entire world.

"Lieutenant. . . ." There was no respect in the title, only stunned repetition. "S–sir. You're . . . under arrest."

Daniel nodded. "Have the MPs meet me in front of the base command building, please." He drove under the raised gate without looking back. The corporal never had time to remember his pistol, holstered at his side.

He picked up his first military patrol car only a block into the base, and two more before he ever got close to Ruskoff's command center. A rifle platoon waited outside, backed up by armored infantry on the roof. Four military police approached his sedan, hands on their pistols, and ordered him out. Daniel complied, slowly, very much aware of how many weapons pointed his direction, keeping his hands in view at all times. The military police cuffed him, checked him for weapons, then shackled his wrists to the front of a leather belt which they cinched around his waist. With an MP at both sides, a hand locked around each upper arm, Daniel Peterson was finally escorted inside.

They led him down a familiar stretch of hallway, through a door and an adjoining office, and held him at stiff attention in front of Legate Viktor Ruskoff. The Legate sat in his chair, hands clamped onto the armrests. His ash blond hair, normally shorn into a tight flattop, wilted as the length grew out. Bags began to darken under his eyes. He said nothing for a long moment, and Daniel held up under the basilisk stare.

"So," Ruskoff finally said. "This is what treason looks like."

No sleep and a starvation diet had done its work on Daniel's face. It had taken a great deal of energy just to shave this morning before leaving the hostel where he'd hidden for two days, thinking. "You have no idea who I am," Daniel said. "Arrest me or shoot me, Legate." He glanced away. "I don't care what you think."

"If that's true, why did you come back? You've disappeared before. Twice before, in fact."

Daniel chewed on the inside of his cheeks, holding his answer until he'd thought about it a moment. His eyes felt scratchy, dry, and he blinked some moisture over them. "Not this time. Whatever happens to me now, I'll see it through without having to look back over my shoulder."

"Very noble of you." Ruskoff certainly wasn't warming to the idea. "Do you know what you've cost this world? Just as the riots begin to settle down, suddenly people are up in arms again. I have fifteen new cases of officers absent without leave. You don't want to know what this did to the enlisted ranks. And I can't tell how many are defections, desertions or are simply dead. The public backlash has been incredible on *both* sides of the Capellan issue. Did you set me up, Michaelson? Crow . . . what the hell am I supposed to call you!"

"Daniel. My name is Daniel."

He seemed to accept that. "Did you?" he asked again.

"Set you up? No. I was set up. Played. Masterfully."

"So now you're innocent?" Ruskoff's sarcasm was plain.

"Ah, I'm guilty as hell, Viktor." One of the MPs shook him, and Daniel twisted around to shake away their hands. They pulled batons, but hesitated when Ruskoff waved them back.

Daniel ignored the MPs and returned to some semblance of attention. "I'm guilty," he said again, "but not of what you think. I was just trying to do what I thought was best." That wasn't quite right. That was Crow talking. "No, I've tried to do what I thought was best for everyone else. I did. But I never meant—"

What? Anyone to get hurt? Too late.

Ruskoff nodded a dismissal to the MPs, who left the office reluctantly. Daniel doubted they went much farther than the adjoining office, ready to take him back into custody the moment the Legate was through with him.

"So if it wasn't you, then who was it? Tsung? Did the Governor's man play me into the enemy's hands? The Dynasty Guard? Who?"

What the hell. "Bannson. Jacob Bannson. Or, at least, it was some of his people."

"What's Jacob Bannson got to do with this?" Ruskoff obviously didn't believe him. "Why would he care about Liao? Answer me, Daniel!"

"Business!" Daniel shouted back with all the strength left to him. "It's all business with him. What he can get as a return on an investment. That's what I was." Daniel fought to recover his poise. "An investment."

"Why you? What did Bannson, or his people, have on you that was so damning?" Of course, the moment he asked, the answer came to him. "The Massacre."

Daniel breathed heavily as his chest tightened. He nodded. "Here on Liao, and on Northwind, I was Bannson's tool. Some mistakes you never stop paying for. Not even when you die."

And Daniel found himself backing up, taking his time to explain—slowly, carefully—the way he'd been approached to let the Confederation DropShip through security protocols. Why he'd done it. What was left to him after. Two years of bloody war. In the chaos, it had been easy to forge a new identity as Ezekiel Crow. Trying to redeem himself by making the "best" decisions on behalf of The Republic, devoting twenty years to doing as much good as possible.

He told Ruskoff about the Conservatory Uprising in 3128, how it was prompted by Confederation agents. *That* made the Legate sit up sharply and take notice. He talked at length about what happened on Northwind and Terra. For the first time in his life, he explained to another person every selfish motivation that drove him to excel, to do better, and what finally backed him into a corner. And what it had cost him. His parents. The trust and respect of his peers. Tara Campbell, who had reached out to him, and had been betrayed.

He'd been talking quite awhile. His mouth was parched and his throat hurt. Daniel ended quickly with his arrival on Liao.

Ruskoff nodded slowly. "So this *is* what treason looks like," he said, though not quite so harshly as the first time.

"I rated everything I got," Daniel admitted, refusing any pity. "This time I wasn't going to play another man's game. I had no aspirations of my own. I just wanted to help. I came clean—clean as I could and have you believe me at all—and hoped it was enough." He swallowed dryly. "It wasn't. And a lot of innocent people died."

He thought a moment. "Well, they would have died anyway, I think. Bannson would have covered those bases. But I helped put it in motion, and got those deaths blamed on The Republic."

Ruskoff leaned over his desk with hands steepled together.

"I've been there," he began slowly. "You take one step beyond the job description, and suddenly people are dead and you can't help but think of what you could have done differently. Usually, the answer is: nothing. And now Liao is burning." He shook his head. "I'm beginning to think this was all put into motion long before you and I ever put on a uniform. But that doesn't matter, does it? What we have to deal with is what happens today."

"And what is happening today?" Daniel asked. He couldn't help it. The responsibility of duty still pricked at him. "Bad?"

The Legate hesitated, then decided it couldn't hurt. "Lord Governor Hidic barely managed to hold on to the industrial centers of Nánlù. The Dynasty Guard struck during the New Year's chaos, but Lady Kincaid stop-gapped them. She took a bad hit from a cockpit breach. Then the Guard suddenly left. No idea why. They pulled out lock, stock and BattleMech while Nánlù's entire defense teetered on the edge. Relocated to Beilù's Northern Ranges."

"I've seen Chang-an," Daniel admitted. "It's every district and suburb for itself right now."

"Governor Lu Pohl—" Ruskoff shrugged. "I'm not certain about her. She's got a small task force sitting inside the White Towers District, appropriated from the surviving militia I had on the capital's streets. I haven't tested their loyalty yet by ordering them out. I might need them up there."

"Need them? For what?" Daniel tried to see where the Legate had mentioned a pending attack. He hadn't. "The Conservatory?" A chill grabbed him. He still felt torn inside that he had been unable to help the students. Unable even to reach Evan Kurst. "I think that would be a mistake."

"It's one thorn in my side that I can deal with immediately." The Legate's hands clenched into tight, white-knuckled fists. "I knew better than to let that fester. Because of Lord Governor Hidic, I've already waited too long, and it's cost us. I bring the Conservatory back under Republic control, the rest of Chang-an might calm enough for the Governor to relax. We may able to restore order."

He might be right, Daniel knew. Maybe it was too far gone for a peaceful solution. "What about me?" Daniel asked.

Ruskoff thought, then shook his head. "I'm not fit to judge you, Daniel. That will be for people wiser than I." He stood, leaning over his desk. His voice hardened. "But I can't trust

you either. I'll keep you on the Reserve for now, under protection, until I am sure you can get a fair hearing. That's the
best I can do for you."

Daniel nodded. "Then it'll have to be enough."

But still a part of him wondered who Legate Ruskoff could
ever find to give him that fair hearing? Just who would de-
clare themselves fit to judge him?

And if anything happened to the Legate, what would become of him then?

28

A Divided House

Sir Ian Valstone, Knight of the Sphere, and elements of the Fifth Hastati Sentinels pushed Confederation forces off the world of Algot this week. Thought to be another major offensive to take the working HPG station, the Capellan drive now looks to have been a feint designed to tie up Prefect Tao's dwindling resources.

—Your World, Algot, 2 August 3134

Yiling (Chang-an)
Qinghai Province, Liao
4 August 3134

"**Y**ou gave it to them!" Evan Kurst shouted as he stormed through the door, into the invitation-only meeting Mai Uhn Wa had called.

The tactical review room was normally used for student debriefing after live maneuvers. Located in a hardened building on the Conservatory's "military campus," it was used maybe twice in any given week during normal university operations, heavier toward the end of an academic year. Normally dressed in MechWarrior togs or a simple jumpsuit, Evan often found the room cold, stark and forbidding. A place he was summoned to be lectured on what he had done wrong and to give an accounting of what he had learned.

Today the room smelled of coffee and nervous cigarettes, filled with a dozen people that Mai felt deserving of a place in the budding House Ijori. Most of Evan's campus cabal, painfully missing Mark Lo. Jenna Lynn Tang stood nearby, but shrank away from the fury that heavily darkened his face. Colonel Feldspar and Field Sergeant Hoi had selected three senior cadets to help cover infantry and tanks. Tori Yngstram. Whit Greggor and two more *Ijori Dè Guāng* cell leaders. These were the people who could be trusted implicitly. Plus the always present Maskirovka agent, Michael Yung-Te.

Evan dismissed them all with hardly a glance.

It was Mai Uhn Wa who could not be trusted.

Word arrived that morning. Using stealth suits, the Dynasty Guard had taken the Cult of Liao's valley stronghold, and had obviously been prewarned of the valley and vault defenses. Evan missed the initial report by hours, busy tearing apart the room "Ritter Michaelson" had used on campus, and then checking his contacts in Chang-an for any news of the traitor. Part of him recognized that Daniel Peterson was only a small part in the Capellan-Republic conflict. Another part wanted to choke the life out of him. If there was one man directly responsible for his parents' deaths, it was Peterson.

But no one knew where Michaelson had disappeared to.

Evan had come back on campus to find the news waiting for him: Sun-Tzu's body *was* in the hands of the Dynasty Guard. Now he stood, shaking. His hands clenched and unclenched.

"You handed over the shrine to Rieves!"

Mai had put together a paramilitary uniform with brown fatigues webbed at the forearms and lower legs with green plasteel mesh. The older man remained visibly calm, even in the face of Evan's accusation. "Our final force strength includes only five BattleMechs, Evan. There is no way to return the *Rifleman* to duty without another week's effort."

Evan locked gazes with his mentor, his Master, at a momentary loss for words that Mai would not even acknowledge the betrayal. "Did you think my network would not report this?" he asked, choking off every word. "I did not want to believe it. But the Guard's DropShip is parked in the valley. Sitting right on top of the farmhouse, I'd guess."

"We are better prepared to field armor and infantry, although our battlesuits are a mixed bag at best and our vehicles weighted to the lighter side."

"Damn you, Mai!" Evan stomped further into the room,

coming up on the display table most of the small committee had gathered around. On it was a map of the Conservatory, with icons spread around the campus to represent a placement of all allied forces. "How many Protectors died because of this? How many did I help you betray?"

"Eight."

It was the first straight answer Mai offered, delivered with a simple matter-of-factness that seemed both cold and cruel. It helped Evan gather his poise again, letting him settle into a righteous anger. "Who gave you the right to make decisions like—"

"You did." This time the House Master did not allow Evan to finish, cutting him off with a hand tearing through the air and a whip-crack shout that silenced the cadet. "I told you then, what you showed me was bigger than either of us. It was mine to deal with as I saw fit."

"Giving his body over to the Dynasty Guard was not what I had in mind. You should have come to me."

"You swore yourself to me, Evan. Of your own choice. I am either Master of your life, or I am not. That is the way of a Warrior House. One leader. One!"

Evan's retort was silenced as Jenna stepped forward to place a hand on his arm. The warning was not lost. For all his anger and the cold emptiness eating away inside his guts, he saw he had not surprised Mai Uhn Wa. Far from it. Mai had waited for him, wanting this to be brought out in front of everyone. Evan glanced about the room as the shift in power played itself out.

Colonel Feldspar did not even look in Evan's direction. Neither did Whit Greggor. Both men silently cast their votes. Evan did notice that Feldspar *and* Hoi glanced at the resident Mask agent, but how they arrived at their decision did not matter. David Parks sat off to one side, mired in his own thoughts. Hahn glanced between Evan and Mai, shook his head subtly as if trying to warn his friend to back off.

So even Hahn had abandoned him.

Evan could not remain in the room. Not now, after openly challenging Mai. Evan had handed his mentor all the keys necessary to become master of the situation, and all because he'd thought—he'd hoped—that he had finally found the path forward. Instead, he'd found a new door being slammed on him. He'd given up the *Ijori Dè Guāng* and his prominence in the uprising. Even his friendships, so painstakingly built, were apparently lost now.

He turned for the door. Jenna moved into his path, but Evan backed her off. "Stay," he told her. "You may be able to help save lives." Then he stepped by her.

"Evan." Mai did not command him to stay. He merely questioned.

Evan paused in the doorway, refusing to face back into the room. Slowly, he unclenched his fists and laid his hands down at his sides. "I remember my pledge, *Shiao* Mai. And now I will wait for your orders. You certainly have no respect for my counsel."

And then Evan left behind his friends, his Master, and his final ties to anything Capellan or Republic.

Making himself unavailable, Evan spent the rest of the day checking inventories and forward postings. He had shut himself out of the strategic council, but a nagging sense of duty pulled at him. He verified that the *Rifleman* could not be repaired any sooner, and hurried the military conversion of a second ConstructionMech into a modified design that might help make up for the Conservatory's light armor assets. That gave them three modified IndustrialMechs. Slow and ponderous, but a threat nonetheless.

Jenna finally caught up with him outside his dormitory. More to the point, she was waiting. Possibly for hours, knowing it was the one place he would return to sooner or later. It had been later, long after dark, and the overhead streetlights were throwing a yellow glare across the quad.

"Want to tell me about it?" she asked, falling into step with him as he headed for the doors.

"No."

"All right." But she continued to follow.

She waited until they were inside, climbing the stairs, then changed her mind. "You know what, it's not all right, Evan." She shook her head, and her braids danced across his shoulders. "Maybe you were first to support the Capellan cause on Liao. Maybe you deserve more consideration because of the *Ijori Dè Guāng* and whatever history you have with *Shiaozhang* Mai." She grabbed him at the first landing and pushed him back against the wall, forcing him to look at her. "But you *do not* walk away from your friends, Evan."

The stairwell wall felt cold where it pressed into the back of Evan's head. He stared up over Jenna's head, at the naked bulb that burned behind a safety grill in the ceiling. "I've spent more time worrying about the four of you than any other threat to me on this world," he said. Today was apparently the day to speak his mind.

It took her aback. "Why? What did we ever demand from you?"

"Not a thing. But it's the first rule of insurrection: trust no one. Mai taught me that. I let myself get close to you. And Hahn, David and Mark," he quickly added.

"Then why didn't you bring us in? David practically begged you, every day."

There was any number of reasons for that. Uncertainty. Unsuitability. Evan jumped right for the throat, though. "Because you four were the first thing in my life that felt *normal*. Something that everyone else took for granted, and I never could. I didn't want to lose that. For any reason. So I tried to walk a line in between my world and yours. And every time one of you pressed a bit too hard about my ... activities ... for days afterward I waited for the roof to fall in."

Jenna blew out an exasperated sigh. "I once asked Mark what he would do, you know, if we ever saw evidence of your involvement with the *Ijori Dè Guāng*. He said that he'd be very disappointed in you."

She laughed a nervous little laugh. "Not that he'd turn you in. He knew you well enough that he understood your politics, even if he disagreed with them. I think he would have argued with you forever, trying to change your mind. But you never let us close enough. Not Mark or Hahn or David." She reached up to grab his chin, tilted his head down so that he *had* to look at her. "Not me."

He sensed the question. "You were with Mark," he said.

"Well, I couldn't wait around for you forever, could I?" Jen sucked in her breath as if she'd said something wrong. Then she smiled, thin and hard. "I was beginning to wonder if you liked women at all. I mean, Hahn is a very handsome man. And available."

Evan opened his mouth to protest, but no words came out. Jen had thrown him right out of the conversation with the ease of a judo wrestler laying hands on someone who'd only thought to spar. Part of it was good-natured teasing—she was, after all, still his friend. But a strong undercurrent of tension ran beneath. Had he really thrown away so many chances, frustrating Jen Lynn Tang as he never allowed her nearer than arm's length?

"If I had known. . . ."

"You would have run even faster, damn you." She curled the front of his jacket into her fists and shoved him back harder against the wall. "And now you're finding another way to run out on us. Evan, you have to start trusting someone sooner or later. Enough to make the hard calls." Then she pulled him into her, rising up on her toes to plant a hard kiss on his mouth.

He drew her scent in like a drowning man fighting for air. Her warmth taunted him, and he grabbed on to her with desperation born from need. One thing. One thing left to hang on to. And Jenna was here. She was here, and warm, and fighting alongside him, not against him.

Evan wasn't certain who finally broke away first. They stared into each other's gaze. She tucked herself into his arm even as he pulled her to his side, and together they finished climbing the stairs to his floor, his room, and their first and last night together.

29

Growing Pains

In related news to the Confederation's war of aggression, word has come from Prefecture VI that the Oriente Protectorate has seized the world of Ohrensen. With the worlds of Park Place and Elnath now threatened, it is unlikely that the Sixth Hastati Sentinels or any help from New Canton, will return to the aid of Prefecture V anytime soon.
— Around the Sphere, Station 64, Genoa,
2 August 3134

Yiling (Chang-an)
Qinghai Province, Liao
4 August 3134

The Liao Conservatory came under full assault just after dawn, the alert waking Evan Kurst and Jenna to a gray, overcast day, pulling them away from each other's warmth. Evan suited up, waiting for Mai Uhn Wa to deny him a place. But whatever their differences, Mai gave him the *Ti Ts'ang* and situated him on point. No doubt Mai wanted someone he trusted holding the center. Someone he could control.

Evan allowed him the first. Not the second.

Leaving behind a shortened company under Jen Lynn Tang's command, the Conservatory fielded one lance of actual BattleMechs and two converted industrial machines. Three companies of armor and infantry spread out in a ragged line around them. Legate Ruskoff anchored the center of The Republic line with his own *Zeus*, an assault 'Mech variant that boasted a PPC, Gauss rifle and plenty of armor.

Evan angled his *Ti Ts'ang* in a short, violent slash across the *Zeus's* path, pulling an SM1 Destroyer and a pair of Maxim APCs in his wake. His targeting reticle burned solid gold, and a series of scarlet lances slashed molten wounds across the *Zeus* from the shoulder to hip. An argent stream of particle cannon fire chased after Evan, caught him, blasted armor into molten shards and smoking coals. Ruskoff saved his Gauss ammunition against a possible charge by the 'Mech killing tank or Evan's strong axe.

But the Destroyer was a ruse. The Capellan forces swung back almost at once.

Missiles from a JES Carrier chewed up ground behind the *Ti Ts'ang's* feet. A Republic Cavalier squad popped out of a tangle of deadwood and thorny brush, jetting up on boosters, but then faded as a pair of Balac Strike VTOLs swooped down like crows on carrion. Evan forced his way into a small stand of bare-branched alder and hunkered down as two Sparrowhawks screamed overhead, laying down strafing fire.

"What are we doing out here?" Han Soom Gui asked on a private channel to Evan. He served as gunner on the Destroyer.

"Wait for it," Evan said, not answering directly. Hahn was a soldier under his command, and the risks were very, very real. He could not afford to think of Hahn as a friend. New alarms wailed as sensors locked onto his machine, and threat icons swarmed forward on his HUD. "Here they come."

Evan had hoped to draw Ruskoff in, exposing the Legate to whatever kind of flanking assault Mai could shake loose. So far the strategy was not working. Ruskoff wouldn't shove his face into the blades so carelessly. But a Republic fire-lance thought it could push Evan back to secure their commander's advance. A *Panther* supported by a full lance of armor drove forward at the small woods.

Evan's infantry had dumped out of their APCs behind cover of the trees, and now a double squad of Purifiers blurred out to surround and worry a pair of Jousts while Evan threw his Destroyer at the *Panther*. Evan slammed down on his foot pedals, launching the *Ti Ts'ang* on a short hop to land between two Scimitars.

His lasers stabbed out in a fury of bloody light, running streams of molten composite into the pale grasses. The 'Mech's titanium ax rose and fell. One Scimitar lost a missile launcher and a long stripe out of its skirting. It spun wildly as the driver fought for control and then ran like hell for the safety of Republic lines.

Evan backpedaled away, pulling his infantry back toward the small wood with him. The Destroyer chased after the retreating *Panther*, then skirted the trees and dodged back to safety.

"Evan," Mai's voice whispered into his ear. A crackle of static washed out his next few words. On Evan's left, the *Panther* fired its PPC at an encroaching pair of VTOLs, causing more interference.

"Say again," Evan said.

"Pull back and slide around to the west. Let Ruskoff forward."

"We have good position here to stall them," Evan said, not challenging the order but making damn certain Mai understood the tactical position.

"Let them come," Mai said again, his tone a touch stern. "I need you out of there in twenty."

Jaw muscles aching, Evan dialed for his small force and passed the order. Infantry loaded up and trailed behind. He and Hahn led a quick retreat north and then west. Every step shook the cockpit, and reminded him that he was moving away from where he thought he was needed. But Mai Uhn Wa commanded.

Control? No.

It came down to trust.

Their first clash had not been the quick, decisive engagement histories always talked about. It opened up a game of kilometers and time as both commanders positioned forces, drove forward with feints, and then followed up with short, vicious jabs. Every so often one of them attempted a long maneuver. Mai Uhn Wa played his people with a conservative hand. Legate Ruskoff had an instinctive feel for battle that too often predicted where the real threat would come.

Now Mai retreated again as artillery shells reached for his command vehicle, whistling down from a heavy, gray sky. Flash and fire spread charred earth into the air, opening three craters in a ragged line just short of the massive crawler. Dirt pattered against the ferroglass shield behind him.

The muted roar of explosions blended into a background of overlapping communications bands and the constant exchange of warnings and commands. Mai let his hindbrain worry on it, too occupied with tracking any of a dozen different threats and trying to coordinate a defensive line that included four different factions. That is, three too many.

"Cavalry-five! Close up that gap." One of Mai's junior aides, fresh out of the Conservatory's Tactics 101 and drunk on authority. He coordinated a mechanized infantry lance sent by Terrence McCarron. A green kid ordering veterans. "Move that hunk of metal!"

Mai turned the back of his command chair to the young firebrand and kicked against a footrest, gliding the swinging boom that supported his chair. He braked to a stop just behind the flustered aide, laid one hand on the boy's shoulder and used his master communications circuit to override that station.

"Cavalry-five, this is *Shiao* Mai." He abbreviated his newly adopted title for the battlefield. "We have Capellan children dying on your forward right. Deploy Fa Shih to slow that *Catapult*. Buy us time."

He toggled off, yanked the headset from his aide's head and pulled the boy back until his throat was exposed and his ear not too far from Mai's lips. "McCarron sent us *three* lances of armor and infantry," he whispered harshly, all pretense of calm and civility vanished. "Nothing turns a veteran bad like lack of confidence in command. If you turn them against me with your insults and boorish shouting, I *will* slit your throat and toss your corpse out as an apology."

"Yes, House Master," the cadet stammered. "*Duì-bu-qǐ!*"

With no more time to instruct the aide, Mai released him and glided forward again. His dark gaze slid across station after station, screen after screen. Here, a lance of militia Condors swung out to flank his modified ConstructionMech. There, a cadet-crewed Schmitt probed forward, found a Triarii infantry position exposed and hammered twenty-mil rounds into their position. Back at his own station, a computer painted colorful arcs across a monitor, estimating parabolic courses from the recent craters, tracking the Republic artillery position.

Slipping behind with every second spent training his staff under battle conditions, Mai routed the data to a different station, shifted command of the Armored Cavalry lances to a new aide, and plugged himself back into the strategic overview.

Just in time.

For the fourth time running, The Republic line surged forward in a well-coordinated press, threatening to encircle Mai's truncated defense. Armor rolled ahead of BattleMechs. Aerospace fighters screamed overhead, strafing the pro-Capellan force. Green cadets wavered, slipped back, trading ground for time. Veterans found themselves exposed, taking heavy fire until Mai ordered them back as well.

Ruskoff knew how to create an offensive, forcing the Capellan defenders to show their weaknesses. But Mai Uhn Wa knew how to expend limited resources for effect. He'd been doing that his entire life.

"VTOL support, flank left," he ordered, passing the command through another aide, directing McCarron's lance of Balac Strike VTOLs on a strafing run which pinned down one side of Ruskoff's line. "Double our missile strikes at the center, make Ruskoff pay for the push. And lay down Fa Shih minefields under that cover."

His people were slow, which cost. Ruskoff's *Zeus* hammered at a Marskman fire-control lance, chewing through armor and setting one tank burning into a small copse of acacia. Smoke roiled into the sky.

A pair of Pegasus scout craft tried to slip in and sting the Legate's 'Mech. They popped half a dozen missiles each, driving Ruskoff away from the retreating Marksmen. They quickly ran into a rain of missile counterfire.

Mai knew the order to swing wide went out too late. Knew there was no steeper learning curve than trial by fire. Both Pegasus craft took scattered hits as missiles blossomed over their sloped sides. One lost integrity on its turret, and a gout of fire and debris blasted out of the ruined top. The hovercraft cut hard, and rolled end over end until it fetched up against a large boulder and burned.

The second hovercraft skated back to safety, but the loss would still be felt.

Mai checked his positions. He saw new lances of enemy red moving up from Ruskoff's backfield; Governor Pohl's forces finally arriving to join The Republic side of the fight. He watched the blue icon that represented Evan's *Ti Ts'ang* loop back and westward, drawing even with the new forces. He weighed the chances and made the call.

"Evan. Advance and engage. Split that line wide open."

He left it at that. Evan would resent micromanaged tactics, and would be right to do so. The young warrior had to be given some room, even from his House Master. He had to be allowed the chance to make a difference. Even if Mai had already decided that Evan could not be allowed to succeed.

Pushing his *Ti Ts'ang* past ninety kilometers per hour, Evan ate up the ground in large strides. To his left, Hahn's Destroyer throttled back to keep pace. APCs of Purifier infantry trailed behind. They dashed forward, fired and faded back left or right to whatever cover they picked up in the local scrub. Light autocannon chased after them, ripping into brush and bark, having trouble against the faster machines.

Mai Uhn Wa had picked a good target of opportunity, where Ruskoff's forces were spread thin in anticipation of reinforcements out of Chang-an. After every pass, the gap widened, and forces at each edge chanced more desperate tactics to hold their line until Governor Pohl's people arrived.

Once again, Evan's small contingent fell back, turning aside early as aerospace fighters strafed by, their autocannon ripping long furrows into the hardscrabble ground. He stepped into an artillery-made crater, which threw a hitch into his step. Fortunately, his gyroscope and the neuro-feedback circuit adjusted.

"Evan," Mai reopened direct comms. "Begin falling back. Slowly. Hold that gap open, but do not punch through."

"*Shiao* Mai. With support, we might bring down the reinforcements and split the Republic line wide—"

"You will *not* engage Governor Pohl's troops. At any cost, Evan. Fall back."

Frustration welled up inside Evan, but he acknowledged the order and passed it to his team. They ducked out of the thin stand and fell back before any Republic forces pressed forward to engage. It left Evan with something extremely valuable in combat operations. Time. A moment with no pressing demands, where he could monitor comms and try to pull larger details from the pressing assault.

"Command, Cav-one. Eastern forces are down one Joust." Score one for the Conservatory.

"Sergeant Hoi is down. Down! His Behemoth overturned on that last artillery barrage."

Not good. Behemoths could make even a MechWarrior nervous, and Field Sergeant Hoi had been helping crew the second of only two such tanks fielded by the Conservatory. That could not be enough to pull his unit back, though.

"Here they come again. *Zeus* leading forward, flanked by two *Jessies* and—"

"—can't see them. Aerospace fighters chewing up our position. We need VTOL support and a MASH pickup."

"Lost one Ranger."

"Two Cavaliers down.

"Someone swing in at grid thirty-six . . . thirty-seven . . . *Vrebrachney*! Southwest side!" That sounded like Whit Greggor. "We're taking heavy—"

"Alert, alert, alert!" A weaker voice broke into the chatter, making up in intensity what she lacked in volume. Icy dread spiked into Evan's guts. "We have contact at forward-post Wilco. Two BattleMechs with support. We need help and we need it fast."

The western picket line. Jenna. The thought of Jen being pummeled by heavy firepower nearly caused Evan to turn his *Ti Ts'ang* for the Conservatory grounds. He paused at the end of his first retrograde maneuver, ready to push forward again or head full flight to Jenna's rescue, on Mai's command. "Identify those 'Mechs," he ordered, preempting Mai Uhn Wa.

"One *Firestarter*. One *Ryoken II*. Principes Guards. Supported by Brutus assault tanks."

So the Guards had sent Ruskoff support, and with better timing than Governor Pohl's laggard forces. How many more lances of the white-and-gold were sneaking through Yiling?

"Evan?" Jen Lynn Tang recognized his voice even without a callsign. "Ijori-one, can you assist?"

Nothing. No call from *Shiao* Mai. No order to press forward, cut for the Conservatory, or simply cease and desist all sideband chatter. Evan hesitated.

"We are falling back under heavy fire," Jen reported. "Double-V, Demon, down already."

Leaving Jenna in a modified ForestryMech, with a few armor pieces and some infantry support. *Maybe* the *Locust* at forward-November could swing down to assist. Maybe that would leave the northern stretch open for a second Principes attack.

"Ijori-one, can you assist?"

"Evan." Hahn's voice blared strong and with a squeal of feedback as he cut in on a private frequency to Evan. "Evan, do we go?"

Damn. Damn Ruskoff for slipping forces through the Chang-an suburbs and Mai Uhn Wa for taking a sudden absence. Whatever the House Master dealt with in the Praetorian, it had better be worth Jenna's life.

"We don't," Evan said on a tight-comms transmission to Hahn. He pivoted his *Ti Ts'ang* south, ready to push-and-fade once again. He toggled for wideband. "We're needed here, Wilco. Cannot assist." He shoved his throttle forward to its stop.

"Copy that." Jen's reply was short. "Any advice?"

Evan clenched his teeth hard enough to grind an edge off one molar. Every muscle tense, he nearly wrenched his BattleMech back around. But he did not. He chose this path far too long ago. He either believed in it, or he did not.

He did.

"Stick and fade, Jen. Buy us time." Not much in the way of advice. "You have your orders." And Evan had his. For better or worse.

30

Blowing Taps

Paladin Maya Avellar made planetfall on New Aragon today, taking charge of a small group of Knights already supporting Prefect Tao's defense of Prefecture V. Paladin Avellar's arrival came one day too late for Knight Jonathan Corrick, who fell in battle on Menkar on the last day of July.
—Damon Darmon, New Aragon, 2 August 3134

Yiling (Chang-an)
Qinghai Province, Liao
4 August 3134

Viktor Ruskoff powered forward, his eighty-ton *Zeus* shoving over trees and crushing thick boles underfoot like twigs on a forest carpet. Sweat ran freely, soaking into his cooling vest. His arm muscles ached, and his neck twinged with dull throbs from holding up the bulky neurohelmet for so many hours. Too long sitting at a desk and not enough time at the gym or in the hot seat of a 'Mech.

A light rain pattered down from Liao's gray skies, streaking his ferroglass canopy with silvered fingers. On the other side of the transparent armor, he watched a new Bellona drive into a tangle of brush and deadwood ahead of him, flushing Fa Shih like a brace of quail.

One of the armored infantrymen rose toward him on jet thrusters, and Ruskoff knocked him from the air with a swipe from the *Zeus's* right arm. The broken trooper fell backward and down into a wild thicket. He did not come out again.

"Zeta lead, this is Principes auxiliary." Captain Danna Shelby, commanding the double-lance loaned to the Legate by Lady Kincaid. "We're getting stragglers on the Grinder. I hope you aren't too far behind."

A Conservatory *Thunderbolt* slashed across Ruskoff's path a half kilometer ahead, smashed a light gauss slug into the *Zeus's* side before ducking behind a large 'Mech hangar. Ruskoff keyed over to the channel shared between Triarii and Guard. "Two klicks," he said, gaining one of the damp ferrocrete roadways that crisscrossed the military campus. "You'll have us on sensors as we strike out from behind these buildings."

And once Ruskoff's main task force stormed the campus grounds, leaving the defenders with no more options than to stand, fight and die, he'd have their surrender or he'd have their asses. Then the student uprising would be ended. Everything but the paperwork.

In the last hour, the arrival of Governor Pohl's forces had finally tipped the balance. The Legate worried at first, when a well-supported *Ti Ts'ang* moved into the gap he'd planned to push the late arrivals into, but then the Capellans fell back, refusing to exchange fire with Pohl's "bodyguards." He mixed Lieutenant Nguyen's scout lance into their midst, cementing that position.

Now the entire force rolled forward, and showed little mercy when Conservatory defenders staged brief and bloody rearguard actions.

A hard choice. A hard path. The Planetary Legate had not wanted this, but Chang–an had to be secured and local support for McCarron's Armored Cavalry and the Dynasty Guard disrupted. Without that, Ruskoff faced a divided government as Hidic and Pohl second-guessed his every order and challenged him for more military control.

Without that, he could not hold Liao for The Republic.

"Triarii four and six, on the left," he commanded, stomping up on the hangar, sending a double set of armored vehicles racing around the western side of the magnificent building. "Two and three on the right."

The quick pincer would hold anything in place long enough for his arrival. Legate Ruskoff levered his shoulder forward into the massive hangar doors, shattering the tracks that held them, bursting them inward.

Techs scrambled out of his way as the "enemy" machine barged inside, leaving their hasty repairs on a wounded ConstructionMech. Ruskoff spent lasers and PPC on the naked exoskeleton. It was all he had time for, as he crashed through the hangar's rear wall and into a firefight.

The *Thunderbolt* had gathered friends in the form of JES tactical carriers. Both hovercraft dumped flights of short-range missiles into one of Ruskoff's Bellonas, staggering the heavy tank. The *T-bolt* spent its light Gauss and short, stabbing lasers into his Saxon APC, chewing apart Cavalier infantry who bailed from the thunderstruck vehicle. The BattleMech kicked out, crushing one trooper against the APC, caving in the vehicle's side.

Ruskoff pulled his crosshairs over the *Thunderbolt*, and was rewarded with an instant tone of full targeting lock. Too close for Gauss, he sprayed the 'Mech with a few short-range lasers and then smashed in at its left side with his particle cannon.

Armor blew off in a mist and in thick globs of burning composite. The *Thunderbolt* staggered, and went down hard. Infantry swarmed forward, but Ruskoff waved them off as he used his PPC to hobble the other 'Mech, cutting into the backs of both knees.

"Three-squad, take the prisoner. Everyone else, leave him and forward!"

No time for the niceties. Not now. Legate Ruskoff had to finish this ill-advised resistance once and for all.

Time was running out.

Evan's small unit was first to break through to the Conservatory Grinder, his sixty-ton 'Mech kicking through the wire-mesh fencing and breaking a hole large enough to drive an armored column through.

From two kilometers out, he'd had good sensor readings on the battle being pressed across the main campus. He watched as Jenna fought for every meter, coordinating her ForestryMech and the wounded *Locust*, saving the armor for quick, violent counters and saving the infantry from a fiery death. The Principes *Firestarter* showed no hesitation in using its massive flamers on academy grounds. Gouts of incendiary gel sprayed out of both arms. Tank crews cooked alive inside their armored shells. A few buildings burned where the MechWarrior had not been cautious enough to prevent collateral damage.

Evan's arrival threw the balance back into Capellan favor. The firefight was brief and dissatisfying as the fast Battle-Mech and the assault tanks immediately withdrew. The *Ryoken II* limped away slowly, all but daring the Conservatory units to follow.

More units broke out onto the parade grounds, some of them chased after by Republic forces. *Shiao* Mai's Praetorian command vehicle crawled out onto the rough-paved Grinder with a swarm of Infiltrators clinging to it, tearing into the control cab. Evan spent a few crucial moments scraping the sides of the mobile HQ.

"Breakthrough on the sou'west grounds."

A militia *Catapult* and a Triarii *Legionnaire* led a host of Republic vehicles and APCs out onto the Grinder. The drive stalled as the Capellan line threw them back on their heels with a massive salvo of concentrated fire. The *Catapult* went down, its cockpit a blackened ruin, but the *Legionnaire* stepped over the corpse of its brother, rallying JES carriers and a Behemoth to quickly hit back and gut a pair of Regulator II's.

Evan nearly struck out to their aid, but too many threat icons popped up on his HUD to justify throwing himself awkwardly around the Grinder.

"*Zeus* and company coming right at us." Hahn was first to call it. He sounded excited. Eager.

"Hoverbikes swing around and tie up the battle armor," another junior officer ordered, bleeding in on one of the sub-channels.

Jenna. "Wilco team, form on my lead." She was dragging one leg on her ForestryMech, but the autocannon looked primed and ready and the huge diamond-toothed saw screamed around on the massive blade.

Evan stood guard over the mobile HQ, driving back any militia unit foolish enough to challenge his speed and the arcing swing of the *Ti Ts'ang's* battle-ax. A trio of wheeled Demons converged on Jenna's ForestryMech, thinking to find her an easy target and not thinking of the *Ti Ts'ang's* faster speed as it grew hotter and hotter. Evan sprinted out, stopped one of the Demons with a foot placed strategically through the front canopy shield, and broke the vehicle's spine with two heavy-falling chops. Jenna used her saw to carve a wheel off one other, and Hahn chased down the wounded tank to finish it with a deadly blast of autocannon fire. The third Demon escaped back to Republic lines, chased by Hahn.

"Think twice before they do *that* again," Hahn decided as the Destroyer skated back into the fold.

Watching The Republic forces drawing up orderly lines at the southern and western edges of the Grinder, Evan wasn't so certain. As the rain grew heavier they became shadowed outlines lit up only by the blue-white lightning flashes of PPC fire. He channeled his circuit to upper command, linking in privately with Mai Uhn Wa and Colonel Feldspar. "They are massing," he warned. And Governor Pohl's troops were taking a strong place near the center of that line. The Conservatory defense had gambled heavily on Anna Lu Pohl showing less backbone and more sympathy with the public outcry.

Shiao Mai evidenced little concern. "We can retreat no further, Evan."

Evan traded long-range sniping shots with a Joust, losing armor along his left arm, but blowing a track from the tank. A recovery vehicle eased forward, fastened a cranelike towing arm to the tank, and dragged it back out of the way. "We could hit them first."

"We could pledge neutrality," Mai countered. He sounded as if he seriously considered it. What would be tantamount to surrender.

"It is too late for that," Evan said. Legate Ruskoff could never allow the Conservatory to stand. Not with the Confederation's return.

Colonel Feldspar's Behemoth pulled back along the Conservatory's rear lines. "Does everyone think that?" he asked. "Our cadets? Their soldiers?"

The *Zeus* strode forward, setting a strong center to come directly against Evan's position. A solid cadre of armored vehicles and infantry swarmed around it. On its left flank the government auxiliaries mixed in with some light, fast 'Mechs and hovercraft. To Ruskoff's right he brought up three assault-class Brutus tanks, the *Ryoken II* and the *Firestarter*.

"Make the offer, Evan."

"*Shiao* Mai. I would not—"

"It has to come from you." He explained no further.

Make this good. Evan toggled for broadband comms, and turned off his scrambling software. "Legate Ruskoff. This does not have to end this way."

As if to deny that, a pair of Pegasus scout craft ran a quick slant out from the Conservatory position, laying out missiles in small, short salvoes. A pair of Gauss rifles struck out from The Republic lines. One Pegasus jumped up from the rough pavement, came down missing half its air skirt, and slid along the ground trailing sparks and fresh gravel.

"It has to *end*." Ruskoff sounded tired, but his voice strengthened as he went on. "This time it has to end my way. Your choices are surrender or subjugation."

"A choice Liao has never recovered from." Evan tried to put a touch of pleading in his voice, and was surprised that it came so easily. "Can't you see that? The Republic has to address the problem at its core."

"End the violence and justify The Republic giving you a damn thing." Fairly final. Ruskoff sounded angry, though not necessarily with Evan. He also had another channel open for passing orders. En masse, The Republic line pressed forward on two different fronts.

Evan stood in front of the command vehicle, ax raised defiantly. He and Mai formed an island of strength around which a few 'Mechs and a healthy group of armor and infantry gathered. Another tight knot of Conservatory defenders formed around Jenna's ForestryMech. The Armored Cavalry was their own entity, and their few scattered units did the best they could to make a coordinated effort to stand and deliver.

There wasn't much room to maneuver, so the cadets and soldiers mingled and mixed and fell back one reluctant pace at a time toward the burning buildings. Evan triggered laser blast after laser blast, cutting at the advancing line and waiting for the final order from Mai Uhn Wa, certain that it would come.

Capellan to the bloody, bitter end, they would go down swinging as a Warrior House—even a nascent Warrior House—should.

Evan chocked open his transmitter, still broadcasting on general frequencies. "You leave us little choice, Legate." He refused to retreat any further, throttling back until he stood straddle-legged and still. He fired a full bank of lasers—even the ones that could not reach—driving his heat up with a heavy spike from the fusion engine, readying himself for the last stand.

A VTOL spiraled down and crashed on the Grinder, burning, roiling greasy smoke into the sky.

"Legate?"

A Republic Shandra overturned with two wheels sheared off.

The defenders had nothing to cheer about. The wounded *Locust* that Jenna had partnered up with took a PPC to the head, a stream of hellish energies flooding the cockpit and turning the control space into a crematorium.

"Legate?"

"*Yóng yuǎn* . . . Liaoooo. . . ."

The battle cry, drawn out into a howl of pride, of determination, cheered the Capellan world as a Scimitar hovercraft speared out from one small cluster of besieged students. Gaining speed, it swerved out from under a missile barrage, and then accelerated right for a tight knot of Republic militia. A *Targe* managed to move fast enough, sidestepping the suicidal hovercraft. A Behemoth moving slowly up from the backfield was not so fortunate.

The two came together in a shattering impact of metal, blades, missiles and fire. It shoved the Behemoth back a few dozen meters, caving in its right side. The Scimitar was lost, left mangled and burning and spread out over the Conservatory's parade grounds.

"Liao! Liao!"

Two more vehicles: the Pegasus tank that had escaped death earlier and a wheeled VV1 Ranger. Both sped forward on charging attacks, braving missile fire and a sudden flurry of energy weapons as The Republic line reacted. The Pegasus disappeared under a wreath of smoke and fire, blasted out of its suicide run. The Ranger clipped the leg of a *Legionnaire*. The vehicle folded up like an accordion, spinning across the Grinder's wet surface until its wheels caught again to flip it over in a death roll. It carried part of the *Legionnaire's* leg with it. The 'Mech toppled in an awkward pirouette.

In singles and pairs, armored vehicles drove out in final charges not once ordered by *Shiao-zhang* Mai Uhn Wa, but arranged by him just the same. Arranged by him, and put into motion by Evan. Each victory added another martyr to the cause. Each death added more weight to Evan's soul.

"It's beautiful, Evan. It's *hùn dàn* beautiful." Hahn's Destroyer swung out from the pack, autocannon burning off its munitions like it had been newly serviced and stocked. "Liao . . . !"

"Hahn!"

The Destroyer skimmed over the Grinder fast enough to leave a spray of shattered rain pulsing in its wake. Evan wasn't going to catch the assault craft with its head start. Still, he raced forward, and the *Ti Ts'ang's* charge triggered something primed and ready in the Capellan force. Most of the Conservatory line surged forward after him.

Now *Shiao* Mai spoke up. Ordering any laggards forward. Calling on true citizens of Liao to make themselves known. To honor the sacrifice of those who had gone before them.

Evan simply wanted to reach Hahn's side, turn him from a suicide strike into a point-blank assault. But Hahn didn't answer his call, too busy shouting "Go, go, go!" into his voice-activated mic. The Destroyer hammered out hundreds of rounds as it sprinted across the Grinder toward Legate Ruskoff's *Zeus*.

Hahn's crew might have brought down the Legate's machine, too, except for the Principes *Ryoken II* that shoved its way forward and planted itself in the Destroyer's path.

Trading weapons fire with a seventy-five-ton BattleMech was hardly conducive to a long life. But at one hundred kilometers per hour, the energy wrapped up in the Destroyer's momentum carried more force than any weapons exchange. Slamming into the *Ryoken's* left leg, it careened around and side-slammed the right as well, folding over the awkward 'Mech and dropping it onto the Destroyer's roof. In a tangle of limbs, cannon barrel, tangled armor and overturned earth the two tumbled together over fifty meters before separating into separate junk piles.

There was hope that Hahn survived. Broken, maybe. Bloodied, certainly. But alive. Evan slackened back on his throttle, not so willing to dive headlong into the enemy line.

He would never forgive himself that moment's caution.

The *Firestarter* had followed its larger brethren to Legate Ruskoff's side. Trailing behind at first, it now planted itself between Evan and Ruskoff, close to the fallen BattleMech and wrecked hovertank. It turned, speared out both arms in the Destroyer's direction, and out of nothing more than pure malicious intent sprayed out twin columns of fiery death to blanket the Destroyer.

"No!" Slamming down on his pedals, Evan leapt his *Ti Ts'ang* into the air on plasma jets, thinking to land a crushing blow against the *Firestarter*. He would be too late again.

A Triarii *Phoenix Hawk*, several hundred meters to Evan's right, turned and stabbed its laser into the *Firestarter's* back. A Regulator II tank in Governor Lu Pohl's small force joined it, hammering a gauss slug in behind the ruby lance, shattering the last of the *Firestarter's* armor and sending it crashing to the ground with the remains of its gyroscope spinning and spitting out of the gaping wound.

The tide turned that quickly. Where Ruskoff's force had held the upper hand, it took one malevolent act to swing a number of shocked warriors to the Conservatory's side. Evan found himself fighting alongside the *Phoenix Hawk* and Regulator II, Jenna's limping ForestryMech and some Armored Cavalry Demons. His *Ti Ts'ang* hacked and slashed and battered its way forward, chasing Ruskoff's *Zeus*.

Ruskoff fell back quickly with a guard of heavy armor and retreating infantry. His assault 'Mech became a dark shadow moving farther back into the gray downpour.

Blood boiling, muscles trembling, Evan still knew a bad fight when he saw it. Throwing away lives to chase after Ruskoff would not bring back Hahn. And there were still heavy forces belonging to the Principes Guard on planet. They would have to be dealt with as well, and not by a crippled *Ti Ts'ang*.

Evan stood at the edge of the Grinder, astride the shattered fence line, and watched as the Republic force fell back in full retreat, but not a rout. Thunder rolled overhead, like an echo of the battle's earlier rage, and rain pelted down in a deepening cloak of false twilight. It pinged and rang against the *Ti Ts'ang's* armored head, streaked the ferroglass shield and puddled on the Grinder's rough ferrocrete surface.

Behind him, it began to quench the greasy fires that raged over Hahn Soom Gui's funeral pyre.

It was a call Viktor Ruskoff had never thought to make. But then, he'd witnessed events in the last five minutes that he'd never thought to see.

... A beaten cadre that stood strong behind its desperate ideology.

... Students choosing the martyrdom of suicide strikes over rational surrender.

... A Principes Guards MechWarrior throwing honor to the winds, executing any chance that the Destroyer's crew might be saved. Those were Liao lives. Liao children. And the Mech-Warrior hadn't cared.

"If he was still with us, I'd burn him down myself," Ruskoff whispered out loud, wanting to hear the words, but careful not to trigger his voice-activated mic. There wasn't anyone out here to talk to. Not even his aide, Lieutenant Nguyen, who had been in the *Phoenix Hawk* and had thrown his lot in with the Capellan horde. Where arguments had not persuaded Nguyen, one act of blind hatred had convinced him.

He toggled over to his command frequencies, connecting back to the Reserve and, through relays, into the satellite system that eventually found Lord Governor Hidic.

Ruskoff was not one to mince words. Even when the news was grave. Especially, when the news was grave. Turning his *Zeus* to stare back through the curtain of rain, he could see not a trace of Conservatory forces. But they were there. He waited for the Lord Governor to identify himself, and then strengthened his own voice with military steel.

His report was simple and damning, as most failures were. "We just lost Chang-an."

31

Friends and Family

"Freedom dawns on many true citizens today. A time long in coming, but one more step on the path back to the Confederation's manifest destiny. Capellans rejoice. Gan Singh has fallen."
—Lord Colonel Xavier McCarron, Gan Singh,
3 August 3134

Yiling (Chang-an)
Qinghai Province, Liao
7 August 3134

In a ceremony prepared over several days, Evan stood among his friends and comrades in arms as the final remains of fourteen cadets were laid to rest at the heart of the Conservatory's grounds.

The battle-thinned ranks stood at silent rest on the circular drive, out in front of the administration buildings. Gone was the old sculpture celebrating Devlin Stone and The Republic's coming to Liao, dismantled piece by piece by volunteer hands and cutting torches since the ConstructionMechs had all been pressed into service. The old metal lay in a scrap heap piled next to one wall. Eventually, it would be reclaimed and recast into a new sculpture. One that honored the sacrifice of all Capellans in the struggle to free their world.

Benevolent oppression, however you wanted to couch the name, was still oppression.

Mai Uhn Wa stepped up to the grave site. He wore simple robes and mantle of green and tan. His wispy beard was trimmed and his gray hair worn loose and flowing around his shoulders.

"As we say our farewells to these brave sons and daughters of Liao, we do so in the light of a new morning, which they helped to purchase with their very lives. We do so with the knowledge that they did not sacrifice themselves in vain. The Conservatory still stands. Chang-an and Governor Lu Pohl are with us. We have so much of what we sought. And yet, we have so much left to attain."

Jenna leaned into Evan, who wrapped one arm around her and to the devil with military protocol. She was a friend. They leaned on each other.

"Even with this heavy cost, Liao still does not enjoy the freedom that Gan Singh has finally come to know. And Styk. We are still held in the grip of The Republic's hand, and it seems they would rather choke us to death than let us breathe one taste of true Capellan liberty. But we shall continue. We shall fight against the smothering embrace of Exarch Redburn and his dying Republic. We shall remain until Liao celebrates once again the right to choose its own destiny."

As Mai Wa continued to extol the virtues of a free Liao, Evan tucked himself into Jenna. He couldn't help thinking about the costs, paid in blood, over so many years.

It reminded him again of the Betrayer, Daniel Peterson. Evan's grip tightened, remembering how the man had dared to lecture him. What did Peterson know about loss? What had really been his game?

Mai Wa headed into the close of the eulogy, drawing Evan back to the somber event. "The highest and most important ideal in any Warrior's life," the House Master said, his gaze finding Evan in the crowd, "is loyalty: to the citizenry he protects, to the state that provides, and to the chief executive of the state, who is the Warrior's commander-in-chief." The sixth dictum of the Lorix Order. One of the founding philosophies of the Warrior Houses. "This also provides one other charge. Loyalty to the people among whom you serve.

"I can say nothing finer of these soldiers, these Warriors, than they proved themselves among the most loyal of us all. We salute them."

Colonel Feldspar called the assembly to attention. Evan felt

Jenna stiffen, but he continued to hold her. Seven infantrymen, Mark Lo and David Parks among them, marched up to
the fore of the assembly. They held rifles in tight embraces.
Jenna turned her face into Evan's shoulder. Rifles came up,
and fired, fired, fired. Three salvoes, echoing lonely around
the campus grounds. A whiff of cordite touched the air and
Evan swallowed dryly.

Colonel Feldspar took the nod from Mai Uhn Wa and ordered the company dismissed.

Evan led Jenna forward, to inspect the small pedestal,
which would be the only grave marker for some time. The
planetary crest of Liao graced its head, followed by the in-
scription *Yù Xiān Guò Guān*. First Through The Breech.

Hahn Soom Gui's name was first on the list. Evan had seen
to that.

"Good-bye, Hahn," Jen Lynn Tang whispered as David and
Mark joined them. If Evan's comforting Jenna bothered Mark
Lo, the stiff-necked infantryman did not show it.

David, however, was shaken. He had dark circles beneath
his eyes and ashen skin. "I'm sorry," he said to Evan, bringing
himself briefly to attention as if reporting to his commanding
officer.

Jenna misunderstood. "There was nothing you could have
done, David."

"It's all right," Evan said. He heard the good-bye. He left
Jenna's side for a moment and embraced his friend. "You did
what you could. And you will always have a place here."

David nodded. He leaned in to kiss Jenna on the cheek and
traded grips with Lo. Jenna's gaze followed after him, confused. "Did he. . . ."

"He's done," Evan said. "Hahn's death was the last straw
for David. He'll never set foot on a battlefield again." Had
that been a fundamental flaw in the soldier's makeup from
the start? Or could he have served with distinction before
being broken under the added weight of rebellion? "How
about you?" Evan asked Mark. "Still with us?"

"To the bloody, bitter end," Mark affirmed. A pledge that
had taken on a life of its own in the last few days.

Jenna gave Mark a hug, whispered something to him. He
nodded to her when they separated. Evan did not ask. It did
not matter. In the end, all that would matter is whether they
won their goal, and how many lives were paid in the cost.

Hahn's was one among several. It brought home the very real cost, though. Evan had used Hahn just as Hahn had used Evan from time to time, supporting his politics. Hahn believed he was right in doing so. Just as Evan did.

Just as Mai Uhn Wa must.

Steering through the maze of mourners, Jenna in tow, Evan cast around for Mai Wa. Found him talking with Colonel Feldspar and Gerald Tsung, as well as a few junior officers. The Maskirovka agent Michael Yung-Te was fortunately absent. He steered over toward the small gathering, his thoughts in a tangle regarding his mentor and Master. Like a sculptor, Mai had chipped away at Evan's rough network to reveal the strength from inside. No denying his success. In the last few days, Mai had also begun to question Evan on the Cult of Liao assets still available to him. Evan had turned over everything, resenting the need to do so, then.

But if Evan believed that he had done right, didn't he also have to accept that everything Mai Uhn Wa had done was only what the veteran officer and rebel leader believed the best path to a free Liao?

"Evan," Mai greeted, nodding respectfully to Jenna to let her know that her company was best applied elsewhere.

He also dismissed another of the junior officers, leaving only Feldspar, Tsung, the two former *Ijori Dè Guāng* members and a man with insignia of the Fifth Triarii. Evan recognized him as Legate Ruskoff's aide, Lieutenant Nguyen. He'd been in the *Phoenix Hawk*, and had fired more out of disgust and shock over the actions of the Principes Guards than in true support of throwing off The Republic yoke.

Evan had not been surprised to hear that Mai had guaranteed Lieutenant Nguyen and his BattleMech release should Nguyen wish to leave. A *Phoenix Hawk* was a venerable design, and nothing to be thrown aside lightly in the aftermath of the battle. The Capellan cadre needed equipment, supplies and warriors. But even more, they needed unity. And *that* they might just have now.

"*Shiao* Mai." Evan began to nod, then bowed formally, a change that surprised both himself and Mai Uhn Wa. "Thank you for this morning. Hahn . . . all of them . . . appreciate it."

"We show our strength in remembering the sacrifices of those before us," the older man said, stroking one hand down his gray beard. Dark, hard eyes surveyed each man in turn.

"Liao was once a strong and united world. It can be again. It will be again."

It startled Evan that his mentor's thoughts closely paralleled his own, though it shouldn't have. Evan had learned from Mai's study of history, just as he had learned from the military academies.

He had also pushed back against both, mentor and military, never fully accepting either into his life. Maybe it was time to change that.

"It might be," he agreed. "If we can accept our differences and put them aside for the greater good."

Nguyen shifted from one foot to the other. "I'm not so certain that I agree that a Confederation vision for Liao is the greater good," he said, reading Evan's words literally. "No matter what Governor Lu Pohl now says."

Evan followed Nguyen's glance to Gerald Tsung. Whatever the man's feelings, he kept them well hidden. "We really have her behind us?" he asked Mai directly, meaning no insult to the Governor's Aide.

"We do. Yes." Mai spoke slowly, eyes clouded as he mentally chewed on Evan's earlier statement. "She has defied Hidic and cast her strength behind a return to true Capellan rule, calling on all residents and citizens to assist Confederation efforts with any and all means as a show of their loyalty."

Which would put the most pressure on landed nobles, who would lose everything if the Confederation returned and judged them not enthusiastic enough. The Maskirovka would quickly ferret out those who had worked against local efforts. Perhaps that was where Michael Yung-Te was off to. Yung-Te would find the Cult of Liao a great deal of help, if Mai Wa decided to grant the agent access.

"It is not an easy path," Nguyen said. "In my head, I *know* that The Republic has been a better steward of this world and its people. I accept that its open form of government is a better system."

"And what does your heart tell you?" Mai asked. But he was looking at Evan as well.

The lieutenant sighed. "That the people . . . our people," he amended, "that they will only suffer more under the forced occupation of The Republic. And that my oath to the people supercedes my oath to the Exarch."

Not an easy choice to make. Not for anyone. "It is time to put the past behind us," Evan said to Nguyen and Mai both, but in different contexts. "Liao needs us all." He bowed his head. "The heart knows where it belongs."

"And that," Mai said, satisfied, "is the essence of family."

32

The Treasure of Daoshen

The whispers grow in retelling. Sun-Tzu Liao has risen. The great Chancellor is rumored once again to have appeared before military leaders on the world of Liao. His presence has strengthened Capellan resolve despite recent efforts by Lord Governor Hidic and Prefect Tao to strangle the newborn movement. Said the Lord Governor at the end of a recent interview, "How does one fight an idea?"
—Reported by Mace O'Ronnell, Stellar Associated Press, 3 August 3134

Thunder Mountain
Sian
Sian Commonality, Capellan Confederation
11 August 3134

Dagger Di Jones did not care for the Capellan Confederation. She hated Sian, and she was ready to stick her knife into Daoshen Liao's throat.

"I have heard the shout for pan-Capellan unity. It echoes across half a hundred worlds, and shakes the foundation of The Republic down to its faulted core." Daoshen clasped slender hands behind his back, voluminous sleeves falling down to cover them.

The two of them waited at a pair of bright steel doors, polished enough to reflect lasers, she'd have guessed. Funhouse images of the two of them stared back, standing at the beginning—or the end, depending on how you liked to think of mirrors—of a short corridor.

With a start, she realized that the images were actually mirror perfect. It was the difference between them that made it comical. Di Jones had angry red hair trimmed short, and brown eyes quick and active. Daoshen Liao had a dusky complexion, dark, dark hair worn loose around his shoulders and falling over his face, with eyes of polished, inscrutable jade. She also looked shrunk down next to Daoshen's two-plus meters, and heavier than she should against his ninety kilos (sopping wet and rocks in his pocket as well as his head).

"It echoes. It echoes." Daoshen liked to mark the passing time with the sound of his own voice. Di wasn't even certain what they waited for. He had given no order, and there was no button to press. "It has even called to my father, who graces our efforts with his favor."

Cracked bread. The phrase shook Di, recalled to mind a world she had tried so very hard to forget, one whose dust she had kicked from her boots twenty years ago. It just fit Daoshen Liao so well. Flaky and burnt on the outside, dried to crumbs within. A brittle husk that cracked under the lightest pressure. She damned the lunatic again for reminding her.

And Bannson, for sending her.

The inbound trip on the *Corporate Raider*—a joke in plain sight, Bannson liked to say—had been long and tedious. Checkpoints and searches. Redundant layers of security that any pirate navigator worth her salt could bypass with one in-system pirate jump. On the ground it got no better: Death Commando escorts, frequent changes in her schedule with no interview given, interminable periods of waiting in small sitting rooms after which a new flunky came to ask her for her business with the Chancellor. At first she gave them Bannson's name only. Ten visits later she gave them the toe of her boot and a helping throw out the door.

Bannson didn't like the way she did business, he could send one of his stiff-suited toadies next time. Hobnobbing with the powerful wasn't her thing. But give Di a 'Mech, and she'd storm hell for Bannson.

Give her a few minutes with the knife tucked up her sleeve in a hold-out scabbard, and she'd *carve* an expression of interest on the Capellan leader's slack features. She wondered how he'd look with just one eye.

Half as well as he does with two.

She smiled, and the Capellan Chancellor craned around to glare. "You doubt that my father returns?"

Yes! "I doubt that my employer has an opinion. I am here to pass along a report, and, no offense, get the hell home." She started to dig the data crystal out of her pocket again, but he turned away. Again. No one would take the bloody thing. "My employer is very upset that his . . . reward . . . has not been offered."

"We are not in possession of Liao, are we." Not a question.

Di breathed a sigh of relief as the metal doors finally hushed open, revealing an octagonal room no larger than a BattleMech gantry lift. It had a wide seam around the entire floor. The walls were white-speckled stone and open to the chamber except for a square metal railing four feet around the entire floor. An elevator down into this Thunder Mountain that Daoshen had talked about on the flight north.

"My employer did not agree to take Liao. He agreed to support your efforts inside the Republic. That's it."

She followed Daoshen into the chamber. No wall held a tracked groove, so the support arm had to come straight up from below, like standing on the head of a giant piston. She didn't care for that idea, but at least this wouldn't be a long ride in an enclosed space with the scarecrow of a leader. Only one of them would have emerged alive.

"How we interpret his agreement is not part of our discussion," Daoshen said.

"Well, he certainly did not agree to any appropriation of his fleet outside Prefecture V." Now that *was* being diplomatic of her. Bannson had actually flung and broken a priceless piece of sculpture on learning that the Oriente Protectorate had seized three JumpShips. On the suggestion of Daoshen Liao!

The lift started down, building speed quickly as Di's stomach lurched. "You discussed that with the ambassador from Oriente, didn't you?"

"He was understandably curious how I moved troops and supplies around so quickly." Daoshen sounded as if he were purring, self-satisfied and smug.

"And so the Protectorate feints at Elnath," Jones said, "is able to grab Ohrensen, and they never show a weakness to the Marik-Stewart Commonwealth. At my employer's expense." The walls blurred past now, and she took a step back.

Daoshen remained where he was, so close to the near use-less safety rail that if Di had wanted, she could have scrubbed the smirk off his face with a good shove. She didn't believe even one of the self-serving tales telling about the Confederation leader's superhuman strength or spiritual vi-sion. She believed that if she had a secure way off-planet just now, she'd make herself infamous throughout the entire Inner Sphere.

"It is a wonderful plan," he said. For a few brief seconds, Di thought that he might be complimenting her on her bloodlust.

How far would this lift descend? "It would be better if my employer were given his due." If she brought it back with her, the appointment of nobility, then Dagger Di Jones was due a reward of her own. Bannson could be very generous when he was in a good mood.

"He is truly so eager to bring his fortunes and assets under Confederation influence? He sees the future drawing close?"

"He can tell which way the wind blows." She resisted the urge to sniff at the air. "And you know the final offer: his for-tune and businesses, minus the tribute already agreed upon, are to be awarded him in hereditary fief." Otherwise, this snake-of-a-Liao could seize everything Bannson owned, inside the Confederation and out, as was the right of the Chancellor over a citizen and unincorporated noble. Bannson was no dummy. He'd have his cake, eat it and lease options on it, too.

Still, he played in an impressive league when he drew an in-side straight against the Chancellor of the Capellan Confed-eration. It was just one of the reasons she had tied her fortune to Bannson's star.

Daoshen Liao still held a few aces up his sleeve, though.

The walls suddenly fell away, and a wave of vertigo swept over Di as the lift plunged down into a massive, well-lit cav-ern of mythic proportions. The lift shuddered as it shed speed quickly. That plus the swing in equilibrium had her grasping the rail, staring out and down and over the ranks of military equipment.

BattleMechs: six . . . no, nine full companies! *Men Shen*. *Blackjacks*. Assault-weight *Yu Huangs* and *Raven* scout 'Mechs. More companies of Po, Regulator and Ontos armored tanks. APCs and aerospace fighters and VTOLs.

This was the place. The place Bannson had told her about. One of Daoshen Liao's treasure troves, kept spotless, no doubt, by a legion of workers who would never—*never*—be allowed out from under Mask scrutiny for fear of what they might say. Di had an image, dark even for her, of those workers and technicians (and yeah, even MechWarriors who had to operate the machines now and then to keep them in working order) kept in a nearby barracks hewn out of the raw mountainside and never seeing the light of day. The salt mines of Sian.

And what of her? Daoshen had once shown this to Jacob Bannson, but why her?

For the first time since setting foot on the wretched planet, Di wondered if she would be allowed to leave.

The lift continued to drop slowly, sliding down the equivalent of a five-story building as it finally came to a smooth rest at ground level. Daoshen lifted a portion of the railing, swinging it back on hidden hinges. "Do you know what it means to serve a master who takes a Lord?" That was how she heard it in his voice: Big L—Lord.

Di let her right arm hang loosely at her side. A slight stretch and the clasp released, dropping a half kilo of finely balanced and laser-sharpened steel into her hand. Daoshen never once looked back. She was no threat. So he thought.

"I'm Bannson's." It was the first time she had mentioned her employer's name out loud. "You don't dare."

Maybe she *was* afraid of Daoshen Liao. A little. Now. But Di wasn't going to bow and scrape before anyone. That was another promise made on the world that *he* had forced her to remember.

Daoshen paused, cocked his head to one side as if he could hear the threat. "Truly? In all the demands you carry in that data crystal, is there a request for citizenship and inviolate status for *any* of his people?"

The crafty spider was giving something away? Di didn't believe that, not for a second. But, she also knew the answer, and so remained mute.

"Go back to 'your employer.' Remind him." He started walking again, leaving Di to wonder and guess of what she should remind her employer. The treasure trove? Daoshen's scrambled eggs in naranji sauce? She *would* have a long talk with him about the inviolate status thing. Oh, yes, she would.

And she might owe Daoshen something for that, someday.

"Remind him, and tell him that when Liao falls, he is to come for his reward. That will be our time to consummate the bargain. He will have earned it. That is the word of Daoshen."

33

Sons of Liao

*In a bold gamble, Prefect Tao has pulled forces out
of a dozen different engagements, conceding some,
stalling others. These have been leveraged against
Menkar and a counterthrust against Foochow, stunning Capellan holdfasts, while heavy aerospace assets
assembled in the space far above New Aragon have
jumped for Palos and Wei to institute a full blockade
of those staging worlds.*
—Jacquie Blitzer, battlecorps.org/blitzer/, New Aragon,
6 August 3134

Lianyungang Military Reserve
Qinghai, Liao
Prefecture V, Republic of the Sphere
13 August 3134

"**D**amned self-centered, obstinate slip of a Capellan whore!"

Daniel Peterson winced as Ruskoff slammed the door and
the frosted glass pane rattled angrily. The Legate stormed into
his office off the Planetary Defense Center like he might assault a city in his *Zeus*. He set himself in a wide-legged stance,
hands balled into tight fists. His burning glare fell on Daniel
first, as if the entire situation were his fault. The disgraced Paladin knew he certainly bore the lion's share of any blame to
be passed around.

But Ruskoff's fury passed over him. It slid by Lady Eve
Kincaid with hardly a pause and then by Colonel James

Lwellen, ranking military officer on Nánlù and another of Lord Governor Hidic's representatives. It stuck to neither of them. The Legate was neutrally mad. Railing-at-the-world furious. Nothing personal.

Daniel knew that feeling; every muscle quivering and the taste of blood in his mouth. He had felt it after the Massacre, before moving on to penance and rebuilding himself as Ezekiel Crow. More recently, he'd seethed with such fury at Jacob Bannson. It took betrayal to raise this kind of anger.

"Governor Lu Pohl?" Lady Kincaid asked.

"Who else?" Ruskoff continued his assault, stomping forward in pursuit of a known objective. He eased past the visitors' chairs—easily done, with Daniel's shoved off a bit farther to one side, away from the line officers—cornered his desk and secured the sideboard bar. He splashed amber into three glasses, colored his own with some dark plum juice, and then poured a fourth glass full of crystal clear and dropped in two cubes from an ice bucket. He carried his own glass to his desk, but rather than take his seat he perched on one corner.

The Legate did not serve, so the officers rose and picked up their own glasses. Lwellen also cut his bourbon with plum. Lady Kincaid preferred hers neat. She also favored her left side, where some shrapnel had ended up after blowing through her cockpit. Daniel did not move, hands clenched tight around the chair's armrests, staring at the remaining glass.

"It's sweet water," Ruskoff said, his voice a touch calmer.

Daniel rocked himself up from his seat. "Of course it is," he said. It was a thank-you, and Ruskoff knew it. But Daniel was also very conscious of the fact that Lwellen moved too far aside to let him pass and Eve Kincaid avoided his gaze on the way back.

Pariah.

Traitor.

Daniel's wrists itched where the shackles had recently come off. He did not return to his chair, drifting farther away from the line officers to lean up against the office wall, instead. His water smelled faintly of naranji and tasted of sweet citrus.

"Anna Lu Pohl will not reconcile," Ruskoff began the meeting. "Lord Governor Hidic and I spent half an hour *reasoning* with Gerald Tsang, and finally convinced him that we would only take the word of the Governor." He sipped, grimaced. "She tied into the video conference and offered us two days' grace before Confederation forces kicked us off Liao."

Lady Kincaid sat up straighter. "Does she really have that kind of control over the CapCons?"

"I doubt it. But she's certainly in with them now. The palace district is guarded by what few militia she trusts and one or two Conservatory cadets." No one asked how the Legate knew this. "The bulk of her 'guard' is operating in concert with McCarron's Armored Cavalry and this recent amalgamation calling itself House Ijori."

"After the dead Warrior House," Daniel volunteered softly. "Mai Uhn Wa is a student and disciple of the lost order."

Lwellen dismissed them with a wave of his hand. "Uppity kids and *Ijori Dè Guāng* terrorists. We've dealt with their kind before. The Dynasty Guard and McCarron's Second are the real threat. The question is, can we meet them here, or do we fall back to Nánlù?"

That was Hidic's question. Daniel tasted his water, but did not swallow, holding it in his mouth for a moment, warming it, thinking.

"I'd like to meet them here," Ruskoff said. "Beilù doesn't have a heavy industrial base to wreck, and Chang-an is here. If we follow Lord Governor Hidic's suggestion, we'll destroy exactly what we want to protect."

Lwellen was not swayed. "And if we lose here, lose big, Nánlù falls to the Confederation by default. We'll have to burn it behind us."

Daniel glanced sharply at the colonel's back. Ruskoff frowned, not liking that idea any more than the disgraced veteran.

Fortunately, it was Eve Kincaid who came to the rescue. "You do that, and the Republic can *never* come back to Liao. I think MechWarrior Flint proved that quite ably by burning our bridges in Chang-an."

Along with the Destroyer and its martyred crew. Daniel gave the Sphere Knight high marks for taking responsibility for the Principes Warrior, but even so she could not quite face the ugliness straight on. Of course, he'd had years to practice looking in mirrors and staring out into sleepless nights.

"The key to taking back Beilù is the Dynasty Guard," Ruskoff said, turning the meeting around to practical considerations. He eased off the corner of his desk, leaving his sweating glass behind on the blotter, and walked over to one wall where he'd tacked up a map. "If we kick out the biggest support propping up the Confederation drive, then Prefect Tao's strategy to blockade Wei and Palos might have time to work. Without constant refreshment, Terrence McCarron and this Mai Uhn Wa will wither and die."

"You're suggesting we leave Chang-an in enemy hands, then, and go after the Guard. But how?" Lwellen pushed his agenda by attacking Ruskoff's. "The Guard owns Hussan, the Du-jin Mountains and now the entire eastern and northern territories. The Capellan pseudomystic babble circulating says that they've received the guidance of Sun-Tzu Liao, which makes sense. Only Confederation inefficiency would have them move their base of operations out of the south and stake out claims on the plains and farmlands."

"It does make pinning them down harder." Given that she'd worked in Nánlù with Hidic, Lady Kincaid still sounded reluctant to agree. "They haven't even moved to defend Chang-an. Why not come again at the local forces protecting the capital?"

Daniel swallowed. "Because we'll lose." He saw disgust in Lwellen's eyes. *It talks.* "McCarron's Second and the Conservatory uprising have won over the people here. Which is why Governor Lu Pohl has gone over."

"You're the expert on treason," Lwellen snapped.

A heated flush prickled at the back of Daniel's neck. "Go on," Ruskoff told him.

"Any direct assault against Chang-an now will be seen as an attack *against* Liao, not for Liao. This has been the Confederation strategy from the start, to win back support from an alienated—and very large—portion of the population. It is time to attack that strategy."

Lwellen tossed off the last of his drink and reached forward to set the glass on the Legate's desk. "How can you attack an idea?"

"With the truth," Ruskoff offered. "Sun-Tzu Liao has not extended any magical protection over the Confederation forces. If he had, the Guard would be invincible. We know they are not. We will prove it. Rout them, and people will begin to doubt again."

"*If* we can pin them down." Lady Kincaid returned to practical considerations. "They must have a dozen staging camps established by now."

"Staging camps, yes." Ruskoff weighed back in. "But there may be one place in particular where they will stand and defend to the death. We've managed to compromise some highly placed members of the Cult of Liao in the last week. The Dynasty Guard has apparently occupied one of their 'holy sites'—the place where Sun-Tzu Liao ascended, apparently."

Lwellen scoffed. "And you think the Guard will defend such nonsense?"

Lady Kincaid hesitated. "They obviously thought enough of that nonsense to pull out of Nánlù. If they hadn't, we would be in worse shape. It may be worth the chance. *If* they allow it."

"If we can, we stand and fight," Ruskoff agreed. "If not, well, we do as we must." He left the map, paced in front of his desk and finally stopped in front of Lwellen. "That includes returning Lieutenant Daniel Peterson to active military service."

That brought Lwellen to his feet in a hurry, though he looked slightly foolish having to stumble shove his chair back with Ruskoff crowding over him. "Oh, that helps our cause, when the Black Paladin and the Betrayer of Liao comes out of retirement to fight for us. It's insulting enough that he is even here!"

Ruskoff had also caught Daniel flat-footed. He found his voice, quivering and shaking back in a dark corner of his mind. "You can't. People wouldn't understand. *They* wouldn't understand," he finished with a nod at the other line officers. He knew why the offer had come, and worried that Ruskoff might unmask himself and what small part he had played in the Uprising of 3128. Not a good idea. The Legate needed a united force. He needed a decisive victory.

"I need him," the Legate said, dismissing Daniel's unspoken arguments. "Lord Governor Hidic has already agreed to sign an order of amnesty." That stunned the entire room. Eve Kincaid glanced sharply toward Daniel. Lwellen sat back down and Daniel sagged back against the wall, his legs suddenly unable to bear much weight.

Ruskoff waited to make certain he had everyone's attention. He most certainly did. "If we are to reclaim the moral high ground, with citizens and Capellan residents both, we need to set an example that redemption is possible. What better way?" The military officer walked over to Daniel, pulled him off the wall and forced him to stand upright. "Daniel is a son of Liao. We can use that in our favor."

"I would like to confirm this," Lwellen said, jumping back to his feet like some kind of military jack-in-the-box. Ruskoff's handling had him rattled and off balance, no doubt as the Legate had intended from the moment he'd walked into the room. Daniel stood silent as the colonel left the room. Lady Kincaid remained.

"You did not have to do this," Daniel said once the door rattled shut behind Lwellen.

"Yes," Ruskoff said. "I did." He left Daniel's side and moved back to his earlier perch on the edge of his desk. He looked at once commanding and compassionate. Daniel had not seen the latter in some time. "I need experienced soldiers, and you're still one of the most able MechWarriors on the planet. And I meant what I said to Lwellen. You might be valuable in proving the power of redemption to the Capellans."

Lady Kincaid leaned forward. "But that's not why you did this," she said. Perhaps guessing, perhaps not.

The Legate smiled thinly. "Not completely, no." He said nothing more on it.

She climbed gingerly to her feet, set her glass next to Lwellen's. "The Black Paladin rides again?" she asked. She stepped over to look Daniel up and down very carefully. In the past few days Daniel had gotten to know people's expressions very well when it came to judging him. Eve Kincaid's was different. She seemed to measure something deeper than his actions. "Maybe," was her final judgment.

Then she limped out the door.

Ruskoff met Daniel's gaze. "If I can forgive myself, I can begin to forgive you. What you do from here is in fate's hands." He glanced at the door. "Lwellen will be finding out any moment that the Lord Governor's promise is contingent on a lot of things, including proof of your rehabilitation and your testimony in a great deal of hearings. So I suggest you absent yourself for the unflattering discussion we will have on the merits of your case. Unless you do not trust me to look after your interests."

Daniel shook his head, throat pinched closed and unable to speak.

"Go on, then, Daniel. Get some rest and come in fresh for our morning's planning session. If we're going to force the Dynasty Guard to stand and fight, we'll need to convince Hidic to back our play with every last soldier he can spare."

"I won't let you down," Daniel promised, finding his voice again. It was stronger this time.

The Legate was less sanguine. "You might," he said. "You might. It's a long road back." But if his doubts included any serious thoughts of rescinding the offer, Ruskoff hid it well. He shrugged, offered a tight smile and an encouraging nod. "But I don't believe it will be for lack of trying."

"No." The fallen Paladin tried on a weak smile, and felt it strain at the corners. "Never that." He already knew that he wouldn't wait until morning. If Ruskoff was extending this very last attempt at redemption, there was one more thing he could do. Something he could not even tell the Legate he intended to try.

Yiling (Chang-an)
Qinghai Province, Liao

Evan Kurst had let Jenna alone as they both worked through their grief. They were there for each other, certainly, but with Hahn's death and David Parks's loss to the Conservatory, they escaped into solitude rather than each other's arms. Just as well. As House Ijori rose from the ashes, there was much to think about.

Now Evan was thinking about rekindling their start at a serious relationship.

Standing in the commons that separated his dormitory from hers, he leaned against the low bend of elm, watching moths dance around the overhead lamps. The bark rubbed rough against his bared forearms, and his feet were cold from standing in the wet, unmowed grass. He walked himself through what he might say. If she gave him the chance. Jen was a strong woman who also knew what she wanted, and might not give him much time to say anything one way or another. Evan had to admit, such forcefulness had its charms as well. He smiled, laughing at himself, joking up the courage for that last step forward.

He never made it. Footfalls padded to an uneasy stop behind him. The quiet was expectant. Evan couldn't help but turn.

Daniel Peterson nodded. "Hello, Evan."

Evan reached for his pistol, forgetting in the sudden burst of adrenaline that he'd traded his cadet corps fatigues for civilian dress. Jeans and a casual shirt. Canvas sneakers. He shoved himself away from the tree, glancing about to see if Peterson had led back an entire Republic team. Nothing. They had the commons to themselves except for one cadet walking on the other side of the lawn. Too far away.

Should he yell for backup? Take a swing at the betrayer? Evan had imagined a dozen different ways this meeting could take place, and right now he was stumped for one of them.

The other man backed up a wary step, ready.

"Easy, Evan. I didn't come here to fight."

Evan took one threatening step away from the elm, hands balled into tight fists. Peterson made no move to defend himself, even though he had several centimeters and twenty kilos on Evan, easily. What was he waiting for? Charge the man. Wrap him around that tree. Do something! Call an alarm— Peterson would never get off the grounds alive.

So if Evan couldn't make himself judge and executioner, he'd leave it to others?

Standing there, shaking, Evan forced himself to relax. Slowly, he unclenched each fist. He had grown beyond blindly striking out, apparently. He had a greater need to understand.

"So," he said, remembering their last conversation, how it ended. "This isn't 3128. But you *are* Ezekiel Crow."

"My name is Daniel Peterson. I think you know that."

"Why are you here?" Evan asked, spitting out each word as if it had a bad taste.

Peterson held a steady gaze. "We didn't get a chance to finish our last conversation. I thought there was still something left to say. Something that might make a difference." He looked around the deserted, darkened campus. "I felt I owed you that."

"You have no idea what you owe me. I've hated you my entire life for what you did. And you had the nerve to stand there and lecture me on the consequences of my actions? All that empty talk about the road to hell being paved by the best of intentions?"

"I did that. I couldn't stand there and watch it all happen again without trying to stop it."

Evan advanced a step on Peterson. "Let it go, you said. Talk this out, you said. You!" The anger was there, white hot and burning at the edge of Evan's control.

Peterson looked ready to turn and walk away. Evan swore that he'd bring the man down and kill him if he tried. But the Betrayer simply checked the horizon, saw that they were still alone and folded his arms over his chest.

"You're not going to listen, Evan, but I'm going to try one last time. I've spent most of my life trying to make good on what I did, but I've never made excuses. And I'm not about to start with you."

"Why not me? What's wrong with me?" Evan felt a cold hollow beginning to eat away at his anger now. He'd let it go for too long. "My parents died after the Night of Screams when a 'Mech—a *Republic* 'Mech!—smashed through our apartment building. That was in the second wave of assaults. Why should I care how many years you lived a lie, trying to make it up to The Republic? What have you done to make it up to me?"

"I tried to help you not make the same mistake I did."

"It's not a mistake unless you never had the conviction to begin with. That's your problem, not mine." His rage was spent, and Evan shook with cold and adrenaline fatigue now. He waited, but Peterson had nothing else to say, apparently. The two men stood looking at each other. "What did you expect, Daniel? Why did you come here? Forgiveness?"

"It's not important anymore, Evan, why I came here. The person I wanted to help is gone."

"No." Evan shook his head. "The person you *thought* you could help never was. My decisions may not be easy ones, but I can live with them." It was *he* who turned away now. Toward his own dormitory. Not Jenna's. He glanced back once, and saw Peterson still standing there. "Can you say the same?" he asked.

No answer followed after him.

34

A Time For Change

*Today, Lord Governor Harri Golan of Prefecture VI
stressed that only through peaceful relations with
neighboring realms can The Republic hope to sur-
vive and thrive in this time of chaos and doubt. The
Lord Governor mentioned specifically his latest attempts to broker a new peace with the Oriente Protectorate, and to stop any similar threats from the
Capellan Confederation.*
— ComStar Interstellar Associated, New Canton,
3 August 3134

Suriwong Floods
Sarrin Province, Liao
15 August 3134

The mobile HQ rocked back and forth as it lumbered up
the clay riverbank. Mai Uhn Wa tightened down the simple
lap belt that strapped him into the crawler's seat. Gray, pre-
dawn light brightened his monitors, and on them he
watched as half a dozen 'Mechs and a rump battalion of
tanks and APCs waded ashore, skimmed across the latest in
a series of shallow rivers, or plowed through one of a dozen
fords.

The Suriwong Floods drained out of Beilù's Northern
Ranges every year as heavy spring melt washed through the
flatlands. The runoff spread into a system of marshes and
bogs, cutting through in a shifting pattern. As the runoff slack-

ened and one particular cut deepened, the Floods would eventually form the Suriwong River. But not yet.

"*Shiao* Mai. I have *Sang-shao* Rieves on video transmission."

Michael Yung-Te glowered down at him. "Now you will see." The agent had refused a secure seat on the observation pad, not wanting to leave Mai's side on the control deck. He stood near one wall, holding on to a hand strap, looking vaguely sick as the crawler continued to roll and pitch as a large vessel sliding over ocean waves. "The *Sang-shao* will not be in a forgiving mood."

Mai nodded, and slid his chair back to an empty station. A nearby tech patched through the transmission, and a darkly unhappy face glared at him from only a few dozen kilometers away.

"You tread on dangerous ground, Mai Uhn Wa."

"That is so. Footing on the Suriwong Floods is tricky at best."

The Dynasty Guard's commander was not amused. "My scouts have reported a large military force converging on our position. Other than yours," the man clarified, preempting Mai's next remark.

"That would be Legate Ruskoff. I would expect a mix of militia, Triarii Protectors, and Principes Guards."

"The Republic is striking at us here? Now? How very convenient."

Mai chose to ignore the sarcasm. "We think so, since we have come here to assist, *Sang-shao* Rieves. If you will deploy from the north, we can link up before Legate Ruskoff hits your valley hideaway."

"A location they should know nothing about! We cannot remove . . . *the artifact* in time." Meaning the stasis chamber containing Sun-Tzu Liao. "It is a technology we are unfamiliar with. But of course, your faithful dog would know that."

Mai shrugged. "However The Republic militia has come here, we are on hand to assist. Shall we pool our efforts, Carson Rieves, or shall we divide our efforts in front of a larger enemy force?"

"Very soon, Mai Uhn Wa, we will determine, you and I, who is in charge on Liao."

"And if we discuss this much longer, The Republic will settle that for us. I estimate fifteen minutes before my forces engage. Without you, we fail." And without the Second McCarron's and the Conservatory cadre, Rieves could not be assured of victory on Liao either. Mai let the officer chew on that a moment. "Or would you rather risk the *artifact* and have to explain its loss to Chancellor Daoshen?"

The idea did not sit well with Rieves no matter which way he looked at it. "You are playing for stakes far above your position," was all Reives said. And then his transmission winked out of existence.

Mai Uhn Wa looked to the Maskirovka agent. "Now we shall see," he agreed.

Evan already had too much to keep straight in his mind. The hastily studied lay of the land—mostly a marshy river basin followed by the soft rolling hills that were Sun-Tzu Liao's final resting place. He juggled Mai's orders for battle, the various level of skill of the men and women under his command, his position on the far right wing of the Capellan line and what would be expected of him. Jenna in her ForestryMech. Mark Lo, who had joined one of the new Fa Shih squads.

The very real fact that the assembled Republic army was twice their size.

Mai's Praetorian command vehicle fed strategic information onto one of his screens. With the Principes Guards and most every militia Warrior that Nánlù could spare fielded in this final strike at the Confederation position, Ruskoff assembled nearly two mixed-force battalions. The Legate's *Zeus* was their heaviest 'Mech, and one of a dozen large machines. The Capellan irregulars could not compete. Even with McCarron's Armored Cavalry and Governor Lu Pohl's commandeered forces. They needed the Dynasty Guard, and *Shiao* Mai could not promise they would deploy.

"Contact," a voice crackled in his ear as forward scouts began skirmishing with Republic outriders. Threat icons burned to life on his heads-up display. "Falling back under heavy fire."

Evan's orders were clear. Draw a large force off The Republic's main body and pull them in toward the Dynasty Guard's position. "Bring them to us," he reminded his small picket force. "Company. Forward at them."

The ground was soft. Too soft for speedy travel unless Evan

wanted to strain a leg actuator or hyperextend a joint. Muddy clay oozed around the *Ti Ts'ang's* feet, sucked at each foot-step and clung to the lower legs in large clumps of reddish gold muck. He moved in lurches and bowlegged steps, hoping they would clear the Floods quickly and find some good open room for maneuvers.

Not quick enough. The scouts in Pegasus hovercraft and Demons arrived first, pulling a pair of VTOL strike craft be-hind them as well as a mixed lance of Destroyers and Bellona.

The wheeled Demons stuck to more solid ground, bouncing and skidding and throwing out long rooster tails of earth. The Destroyers had every advantage, and pounced on the wheeled vehicles just short of safety, turning one into a burn-ing wreck before Evan could throw enough forces forward to aid them.

Long-range missiles and a few light autocannon sniped at the patrol, but the Destroyers weren't foolish enough to close with a combined-arms company. A pair of McCarron's Balacs chased off the strike 'copters, and Evan's force shook out into a ragged line to pursue.

"Don't wait for us," Jenna said, bringing up the rear in her ForestryMech accompanied by a few slower assault tanks. "Sixth squad, on my lead. We're pulling for the headlands." She veered off.

If Jenna could clear two shallow rivers and a small swamp, she could shortcut over some drier land and act as a safety force toward which Evan and his abbreviated company could run.

"Watch your back," Evan told her, but his mind already looked toward his flanking strike against Ruskoff's column.

He barely heard her say, "You do the same."

Jenna's force broke away, following a ridge of mostly dry high ground. Evan let her go with a small twinge of concern that he quickly buried. There was still plenty left for him to worry about, after all. Including what they could do if the Dy-nasty Guard did not show. There had to be something. He just didn't see it yet.

35

Both Sides of the Line

Gan Singh's provisional government, advised by
Sang-shao Xavier McCarron, has asked for Senator
Jiu Soon Lah to return to the world and accept a
post as the new planetary governor under Confeder-
ation rule. Governor Jean Littlefield resigned after
Gan Singh's final surrender, and was allowed to
leave the system.
　　　　　—ComStar Interstellar Associated, Gan Singh,
　　　　　　　　　　　　　　　　　　　　7 August 3134

Suriwong Floods
Sarrin Province, Liao
15 August 3134

Artillery fire tore up the Floods around Evan Kurst, geyser-ing up water and fire, muck and smoke. An oily haze churned across the low-lying hummocks. A downed Balac Strike VTOL burned on an island of cottonwood and willows—black soot and gray ash swirled together in the air. Missiles rose and fell in their sharp, violent arcs, and the hard light of laserfire slashed back and forth between BattleMechs, armored vehicles and infantry.

Evan's forward probe hadn't split The Republic force, they'd turned it. Legate Ruskoff wheeled around to throw everything at them, and Evan's small company was forced far back from the main Capellan line. The Legate first thought they were the Dynasty Guard. Mai's command vehicle unscrambled a few intercepts to that effect, including one broken transmission that the House Master played for Evan.

"Legate, I . . . these vehicles. That *Tian-zong*. Conservatory forces! Ijori . . . come out of Chang-an."

Evan recognized the voice instantly. He'd never forget it. Daniel Peterson was fighting on the field!

The only 'Mech engaged near House Ijori's *Tian-zong* was a Triarii-painted *Tundra Wolf*. Evan circled around on its position, weathering a storm of missiles and laserfire to challenge the Betrayer. His *Ti Ts'ang's* heat-accelerated myomer allowed him to close, hacking large chunks of armor away from Peterson's chest and side.

But the disgraced veteran was not without some support. A Principes armor company led forward by the on-planet Knight—Lady Eve Kincaid—came to Peterson's rescue and drove back the Ijori forces. Her *Mad Cat III* savaged two of Evan's Condors. A pack of hoverbikes peppered his *Ti Ts'ang* with laserfire, chasing Evan back toward safety.

Triarii and militia squads piled up to the west. The Knight and fallen Paladin held the north. Eva's position looked desperate. Then fate intervened in the voice of an Armored Cavalry scout patrolling far to the northeast.

"The Dynasty Guard! They're deploying out of the hills!"

More welcome words Evan had not heard. The Republic force got the news at nearly the same time, apparently, with Lady Kincaid splitting away for a hard run northwest. She drew several hovercraft with her.

Evan pulled his crosshairs over the *Tundra Wolf*, preparing another charge. He sparred against the *Tundra Wolf's* heavier weapons, trying to hold Peterson's attention as the Ijori *Tian-zong* slogged forward with a squad of Regulator II heavy tanks.

"All nearby units, this is Ijori-five." Jenna! "Praetorian is under assault. We need backup. Home in on transponder three-eight-one."

Tori Yngstrom moved up on his position. Her *Tian-zong* belted out Gauss slugs from each arm. "We can hold here, push them back toward the Dynasty Guard. Get to *Shiao* Mai!"

Evan was the logical choice, his *Ti Ts'ang* was the faster 'Mech. He had walked away from Peterson in Chang-an, and that had been one of the hardest decisions of his life. This time, there was no choice to make. His House Master needed him.

Evan pulled back, grabbing a Destroyer and two nearby Condors, as well as a loaded Maxim APC arriving from the south. "Three-eight-one," he ordered his new ad hoc unit. On the command frequency, he broadcast, "Ijori-one, en route."

Six kilometers struggling through marshes and muddy rivers cost Evan nearly ten minutes as he homed in on the mobile HQ's directional beacon. He learned on the way that it was Ruskoff's *Zeus* pushing forward to trap Mai Uhn Wa in an encirclement. Jenna opened a door, her ForestryMech dicing up a pair of Joust crawlers. The Praetorian escaped with armor and infantry assets to make rendezvous with Evan's force.

Not soon enough. The *Zeus* followed and caught up with the fleeing command unit, called in artillery fire to pin it down. Evan listened in on the battlefield chatter coming from just ahead. He ran his *Ti Ts'ang* up a steep rise that thrust out of the swampy flatlands, cleared its summit and then leapt far out over the Suriwong Floods.

Jenna's ForestryMech was nowhere to be seen. Mai Wa's Praetorian struggled along a spine of rock and clay, protected by a *Locust*, some Armored Cavalry, and two wheeled APCs dumping out Purifier troopers and Ijori irregulars.

Still airborne, Evan identified a *Zeus* and a *Pack Hunter* leading forward a mixed bag of Republic armor and infantry. More threat icons gathered on his HUD's horizon.

He came down into a shallow river, splashing up great sheets of water and sinking the BattleMech's feet meters into soft, grabbing clay. Stuck. His arrival threw back the *Zeus*, which turned away reluctantly like a snarling beast deprived of its prey. One PPC snaked manmade lightning across the stirred Floods, ripping a long, jagged gash up the side of Evan's *Ti Ts'ang*. Gray-green heat sink coolant spurted out of the wound like arterial blood.

A squad of Triarii Scimitars swept in to harass him with missiles. Fire blossomed along both legs as Evan worked his feet loose from the muck. He walked his *Ti Ts'ang* up onto a rocky bar and set himself in a wide-legged stance. His hovercraft and the HQ's remaining defenders flocked to Evan's side, driving back the Scimitars.

"Wedge formation," Evan ordered, buying time for his House Master. Artillery fire continued to hammer down behind them, walking in closer with every round. "Cavalry, double up on my left. Ijori, thin ranks and envelop on my right."

A risky call. Evan had little more than a reinforced company to work with. McCarron's soldiers made for a good anchor on his western flank, but thinning the rest to the east was chancy. They weren't veterans. They were hardly more than cadets.

They certainly were not an elite Warrior House. Not yet.

"Ijori-five. Jenna. Can you rendezvous?"

Silence answered him and a push by the *Zeus* occupied him for a moment. Fire and shrapnel swept the center of his line in alternating waves. Evan's BattleMech dropped to one knee under the barrage, but it stood again.

"Jenna?"

"Evan." Mai answered him. "Ijori-five is down."

"Confirm!" Evan snapped at his Master, letting his own feelings get in the way. Not now. Not like this.

"It is confirmed." Mai showed no more warmth. "We've lost a *lot* of good people already. No news on casualties, or survivors."

The news cost Evan several seconds, wondering if Jenna might still be alive, thinking about the things he had not gotten a chance to say to her yet. The battle did not wait for him. Greasy smoke from a burning APC hid the Ijori irregulars who moved up quickly, rocket launchers across their shoulders. A pair of Triarii *Stingrays* slashed across the battlefield, catching the *Locust* in a broadside salvo of lasers, and a lance of Mk II Scimitars scooted in under that cover and slashed at the Armored Cavalry with lasers and missiles.

One of the Po II heavy tanks turned and snap fired, taking the nose off one Scimitar with a well-placed Gauss slug. The hovercraft dipped nose down into a thin gruel of mud, caught in the Suriwong's grip, end-overed and then splashed down on its side.

It wasn't Terrence McCarron, but the shot was certainly worthy of the veteran. Evan glanced at his HUD, checking ID tags. "Cav-six. Can we call on your commander?"

Again it was Mai Uhn Wa who answered, overriding from the command vehicle. "Terrence McCarron is holding, barely, on the eastern edge of the Floods."

So there was just him. Hahn dead. David finished. Mark Lo separated by the press of battle and Jenna left behind. The Dynasty Guard pressed forward, but slowly, slowly. And now, no Cavalry to the rescue.

Artillery tore a spit off his island, pinging and slamming rocks into the *Ti Ts'ang's* lower legs. Evan checked his heat curve and spent half of his lasers at a Demon that tried to edge forward around the base of the same rising slope he'd come over only minutes before. A few vehicles crawled up from the Capellan backfield, but there wouldn't be much else. Except Legate Ruskoff. He would be coming.

If Evan did not move against him first!

"Ijori-one. We have movement on the enemy line. Your orders?"

Evan watched the red icons shifted, *Zeus* taking up a spearhead position, flanked by a limping *Pack Hunter* and a scarred *Vindicator*. Armor crawled alongside or raced forward on cushions of air. Infantry leapt and ran and clung to the sides of vehicles. Ruskoff feathered most of his forces out to the east as well, matching Evan's line.

"Ijori-one. What are your orders?"

He saw the maneuver in his mind's eye. Feint into the eastern enemy, and then drive into the middle with whatever he had left. Sweat beaded on Evan's brow that had nothing to do with his saunalike cockpit. A flush rose from the back of his neck. This is what Hahn had felt, he knew, in those last moments. All or nothing.

"Ijori-three?"

Mai Uhn Wa also sounded concerned. "Evan?"

Evan bumped his throttle forward, walked his *Ti Ts'ang* to the end of his little island and straddled the artillery crater. He pulled his crosshairs over the *Zeus*, and adjusted his grip on the sweat-slick control sticks.

"We charge," he said. "Everything we have left, for House Ijori."

Daniel Peterson struck with lasers and missiles, flailing about his *Tundra Wolf* with desperate attacks as a mixture of Dynasty Guard and Ijori warriors sought to rush his position. Infantry scrabbled at his lower legs, trying to gain purchase. Fire wreathed the BattleMech's upper chest as a new spread of missiles hammered into him, and lasers scourged its back.

No one moved to his aid this time. Lady Kincaid was pinned under heavy fire, and the flanking vehicles turnkeyed to him by Ruskoff had fallen back under Lwellen's orders. No use throwing good after bad. Wasn't that what the militia colonel had said in planning?

Daniel had no intention of making it easy.

Kicking aside Fa Shih troopers and a JES tactical carrier, the ex-Paladin cleared his own path toward the relative safety of the allied line. Given a choice, he would have set himself for the western flank where Eve Kincaid wielded two companies of Principes Guards like a surgical tool. For better or worse, he fell in closer to the allied center. There, Colonel Lwellen's *Catapult* maneuvered from side to side to avoid the press of Carson Rieves's assault-weight *Yu Huang*.

It was a sparring match that only had one conclusion. Nothing stood up under the kind of pounding an assault 'Mech could inflict, except another assault 'Mech. The Dynasty Guard owned every advantage except for the raw determination of Republic forces to hold off a Capellan victory.

"If we had our full numbers massed here, we'd have them."

But they didn't. The Republic force had split its strength against "House" Ijori, thinking they had found the Dynasty Guard. How had the Conservatory forces learned of this assault, coordinating their own arrival so well? Daniel could only imagine. An informer? Misinformation leaked through to Legate Ruskoff? Whatever the ruse, it had worked. Now the fall of Ijori was the pivotal point to the entire battle and the very defense of Liao. Break the nascent Warrior House, and The Republic could sweep all forces north against the Dynasty Guard.

Which meant holding the line, here, in the foothills above the Suriwong Floods.

A pair of lasers stabbed into Daniel's back, bringing him up short of The Republic lines, forcing him to turn and deal with a pair of Demons. His Tactical Missile System automatically selected down to short-range warheads, slamming blossoms of orange fire into the side of one vehicle. His lasers slashed apart one tire and cut through the axle behind it. The fast-attack vehicle slewed over, dug a fender into the soft ground, and rolled into a crashing death.

The other vehicle sped back to the side of an approaching *Wasp*. Daniel throttled into a slow, backward walk, protecting his thinning rear armor.

Which set him in the no-man's-land between Republic and Confederation lines, alone, when the warning crackled across communication channels.

"Down! The Legate is down!"

Daniel froze over his controls, earning him a ruined right arm actuator as the *Wasp* sprinted in, stung at him with lasers and machine guns, and raced away again. He tried to snap fire a return salvo, but the lighter 'Mech's speed and stealth armor made targeting lock impossible.

At least it got him moving again. He faded back from The Republic line, torn between the battle here and the man who had offered him a hand.

"*Zeus* is back up," the report came, but it was no time for breathing easy. "Limping . . . *Ti Ts'ang* and infantry swarm attacks." Evan Kurst! "Taking heavy fire. *Tā mā dè*! They're all over us."

The *Wasp* continued to strike at Daniel, always moving for his flanks. A Demon and a pair of Condors now trailed in its shadow. Daniel fired again, and again. He turned his *Tundra Wolf* south, then back north again. He had a fairly clear field to the southwest. . . .

"What are you waiting for, Peterson?" It was Lwellen, still struggling along in the face of the *Yu Huang's* deadly assault. "Legate Ruskoff is in trouble. Pull him out, man!"

Lwellen passed other orders as well, detaching VTOL assets and a squad of JES tactical carriers to his command. It wasn't much, but they would be able to move fast. They came toward him at flank speed, chased by Confederation units split off to prevent any aid from heading south. *Sang-shao* Rieves did not want reinforcements coming north.

"Go, Daniel." Lady Kincaid. Her voice sounded strained. She led the Principes Guards forward, driving through a wall of Confederation heavy armor to try and bring some relief to Lwellen. "You won't make the difference here."

The *Wasp* came at him again. Daniel turned into it, preempted its assault by hammering the area with missiles from his XX-rack and ATM launcher. When the stealth-equipped machine staggered out of the destructive rain, he shouldered it aside and left it sprawled over the scarred earth. A pair of *Jessies* smashed it down again on their way by, slamming a curtain of short-range missiles across its back.

Then they were moving south and west, away from the foothills and back into the Suriwong Floods. A *Tian-zong* fired gauss slugs at him from long range, missed. The Ijori 'Mech struck out at sixty kilometers per hour in pursuit, but could not even keep up with the Dynasty Guard armor sent by Rieves.

It was a race to see who would reach the southern battle first.

If Viktor Ruskoff could hold on for their arrival.

The Ijori charge had smashed into Ruskoff's line like a sledgehammer, putting forward every effort to bring down the Planetary Legate. Evan smashed the *Zeus's* gauss rifle into useless scrap, and put a deep ax wound into the assault 'Mech's knee as well. The *Zeus* went down, and a mix of Purifier and Fa Shih attempted to reach the stricken 'Mech.

Then a savage counterthrust by the militia *Vindicator* and several Brutus assault tanks drove Evan back. He lost his Purifiers to heavy bombardment by a JES II strategic carrier. The Fa Shih barely made it out ahead of a hunter-killer pack of hoverbikes.

The Capellan force hammered forward again, trying to reach the wounded *Zeus*. But The Republic defenders had stood up under their first assault. They were better prepared for the second. The third. Artillery fire fell haphazardly now as a see-saw offensive spread forces all across the Suriwong Floods, leaving some vehicles stranded, others burning.

There always seemed to be more, though, as reinforcements on both sides of the line streamed in for Ijori's last stand.

"Ijori-one, be advised: Dynasty Guard has broken The Republic cordon!"

Not even the unflappable *Shiao* Mai could hide his excitement. With the Guard *finally* loose in the Suriwong Floods, Capellan forces tying up Ruskoff's command had a chance. Mai and House Ijori had a chance. It all came down to time.

Hours, perhaps minutes.

A Republic VTOL, swooping in from far afield, strafed over Evan's small spit of rocky land. Touching off his jump jets, he rose on streams of plasma and swatted the fragile craft out of the air with his battle-ax.

He landed in a ready crouch, knuckles white as he gripped his control sticks with renewed strength. From The Republic backfield, Ruskoff's *Zeus* limped forward once again.

"Hold the line," Evan reminded them all. His voice tightened. "Hold."

His *Ti Ts'ang's* lasers speared one Republic minigun cycle

as it tried to jump between two rocky upcroppings, crisping machine and rider and dropping them into the sluggish waters.

A pair of new *Jessie*s slid around a willow copse, chasing a Cavalry Condor out over deeper water. The Condor took heavy missile strikes against its skirting, foundered and sank.

Then dozens of hard-hitting fists pummeled Evan's *Ti Ts'ang* across the head and shoulders, driving it to one knee. A *Tundra Wolf* crashed out of the nearby willow copse, spreading missiles through the air as if newly restocked. The ATM warheads blossomed new fire around Evan's position, shaking him violently against his harness, but he held into his seat with a determination born from knowing his attacker.

Daniel Peterson had returned.

Burning Cold

The streets of Chang-an have never felt so quiet. Reports concerning the fighting in the Suriwong Floods are mixed. Tensions run high. It feels as if the entire city, the entire planet, is holding its breath. Waiting for the news.
　　　　　　　　　—Station XLDZ, Liao, 15 August 3134

Suriwong Floods
Sarrin Province, Liao
15 August 3134

Missiles hammered into the side of the *Ti Ts'ang*'s head, ringing in Evan's ears like the sounding of a deep gong. Shaking him. The straps of his harness bruising his shoulders, across his chest, digging the buckle into his gut.

The saunalike atmosphere of the cockpit dulled his senses and the world swam in front of him. Sweat stung at the corners of his eyes and burned on his lips.

Gravity pulled, dragging him downward with such steadfast force that it felt as if the sixty tons of BattleMech strained in Evan's muscles. So easy to let go. Sprawl the *Ti Ts'ang* full out, then labor back up afterwards.

Instead, Evan Kurst straightened in his seat, willing the ten-meter-tall machine to follow him as it came up off one knee. He took a step forward. Another. He walked the machine out of a haze of gray smoke and fire, wading into ankle-deep water and pulling his crosshairs over the *Tundra Wolf's* outline. Ruby fire stabbed out into the other 'Mech, splashing armor into a mist of gray droplets.

"Ijori-one," Mai broke in over the communications band. "Enemy converging on your position."

"Let them come," he croaked. He drove his heat up another degree, firing a full spread of lasers.

Daniel Peterson answered with his own energy weapons, carving deeply. Then Evan's 'Mech rocked to the side as Ruskoff's *Zeus* slammed a PPC into the *Ti Ts'ang's* shoulder. And another. Armor flashed into a molten, fiery mist and ran in quick flashfloods of melted composite. It dripped to the ground or resolidified in waxy gray sheets along the *Ti Ts'ang's* skirted waist.

Computer estimates painted his damage schematic nearly black from head to foot. He had a few tons of armor clinging to his 'Mech, but not much more than that. He'd lost three heat sinks, and the scorching heat baking his lower legs could only mean a breach in his engine shielding. In short, Evan's machine was a walking skeleton.

Swallowing dryly, wishing for even the smallest taste of the Floods that surrounded him, Evan coaxed life into his throat. "Not much longer now, *Shiao* Mai."

If the House Master agreed, it did not show in his voice. "Cavalry-five, forward and flank," Mai Wa ordered, wheeling the last of the heavy armor around in a pincer maneuver. "Scout lance, fall back. Infantry, ground and hold."

The Armored Cavalry drove back Peterson's *Tundra Wolf*, hammering into his side with heavy-hitting Gauss slugs. Artillery tore into one Regulator, smashing it beneath the muddied waters, but Mai kept the remaining tanks on Peterson until his retreat formed a new break in The Republic line. But not for long. Into that split limped the *Zeus*, with a pack of hoverbikes clinging protectively to its shadow.

The *Zeus* came on steadily, with the kind of determination only an assault 'Mech carried with it.

"Evan," Mai commanded, "you are under orders. Not to die until I tell you."

Another PPC slammed into Evan's left side, drilling deep. Some of the hoverbikes throttled forward, ready to engage. Evan's lasers crippled one, and sent another running.

He checked his HUD. One Condor. A handful of Fa Shih.

A stripped-down *Ti Ts'ang*. They weren't going to stop Ruskoff's *Zeus*. But he was under orders.

Two hundred meters. Another PPC blast stabbed him low in the torso, carving into his gyroscope housing. The *Ti Ts'ang* folded over as if gut punched. It wavered on unsteady legs. Evan strained against his controls, contorting his body to give the gyro-struck 'Mech some additional force of balance. While he was doubled over, another PPC stream missed high, and a new brace of warheads from Peterson's *Tundra Wolf* slammed into his back, one of the few places he still had good armor.

Slowly . . . slowly Evan straightened back up again.

He scoured armor from the *Zeus* with every laser left him. One fifty. Throttling into a hobbling, backward walk, he fast-cycled his lasers and chewed into the assault machine again. The *Zeus* didn't look too much better than Evan's Capellan design, but it was still an assault 'Mech. You didn't stop that kind of momentum with a few lasers.

A Scimitar raced by on Evan's left, heading past to worry the Cavalry's backfield. Two hoverbikes slewed over the water like pond skippers, firing at some scattered Fa Shih infantry.

The Fa Shih!

Evan saw Mai's plan even as the Master of House Ijori put the final pieces into play. "Infantry, forward and swarm. Evan, hold off that *Tundra*!"

As Fa Shih broke from the ground, rising on fiery jets, Evan saw the *Tundra Wolf* throw itself forward into the embrace of McCarron's heavy armor. Ruskoff recognized the danger as well, but too late. The Ijori Condor powered forward to smash into Ruskoff's hoverbike squad, spitting missiles out in a furious assault. The center of the battlefield erupted into new chaos as infantry, armor and 'Mechs all came together in a tangle of weapons.

Evan had one last act left to him. Slamming down on his foot pedals, he launched his *Ti Ts'ang* on an uneven, wobbling flight that arced above Peterson's next missile barrage, over a deeper channel of the Suriwong, and then right back down into the muddy clay. Planting himself between Peterson and Ruskoff.

"Be ready," Ruskoff had warned Daniel. The collapse of the Ijori line had looked imminent, despite Evan Kurst's refusal to simply go down under scathing weapons fire. "Be ready to push forward."

Daniel had only backed off under the Cavalry press under orders, saving his armor for the final assault that would cut out Ijori's heart. More reinforcements had come up from the Capellan backfield, giving Mai Uhn Wa's mobile HQ some protection, but not enough. Not against a *Zeus* and Daniel's *Tundra Wolf* leading the final charge of Republic forces. If Mai Wa had any chance to worry the heavier BattleMechs, he would have to mass up a decent infantry screen. . . .

No.

Turning from the waist, Daniel stared out through his ferroglass shield. He saw movement, counted a few indistinct shadows crawling over the ground, and was opening his mouth to warn the Legate when Fa Shih troopers rose from concealment and jetted out over the Suriwong Floods.

Daniel did not stop to think. He spent one last flight of missiles at Evan Kurst, then throttled up to his best speed, striding forward into the Cavalry's heavy armor. Legate Ruskoff was in trouble, and Daniel had to act.

"Forward!" he ordered. "To the Legate's aid!"

The trio of Regulator II's pounded Daniel from both sides as he broke through their cordon, smashing Gauss slugs into the better armor of his flanks and his right leg. He stumbled forward under the hard shoves, but stayed on his feet. His ATM launcher pounded one Regulator, opening up its crew compartment so that his lasers could stab deadly energy down inside.

Another of the armored tanks drove into his path, and he kicked it aside, caving in one side of the sleek vehicle.

Then Evan Kurst's *Ti Ts'ang* dropped out of the sky, lasers spiking hard, ruby energy into the *Tundra Wolf's* face. Daniel's vision swam with laser blindness, and he nearly lost his footing. Fortunately, the polarized ferroglass took most of the glare. He slowed, recovered, and blinked his vision clear.

In time to see Viktor Ruskoff fall.

No one was going to reach the Legate in time. Under the full fury of an infantry swarm, Ruskoff had seconds—heartbeats—before the Fa Shih cracked his cockpit and took him prisoner . . . or took his life. Anyone close enough had to go through Kurst's *Ti Ts'ang*. At the least. More Ijori units pressed now, thrown forward by Mai Wa in an attempt to permanently sunder The Republic line.

"Right flank, curl inward!" Daniel ordered at once, taking local control. "Recover the Legate. Forward units press Ijori now!" A solid gut-punch might push some of the Ijori forces back, giving Daniel time to rescue Ruskoff. If Mai Wa was threatened—was taken—the battle might even be salvaged.

Too late. It was all too late. Only a few Republic units surged forward at his order to rescue Ruskoff. Fewer backed Daniel's move toward the center of the fray. Most milled about uncertainly.

Then Evan Kurst stung at him again with lasers. Daniel slammed the medium-weight machine with everything he had at his disposal as he slashed across Evan's path, missiles and lasers scouring armor and shaking the sixty-ton machine hard. As fast as his weapons cycled, he struck again, and again. Kurst went down under the barrage, but immediately began to struggle up again.

A pair of hoverbikes swung away from the *Zeus*, rallying to Daniel. One of them burst into flame and shredding metal when a Regulator II's Gauss rifle gutted it. A JES tactical missile carrier also caught up with Daniel, to accompany him on the desperate run.

Daniel wanted to believe they might be throwing themselves forward because of him. Wanted to believe it, but would not let any more good men be wasted on his account.

Planting his right foot firmly, he managed one last scourge of lasers against a nearby Regulator. Then Daniel throttled up and twisted his controls to do an about-face launch into a full run, stepping into the middle of a Purifier squad converging on his position. Turning his back on the still struggling *Ti Ts'ang*, Daniel plunged into the oncoming mass of Ijori troops and surged forward, weapons blazing as fast as he could cycle them.

Daniel Peterson or Ezekiel Crow—he was a Knight of Liao now, and he was attacking!

The unconventional move caught Ijori off balance, and let him make several hundred meters before the first tank boxed him in. A Po II. A score of short-range missiles hammered across its length, scouring away armor, and it was then that Daniel noticed the *Jessie* sticking by him.

Crosshairs flashed red and gold as Daniel second-guessed

his targeting system and pulled into several flights of missiles, ATMs and lasers. He left the Po II a smoking wreck.

Sensor alarms wailed for attention. A Gauss slug smashed into the back of one leg.

Two missiles tapped the back of his *Tundra Wolf's* head.

The cockpit shook like a cement mixer, jerking Daniel about like a rag doll. He saw the ejection controls out of the corner of one eye, knew he could have his hands on them in an easy reach. No. More trading of weapons fire. More return pounding.

He plowed past the Po II, his mind set on the Praetorian mobile HQ. He knew Evan Kurst was behind him, throttling into pursuit, but he had a good lead. Without stopping he kicked in the side of a Marksman tank, and spent his lasers into a scattering of Fa Shih battlesuits.

More hammering, coming from all sides as House Ijori moved forward to contain him. Surviving Fa Shih leapt up and grabbed handholds where they could. Evan Kurst reached out at range with his lasers, but was too far behind him.

Warning lights and alarms fought for attention as he lost armor, shielding, his missile launcher and a few heat sinks. Temperature soared and his vision swam. Only the cooling vest's maximum capacity kept him conscious now. Didn't matter.

New target. Full salvo. A Joust rolled over in explosive flame.

Next. Full. VV1 Ranger.

Giggins APC.

Schmitt.

More frenetic fire, and one of his restraining straps tore free. He pressed himself into his seat by pressing both steering pedals to the floor and holding himself in. Ejection controls. No.

Somewhere along the way he'd lost the JES tactical carrier. He could no longer be certain when, or where. The HUD was a tangle of threat icons and his damage schematic showed his systems as more memory than fact. He put the finishing touches on the DI Schmitt. Stepped over it.

And a hard shove nearly sent him sprawling as Evan Kurst's ax bit into his back, caving past armor and striking a deep cleft through his reactor shielding.

Sweat stung his eyes as Daniel Peterson hauled what was left of his BattleMech back around. He'd fought his way almost entirely through the House Ijori force. Vehicles lay scattered and ruined behind him. But right along that same path had come Evan Kurst in his *Ti Ts'ang*, followed by a number of hovercraft and infantry carriers.

Daniel levered out his right arm, lasers probing, but Evan beat it aside with the flat of his ax blade and then chopped down again. And again.

The titanium edge on the ax took his right arm off at the elbow, and opened up another deep chest wound. Laser fire and several Gauss slugs slammed into him at once, rocking him back several paces. Fusion-fed flames licked out of multiple rents in his armor, blackening the bottom edge of his cockpit shield.

He fed what few weapons he had left into the wall of onrushing forces. He couldn't breathe.

His boots stuck to the floor as their soles began to melt.

More lasers. Flames licking higher. Throttling forward, Daniel Peterson made two steps before Kurst spent one last crushing blow against the *Tundra Wolf* and its reactor finally let go. Golden fire burst up through the plate decking and speared out of a dozen wounds fatal to his BattleMech.

Ejection controls. . . .

No.

An unhealthy glow sparked inside the *Tundra Wolf's* chest wound as the reactor vented spilled plasma through the cleft. Dark smoke roiled up and around the ax head. With the last of his strength, Evan Kurst wrenched the weapon free. No time to do anything more, except stand there.

The explosion ripped apart Daniel Peterson's BattleMech with a savage fury Evan had never experienced quite so close. Golden fire splashed across his ferroglass shield, running molten fingers of melted composite down both sides. An acrid stench filled the cockpit, pulled down into Evan's lungs where it burned like live coals. For an instant, it felt like every last molecule of oxygen had been sucked out of the cockpit, and a silence descended.

Then a magnificent roar screamed in Evan's ears, pressed around his skull. His entire BattleMech was lifted up and hurled through the air. He couldn't breathe, couldn't see. He felt the *Ti Ts'ang* hit, laid out onto its back. His helmet smacked the back of his command chair with whiplash force, and pain exploded at the back of his head.

All was quiet.

Evan thought he was dead, pulled down into the abyss after Daniel Peterson. The man had warned him, after all. They were so very much alike, of course they would meet the same fate. Except that Evan remembered . . . he was under orders. Not to die until Mai told him to. He forced open his eyes, and worked carefully on focusing them.

He stared up through a cracked, half-melted ferroglass shield. Blue. White cloud. A Purifier infantryman stood on the bridge of the *Ti Ts'ang's* brow, looking in to see if the Mech-Warrior was all right.

It was all Evan needed to see. With Ruskoff captured or killed, Peterson gone, the Dynasty Guard chasing down from the north—there could only be one final conclusion to the day's fighting. The week's campaign. The month's struggle.

Evan rested back into his command couch, and stared up into a free Liao sky.

37

Homecoming

As Republic troops march into DropShips, departing Liao under an amnesty granted by Sang-shao Carson Rieves, the crowd's mood remains mixed. There is a feeling of wonder, and one of apprehension, as port workers and cheering crowds and even a few well-guarded protestors stand in the shadow of the main administration building and glance up at the green ensign waving overhead with its gauntlet and sword. The flag of the Capellan Confederation flies once more over Liao.

—ComStar Interstellar Associated, Liao,
22 August 3134

Chang-an
Qinghai Province, Liao
25 August 3134

Mai Uhn Wa stood at an open library window in the Governor's mansion, drinking in the afternoon breeze. He accepted a small glass of plum wine from Gerald Tsung, but did not sip. The view out the third-floor window was intoxicating enough.

Outside the White Towers District, strings of firecrackers rattled inside garbage cans. People paraded through the streets with caricature heads of Daoshen Liao, Anna Lu Pohl, Confederation soldiers with their Han-influenced helmets and papier-mâché BattleMechs raised up on poles. A long, serpentine dragon jumped and twisted through an intersection, running along on a hundred human legs. It was like an extended New Year's celebration. Only instead of riots, the Capellan people were truly reveling.

Michael Yung-Te slipped up beside him, the Maskirovka agent as unassuming and dangerous as ever. "Carson Rieves is in the palace, *Shiao-zhang* Mai. Perhaps you should rejoin us?"

Shiao-zhang. The title sounded better forced from the lips of the Mask agent. Mai Wa looked outside once more. It felt only right to sample the true New Year. But *Sang-shao* Rieves would not be in a forgiving mood, and it served no purpose to anger the man further without great need.

House Ijori was still in its infancy. Infants were vulnerable.

He set his wine glass on the window ledge, trading the celebration for the awkward attempts at small talk as Governor (pro tem) Lu Pohl and Gerald Tsung danced awkwardly around the room's white elephant. Viktor Ruskoff stood at full attention, holding himself stiffly apart from the others. *Sang-shao* Rieves kept the Legate available, although soon Ruskoff would be allowed to follow Lord Governor Hidic to Genoa. A good place to reestablish The Republic government for Prefecture V. The tunnels and warrens of Genoa would be a tough nut to crack.

Taking Liao, for all of The Republic's efforts and five decades of social engineering, had really been quite easy. The people, after all, were always the true power.

The people had wanted—and waited—to be freed.

The door banged back against a protective stop and the Dynasty Guard's commander barged into the room as if storming a battlefield. Two large infantrymen followed him in. One kept a hand on the butt of a very large pistol.

"Mai Wa!" Rieves nearly rushed the House Master. "You have ten seconds to explain yourself or be shot as a traitor."

The elder man stroked his long, wiry mustaches and the wispy beard he still refused to shave. "I *am* a traitor," he reminded the other officer. Daoshen Liao's denouncement still stood. "I serve the Confederation."

"And that includes conducting more crimes against the State?"

"I am not sure which crime you refer to, *Sang-shao* Carson Rieves." Mai remained properly deferential to the true power on Liao. Governor Lu Pohl would administer the world only so long as it suited the senior officer's needs.

"*Tā mā dè* you're not!" The crude insult, thrown out so freely and with real ire behind it, startled even the Maskirovka agent. But Rieves did not miss the implied warning, and restrained from barking out anything revealing in front of Ruskoff or the others. "The . . . the artifact. Your cultists raided the vault."

This time Michael Yung-Te was startled for another reason. So Carson Rieves *had* informed the local Maskirovka agent of Sun-Tzu Liao's survival.

"I have no cultists in my House," Mai said evenly. The distant echoes of more firecrackers drifted into the room.

Rieves's hands were opening and closing, as if wanting to fasten themselves around the neck of Mai Uhn Wa to wring the answers from him. "Where is the body, Mai?"

"Ah, the statue." Mai nodded. "Yes, I heard about your discovery. I have to say, the rumors of Sun-Tzu Liao's return certainly fueled a great deal of local fervor. And inspired our troops. Soon, I imagine, word will even reach Chancellor Liao that his Illustrious Father, the Ascendant, favored us with a brief visit."

Mai frowned. "But you lost it, you say? That might be . . . unfortunate."

Realization was replaced by dawning horror as Carson Rieves ran through several possibilities in his own mind. Mai watched him shift rapidly from prosecutor to protector of the faith. He covered his earlier gaffe with a lightning strike in a new direction, turning on Ruskoff. "Then I should assume the militia destroyed our . . . archeological find? You promised a peaceful withdrawal once Hidic fled."

Ruskoff braced up under the assault. "We have met every term thrust upon us," he said, biting off every word. "If you have partisan troubles, you are welcome to them, Rieves." He shrugged, smiled. "Maybe in a few months, the local population will help throw *you* off planet."

Rieves smirked, but it was forced. "I doubt the people of Liao will much complain about the return of Confederation rule." His gaze did not shift to the Maskirovka agent. It did not need to. "Whatever they give up, it will be a small price to pay for what they gain. The return of their heritage. Liao is Capellan once more."

Another shrug. "If you say so."

Seeing the two of them warming to an argument, Mai Uhn Wa drifted toward the still open door. Michael Yung-Te caught him by the elbow and pulled him aside.

"Are you mad?" the Mask agent whispered harshly. "You have rehidden the body of the Chancellor's father, and you expect to get away with this?"

Mai spent a level gaze on his keeper. "You should speak with *Sang-shao* Rieves again. He will admit that the *statue* really is of no importance. In fact, it might be best for all that the *visitation* is left to rumor, not a report. Or would you like to tell Daoshen Liao that his father's body was recovered, and lost again?"

The agent recoiled. "You ask me to involve myself—"

"I think you already know that you do not want to involve yourself. Not in this, Michael Yung-Te." Mai let a spark of strength show in his dark, dark eyes. He was perfectly ready to answer for his decisions, and he would drag several of the ranking men and women on Liao down with him if he needed to.

Yung-Te's expression was a mixture of anger and disgust. "What gives you this right?" he asked.

"I am a traitor," Mai Uhn Wa said again. "And I serve the Confederation." And then he quietly left the room.

Evan Kurst found himself once again outside Lianyungang, standing at the edge of the Cavalry River scarp. He stared out over the forest, which stretched for hundreds of kilometers on all points south and west. He had stood here the night Mai Uhn Wa had abandoned the *Ijori Dè Guāng*.

So much had changed. It was not night, and Evan waited for no DropShip to come. In the timber below, several ForestryMechs began clear-cutting from the cliff base. He couldn't see them, but he could hear their diamond-edged saws and smell the wood smoke from a hidden slash burn.

Behind him growled heavy machinery and the *beep-beep* of back-stepping Construction machines.

And at the cliff edge, fifty meters off to his right, spotters worked carefully, checking the mounts and tackle that supported the engineers lowered halfway down the escarpment face. Soon another blast echoed out over the lower flatlands as natural crevices were widened and hollowed out into deep, stable caverns.

Footsteps behind him. Evan stepped back from the cliff edge, but did not turn as Jen Lynn Tang walked up to him with a noteputer listing the day's plans and checklist.

Evan had to sign off on each team's progress for the day with Mai Uhn Wa not yet back from Chang-an. He thumbed open the file and recorded the progress of the ForestryMechs and blasting teams and the earthmovers that were still working to level the grounds on top of the plateau for House Ijori's planned stronghold. It looked like any construction site he'd ever seen. But in his mind's eye he saw heavy, reinforced walls and a compound of simple buildings serving the House mansion.

Below the cliff would be BattleMech hangars and the motor pool. The business side of a Warrior House.

"It will be good." Good to have a place to feel secure. The Conservatory would never be that again, not for any cadet of the last year. Maybe the Confederation could revitalize it again. Maybe not.

Jenna nodded. "I know." It wasn't the first time he'd spoken of it aloud, as if trying to convince himself.

She remained deferential and distant, still waiting for Evan to come back to her after their victory on the Suriwong Floods. Since being pried out of the cockpit of the broken *Ti Ts'ang*, however, Evan had maintained a careful attitude. Even the news of Jenna's surviving the death of her unit hadn't chipped much of his resolve free. They were brother and sister now as well as lovers. Warriors of House Ijori. He needed time to come to terms with the first before again considering the second. She knew this.

She was being kept fairly busy herself. Jen was currently working on recruitment and indoctrination for the resurrected Warrior House. Finding the right disciple-cadets and learning how to groom them into the next generation of warrior-philosophers would be a daunting task.

Mai Uhn Wa played each person to his or her strengths.

"Did you discover anyone today?" he asked.

Jenna smiled, glorious and proud. "You would not believe it. Two sixteen-year-old twins who had already been tagged by The Republic as problem children. Their problem, as it turned out, was fighting back against hazing for being too Capellan in their ways. Well, now they can bask in a little hero worship before coming here to live."

Twins? Interesting. "And the younger brackets?" Evan opened up new files.

The age groups ranged to as young as eight. Eventually, such precocious children with the right qualifications would be invited to attend summer schools for philosophy. The best and brightest would be wedded to House Ijori at age twelve. And in only one decade Ijori would have a program that matched other Warrior Houses.

"A few," Jenna said. "It's harder, but we'll be ready." She paused. "Have you thought about this? What it will be like to divorce such young children from their families?"

He had. But not in the way she meant. Evan was one of those children, cast adrift into a surrogate life. These new children would have what he had never been given. A choice. "Only those who decide for themselves," he promised her. "That is the only way it *can* work. *Shiao* Mai knows what he is doing." As did Evan. Now.

"All right. Keep it between you for now. But Evan, let me in on one thing, will you?" An echo of 'copter blades rolled over the small plateau. "Why are we blasting tunnels into the cliff face?"

She sounded eager. Enthusiastic. And eventually, Mai Uhn Wa or Evan would let several of their key people in on House Ijori's secret charge. But Jen Lynn Tang had waited too long to ask this day. The thunder of military rotors grew louder. Evan turned and found the Sprint VTOL, growing larger as it flew in from the northwest. "The Master returns," he said simply. "We should go welcome him home."

He hadn't planned on it, but Evan reached out as he went by to snag her hand and pull Jenna along at his side. It seemed such a little gesture, but one he needed to make, for her as well as for him. After so long, Evan finally had found what The Republic had taken from him.

A family. A House.

A home.

EPILOG

Noble Victory

*Lord Governor Golan of Prefecture VI has traded
away the worlds of Yunnah and Second Try to the
Capellan Confederation. In return, Chancellor Liao
pressured the Oriente Protectorate to end hostilities.
Prefect Tao demands that strict measures be taken
against the Lord Governor for his policy of appease-
ment, as the gift of worlds circumvents his strategy of
a military blockade against Palos and Wei.*
— ComStar Interstellar Associated, Liao,
2 September 3134

Celestial Palace
Zi-jin Chéng (Forbidden City), Sian
Sian Commonality, Capellan Confederation
23 September 3134

Jacob Bannson stewed outside of Daoshen Liao's ceremonial temple, waiting for the Chancellor's return, sweating
through an imported suit that cost him several thousand Liao-
bills. From one of the finest tailors on Highspire, influenced
by the Mao jacket but cut for a modern man of business, it did
nothing for him in Sian's summer heat. He and his entourage
were quietly miserable. The temple's white oak siding reflected most of the sun's strength back into their faces. The air
shimmered. There was not one lick of shade on this side of the

temple, a fact certainly not lost on the inscrutable leader of the Capellan Confederation.

Daoshen Liao. The Great Soul. Soon to be Jacob Bannson's liege lord and master.

Well, his liege lord, anyway.

Retainers fetched him iced water, talcum and towels, whatever he commanded at a snap of his fingers. His own people, brought with him from The Republic, were also decked out in the finest clothes as befitting the court of a traveling lord. The corporate leader had taken to heart Daoshen's *suggestion* that he arrive in style, and so he had. And for the indifferent reception he'd received so far, was glad of it. *His* people, at least, were well practiced in calling him *sire*.

Most of them. The rest would learn. Di Jones, for instance, bent and scraped for no one. Though even she might have to bend to the necessity once Daoshen Liao made it official. The flame-haired raider had chosen to remain on his DropShip rather than spend another moment in Daoshen's company, but she had her assurances of inviolate status. She'd come around.

So what would it be, a simple Lordship? Daoshen promised a reward "commensurate with services rendered to the Capellan Confederation." Well, Liao had fallen even as Bannson began to think it wasn't in the cards. Mandrinn? Was Duke too much to hope for?

If not now, then some day. Once Bannson opened up a new opportunity, he never let it go. Nobility had been the one thing closed off to him. Now he had earned that as well.

The temple's heavy doors swung open, bringing a temporary breeze of refreshing coolness as the interior chill bled out and died under the summer sun. Temple priests stepped into the golden heat, holding back the doors. Not one drop of sweat appeared on their shaven pates, Bannson noticed. His eyes searched the gloomy interior, and found an Asian woman decked out in a slender dress of Asian style. An imperial cheongsam. Brocaded silk of dark, dark ruby red with a detailed design of phoenix and dragon, Mandarin collar closed over a keyhole slit that plunged into a deep neckline.

She looked Bannson over carefully with dark, veiled eyes that gave away nothing. Her gaze had a tangible presence, penetrating. A flush gathered at the back of his neck, but the

CEO gave away nothing as he stared back, matching his will against hers. Finally, she nodded once. "He will suffice."

Not the most glowing endorsement. Bannson bristled, then forced a calm on himself as Daoshen Liao stepped up beside the beauty. The Chancellor could not have been waiting much farther into the temple. Once again, Bannson marveled at the Chancellor's ability to remain cloaked.

"Chancellor." Bannson hesitated, unsure of the protocol here, and submitted himself to bowing from the waist. His people, well-schooled to follow their master's lead, dropped into deeper bows and formal curtsies. "I am honored to stand in your presence again."

Daoshen folded his hands into the voluminous sleeves of his ceremonial robes. He wore black silk, trimmed in gold. No patterns decorated the fabric. Very understated for the Chancellor. "It is we who are honored, *zhàng-fu-xiàng*-Ki-linn. It is a joyous ceremony that awaits us."

Ceremony? Daoshen was prepared to be more gracious than Bannson had hoped. He untangled his title with great care, not wanting to miss one nuance. He didn't.

. . . husband . . . to. . . .

The CEO glanced quickly to the waiting woman, her formal dress and back to the Daoshen. "Chancellor! You do not mean. . . ." For the first time in years, Bannson found himself at a loss for words.

"Our cousin." Daoshen nodded to the beauty who remained watchful behind her passive mask. "Twice removed, but a blood descendant of our father's sister. Ki-linn is a Mandrissa of our court, given new landholds on Wei as well as hereditary estates on Highspire. We expect you will be very happy."

Ki-linn . . . Liao! One of Daoshen's blood, considered divine among the Capellan people. The Chancellor proposed marriage!

"This is how you keep our bargain?" he asked, outrage boiling just below the surface.

The leader's eye narrowed into dangerous slits. "How else would you become a noble of our realm?"

Bannson dialed back his anger, knowing it could only serve Daoshen's plans to let the dark emotion rule him. "By appointment. By fiat through service." Marrying into nobility, he would forever be tied to his wife's status. His accomplishments would be rewarded to *her*.

"And we have offered you a greater reward. As promised." Daoshen stared ahead stoically. No hint of mocking, of condescension, touched his voice or his expression. "We do not recall you setting restrictions on how we granted your wish."

Trapped. Bannson had left one fatal flaw in his plans. He had *assumed*. But when would he ever have considered the idea of Daoshen Liao, God Incarnate of Sian, arranging a marriage into his family? Masterful, he had to admit. Bannson's personal holdings held inviolate status, even after his death, but by Confederation *and* Republic law, a spouse held many entitlements that could undermine the safeguards put into place.

And to turn down such an offer? That was likely to be more immediately hazardous to his health.

Bannson had trained himself over his entire life to make the tough calls. "The Chancellor is indeed a generous soul," Bannson said formally, without warmth. He bowed again to Daoshen Liao, and then deeper to his expectant bride. She nodded back curtly and disappeared back into the temple. Bannson blotted sweat from his brow, and joined the Chancellor in the shade of the temple's interior.

"We still sense a lack of enthusiasm," Daoshen said. Not as a rebuke, though. A feeler? Something new being offered?

"Understand, Illustrious One, that I am quite surprised by your . . . solution. I have lived my life earning my own way. Marrying into such a great reward runs contrary to my nature." He smiled weakly. "I'm certain I will get over it." If Daoshen did not help him over it first with a Maskirovka assassin in the night.

"You worry too much about such things, Jacob Bannson." It seemed that Daoshen answered what was left unspoken as well. Now the ghost of a smile did trace the Chancellor's lips. "But as our wedding gift, there may yet be something we can arrange. *If* earning your nobility by fiat means so much to you."

Bannson smiled thinly. "At the Chancellor's pleasure," he agreed. His mind raced, picking over every word with great care. He did not make the same mistake twice.

"That is well," the Chancellor said, smiling fully now as they moved into the temple, and the waiting ceremony.

"We have another task for you."

About the Author

Loren L. Coleman began writing fiction in high school, but it was during his enlistment in the US Navy that he began to work seriously at the craft. In the last ten years he has built up a personal bibliography that includes (around the time of this printing) thirteen published novels, a great deal of shorter fiction work, and involvement with several computer games. *Endgame* was his ninth BattleTech novel and the finale to the original BattleTech series. *By Temptations and By War* is his second MechWarrior: Dark Age novel. He is also the author of *Into the Maelstrom*, the first novel of the Vor series, and *Rogue Flyer* in the fascinating universe of Crimson Skies.

Loren Coleman currently resides in Washington State. He has a personal Web site at www.rasqal.com.

The *Blade* BattleMech miniature stands approximately 2–3/4" tall.

A MechWarrior® By Temptations and By War Novel Exclusive!

Limited Edition Ezekiel Crow *Blade* BattleMech® Figure...

Get your own *Blade* BattleMech miniature, piloted by the Paladin of the Sphere Ezekiel Crow. This Limited Edition game piece is from the runaway hit collectable miniatures game, **MechWarrior: Dark Age**. The Ezekiel Crow 'Mech® is available only through this exclusive offer.

Don't miss your chance to get this rare figure!

AVAILABLE ONLY WHILE SUPPLIES LAST!

ORDER YOURS TODAY!

NAME: [ ]   DATE OF BIRTH: [ ]

SHIPPING ADDRESS: [ ]   APT #: [ ]
(If using credit card, will ship only to credit card billing address.)

CITY: [ ]   STATE/PROVINCE: [ ]

ZIP/POSTAL CODE: [ ]   DAY PHONE: ([ ]) [ ]-[ ]   VISA: [ ]   MC: [ ]

CREDIT CARD #: [ ]   EXP. DATE: [ ]/[ ]

EMAIL: [ ]

Do you wish to be added to our mailing list? YES: [ ]   NO: [ ] _____
Card Holder's Signature

Ordering Information	**Price***	**Qty****	**Total ◊**
U.S. Addresses:	$ 5	_____	_____
Canadian Addresses (credit card only):	$ 6	_____	_____
Other Addresses (credit card only):	$ 10	_____	_____

* All prices include shipping and handling and tax.   ** Limit two figures per order.   ◊ Total price = price x quantity

**Send this ORDER FORM with PAYMENT and
ORIGINAL NOVEL CASH REGISTER RECEIPT to:**

Ezekiel Crow 'Mech Special Offer
WizKids, LLC
12145 Centron Place
Cincinnati OH 45246

Available only while supplies last. Orders must be received before December 31, 2004. Do not send cash! Limit two figures per order. Make checks and money orders payable to WizKids, LLC, and allow 10–15 days for personal checks to clear. No personal checks or money orders accepted on orders shipped outside the U.S. International orders will be processed only with credit card payment. All payments must be in U.S. funds. Please print clearly. All orders must include this original order form, payment, and original novel cash register receipt to be processed. Actual figure may vary slightly from figure shown. In the event the offer is sold out, all orders received after the sell-out will be returned to sender unopened. Allow 8–16 weeks for delivery.